MW00826967

Also by Pam Jenoff

#BookTok is raving about *Last Twilight*

"Historical fiction at its finest! *Last Twilight in Paris* was imposs…
impeccably researched, and one of the most engaging books I'v…

—Fay Silverman, @nobookmark_noproblem

"A fast paced story full of heart, hope, twists and turns, betray…
and love that will have you hooked from the first page!"

—Ashley Sickora, @thepageladies

"An unforgettable tale of love, loss, hope, and survival."

—Alexis K, @_alexisinwonderland

"Full of hope, heart, betrayal, love and so much more."

—Red, @redbookreview

"An irresistible blend of romance, espionage, and bravery. The story pulls you in
from page one, delivering pulse-pounding suspense and heart-wrenching emotion."

—Zivorad Filipovic, @zivorad.filipovic

"*Last Twilight in Paris* describes motherhood in a way that only a mother
with grown children can. I felt so seen and so understood."

—Katie Wascisin Hathaway, @simplefairy_book_magic

"Another gem by Pam Jenoff! The beauty of Jenoff's historical fiction
is that we learn pieces of history through her books."

**—Andrea Peskind Katz, Great Thoughts Great Readers
Facebook group**

"A beautifully written story that sheds light on a lesser known
part of WWII history. Fascinating and heartbreaking."

—Becky, @beckybingbooks

"This book is a must read. You will be rooting for the characters as this
fast paced book takes you on an incredible and historical journey."

—Cori, @clp412

"It blends romance, mystery and suspense against the background of a wa…
that never fails to create high emotions in the reader."

—Pamela Zinnel, @bookwormpbz

"Jenoff was able to take one of the most devastating times in history and…
beautiful story! This is a story of heartbreak, loyalty, love, mystery and…

—Jenna Weaver, @book_loverrr99

PAM JENOFF

LAST TWILIGHT IN PARIS

PARK
ROW
BOOKS

PARK™
ROW
BOOKS™

Recycling programs
for this product may
not exist in your area.

ISBN-13: 978-0-7783-0798-3
ISBN-13: 978-0-7783-8771-8 (International Trade Paperback Edition)

Last Twilight in Paris

Park Row Books
22 Adelaide St. West, 41st Floor
Toronto, Ontario M5H 4E3, Canada
ParkRowBooks.com

Printed in U.S.A.

For my family. For always.

Prologue

Helaine

Paris, 1943

Darkness.

Helaine stumbled forward, unable to see through the black void that surrounded her. She could feel the shoulders of the others jostling on either side. The smell of unwashed bodies rose, mingling with Helaine's own. Her hand brushed against a rough wall, scraping her knuckles. Someone ahead tripped and yelped.

Hours earlier, when Helaine had been brought from her underground cell at the police station into the adjacent holding area, she was surprised to see other women waiting. She had not encountered anyone since her arrest. She had studied the women, who looked to be from all walks of life, trying to discern some commonality among their varied ages and classes that had caused them to be here. There was only one: they were Jews. The yellow star they wore, whether soiled and crudely sewn onto a worn, secondhand dress or pressed crisply against the latest Parisian finery, was identical—and it made them all the same.

They had stood in the bare holding area, not daring to speak.

Helaine was certain that her arrest had been some sort of mistake. She had done nothing wrong. They had to free her. But even as she thought this, she knew that the old world of being a French citizen with rights was long gone.

An hour passed, then two. There was nowhere to sit, and a few people dropped to the floor. An elderly woman dozed against the wall, mouth agape. Except for the slight rise and fall of her chest, she might have been dead. Hunger gnawed at Helaine and she wished that she still had the baked goods she purchased at the market just before she was taken. The meager breads, which had seemed so pathetic days earlier, now would have been a feast. But her belongings had been confiscated upon arrest.

Helaine looked upward through the thin slit of window near the ceiling. They were still in Paris. The sour smell from the city street and the sounds of cars and footsteps despite the curfew were familiar, if not comforting. How long they would stay here, she did not know. Helaine was torn. She did not want to remain in this empty room forever. Yet she also dreaded leaving, for wherever they were going would surely be worse.

Finally, the door had opened. "Sortir!" a voice ordered them out in French, reminding Helaine that the policemen, who had brought them here and who were keeping them captive, were not Germans, but their own people.

Helaine had filed into the dimly lit corridor with the others. They exited the police station and stepped outside onto the pavement. At the sight of the familiar buildings and the street leading away from the station, Helaine momentarily considered fleeing. She had no idea, though, where she would go. She imagined running to her childhood home, debated whether her estranged mother would take her in or turn her away. But the women were heavily guarded and there was no real possibility of escape. Instead, Helaine breathed the fresh air in great gulps, sensing that she might not be in the open again for quite some time.

The women were herded up a ramp toward an awaiting truck. Helaine recoiled. They were being placed in the back part of the vehicle where goods should have been carried, not people. Helaine wanted to protest but did not dare. Smells of stale grain and rotting meat, the truck's previous cargo, assaulted her nose, mixing with her own stench in the warm air. It had been three days since she had bathed or changed and her dress was wrinkled and filthy, her once-luminous black curls dull and matted against her head.

When the women were all inside the truck, the back hatch shut with an ominous click. "Where are they taking us?" someone whispered. Silence. No one knew and they were all too afraid to venture a guess. They had heard the stories of the trains headed east to awful places from which no one ever returned. Helaine wondered how long the journey would be.

As they bumped along the Paris streets, Helaine's bones, already sore from sleeping on the hard prison cell floor, cried out in pain. Her mouth was dry and her stomach empty. She wanted water and a meal, a hot bath. She wanted home.

If home was a place that even existed anymore. Helaine's husband, Gabriel, was missing in Germany, his fate unknown. She had scarcely spoken with her parents since before the war. And Helaine herself had been taken without notice. Nobody knew that she had been arrested or had any idea where she had gone. It was as if she simply no longer existed.

To distract herself, Helaine tried to picture the route they were taking outside the windowless truck, down the boulevards she had just days earlier walked freely, past the cafés and shops. The familiar locations should have been some small comfort. But this might well be the last time she ever came this way, Helaine realized, and the thought only worsened her despair.

Several minutes later, the truck stopped with a screech. They were at a train station, Helaine guessed. The back hatch to the truck opened and the women peered out into pitch blackness. "Raus!" a voice commanded. That they were under the watch of Germans now seemed to confirm Helaine's worst fears about where they were headed. "Schnell!" Someone let out a cry, a mix of the anguish and uncertainty they all felt.

The women clambered from the truck and Helaine stumbled, banging her knee and yelping. "Quiet," a woman's voice beside her cautioned fearfully. A hand reached out and helped her down the ramp with an unexpectedly gentle touch.

Outside the truck it was the tiniest bit lighter and Helaine was just able to make out some sort of loading dock. The group moved forward into a large building.

Now Helaine found herself in complete darkness once more. This was how she had come to be in an unfamiliar building, shuffling forward blindly with a group of women she did not know, uncertain of where they were going or the fate that might befall them. She could see nothing, only feel the fear and confusion in the air around her. They seemed to be in some sort of corridor, pressed even more closely together than they had been. Helaine put her hand on the shoulder of the woman in front of her, trying hard not to fall again.

They were herded roughly through a doorway, into a room that was also unlit. No one moved or spoke. Helaine had heard rumors of mass executions, groups of people gassed or simply shot. The Germans might do that to them now. Her skin prickled. She thought of those she loved most, Gabriel and, despite everything that had happened, her parents. Helaine wanted their faces, not fear, to be her final thought.

Bright lights turned on suddenly, illuminating the space around them. "Mon Dieu!" someone behind her exclaimed softly. Helaine blinked her eyes, scarcely daring to believe what she saw. They were not in a camp or a prison at all. Instead, they were standing in the main showroom of what had once been one of the grandest department stores in Paris.

1

Louise

Henley-on-Thames, 1953

The fog is rolling in low across the Thames as I shutter the secondhand shop on Bell Street for the night, the mist weaving its
way, tentacle-like, into the alley where my bicycle leans against
the side of the gray brick building. The sudden gloom seems
to signal a change, the start of something ominous. I draw my
woolen scarf closer around my neck against the brisk September air, then climb onto the rickety shopper and begin to pedal
home.

I navigate through the town center, then left on Hart Street
and toward the base of Henley Bridge, welcoming the stillness.
There's no one out at this late hour to require a greeting or stare
at me oddly. When I moved here seven years ago after marrying Joe, the bucolic Oxfordshire town had at first seemed like
a haven, a welcome refuge from my mum's dismal flat in South
London. Only later would I realize how small the town actually was, how stifling it would become.

Ten minutes later, I reach home. Our low, two-story house
on the outskirts of town at the end of Wargrave Road is iden-

tical to the half-dozen others in the row, gray brick with a tiny front yard just large enough for a single rosebush each. It is situated in one of the new housing developments that had been erected hastily after the war. The site had formerly been a crater where a bomb had fallen, and I sometimes breathe deeply and imagine that I can still smell the gunpowder.

Though the house appears well-kept from a distance, closer I can see the little faults, even in the near darkness, the cracks at the foundation, a bit of trim around the window that is beginning to fall. I glance at the coal bin and make a mental note to ask Joe to fill it, in the morning of course. He will be on his third brandy or perhaps fourth, so he won't remember if I mention it now.

Inside, the house is still. Joe is asleep in his chair, reliving the battles he fought, as he does every night. His newsboy cap sits on the table and he is still wearing his white dress shirt from his long day at the accountancy firm, sleeves rolled. Joe's auburn hair remains military-short, though his face is a bit fuller now with age. I lift the tilted glass gently from his hand and stub out the cigarette, a Player's Medium, in the ashtray. Though I worry about him drinking too much, I don't begrudge him the temporary escape liquor provides. At least he drinks at home, bottles purchased from the off-license, rather than getting pissed at The Old Bell or one of the other pubs like some men in town do, staying until closing or even later for a lock-in and stumbling home at all hours, embarrassing their wives.

I touch his cheek, then nudge him gently. "Go up to bed, dear." Joe rousts himself, mumbling unintelligibly before shuffling off. I watch with a pang of sadness as he retreats.

Joe had served in the British army during the war and had spent more than four years on the ground in active combat. *Lucky*, some call him, because he was never captured or even wounded. I can see the scars brought on by living under that kind of strain, though, watching friend after friend killed, never knowing if each day would be his last. Neither Joe nor I had ever talked in detail about what either of us had done during the war. It lies silent and unspoken between us, a dark divide.

My mind reels back to the other day when the children had been playing hospital. They were using an old gauze bandage, wrapping it around a doll. Seeing this, Joe, usually so even-tempered, had become distraught. "You're wasting medical supplies!" he cried. "Don't you know that some people don't have enough of those?" His eyes had been wide with horror as he surely remembered men bleeding out when there hadn't been bandages to save them.

I had taken his arm. "It's okay. That's just an old scrap of cloth. It really can't be used for anything else."

His eyes seemed to clear then. "Yes, of course. Sorry." He retreated, his old calm returning. But I could see in that moment the deep places where he hid his anger and pain.

Eight years have passed since the war ended and Joe came home, far longer than he was over there. *Time to get on with it,* stiff-lipped English folk seem to say. And Joe has gotten on with it, putting his bravest face on to mask the pain. He goes to work and keeps the garden neat and pays the bills, everything that a good husband and father is supposed to do. Only I'm close enough to see the scars that will never fully heal, and I wish there was more I could do to help him.

I walk to the kitchen and pick up an empty packet of crisps from the counter, left there by one of the children, no doubt. I consider being annoyed and then decide it isn't worth the trouble. I move around, cleaning and straightening. It is late and I'm exhausted; tidying up might have waited until morning. But my own childhood had been a never-ending stream of empty beer bottles and unkempt rooms, and I don't want that for my family. I simply cannot rest unless things are in order.

When I have set the kitchen to rights, I walk into the living room and sit down by the low table to work on the jigsaw puzzle that Joe gave me for Christmas, depicting a lovely image of the Welsh countryside in summer. I pick up a piece and study the jagged, half-done puzzle, finding a spot and trying it. The piece snaps satisfyingly into place. That is the thing I love most about puzzles. Something that moments earlier had made no sense at all now fits. I reach for another piece. I should go to sleep, I know. But these few minutes of solitude are worth more.

Five minutes later, I tear myself away from the puzzle and start upstairs. In the nursery (a fancy word for the children's shared room, which is just large enough for two single beds), the twins, Ewen and Phaedra, are sleeping soundly. I pick up a *Beano* comic from the floor and place it on the nightstand. *Winnie-the-Pooh* lies open, spine up, and I regret not making it back to read to them before bedtime. I normally only work when the children are at school, wanting to be home for them in the afternoons and evenings. Joe doesn't mind my helping at the shop, as long as it doesn't interfere with taking care of the house and children. But Midge had asked a favor, something came up and she was called away suddenly. Could I stay and close up and straighten things for the night? So I'd left dinner and Joe agreed to put the children to bed. At first, I'd worried whether he could manage it. But despite his demons, Joe is good at being there when I need him to be. I stayed longer than I had planned to after closing the shop, getting lost as I so often did when sorting through the objects and imagining the stories behind them.

I adjust the children's bedclothes to ward off the persistent cold of the second floor, then remove the hot water bottles, which have gone tepid. Downstairs is warm enough from the stove, but upstairs the electric fire does little to stave off the chill. I pause, studying their faces lovingly. Born after the war, Ewen and Phaedra sleep with the peaceful minds of ones who have never been woken and hurried to bomb shelters for nights on end. For me, doing without has always been a kind of default state, first from my poor childhood and later the Depression and then the war. But despite the shortages and rationing that carried into the postwar years and are only just now ending, my children have no memory of a time of worry or doing without, and for that I am grateful. I kiss them each on the forehead and then tiptoe from the room and down the hall.

I slip into bed beside Joe and move close to him for warmth, leaning my forehead against the wide expanse of his back as I often do for comfort. I had met Joe in a London dance hall before the war. He was a college student and a rower, tall and confident. I was never quite sure what he saw in me, a girl who worked in one of the shops with no higher education or family background. But we had a connection and made each other laugh. We went for drinks and to the movies in Leicester Square and talked of a future together after he graduated.

Then the war broke out. Before Joe deployed, he abruptly ended things with me. I was gutted. Other couples were going forward and sealing their love with hurried weddings. Why not us? "I just don't want you to rush in with me out of some sense of obligation," Joe explained when I asked. It was our last night together and we stood at Embankment, looking across the Thames at the blacked-out buildings on the South Bank. We were breaking curfew, but I didn't care.

"It isn't like that," I protested.

"And I don't want you to spend your whole life mourning for a bloke you knew a quick five minutes." He was afraid of not coming back. He was afraid of hurting me.

Joe *had* come back, with the same affable grin, appearing unexpectedly one day on the doorstep to the shop where I was working, looking much the same except for a bit of gray at the temples. His hat was literally in his hands, the trilby filled with flowers and an engagement ring at the bottom. "I'll never leave again," he promised, sensing my unease. We married a few months later and moved out to Henley, close to where he had grown up. It wasn't impetuous. Joe had seemed solid and stable, the very opposite of everything I was trying to outrun. I knew he would love and care for me. Only later did I see the scars. I had been so glad for his safe return that I had not seen all of the ways in which he was not okay.

He is not asleep, I can tell, for he does not toss fitfully from nightmares. Instead, he lies too still. I wish he might turn to me. I could reach for him, I suppose, if not for sex, then at least for a cuddle or to talk long into the night in low voices as we once had. But something stops me. Instead, I turn to my own side of the bed and drift to sleep.

The next morning when I wake, Joe has already left for work. Despite his struggles, Joe has always kept to a strict schedule, rising and setting out for the station and the commuter rail to Oxford before dawn. I sometimes wonder if it is to avoid the noise and chaos of the children in the morning.

I set out their breakfast, two bowls of Weetabix and the fresh milk from the glass jar that the children prefer to the paper cartons of long-life milk that are doled out at school. I go upstairs to wake them, pausing to inhale their sleepy scent. "Time to get up, luvs." Then I carry on with the morning chores while they rouse and dress. I lift the laundry, wet and heavy, from the first tub and through the press into the second, the smell of bleach tickling my nose. I set out the empty glass bottles, as well as some old pots for the rag-and-bone man.

Back inside, I glance down at a copy of *The Times* Joe left from the previous day. The headlines are about the Soviet Union and a possible rail strike in the north. I remember the days when the paper carried only news about the Second World War and I still half expect to see those. But no one wants to talk about that anymore.

When I have done as much around the house as I can, I fix myself a cup of Yorkshire tea, savoring the last bit of quiet. The children stumble down the stairs a few minutes later, dressed but unkempt. Phed is a little fairy of a girl, all blonde and pale, wide-set eyes and a charming gap between her front teeth. Ewen is solemn, with manlike features and a somber expression that tell exactly what he will look like when he grows up.

I hurry the children through eating their breakfast and then putting on their socks and shoes, reminding myself not to be cross when they dawdle. This morning Ewen has a sniffle. "I don't wanna go to school!" he whines. For a second, I debate whether I should keep him home. I do love when we curl up by the fire on a chilly day, with nothing to do but read and work on puzzles together.

This morning, though, I'm restless. Selfishly, I don't want to give up my time at the shop. "How about if I put an extra chocolate biscuit in your lunch?" I offer. Ewan sniffs and nods, miraculously healed by the bribe. I'm secretly relieved when he puts on his coat and starts for the door without further complaint. I grab another biscuit for each child, pushing down my guilt. I try to feed them healthy, wholesome foods, but it is a losing battle. The children's magazines advertise soft drinks like Tizer and the kids beg for the boiled sweets like barley sugars and licorice their friends have, even though I warn them they will get holes in their teeth.

We leave the house and start into town. It is a brisk September morning, and the leaves on the poplar trees that line the road seem crisper, signaling that they will soon begin to change. Phed runs ahead in her Mary Janes, but Ewen drags his feet, scuffing his saddle shoes. I fight the urge to scold him for dawdling. "If you hurry, you'll have time to play hopscotch before the bell," I say instead, exhaling silently when his pace quickens and he scurries to catch up with his sister.

Fifteen minutes later, we cross Henley Bridge, sculls and pairs gliding beneath us on their morning rows. Boathouses dot the far bank of the river. Rowing, which had dwindled when the young men were away at war, has come back with the force of fauna blooming after a forest fire. I think sadly of Joe. He rowed at uni until the war ruined his knees. Now he is forced to look on as a spectator at the sport he had once loved, and I suspect he avoids coming to town for this very reason.

When we reach the school, the children run to their friends, who are playing tag and marbles. Ewen's legs are like sticks beneath his shorts, but Phed's are plump, cherubic. Through the classroom window, I can see the twins' teacher, Miss Eakley, filling the inkwells for the dipping pens.

I drop the children off without lingering, pretending to be in a hurry so that I won't have to make small talk with the other mums. I just have so little in common with them. It is not only that I came from somewhere else while so many of them went to school together. They seem like alien beings, these women who are so content with child-raising and chores, only the occasional garden club or card game to break up the monotony. Surely, they had done other things during the war, too, but they gave it up so easily, as if it had never happened at all. Funnily, I envy them. Why can't I be content with this life?

Leaving the school, I set out for the shops to purchase groceries for that evening's supper before heading to work. At the butcher's, women queue for meat, the sawdust from the floor clinging to the hems of their dresses. Once in a great while, Joe will drive me into Oxford to do a big shop at Sainsbury's, but day-to-day here, it is still separate stores for most of what we need. I pay, grateful that I do not have to worry whether I have enough. Joe's paycheck is adequate for what we need and a few modest treats. Joe is generous with money, giving me an allowance and a few extra quid if I need it without asking why.

As I leave, I catch a glimpse of myself in the shop window. I've never been able to manage the makeup and rouge and mascara and the thousand ways women were meant to mimic the Hollywood starlets. Fortunately, I'm blessed with decent bone structure and can get away with just lipstick and powder most ordinary days, some pancake makeup and eye shadow on special occasions. I don't even try to wear the formfitting shapes that are all the rage these days with the New Look or totter around on the heeled shoes that have replaced wartime work boots for most. Though childbirth had not been onerous, I still feel the tugs of a body that will never quite be the same.

I carry the groceries home and put the cold items in the icebox. Thankfully, the cottage had come with some of the modern conveniences. And what it didn't have, Joe had added. When we moved in, he insisted on everything fresh and bright and as far from the past as possible—as if all of the shiny metal and chrome might chase away the painful memories. I wanted to tell him that it would do no good, but he would not listen and so I let him try.

I set out once more for town, my arms lighter without the groceries. When I reach the store, Midge is already there, rifling through a box. Midge's, as it is called per the faded sign out front, is a charity thrift shop, its slanted wooden shelves overflowing with secondhand goods. People bring in the things they don't want anymore, household items mostly, odds and ends. I help Midge to sort through the items and display for resale what is in suitable condition. Then others can come in and buy things at a reduced price, a service on both ends. I like the neatness of it all, sorting things into piles and setting them right. Like the jigsaw puzzles, it helps give me a sense of order and calm. I often wonder, too, about the people who owned the objects and the stories behind the items I hold in my hands.

Midge turns and starts to lift a new crate from a shelf with effort, and I hurry to help her set it down on the counter. "Let me help." Midge has to be close to eighty, a tiny slip of a woman. She moves with greater effort now among the clutter. That was how I had sold the idea of working at the shop to Joe, saying that Midge needed the help. In fact, the job is more for my own benefit. I love to get out of the house and lose myself tinkering with objects from the past.

"Sort this one, luv." Midge gestures to the crate, which has two broken slats. "Seems mostly to be odd bits, probably nothing worth saving."

"Probably." I slide the crate down onto the floor.

"How are the little ones?" she asks.

"Needy," I blurt, regretting it at once. I'm lucky, I know, to have a beautiful, healthy family. It is the very thing I wanted, growing up alone with my mum in London as a child. "It's just a lot sometimes."

"It's a lot," Midge agrees. "When my Johnny was young, some days lasted forever. And then those days were gone." There is a note of sadness in her voice. Midge had a son, I recall then, who was killed in a car accident before the war. Her husband, unable to bear the loss, had taken his own life after. She is completely alone.

"Midge, I'm so sorry. I didn't mean to upset you."

She shakes her head. "It's not the upsetting that is the problem. And Joe, how's he?"

I hesitate before answering. Midge and I are not particularly close, and it feels strange to talk to her about such things. At the same time, I'm grateful to have someone to confide in for once. "He's the same. He's so sad, and I wish I could help him. It's not just him, though. It's me. I miss who I used to be, if that makes any sense."

"It does. You can't be any good for him until you've sorted out yourself. Have the two of you considered getting away together?"

"Not really." Except for an annual seaside family holiday to Brighton, we never leave town. I remember fondly a moment last year when I stepped away and treated myself to a candy floss I did not have to share, watching the seagulls swoop above the promenade as I ate it. "It's difficult with the children."

"You should think about it."

"I will. I promise."

I carry the crate to the tattered cozy chair in the corner by the woodstove before sitting down. Rifling through the first few items, I consider putting the whole thing in the rubbish bin. There are some cracked glasses and a detached telephone receiver. True junk and likely nothing salvageable.

I run my fingers along the bottom of the box, checking for any coins. My hand rubs against something metallic. A chain. I pull at it, but it sticks. I clear the remaining objects from the box to get a better look. There is a gold link necklace, delicate yet sturdy, hooked around the base of the wood crate. I dislodge it and hold it up to the light. On the chain is a charm shaped like a heart with a jagged edge, as though half is missing. But the metal is intact, suggesting an entire separate piece of jewelry is out there somewhere that might make up the second half.

The shape is familiar. My breath catches.

"Look at this," I say, carrying the necklace to Midge. She takes it and turns it over with the expert hand of one who has been sorting longer than me. There is an inscription on the front, so faded among the scratch marks it is almost impossible to read. I can just make out the words *watch* and *me*.

"What do you think this means?" I ask Midge, who shrugs.

"I'm not sure. Doesn't look to be worth much, but I've never seen anything quite like it."

"That's the thing," I say slowly. "I'm virtually certain I've seen this necklace before."

❧

London, 1944

The Red Cross center, a converted dance hall in Southwark, was hot and stuffy. The wooden benches that ran along rectangular tables were packed with volunteers jostling cups of ersatz coffee and trying not to spill them on the care packages they were filling. A halo of cigarette smoke lingered around the top of the room.

"Pardon me," I said as my elbow bumped against an older woman seated beside me. The woman gave a faint harrumph and continued trying to close the too-small box she had been given. The packages were meant to contain cocoa and condensed milk, a tin of sardines and a bar of chocolate. There was also sugar and margarine and a bar of soap, which I feared would make the whole thing smell of lavender.

I'd decided to volunteer for the Red Cross after an incident a few weeks earlier. One day as I walked across the city, I saw a young girl sitting on a pile of rubble. She wasn't crying, but rather sitting numbly, wearing one shoe and holding a scrap of a blanket. I walked up to her. "Are you hurt?" She didn't answer and I realized that she was in shock. I found a nearby police officer and turned the girl over to him. As I walked away, I was remorseful that I had not done more. *Parents killed in the bombing*, I was told when I went to the police station the next day to inquire about her well-being. *Sent to an orphanage*. I wish that I might have taken in the girl myself, but I was barely getting by just taking care of my mum. Still, the image of the girl lingered with me for days. My own childhood had been difficult enough with a single mother. How much harder would it be with no parents in wartime?

After that, I became aware of the suffering around me more acutely. Simply trying to survive the war no longer felt like enough. I remembered a poster I had seen during one of my long nightly walks along the Thames that I took as a means of escaping the tiny flat I shared with my mum. I went back and found the notice pinned to a wall, fresh against the faded posters exhorting women to "Make Do or Mend" and keep the curtains closed for the blackout, and to send their children to the countryside to escape the Blitz. *Volunteers Needed at the Red Cross Center*, it read.

So I had turned up the next evening and was seated without ceremony or introduction at one of the long tables to pack boxes. I looked across the table now. The women who volunteered at the Red Cross came from all walks of life, singletons in their twenties like myself, and mums and grandmothers who wanted to do their bit. Here we sat elbow to elbow, packing boxes, the fine ladies from Kensington and Mayfair, and girls like myself, whom they wouldn't have so much as looked at outside of wartime. We chatted among ourselves, eager for a few hours' company to forget the dreariness and hardship. It didn't matter if you came from a one-room flat in South London, where your mum took in laundry and men and drank her days away. Some (not me) dressed as though they were going out for a night in the city, brought wine or pastries to share among us, if they had any to bring. One of the few things I did not hate about the war was the way it served as a kind of equalizer. More was possible now, no matter where you came from.

There was a man who sat in the corner, puffing on a pipe and supervising us without speaking. Someone had mentioned that he was from the International Committee of the Red Cross. I wondered why he was here and not deployed, like most men his age. He must have been a few years older than me, though his dusty wool sports coat with leather patches at the elbow made him appear more mature, attractive in a professorial sort of way. He looked in my direction suddenly and our eyes met. I turned away hurriedly, feeling my cheeks flush. I had a boyfriend, or at least I had until Joe had left for the war. He hadn't wanted me to worry while he was away or mourn him if he didn't come back. So while others had been in a hurry to get married before deploying, he'd broken up with me.

Sudden rumbling caused the building to shake. "Blimey!" one of the women cried. A collective murmur rippled throughout the room as dust and bits of plaster began to fall from the ceiling. Some of the women reached for the gas masks they'd remembered to bring, but mine was back home in our flat, useless now. Should we make our way to the air raid shelters? I worried about my mum, who was undoubtedly sleeping off a day of drinking gin. More than once, I wondered if I would return to find a crater where our dismal flat had been. She would never know what hit her, which would be a blessing. I felt guilty at the thought.

When a few minutes had passed and no further explosions came, the women resumed work on the care packages.

Forty-five minutes later, when the last box was filled, the women stood to leave. I walked over to the coatrack. Behind it there was a bulletin board with the volunteer schedule and some other routine announcements. I scanned the familiar notices, seeing nothing new. Reluctantly, I put on my coat and began the long walk home.

2

Helaine

Paris, 1938

You almost never know when it is the last time.

One Sunday, when Helaine was five years old, her father took her on their weekly outing to the Parc Monceau. They flew a kite until the string became tangled in the branches of an oak tree from the brisk September wind. Then her father bought a bag of salted nuts, and they sat by the pond, watching leaves and bits of newspaper blow by and send the pigeons scattering. Helaine leaned against the scratchy wool of his coat sleeve, smelling the lingering pipe smoke. Finally, she complained that she was tired, and they started for home.

She would not leave the house again. The next week, she died.

Almost died, Helaine corrected herself as she did her mother, every time she told the story. Maman always pressed her hand to her chest and fluttered her eyelashes, as though she was about to lose consciousness herself. She insisted that Helaine had stopped breathing and that the doctor had declared her heartbeat gone, his next sentence of condolence cut short by Maman's singular wail.

Helaine had been looking forward to starting school in just one week's time. Her new bag and shoes sat by the door waiting. But the fever came without warning. One moment she was fine and the next day bedridden, scarcely able to move or speak.

Helaine lay in bed, clinging to life, for weeks. Doctors came and went, shaking their heads apologetically and explaining that there was nothing more to be done. The Chief Rabbi of Paris called at their house to offer prayers.

Then, just as improbably, Helaine returned. She coughed and opened her eyes and sat up, the fever that had held her in its grip suddenly broken.

Except it wasn't. The effects of influenza, which had swept through Paris and hit Helaine with stunning force, were long-term. Her heart was weakened and susceptible to infection. She struggled to walk even a few steps.

From that moment, Helaine's world changed entirely. Her family no longer traveled. Helaine had vague memories of before she became ill, of grand summer vacations in the south of France, winter ski trips to St. Moritz. Suddenly, all of that stopped. Visitors to their home became practically nonexistent. Before Helaine's illness, they had several servants. They were all let go to keep germs farther from her. Instead of Helaine starting school that fall, her parents hired a tutor. She watched enviously from her window as other children walked back and forth to school, yearning to feel the pavement beneath her feet and the sun on her face, unencumbered by a window sash.

It had been more than thirteen years since she had taken ill, and still she remained inside. Helaine, eighteen now, peered out the window at the grand street below. Though she had little to compare it with, Helaine knew from a young age that their home, a four-story town house with a courtyard, was extraordinary. Even in their elegant neighborhood in the 9th arrondissement, referred to by some as the "Beaux Quartiers," the wide, gleaming house stood out like a shining jewel. Down the street, a moving truck idled along the pavement, the logo *Le Castagne* emblazoned on its side. As a young child, Helaine had always taken in the appearance of movers with curious enthusiasm, hoping that she might be getting new neighbors with a child her age. After her illness, though, her interest waned. Even if a child moved in on their street, she would not be allowed out to play with them.

Helaine looked away from the window, turning from the world that could not be hers to the one she was forced to live in. Once Helaine could no longer go outside, her mother had set out to make their already opulent house a place that Helaine would never want to leave. As a result, their home was a marvel of comforts. The walls were bright and decorated with cheerful paintings of faraway places. The furniture was softly upholstered with downy pillows Helaine could sink into until she was almost lost. Every book or toy Helaine wanted was hers for the having. As she had grown older, Helaine chose fabrics for her dresses, and they were made and brought for her to try on. But what good was having beautiful clothes with nowhere to wear them? It was as if she lived in a gilded cage.

She was sitting in the library now, her favorite room in the house, with her feet tucked up beneath her in the window seat. Walls of books climbed to the ceiling, so high that a small rolling ladder was needed to reach the top shelves. Helaine had been permitted for as long as she could remember to roam the shelves freely. No one ever said a book was too grown-up or that she shouldn't read it. Her mind was as free as her body was trapped and so she learned to read early and voraciously. Here, the only limit holding her back from discovering the outside world was Helaine herself. There was a kind of pain in reading about all of the places she could not see beyond the walls of their house. But in these books, she could be anyone and go anywhere, and she gratefully took the ride.

In her hands, she held a small, leather-bound journal, one of her most treasured possessions. Helaine didn't just read stories; she loved to write them as well. She wrote about a girl called Anna, her strong alter ego who could travel and do magnificent things. Helaine sent her on many great journeys. For the past few days, she had written about Anna visiting Italy and seeing the Spanish Steps and Colosseum, sights that Helaine herself had only dreamed about. She had created a friend, Sofia, whom Anna had met in Rome, and now the two girls were debating if they should head to Lisbon or Athens.

Not sure of the answer, Helaine closed her journal and picked up *Little Women*, which she was reading for the third time. Normally, she preferred more adventurous books, like *The Three Musketeers*. But she identified with Beth's confinement and the way that Jo felt torn between home and seeing the world. Helaine looked out at the Paris streets, which seemed to beckon. Why not go outside? she thought suddenly. She had no physical impairments anymore and she had not been sick for years. Rather it was the fear of illness (her parents' fear, really) that kept her from living fully.

Helaine heard footsteps down the corridor and knew without checking that it was Maman. It was not just the lightness of her step. Her mother was the only other person who was ever there. Papa traveled the world for his business. When he did come home, he would first quarantine in a small flat off Rue Petrelle so as not to bring germs from his travels and make her sick.

Or so he said. Helaine knew that really he went there to meet his lover. Her mind reeled back to when she was eight and saw Papa's limousine pull up on the street in front of their house. Her heart had skipped a beat. Papa always brought fun and light, the whiff of foreign countries and a welcome break from her solitary confinement. And gifts. Helaine watched with anticipation as the rear door of the limousine opened. As the top of Papa's familiar hat appeared, she glimpsed something else through the car door. A woman's leg. The dress hem and shapely calf beneath seamed nylons were unmistakably feminine. At first, Helaine assumed that it was her mother. Maman was downstairs, though, and the leg bore no resemblance to her own matronly form. Helaine could not ignore the fact then that her father was unfaithful. Even though she did not know exactly what that meant at such a young age, somehow she understood.

Helaine's father was not an unkind man. He provided them with every material comfort. But so many French men, especially wealthy ones, kept lovers on the side and there was nothing to be done about it. Maman pretended not to notice. That was the charade and they all maintained it. Helaine often wondered if it was her illness and the burden of caring for her that had ripped her parents' marriage apart, or if the infidelity was culturally inevitable.

Restless now, Helaine walked from the library toward the kitchen. As she passed the china cabinet in the hallway, she spied her grandmother's tea set. Sadness rose in her. One of the things she missed most after getting sick was going to her grandmother's house, a dusty mansion in Neuilly-sur-Seine with an attic that had endless trunks for a child to explore. Helaine's grandmother died when Helaine was nine and Helaine never got to see her or visit her house again. They had just a few things of hers, including the silver tea set.

Looking at the tea set now, it seemed to represent everything Helaine had lost, her grandmother, her freedom. *Her life.* She had accepted her solitude, but as she had gotten older, her desire to explore the outside world had grown. It burned inside her now, hotter than ever. She could not go on like this any longer. Impulsively, she returned to her room, changed clothes and found her coat. It was a size too small, and she had never actually worn it.

She walked downstairs to where her mother was just pulling a tray of croissants from the oven. Though they could afford an army of servants, Maman insisted on doing everything herself for Helaine, cooking healthy meals, overseeing her education and her care. Sometimes Helaine found her mother watching her as she slept. She would reach out and touch Helaine, as if to make sure she was still there. Her mother was constantly in motion. Helaine had no early memories of her sitting down. Only later would Helaine realize that her mother's perpetual movement was not only to help and care for Helaine, but to stave off her own loneliness.

Helaine's mother came over and put her arms around her. Helaine buried her nose in the familiar place in her mother's neck, inhaling her sweet scent. Maman smelled like cherries and vanilla, and Helaine never quite knew if that was natural or perfume or the aroma of the delicious baked goods she always made. Helaine always felt in her mother's embrace not just love, but the sadness of all of the things she had not been able to give her, her freedom, or at the very least a sibling as company. Helaine knew that there was disappointment mixed in as well. Her parents didn't talk of the hopes they had for her if she had been healthy, but she could see it in their eyes. They wanted Helaine to marry someone important and carry on the family name with her children. But all of that was gone now. She had been told that the illness she suffered as a child had left her unable to have children of her own. She was an empty vessel, a should-have-been.

Helaine's mother held out a croissant to her. Normally, Helaine loved the flaky, buttery treats, but today she had other things on her mind. "No, thank you." Her mother's expression was puzzled; it was not like Helaine to turn down one of her delicious baked goods. Then, seeing Helaine's coat, her brow furrowed.

"I'd like to take a walk," Helaine said, scarcely managing the words. It was not the first time Helaine had thought about going. But something, the fear of it angering her parents or perhaps of it being too much, had stopped her from pushing to go.

Now, though, something felt different. She was driven to see the outside world.

Helaine's mother looked at her as though she had suggested juggling knives. "But how can you possibly?"

"Just a short walk," Helaine replied quickly. "It's early, so there won't be many people out."

"It's too dangerous," her mother protested. "You might catch something and get sick." Helaine watched as her mother's eyes grew dark, and Helaine knew that she was remembering the fear and sadness of Helaine's childhood illness once more.

"I will be safe. The doctor said fresh air will do me good."

"He meant short walks around the garden. Not running the streets of Paris."

Still, Helaine would not be dissuaded. "Once around the block. I'll go now, early in the morning when no one else is out. Please. I cannot stay in this house forever." Helaine's voice rose uncharacteristically. She and her mother had never fought. Helaine asking to walk was their first disagreement now, though, a fissure.

Helaine's mother stared at her skeptically and Helaine was certain she would refuse. "Fine," she relented. Helaine looked at her mother with disbelief. Helaine was eighteen years old now, though. She could hardly keep her prisoner. "But just down the street."

"And back straightaway," Helaine replied, doubting the promise even as she made it.

"Shall I come with you?" her mother asked.

"No," Helaine said quickly, regretting it as a hurt look crossed her mother's face. It was not that Helaine disliked her mother's company. To the contrary, they had been one another's only companions for a long time now and had always gotten on well, moving like two appendages of the same body in their shared space. But this was about freedom, and to Helaine, having her mother beside her, hovering and worrying, was the very opposite of that.

"You shouldn't go by yourself," Maman pressed.

"I *need* to do this myself." Helaine feared that her mother would insist on going.

To Helaine's surprise, her mother did not argue further. "Fine," Maman said again, her voice begrudging. Helaine realized then that her mother liked their solitude and being shut off from the world, because she felt safer where she could control everything. Almost everything. "But come back in a few minutes or I shall have to come looking for you. And be sure to leave yourself enough strength for the journey home." Helaine's mother walked from the kitchen and a moment later returned with a blue wool beret. She put it on Helaine's head and pulled it low, drawing it so close around her ears that it squeezed. Her expression was solemn and intent, as if by that one gesture she could keep Helaine safe. Then she handed her a few francs. "In case you need anything," she added. Helaine wanted to point out that she was only going down the street, but she knew that to her mother, Helaine going even that short distance felt far and unpredictable.

"Thank you." Quickly, before Maman could change her mind, Helaine walked from the kitchen. She started down the stairs, half expecting her mother to come after her. But the house behind her remained still.

As Helaine stepped outdoors into the chilly March morning, her excitement grew. She had looked down at their street through the window so many times over the years, but to be standing on it was something else entirely. Everything seemed so much brighter and crisper, the colors of the early spring flowers in the window boxes more vibrant. Helaine ran her hand along the iron gate in front of their house, savoring the feeling of cool condensation against her skin.

But she only had a short while; there was no time to linger.

Helaine started for the corner, then hesitated, considering which route she should take. She needed to pack the absolute most she could into her brief walk. She set out east in the direction of Rue de Paradis, with its cluster of lively storefronts. The world looked so different from the outside than it had from her window. She drank in the still-shuttered cafés and shops, which would have seemed dull and ordinary to anyone else, like water after a drought.

When Helaine reached the intersection, she paused. Her heart raced and her lungs burned. Her legs felt a bit wobbly and she eyed a bench across the way, fighting the urge to go to it and sit down. The cobblestones were slick beneath her feet. Helaine hesitated, her mother's doubts reverberating in her mind. Maman was right, Helaine decided. She could not do this. She was in no shape. But Helaine somehow sensed that if she did not continue on now, she would be a prisoner forever. She took a deep breath and, with renewed determination, stepped forward.

And with every step, Helaine felt a bit stronger. Once she started again, she did not stop. Her confidence grew. Helaine thought she might grow tired. Instead, the exertion brought a certain kind of energy and elation. She was strong enough after all.

Helaine turned onto a wide thoroughfare lined with grand shops. She paused in front of an elegant department store. *Lévitan*, the engraved brass sign atop the marble entranceway read. She had a vague memory of being there once before she had taken ill. She could not have been more than three or four at the time.

Helaine peered through the glass window. The store had loomed large in her memory during the years of her confinement, hazy images of soaring ceilings and counters of fine goods as far as the eye could see. Some memories, she found, were outsized in her mind's eye and looked smaller with the distance of years. But the department store with its terraced balconies and grand displays was as elegant as she had remembered.

Helaine wanted to stroll the aisles. But it was not open yet, and even if it had been, she had not brought money with her beyond the few coins her mother had given her. Perhaps she could persuade Maman to come with her and they might browse together, making up for the years they had lost.

Helaine continued on past the department store. She yearned to keep going and never stop. But Maman's words reverberated through her head: *leave yourself enough strength for the journey home*. Helaine didn't want to stay out and worry her mother either, for fear of risking her anger and not being allowed to go again. Reluctantly, she started back. Her blood surged warm with excitement. Helaine knew after that she would walk these streets every single day for the rest of her life.

Helaine returned home, exhilarated. Next time, she resolved, she would go farther. Maman leaped to her feet when Helaine entered, her brow furrowed with concern. "How was it?"

"Wonderful." Helaine smiled.

But her mother did not share her excitement. "That was too much," she fretted. "You went farther than just down the street." Her tone was less accusatory than concerned. "Your cheeks are flushed. I will draw you a bath. You must be exhausted." And somehow, hearing the words, Helaine was.

The next morning, Helaine awoke early. Though her limbs ached a bit from the previous day's walk, she was filled with anticipation about the prospect of going again, and farther. She slipped from the house before her mother awoke. Maman had given permission the previous day, but Helaine feared she might say no if she asked a second time. It was not yet light as Helaine set out in a different direction, eager to explore. The still-damp streets sparkled and the pavement gave off an ancient smell, like a secret whispered. The bistros were still closed, but the proprietors were setting down the wicker chairs and drying the small round tables. Helaine walked faster now, turning new corners, heedless of how far she went or the possibility of getting lost.

Halfway down an unfamiliar street, Helaine heard music coming from an open window of a house. At first, she thought someone might be playing a gramophone or radio, though it seemed too early for that. Then, hearing the clearness of the sound, she realized that someone was actually playing. She walked toward the window, curious. There was a man seated alone in a semicircle of chairs, playing some sort of chamber music on a cello. Helaine knew that she should not be spying on him. But she was drawn to the richness of the sound. Her eyes fixed on the cello and the way the bearded man who played it ran his hands over the large instrument, caressing it.

Then the cellist looked up abruptly and his eyes met hers. He had seen Helaine watching him. She pulled back from the window and started away swiftly. The music stopped. She hurried down the street.

"Wait," a voice called from behind. The man had come to the door, followed her. She noticed as he neared that he had a slight limp. What had she been thinking, Helaine berated herself silently, peering into a stranger's house?

She started quickly away once more. Her foot caught a crack and she fell, smacking her hands against the pavement. Feeling the pain, she let out an involuntary cry. She was not badly hurt, though, and for a moment, she considered running. But Helaine did not have the stamina to go for long and the man could surely catch her if he wanted.

He loomed over her now, tall and broad-shouldered. Longish brown hair brushed into his eyes. His face was lined with concern. "Are you hurt?"

Helaine shook her head, for although her knees still stung beneath her dress, she could tell that the skin was not broken. "Just clumsy," Helaine managed, feeling her face flush.

The man reached down to help her up. Helaine pulled back,

afraid. But the man's cheeks were rosy and his wide smile genuine. In his expression, there was not the slightest bit of guile.
Helaine was certain in an instant that she could trust him. She
took his hand. His fingertips felt calloused and cracked, but the
palms were smooth and strong.

I know him. That was Helaine's first thought as she stood and
looked up at the man, though of course that was impossible.
She had not left the house or met anybody in years. But there
was something instantly recognizable about him. Helaine was
struck by his features, which reminded her of puzzle pieces that,
although each one was distinctive, formed the perfect image
when placed together. His full lips were framed by a goatee and
the flecks of gray said that he was older than her, though she
could not tell by how much. His expression was a mixture of
warmth and concern.

"Not at all. These sidewalks are a disgrace. I saw you at the
window," he added.

Her cheeks flushed. "I'm sorry, I shouldn't have been there."

"I'm glad you were. What good is music if people do not listen? Do you play an instrument?"

Helaine shook her head, thinking of the piano in her living room. There had been no one to teach her. "You should
get back to your music." Helaine started to leave, eager to get
away and yet somehow oddly reluctant. This man was one of
the few people she had met outside of her family and she was
curious to know him.

"Wait," he said. Helaine turned back. "I was actually just fin-
ishing. Will you have coffee with me?"

"No," Helaine answered too quickly, caught off guard by the
unexpected invitation. She immediately regretted her response.
But the question seemed a silly one, for surely there were no cafés
open at such an early hour. The man looked instantly saddened.
Helaine loved the way his face seemed to shift rapidly, telegraph-
ing his emotions without pretension. Helaine had grown up in

a world of reserve and conventions, and the stranger's directness was a breath of fresh air.

"Are you certain?" he pressed.

She faltered. Part of her wanted to accept and get to know him. Talking to someone she had met by happenstance was one thing, though. What he was suggesting sounded almost like a date. "I'm sorry, I can't. I have to get home." It was the truth. Helaine hadn't told her mother that she was going out this time, and if Maman woke up and discovered her gone, she would be alarmed.

"Well, I will be in this same spot tomorrow rehearsing and I hope you will walk this way once again."

Helaine nodded. She could not imagine why he would care so much if she met him again. Did he like her? Helaine's cheeks flushed and she started away, hoping he had not noticed. "Wait!" he said again.

Helaine half turned back, keeping her head low. "Yes?"

"What's your name?"

"Helaine," she replied, lifting her head slightly so that her eyes met his. "With an *e*." It was only after she hurried away that she realized she had not learned his.

When Helaine awoke the next day, the sky was gray above the slate rooftops and a faint drizzle misted the windowpanes. She hoped to slip from the house once more, but Maman was already in the kitchen, kneading dough. "You can't possibly go out in this," Maman fretted.

"A short walk," Helaine said. "I will carry my umbrella and bundle up. I have to go," she added. "I left my scarf on a bench." This was, of course, a lie.

"Oh, Helaine!" She thought her mother would be mad at her for losing her expensive silk scarf. But Maman was only concerned for her. "I can send someone for it. It probably isn't even there anymore."

"No, I know just where I dropped it. I need to go myself."

"Just straight there and back. The weather is dreadful."

She gave Maman a kiss on her cheek, as if the press of her lips could erase her mother's worries. Despite their family's wealth, Helaine's mother did not have the easiest of lives, and the last thing Helaine wanted to do was worry her more.

"You'll hurry, won't you?" Maman pressed. Helaine left without answering, swiping a parasol from the coat stand before hurrying out the front door.

As Helaine retraced her steps from the previous day, it began to rain more heavily, sending the last few well-heeled pedestrians still on the sidewalks scurrying like ants. Drops rolled off the edge of the umbrella, splashing her coat and seeping down the back of her dress. Her shoes grew damp from the dirty puddles that kicked up from the pavement as she walked. For a moment, Helaine considered turning back.

When Helaine reached the building where she had seen the man play, the window was closed. Helaine peered through the glass, worried that perhaps she had the wrong address. The chairs where the musician had sat were in the exact same arrangement, though. Only this time, they were empty. She turned away, feeling foolish.

"Helaine-with-an-*e*!" a voice called. She spun to see the man from the previous day coming toward her carrying a basket, his gait awkward. He did not have an umbrella, and his hair and beard dripped with rain. "I'm sorry I was late. I went to get these." He held up a bag of pastries. He reached to open the door to the house, but it was locked. "Bah!" he exclaimed. Then he looked around. "Come with me."

"But…" Helaine began to protest as he led her across the street to a small park. Did he expect them to sit outside in the rain? She followed him to a clearing off the main path where a thick canopy of trees created a kind of shelter. He dried off one of the large flat stones beneath the trees and gestured for her to sit.

Helaine hesitated, imagining Maman's disapproval when she

came home with her dress soaked. Her hair was already curled with moisture, though, and her stockings damp beneath her feet. As she sat down, he smiled. "I didn't know if you would actually come." He had doubted her return, just as she had his.

He pulled a white cloth from the basket and spread it before him, then produced a coffee press and two cups. He poured her a cup from the carafe, then removed two chocolate croissants from the bag. Helaine was surprised. She had not expected him to return to meet her, much less bring a picnic. It seemed in that moment the nicest thing anyone other than her mother had done for her in her entire life. "You wouldn't come for coffee, so I brought coffee to you," he explained, seeming to read her thoughts. "I'm Gabriel."

Helaine took the cup he offered, still surprised that anyone would go to such trouble for her. "A pleasure to meet you." She took a bite out of the croissant. "Delicious."

They ate in silence for several seconds, Helaine studying his face out of the corner of her eye. His beard was somewhat un-kempt and flecked with premature gray and his curly hair was tousled. He wore no coat, despite the rain, and his clothes were a bit rumpled, as if he had picked them up off the floor instead of hanging them. "Do you live there?" Helaine asked when she had finished chewing. She gestured across the street to the house where she'd heard him playing the previous day.

"No, that's the studio where I rehearse. My flat is in the north of the city in Montmartre." Helaine had visited the area a few times as a child and had vague memories of the artistic neigh-borhood, set on a steep hill beneath the white domes of Sacré-Cœur and brimming with cafés and galleries.

"I walk sometimes and listen to the sounds when the park is still. I'm a cellist with the Orchestre National," he added. He-laine was awed. In the world where she had grown up, there were bankers and businessmen and lawyers. Practical jobs, her mother would say. She had never met anyone before who worked in the arts.

"And you?" he asked.

Helaine faltered, wishing that she had something equally grand to say. "I just live with my parents." She considered telling him about her illness, a kind of alibi for why she had not done more. But she didn't want him to think of her—or treat her—any differently. "I do like to read and write."

"You should become a journalist," he replied. As if it were that simple. What made him think she could do such a thing? "Report on the war in Spain. It's a terrible thing, the way the people are suffering. Do you know much about it?"

Helaine shook her head. Although she read constantly, it was primarily fiction. The real world, from which she had been cut off for so many years, had always felt like someone else's problem. Until now. The events of the outside world suddenly loomed large and it seemed important to learn about them. "Tell me."

Helaine listened, rapt, as Gabriel talked about the conflict in Spain between Franco and the loyalists and the way people were suffering and dying, why it mattered. "You should take time to read about it."

"I shall," Helaine promised. "We do get a few newspapers. *Les Echos* for its financial reports, and anything with news of the Jewish situation abroad."

He tilted his head slightly. "Your family is Jewish?"

"Yes."

Gabriel's face turned somber, and he did not speak for several seconds. Perhaps he was one of the French who did not like Jews. Although Helaine's family was one of the oldest and most respected Jewish families in Paris, there was an unspoken divide because of the anti-Semitism that ran through some parts of French society. This had been truer than ever in recent years, when far-right politicians stirred anti-Jewish rhetoric, and political cartoons and editorials in the paper blamed the Jews for

France's woes. She worried that Gabriel would not want to see her anymore.

"There is a great darkness spreading across Europe," he said finally. Helaine nodded. He did not dislike Jews; she could tell instantly. Rather, he was worried for her. The news of what was happening across Europe was impossible to ignore, even for someone like her who had been isolated from the outside world. Hitler had claimed power in Germany and was trying to take control of Austria. And no one, not France or England, seemed willing to stop him. Gabriel continued, "I'm afraid that much of it has been directed at the Jews, unjustly of course. Has your family considered leaving?" he asked.

"No." Helaine was caught off guard. "Our family has been in Paris for centuries. How could we possibly leave?" She turned the question over in her mind, considering it for the first time. Her parents treated her like a child, told her so little. Perhaps they *had* considered emigrating and not mentioned it to her. The thought of leaving her childhood home and setting out for parts unknown filled Helaine with both sadness and excitement. But she brushed the thought aside just as quickly. Helaine's parents didn't even want her going out of the house. They would never contemplate leaving the country.

"This is Paris," Helaine said firmly, trying to close the subject. After all, they were in the capital of France, one of the oldest and most sophisticated cities in the world. "Things like that can't happen here."

Gabriel looked as though he wanted to argue. "Yes, of course," he said, but Helaine could tell he didn't mean it. Annoyance rose in her. She had spent her whole life being placated and condescended to, and she feared now that Gabriel was going to turn out to be just like everyone else.

"You think differently?" she pressed, now unable to leave it alone.

"I think," he replied gently, "that nothing is what it once was. We can't assume. But I don't want to quarrel."

Neither spoke for several seconds. The rain was falling heavier now, the steady torrent of drops too much for the canopy of leaves above to withstand. "I should go," Helaine said, not wanting to worry her mother further by staying out in the downpour. They stood and she helped him pack up the picnic. When they finished, they stood facing one another. "I hope that I shall see you again," she said.

"You can count on it." He looked deeply into her eyes. Helaine turned away, feeling her cheeks flush. "Of course, that would be easier if you would tell me where you live." Helaine did not reply. "Shall I see you home?"

"No, thank you." She could not risk her mother seeing her with Gabriel. "But I'll come again tomorrow." She turned and left, feeling Gabriel watch her as she went. As she started for home, she could not escape the certain feeling that something new and strange and wonderful in her life had begun at last.

3

Louise

Henley-on-Thames, 1953

I take the necklace back from Midge and hold it in my palm, hand trembling slightly. "Do you know where it came from?" I ask her.

"No idea, luv. I'm afraid I've never been much for jewelry."

"Me neither. It looks exactly like one I saw during the war, though." There is even a nick in the top arch of the heart, just as I remember it.

Midge runs her finger over the chain, still indifferent. "I suppose we could sell it for the metal." I feel a tug of disappointment that Midge does not share my curiosity about the object. But how can she, really, when she had not been there?

"Do you mind if I keep it?" I ask, surprising myself. I haven't wanted anything from the shop before. Though I enjoy sorting through the boxes, I've never really cared about belongings. "I can pay you for it if you want."

Midge waves her hand. "No, go on and take it. It's one less thing I've got to bin."

"Thank you." I slip the necklace into my purse. Then I return to work and resume sorting through the other items in the crate. But my mind keeps returning to the necklace. I pull it out again, wishing that I had seen the one from the war more closely and that I had a better image of it in my memory. As I study the gold, and the engraved letters on it, though, my certainty grows: this is not a necklace like the one I saw during the war. This *is* the same necklace. How has it come to be here, after disappearing from Germany more than eight years ago?

I want to bring it up to Midge again, but I know she won't understand my curiosity any more the second time than she did the first. Instead, I look through the crate it came in to see if the other items are somehow related to it. There is a broken alarm clock and a pair of cracked leather gloves, but nothing that seems significant or related to the necklace.

I finish the first crate and start on another. The morning passes quickly, and when I look up, it is nearly noon. I stand and return the last crate I'd worked on, now empty, to the shelf, then prepare to leave. "I will see you tomorrow," I say to Midge. Then I turn back. "The crate that necklace came in…do you have any idea where it came from?"

Midge seems to think for a second. "Probably the donations bin out back like most everything else." Anyone could have left it there, I realize, discouraged. I turn to go. "You know, my sister, Millie, owns a jewelry shop in London," Midge calls after me as I near the door of the shop. "She would probably know more about the style of the necklace or maybe where it was made."

"You have a sister?" I realize how little Midge and I know about one another.

Midge nods. "She has a tiny little place off Portobello Road. Not more than a cart, really. But she knows jewelry and she might be able to help place the necklace, if you wanted to make a quick trip into the city to show it to her."

As I contemplate an errand to London, all of the why-nots bubble up: my job at the shop, the things I need to do at home, not to mention being there for the children. "I'll think about it, thanks," I say. Then I walk through the doorway and start for home.

Later after I have washed up from dinner and played a game of snakes and ladders with the children, I begin to draw their weekly bath, my thoughts returning to the necklace. It might be one of many that were made at the same time, not particularly unique. But it is the words, *watch* and *me*, that stop me in my tracks. How many identical charms bearing this phrase can there possibly be?

As the children splash in the tub, I pull the necklace out to examine it once more. "Pretty!" Phed cries, reaching out with wet, soapy hands. I lower the necklace to show her and she runs her finger over the surface. "May I have it?"

I pull the necklace back and dry it with a flash of irritation. Can a single object not belong to just me now that I have children? It often seems that I am not allowed to have anything at all for myself. But Phed is just a child and her need to possess understandable. "No, darling," I manage, tamping down my annoyance. "It doesn't belong to Mummy."

After the children have gone to bed, I carry the necklace downstairs, over to the chair where Joe sits reading the newspaper. "What do you think?" I hold out the necklace on my open palm for him to see. Joe looks up and blinks, as though not quite sure what it is. "I found it at the shop. Interesting, isn't it?"

"I suppose," Joe says with indifference. He does not know much about my experiences during the war years, or where I might have seen the necklace before, or why it matters so much to me, and I find myself wanting to share more with him, to let him in.

"I wonder where it came from," I press. "Europe, before or during the war, most likely."

I wait for him to ask why I suspect that, but he does not. "Then whoever owned it is probably dead." His voice is flat.

There is a silence between us. "I'm sorry," he says stiffly. "It's just that the last thing I want to talk about is the past."

"The thing is, Joe." I swallow, trying again, "I think I have seen this necklace before."

He looks at me sideways. "You mean, like in a shop or something? Because I'm sure I can find you a new one for Christmas. You don't need to wear someone else's old junk."

I smile fondly at his willingness to get me whatever I want. Despite his own struggles, Joe loves me and he is doing the very best he can. Then my amusement fades; what is broken between us cannot be fixed with jewelry. "That's very kind, but that isn't what I meant. You see, I think I saw this necklace during the war."

"Oh." There is a thud in his voice and I realize too late that bringing it up was a mistake. "That seems unlikely, doesn't it?"

"I guess so." I find myself, as I had so many times in my younger years, walking back my curiosity, not wanting to overstep.

No, Joe is not one to appreciate the significance of the necklace. He takes life day-to-day and at face value, and that is all that he can manage for now. I remember what Midge said about her sister, Millie, and her jewelry shop. Suddenly, a day in London feels like the most appealing thing in the world.

"I might pop into the city tomorrow and go to the shops," I say casually to Joe. "It's been ages." I wonder if he might ask why, or perhaps even offer to join me for a day out.

But that was the old Joe. Now he simply nods. "That sounds nice. You'll be home in time for the children?"

The next day, I drop the children off at school a few minutes early, then head straight for the shop. I find Midge in the back, making tea. "You're early," she remarks. "Fancy a cuppa?"

"No, thank you." I pause. "I was thinking I might run down to London and show Millie the necklace. That is, if you can spare me for the day."

"I can." She sets down her teacup and scribbles an address on a notepad. Then she tears off the address and gives the sheet to me. "Give her my love, won't you?"

I start for the station. As I board the train for Paddington along with a few suited men commuting into the city, I look over my shoulder guiltily. The trip seems frivolous. What do I hope to learn, really? But it has been so long since I've had a day to myself. I'll be gone just a few hours and back in time to pick up the children. I only hope that the school nurse won't try to ring and say that Ewen's cold has turned into something worse and that I need to fetch him early.

The train pulls from the station and gradually gains speed, the town and Thames fading in the distance. Farther into the countryside, the fog lifts, revealing gently rolling meadows dotted with cows and sheep, broken only by the occasional farmhouse. A man pushing a sandwich trolley comes through, and my stomach rumbles. I'd fed the children breakfast but had not myself managed to eat this morning. I purchase a sausage roll and unwrap the paper to reveal an anemic-looking sandwich inside.

Forty minutes later, the countryside gives way to the outskirts of London, planned housing developments comprised of clusters of row homes, many still under construction. Then we reach the outer limits of the city proper, factories and closer streets and narrow brick town houses that seem to lean against one another. When the familiar skyline appears through a haze of coal soot, a mix of anxiety and anticipation rises in me. London was the city of my childhood and all of the painful memories come rushing back now. But I am not that girl anymore, I remind myself. I am a grown woman now, a wife, a mum. The old ghosts can't hurt me anymore. And at the same time, London has always brought an air of possibility that I cannot quite bring myself to hate.

The train wheezes into Paddington, wheels screeching as it slows to a halt alongside the platform. I rise and shuffle off with the other passengers. Outside the station, I pause in front of a Barclays bank, trying to get my bearings. I have not been in London in a few years, and for a moment, I am overwhelmed. Portobello Road is in the Notting Hill neighborhood, west of London's city center, too far for a walk. I consider going to the taxi stand; I have the coins in my purse. But the old, frugal Louise, who had never quite left me, rises stronger now that I am back in the city. I tuck my chin and set off down the escalator to the Tube. At the bottom, I shudder in the deep cavernous space, assaulted by memories of long nights spent here during the Blitz, sleeping upright on the hard ground and fearing that every explosion might be the last.

I emerge from Notting Hill station twenty minutes later and make my way toward Portobello Road. The familiar, sooty air fills my nose. As I set foot on the pavement, the bustle of the city wraps around me like a cloak, and my stride grows longer.

I make a turn at the corner, and then another, feeling my way. Portobello Road hosts an open-air market two mornings per week, but it isn't a market day and the streets are quieter without the vendors and their makeshift stalls and wheeled carts.

I find the address Midge had given me, a tiny jewelry store sandwiched between a bookseller and an antiques shop. As I open the door, a bell tinkles above, announcing my arrival. I start toward the counter at the back of the narrow shop, then stop short. Millie is a carbon copy of her sister—it is as if Midge had been plucked out of the village and placed here smack in the middle of London.

"I'm Louise," I begin, trying to figure out the right way to explain why I've come.

But Millie waves her hand. "Midgey rang me this morning that you were coming. I'm Millie."

"Midge didn't mention that you are twins."

"We aren't." I'm surprised once more. Their resemblance is so close. "I'm eleven months older. The necklace," she adds abruptly. "Let me see it." Though the sisters look identical, Millie's raspy voice is nothing like Midge's bright chirp. I pass it to her, feeling an odd pang of remorse as it leaves my hand. Millie studies the necklace. "Ah, yes, this is a Mizpah charm."

"Mizpah?" I repeat the unfamiliar word.

"Mizpah is Hebrew and it means 'watchtower.'"

"Is that why it is engraved with the word *watch*?"

Millie shakes her head. "Not exactly. The charm is inscribed with a biblical phrase from the book of Genesis. 'The Lord watch between me and thee.' It is part of a longer biblical prayer, 'The Lord watch between me and thee when we are absent one from another.' But usually just the first part is engraved because the rest is too long. The charm splits into two parts, so you are only seeing half of the inscription." I nod, trying to take in all of the information.

"So, the necklace is Jewish?"

"No, Mizpah jewelry is actually English. The tradition dates back to Victorian times. People, couples or lovers mostly, would give the other a half when they were to be separated in hopes of reuniting the two halves. It became quite popular during the First World War between soldiers and the women they left behind."

"English?" I repeat. "But I saw one of these in Germany that looked exactly the same." That the necklace was in fact English made it even less likely that I had seen it during the war.

"There's another half to this necklace—or was, at least, when it was made," she points out.

"Yes, I know. But this is the half I saw during the war. It has the same half of the inscription. I think it's the same one."

"It's possible. An English soldier might have been carrying it with him when he went over. But unlikely that it was this exact one. They are very common and there are plenty that look alike."

"Oh," I say, deflated. The necklace probably has nothing to

do with the one I saw. If I saw one at all. Suddenly, everything I went through during the war seemed hazy, like something I imagined or dreamed.

Millie hands the necklace back to me. "I'm sorry not to be of more help."

"Thank you."

"Give Midgey a hug for me."

"I shall," I say, envying their sisterly bond, something I never had. I start from the shop and down Portobello Road, the promise of answers evaporating like a chalk drawing on damp pavement in one of the Mary Poppins stories I read to the children. The necklace had been a fun diversion, nothing more. What had I expected? It is time to go home. Regular life descends upon me, gray and suffocating, and as I walk back toward the station, the first drops of rain begin to fall.

ↃↃ

London, 1944

I walked into the Red Cross volunteer center one evening, soaked from a heavy rain that had come on without warning during my commute. My wet clothes stuck to me, giving off that smoky smell that seemed to cling to everything after the nightly air raids. As I hung my coat on the rack by the door, a crisp new sheet of paper in the top right corner of the announcements board caught my eye.

Couriers wanted immediately.

I paused, interested. Then I read further. They were looking for people to go across to the Continent with a Red Cross delegation by ship and deliver the packages we made. I hadn't considered until that moment how the boxes we packed, once they left the volunteer center, made their way into the hands of the prisoners of war who needed them. It made sense; someone had to deliver the packages. Still, it seemed there ought to be a better way to find people qualified for such a task than simply putting up a sign.

Was I qualified? I turned the question over in my mind as I walked across the room and sat to begin filling packages. I had stayed in school until I was sixteen. I might have gone longer now that public education was free, but I had to work to support my mum and me and feed us and keep her off the street. I had done well in school, though, preferring the real subjects like math and science and languages to the domestic arts, where they steered girls. I knew that I had skills and smarts, and in another life, I might have been someone. No, even before the war, something inside me sensed that there was more to be had, if only I could figure out what that was.

Later that evening, after I had finished working and went to get my coat, I found myself drawn back to the flyer seeking volunteers. I walked to the man who sat at the desk in the corner. "Can you tell me more about the courier position?"

He looked up from the papers he had been reading. "You interested?" His voice was skeptical. I had not formally met him or spoken with him before, but I had seen his tall, angular figure crossing the room in long-legged strides, helping to lift a stack of boxes or making sure the volunteers were doing the packing correctly so that nothing broke or spilled in transit. He had brown hair that curled at the collar and a lock in front that refused to be cowed, but instead fell into his eyes.

"I am. I'm called Louise and I'm one of the volunteers who has been packing."

"Louise Emmons. I know who you are." I was surprised. I'd never spoken to him before. "I know everyone who works here." I considered whether I found him arrogant, but his voice was affable and his smile warm. "I'm Ian Shipley and I'm from the International Committee of the Red Cross. The position provides me with an exemption from military service because of its importance to the war effort," he added quickly.

Up close, he was more attractive than I thought previously, with hazel eyes and a slight dimple in his chin. Handsome, but not in a conventional sort of way. He had craggy features and eyes set a bit too narrowly, long eyelashes and a smattering of freckles that showed exactly how he had looked as a boy. I stilled myself. I'd already had my heart broken once by Joe when he left for the war, and I didn't intend to get anywhere near a man again.

But I was curious about the work. "The International Red Cross?"

"That's separate from the British Red Cross," he added. I had not until that moment realized there was a difference. "We're charged with getting the packages delivered and we are looking for a few able-bodied people to help. Women, in this case, since most of the men who could do the job are already off fighting. And we've got more prisoners than ever to reach." I nodded gravely. "Our men are suffering over there and it's critical that we get aid to them as quickly as possible." There was an intensity to his voice now. This was not just a job to Ian, but a mission.

"It's terrible work," he continued bluntly. "We'll be going behind enemy lines without a weapon or other protection and the pay is awful." I searched for some sign that he was joking but found none. He sounded as though he was trying to talk me out of going—which only made me more determined.

"If that sounds like too much, you can just stay here and pack boxes," Ian added. There was an irksome dismissiveness to his voice. Suddenly, staying here and packing boxes was the very last thing I wanted to do. I was seized with the urge to get out of London, out of England, and contribute more.

"It's not too much. How long would I be gone?"

"It's a quick trip, a week at most. Do you think your husband would mind?"

I bristled at the question. I was quite certain that no one asked the wives if they minded when their husbands went off to war.

"I'm not married," I said, hating the way it came out like an admission. I wanted to add that it was really none of his affair, but I refrained.

Joe flashed before my eyes. What would he say about my going if he were here? I brushed aside the thought. He was gone and the decision was mine alone.

"Just as well," Ian replied. "They probably wouldn't let a married woman do this job."

"That's rubbish." Married women were doing so many things during the war, manning antiaircraft guns and serving as nurses and who knew what else. Surely, they could do this as well. "I'd have to ask for leave from my day job at the glassworks."

"This is for the war effort. I can make that happen for you. Do you speak any languages?" he asked.

"My French is self-taught, but quite good." I was not bragging, just being honest. I had learned on my own from books I'd purchased from the secondhand shops or borrowed from the library, dreaming of someday seeing the world.

Ian smiled, revealing a lone dimple in his left cheek. "Excellent." He clapped his hands, then rubbed them together. "So, what do you say?"

I considered the question. The idea of volunteering to go to war-torn Europe was audacious. I'd never left England before. I had no experience or training. I had taken the job at the Red Cross because I wanted to help. Yet volunteering to pack boxes for a few hours in the evenings had never seemed enough. Now here it was before me, a chance to go across and make a real difference. To do more. I had doubts, of course, about the danger of going over into occupied Europe and whether I could do the job. I pushed them down.

"I'm interested," I replied. "Tell me more about the work."

Ian gestured for me to sit down opposite him at the small desk in the corner from which he managed the volunteers. He pulled out a flask and poured some liquor into a small metal cup and offered it to me. I hesitated for a beat; I've never been a drinker, especially not after seeing what it had done to my mum. But I accepted the cup reluctantly and took a sip, feeling the strange way the liquid burned my throat as it went down. When he offered me a cigarette, though, I shook my head—one new vice was enough to try for now.

"We used to go across the Channel by boat, deliver packages to the various POW camps and come home. It was pretty straightforward. Only now the British have blockaded Europe."

I nodded. I had read about it in *The Times*. Churchill was hoping to stop the flow of goods in an effort to bring the Germans to their knees. But the very same blockade that was intended to harm the Germans made it impossible for the Red Cross to get food and other supplies to the POWs in German camps. Ian continued, "Early in the war, Churchill had issued a strict edict that no relief shipments were to be sent over whatsoever. He thought the supplies would fall into the wrong hands and inadvertently help the enemy and lengthen the war. Then Dunkirk happened and the capture of thousands of British soldiers, including some from prominent families, forced him to rethink." Ian's voice crackled with intensity. "But we can't go across the Channel, so we have to sail down to the south of France and bring the packages across by land." My head swam at the magnitude of the journey he was describing. What had I gotten myself into? At the same time, I felt a twinge of excitement at being part of something so important.

"Will we be going to the front?"

"No, just to POW camps in occupied France." *Just.* I could hardly imagine it. Ian refilled my cup with scotch, and I took another gulp, feeling my cheeks go warm. "But really, we need to go as far as we are able to get aid to those who need it." I took in his words, captivated. It was more than just his appearance that made Ian attractive. He was driven by the work with a kind of passion and principle that was irresistible.

Across the room, I saw two of the older women who were leaving looking in our direction and whispering, heads tilted conspiratorially. "I think they're talking about us," I said.

He shrugged. "Let them talk. So are you in?"

Straightening my shoulders, I realized that I very much was. "Yes."

He stood. "Get your belongings, no more than a satchel. Then come back here. We leave for Southampton at dawn."

4

Helaine

Paris, 1938

After the day they had tea in the rain, Gabriel and Helaine met in the park every morning at the same time, as if by unspoken agreement. Sometimes they sat and fed bits of bread to the ducks in the pond. Others days they would walk, Gabriel leading her through winding backstreets and charming passageways, revealing a secret Paris Helaine had never known existed. As they strolled, Gabriel and Helaine talked endlessly. When it rained or grew windy or cold, they would find shelter in a café or browse a dusty antiques shop.

One afternoon, as they walked along the quay, the smell of roasted chestnuts tickled Helaine's nose. "Would you like some?" Gabriel asked, and he purchased a bag. They shared it, their fingers brushing as they reached for the warm pieces. A breeze blew a brackish smell across the Seine.

"Did you grow up in Paris?" she asked.

Gabriel shook his head. "My father was French, but my mother was English. I was raised in Dover and spent summers in Normandy." Then he paused. "When I was eleven, my father died suddenly."

"I'm so sorry." Helaine could only imagine how difficult the loss must have been.

"After that, my mother moved us to London. She wasn't the same, though. She took a bad turn." Helaine was not entirely sure what that meant, but it did not seem right to ask. "I used to roam the city, sneaking into concerts and shows because I couldn't afford a ticket." He smiled at the memory. "Every so often I would steal some penny candy from one of the shops to take back to my younger sisters."

"Are they still in London?"

"One is, I think. I'm not certain what became of the other. I'm afraid we've lost touch."

"That's too bad." Impulsively, she put her hand on his arm. The gesture was forward and she started to pull back. But he took her hand and held it as they walked.

"And you?"

"I'm an only child." But she omitted the part about her illness, not wanting him to think her flawed or weak.

Helaine worried, as the weeks of secretly meeting Gabriel on her walks continued, that her mother would realize what was going on. Surely Maman would notice the way her daughter's eyes danced or how she skipped merrily out the door. But Helaine took care never to be gone for more than an hour. If Maman attributed the flush in Helaine's cheeks to anything more than the cold or detected a hint of cologne on her coat when she returned, she said nothing.

One rainy day, after Helaine and Gabriel had stopped for coffee, they stepped out on the still-damp pavement. "The sun is coming out," Gabriel remarked. Though drops still fell from tree branches, the sky had brightened just a little.

"I wonder if there's a rainbow," Helaine mused, peering at the sky through the trees.

"The best place to see those is from Montmartre, with the whole city laid out below. Have you been there?"

Helaine shook her head. "Not since I was very young." The only view of the city she had seen for many years was from her bedroom, though she could not tell him that.

"But you must." He held his hand out. "Come with me to see."

"Now? I'm expected at home."

"Then meet me tonight. The evening view is even more breathtaking."

"But I can't..." Helaine started to protest. Gabriel brought his finger to her lips as if to silence her. The warmth of his touch, as well as the sudden, intimate gesture, stopped Helaine. Then just as quickly, he kissed her lightly. She froze, too stunned to move or respond.

Before Helaine could kiss him back, Gabriel pulled away. "I'm sorry if that was forward of me." She did not respond. It *had* been forward. They had known one another for just a few weeks. Some part of her wanted to run from him. And at the same time, she was desperate for him to do it again. Helaine had read about being kissed, dreamed about it. Now it had happened to her, though, and it was everything she had imagined and more. For the first time in her life, Helaine felt like a real person with skin and blood and breath. And desire. A longing she had never felt yet somehow understood welled up inside her.

"Meet me tonight at ten," he urged as they were about to part and go their separate ways. "Don't answer, but think about it. We all get to choose how we spend our days—and nights," he added. "I hope you will choose to spend this one with me." The words reverberated as he walked away.

Helaine considered his invitation on her walk home. She would have to sneak out. Her mother, if she ever found out, would be incensed. But Helaine could no longer stay caged. A life chained was not a life; she knew that more than ever now that she had tasted the outside world. What was the point of re-maining healthy if not to live?

That evening after Maman had gone to bed, Helaine slipped silently from the house, feeling almost like a criminal. Yet some selfish part of her was too happy to care. She walked to the edge of the park where Gabriel was waiting. He kissed her on the cheek, and she instantly wanted more. But he took her arm and started down the street. "It's a bit far. Do you mind the walk?" Helaine shook her head. With him, she felt as though she could fly.

Gabriel swept her through the streets of Paris, pointing out interesting architecture, telling stories about the streets they passed. She listened, rapt. Despite his limp, he walked briskly and it was an effort to keep up. Their conversation was so lively that Helaine scarcely noticed how far they had walked.

As they neared Montmartre, though, the streets climbed up-ward. They ascended the steep stairs of Rue Drevet and she struggled to breathe evenly, remembering that she had only been out walking for a few weeks and was in no shape for such a climb. She tried not to think about how far they were going or how she would possibly get back. At least it would be downhill. Finally, he stopped before a tall, narrow building that seemed to slope against the one adjacent to it. "My garret is here," he said. "Would you like to see the view?"

Remembering their kiss, Helaine considered whether he in-tended more by inviting her inside. Part of her wanted him to. Her mother's disapproving look appeared in Helaine's mind and she pushed it away. "I would like that very much."

Gabriel opened the door and she followed him up one flight of stairs, then another and another to the very top floor. She fought to catch her breath as he let her inside. His flat was tiny, with a sloping roof and a tiny kitchenette in the corner. There did not appear to be a toilet and Helaine assumed he had to use the one they had passed on the floor below. She wondered if, despite playing for the Orchestre National, this was all he could afford.

"You live here alone?" Helaine asked.

"I have no family. It's just me." There was a loneliness in his voice and she thought of her own family. She had been in her house with only her mother, her father often gone. However, there was undeniably a great deal of care and love. She had often been lonely, but never alone. "But my father was a great musician and he left me this cello." Gabriel walked to the instrument case in the corner and ran his hands over it tenderly. "I had not been interested in music while he was alive. I started to play only after he was gone, as a way to connect with him. I found that I loved music. I only wish I had discovered it sooner."

"He would be very proud of you," Helaine offered.

Gabriel nodded solemnly. "I started playing when I was older than many but immediately found I was talented." He was not bragging, just stating the truth. "I outgrew my first instructor within a year. He said there was nothing else he could teach me. The second was the same. As soon as I was old enough, I returned to Paris to learn. And I spent a year at Juilliard in New York."

"You've been to the States?" Helaine asked with amazement. He nodded. "What was it like?"

"Overwhelming. Brilliant. I'll take you and show you someday." It seemed presumptuous of him to speak of future plans when they had known each other such a short time. But Helaine didn't mind. "After graduation, I came back. Attending the finest music school and finding work as a musician were two very different things, I quickly learned. I was accepted to the Orchestre National, but that still does not provide a livable wage. So I make my own music, and I play various engagements and teach lessons to pay the bills. But I've gone on too long. You came for the view."

Then he flung open the window sash to reveal a brilliant

panorama of the city below. Taking in the sea of lights, Helaine understood then why he stayed.

"What do you think?" he asked.

"It's spectacular," she replied. The entire city of Paris glittered beneath them. He leaned in close, and she could feel warmth behind her, and his breath on her hair. She turned and looked up at him, their lips just inches apart. Helaine worried for a second time about the propriety of being alone here in his most intimate space. But this was exactly what she wanted. She leaned in, this time kissing him. Neither of them pulled away, their embrace deepening.

Then he hesitated. "Helaine, are you certain? We only just met a few weeks ago. I wouldn't want to take advantage." Helaine kissed him again.

A few seconds later, he pulled back. "Shall I play for you?" The cello, she remembered, as he walked to the corner and pulled out the instrument. He sat in a worn chair in the corner, cradling the instrument between his legs. Before happening upon the house where Gabriel was practicing that first day, Helaine had never seen anyone play a cello, or any instrument at all, other than during some brief piano lessons as a child before she became sick. Gabriel's music wove a tapestry that seemed to float from the apartment and out across the skies of Paris. She marveled at the way he seemed to pull sounds from the instrument.

Gabriel did not seem to hold the instrument as much as cradle it in a way that was almost sensual as his long, tapered fingers ran along the strings. He looked up, still playing, and as his eyes met hers, Helaine was certain he could read her mind. Feelings that she had only imagined rose up, threatening to overwhelm her.

He finished the piece and lifted his head once more. Wordlessly, Helaine walked to him and took the instrument, leaning it gently against the wall. Then she slipped into the space where the cello had been, folding herself into his embrace. In that moment, for the very first time, she was home. They kissed one another, and this time, there was no stopping. It was the kind of love Helaine had read about in storybooks, instant and complete, as though their souls had been imprinted on one another for a thousand years.

Helaine drew him to the bed. "My love, not like this," he protested.

"Exactly like this," Helaine insisted. She was confused. She thought he wanted this as much as she did.

"You deserve more."

But Helaine didn't care. She had spent her entire life reading about such things, dreaming them. Waiting for them. Now here Gabriel was in the flesh, like some sort of hero in one of her stories. Only he was real and he wanted her. "This *is* more," she whispered. "This is everything." His willpower seemed to crumble then, and his lips were on her neck and her body. She closed her eyes, swept away by a mixture of joy and desire beyond anything that she had ever imagined.

Afterward, they lay in a tangle of limbs and strewn clothes and fell asleep without speaking. Helaine awoke sometime later. She did not immediately know where she was. Then, remembering, she grew alarmed. How much time had passed? She had to get home. It was not yet dawn, though. Her mother would be asleep.

Helaine sat up and started to gather her things to get dressed. Then she noticed Gabriel was not sleeping, but lying with his eyes open, looking out across the pinkening Paris skyline. His expression was troubled and she worried that he might regret what had happened between them. "What is it?" she asked. "Is something wrong?"

He turned toward her and took her hand. His lips parted and he uttered the two words Helaine had never expected to hear in her life.

"Marry me."

Helaine was stunned. She did not know what to say.

"Marry you?" Helaine echoed with disbelief. "We've only

known each other a few weeks." Marriage had always seemed something for other people, not someone as weak and isolated as herself. Even these past few weeks, as she had been swept away by her infatuation with Gabriel, she had not dared to dream of such a thing.

Gabriel kissed her firmly on the lips. "With some things, you just know."

Helaine's mind whirled. Just weeks earlier, she had been isolated at home, knowing no one. Now this man was before her with open arms, asking her to share a life with him. She marveled at how her world had changed so much in an instant. And even though his words sounded ridiculous, some part of her understood.

"Darling," he pressed, "war is coming." Helaine had heard whisperings of which he spoke. Germany had annexed neighboring Austria and was threatening aggression against its neighbors that would surely draw France into conflict. Gabriel continued, "Everything will change and we should take this moment while we can. Tomorrow is promised to no one," he added. "Especially not now. Let me talk to your father and ask his permission," he offered.

"You can't…" Helaine faltered, because how could she explain her family? Her mother constantly hovering, her father seldom present but always controlling. Both were singularly obsessed with keeping her safe—and home. In their eyes, a man sweeping her away was almost the worst thing that could happen.

"Am I so unlikable?" he joked, feigning hurt.

"No, of course not. But my parents are difficult."

"Your parents are very protective," he offered. "It's understandable, as you've said, being the only child."

"It isn't that." Helaine considered once more telling Gabriel about her illness but decided against it. He was the first person ever to see her as whole and unbroken, and she was desperate to hold on to that for as long as she could.

"Then I shall ask only you." He took her hands in his and gazed at her deeply, his eyes two cerulean pools. "Will you be my wife?"

Helaine wanted to say yes. She could see a life with Gabriel and all of its potential for joy.

But she knew it could never be. Even if he knew the truth about her, they would always have their differences. Gabriel was undoubtedly gifted, but he was a struggling artist, and he wasn't Jewish. Though Helaine did not mind these things in the slightest, she knew that her family would never accept him or give them their blessing.

"I'm sorry. I can't." Tears flooded Helaine's eyes, spilling over onto her cheeks.

"Why not?"

Helaine hesitated. He had to know the whole truth now in order to understand why it would be so very hard for her parents to let go. "You see, I was very ill as a child, and my parents, well, they kept me home so that I would not get sick again."

"All of the time?"

"Yes, until very recently." Describing her childhood, Helaine felt like an oddity in a museum.

"I'm sorry. That must have been dreadful."

"In some ways, yes. They meant only the best, but it was very hard. Anyway, to tell them now that I want to marry someone I've only just met…they would forbid it."

"But, Helaine, it's your life."

"I know. And I'm sorry." Overwhelmed, she stood, finished dressing and gathered her things. "You should forget me." She kissed him, her tears falling between their lips. Then she turned and ran from his flat.

Helaine fled down the stairs, trying to block the sound of Gabriel calling her name from her ears. She reached the darkened street and began to run, turning this way and that, trying to retrace the route they had taken in reverse, going this time from Montmartre to the city center. She got lost, though, and a few minutes later, she had to stop to catch her breath under a yellow streetlight. She looked back over her shoulder, half hoping Gabriel had come after her. But the pavement behind her was empty and still.

Forty minutes later, Helaine reached her house. She prayed that her mother was asleep and that she might slip in undetected. However, in the grand foyer, she noticed a black umbrella in the stand that had not been there when she left. *Papa.* Helaine questioned if his return was unexpected. Then remembering how her mother seemed more tense the day before, she knew that it was not. Maman always cooked and cleaned more fiercely than usual before Helaine's father came home, like preparing for inspection by a general. It was as if she thought that a perfect house and some delicious treats might magically transform them back to the family of yesteryear, before all of the troubles began.

Steeling herself, Helaine started up the stairs into the sitting room. "Hello," she said, trying to sound natural, as though there was nothing at all odd about her being out, or coming home so late.

"Where were you?" Papa roared, his normally kind face a mixture of concern and anger.

Who are you to ask? Helaine wanted to retort. *You who are never here.* Her mother's concern made sense, but Papa's seemed unearned. Of course, Helaine did not dare. She searched for an explanation that would make her coming home this late all right. "Just out for a walk," Helaine replied lamely at last. She looked to Maman for some sort of assistance, but her mother's eyes were cast downward.

"A walk? You've been out all night." Helaine's father turned to her mother. "You knew about this?"

"Helaine wanted to go outside one morning," Maman explained meekly.

"You let her go out? By herself?"

"It was just a few times for a short while."

Before Helaine's father could berate either of them further, there was a knock at the door. He went to answer it, his expression perplexed. Who could be calling unannounced at such an hour? Knowing, a sense of dread formed in the pit of Helaine's stomach. Still, as she watched from the top of the stairs, she was stunned by the sight below.

There, in the doorway to their home, stood Gabriel.

"Yes?" Helaine's father said, trying to be polite over his surprise and irritation at being disturbed. People did not visit unannounced, and certainly not in the middle of the night. "Who are you and what are you doing here?"

Helaine froze, wishing she could melt into the floor. Gabriel had come for her. "I apologize for calling at such an hour," Gabriel began politely. Then, seeing Papa's glowering expression, Gabriel squared his shoulders. "My name is Gabriel Lemarque and I've come to ask for your daughter's hand in marriage."

Helaine stared at him in disbelief. Even after she had run away, Gabriel still wanted her. He must have followed her home. And he was courageous enough to come to their grand house and ask her imposing father. Papa looked aghast. "Helaine? But you don't even know her! How could you possibly?" He turned to Helaine, as if seeking confirmation of this. Then, taking in Helaine's eyes, he seemed to understand all that had transpired in his absence.

"I do know him, Papa." Helaine walked down the steps to the foyer, where they both stood. If Gabriel could be brave, then so could she. Helaine reached around her father and took Gabriel's hand and urged him through the doorway, into their home. "And yes, I want to marry him." Helaine realized as she said this last part how true the words were.

"You do?" Gabriel's eyes met Helaine's and held them. She nodded.

"Impossible!" Papa thundered. He turned to Gabriel. "You need to leave now."

But Gabriel remained, feet planted, firmly by Helaine's side. "Papa, Gabriel and I have feelings for each other," Helaine offered.

"How long have you even known one another?" Papa demanded.

"Only a short time, but…"

"We are in love," Gabriel finished for her, his voice unabashed. Hearing the words for the first time, Helaine knew that she felt the same.

"Ridiculous!" Helaine's father turned to her mother, who had come down to the foyer as well. "Did you know?" Maman shook her head, too astonished to speak. Her eyes were wide with puzzlement. "But how did you even meet?"

"I passed by Gabriel's studio when I was walking. He's a cellist."

"A musician?" Papa's expression grew even darker. He turned to Helaine's mother. "You see what came of letting her go outside?" Helaine could see Maman's regret that she had let Helaine take walks in the morning and that this was what it had wrought.

Watching her mother's eyes flicker with fear, Helaine felt guilty at the trouble she had caused for her. Helaine knew then that fear had kept her mother every bit as much of a prisoner as the walls of her childhood home had kept Helaine herself. "Papa, this is not her fault! I am eighteen, no longer a child. I want to live my life like a normal person."

"But with your condition, you are not like other people." Helaine's father turned to Gabriel. "She's sick. Didn't she tell you?"

"*Was* sick," Helaine countered. "And I did tell him. As I said earlier, Gabriel, I'm fine now." Helaine worried again that Gabriel would not want her. She had been a burden her whole life. Who would want to take that on? She braced herself, preparing for him to turn and go.

Instead, Gabriel moved closer. "Thank God you are well." His voice was full with relief.

See, Helaine said silently, looking at her father with defiance. *Not everyone sees me as broken.*

But her father would not be placated. "Helaine, he's a musician." The last word came out with disdain. "How will he support you?"

"Gabriel is an acclaimed cellist. He plays with the Orchestre National in the finest halls of Europe."

"Bah!" Helaine's father waved his hand.

"We ask nothing of you, sir," Gabriel said, a quiet dignity in his voice. "We will make our own way."

Ignoring him, Papa spoke again to Helaine. "Surely you can't mean to give up all of this for him?" That, Helaine realized, was exactly what she meant to do. There was more joy in sharing Gabriel's tiny apartment and the freedom of the city than in this enormous, cold house where she felt so caged.

"Is he even Jewish?" Papa demanded.

Helaine hesitated. "No, monsieur, I am not," Gabriel replied. For Papa, this was another strike against him.

"I'm going to marry him, Papa," Helaine replied firmly. "We would like your blessing."

"Troubles are coming," Papa said, his voice ominous. "This is no time for rash decisions."

"I know all about Hitler and the rise of fascism," Helaine retorted.

Her father looked surprised. Helaine knew he did not think she was aware of such things. Only then did he seem to realize how deep her connection to the outside world had become. He turned to Maman with a look of recrimination on his face. "I trusted you to keep her safe."

"Safe and hidden are not the same thing," Helaine interjected. "I want to see the world." Suddenly, Helaine was angry as well. They had spent their whole lives playing at the charade her parents had created. Now she had something real and true and good for the first time in her life, and they were blaming her for it. Why couldn't they be happy for her? "Maybe you would have known that if you were ever here."

"Helaine," her mother warned sternly, "you won't be disrespectful."

Helaine looked at her mother with disbelief. Papa had betrayed her over and over. Was she really standing up for him? Through it all, her mother still loved him. And even in their most painful moment, Helaine knew that her father loved her and that his anger came from a place of concern. Helaine softened. "Papa, please. I don't want to quarrel. But I love Gabriel and I will be marrying him."

Papa's expression grew angrier. Love or no, he was a powerful man and not accustomed to being crossed like this. "Then you will do it without my blessing." He faced Gabriel. "Get out of my house. And you—" he turned back to me "—will stay here."

Gabriel gave Helaine a long, sorrowful look. "I'm sorry." He turned to go.

"Wait!" Helaine cried. Then she hesitated, feeling all eyes on her. Her entire future seemed to hang in the balance of what she did next. Helaine's spine straightened. "If he goes, I go, too."

Helaine expected her father to force her to stay, or at least forbid her once more from leaving. She drew herself up to her full height of five feet two inches, but to her surprise, he seemed to crumble. "Then go." Her father turned slowly, painfully away. Despite all of the acrimony between them, Helaine's heart broke.

"Darling, please," Helaine's mother said, pleading in vain with her husband to show reason and reconsider. "Helaine is our daughter, our only child." Helaine's mother put her hand on Papa's arm as he passed her going up the stairs, but he shook it off. Helaine hoped that her mother might protest and stand up to him. But she had never had that kind of strength. Instead, she pleaded with Helaine now, tears streaming down her face. "Laina, don't go."

Looking around the house, Helaine felt a sense of guilt. Her mother had undoubtedly stayed all of these years for her. Now she stood alone. *Don't leave me,* her face seemed to say. With Helaine gone and Papa away so much, she would be truly by herself. But she could accept Helaine and Gabriel and choose to be part of their lives. She was siding with Helaine's father despite his years of betrayal—and it left Helaine with no other choice.

Helaine longed to have Maman wrap her in her embrace one more time, to bury her nose in her mother's neck and breathe her sweet smell. Helaine did not want to lose her family. But there was no choice. Her father was not going to relent. And if she let Gabriel walk out that door without her, Helaine would spend her whole life a prisoner, alone.

"I'm sorry," Helaine said to her mother. Then she turned to Gabriel. "Wait here."

Helaine ran up the stairs and into her room one last time before anyone could stop her. Her childhood things screamed at her, begging to be taken. But there wasn't time to properly pack. She grabbed a change of clothing and some toiletries and stuffed them in a bag. Helaine's hand rose instinctively to her neck, where she wore a half-heart locket. Helaine's grandmother had sent it to her during her childhood illness. Helaine had worn one half and her grandmother had worn the other, creating a kind of connection between them when they could not see one another. After her grandmother's death, Maman had given Helaine the second half of the necklace. She took the second half of her grandmother's locket now and put them in her pocket.

Then, steeling herself, Helaine turned and left the room. She walked downstairs to the foyer. Maman was gone and only Gabriel awaited. She started to follow him out the door. Then something on the low table in the foyer caught her eye. There were several francs that had not been there previously. "Your mother left that," Gabriel said in a low voice. "I think she wanted you to take it."

Tears sprang into Helaine's eyes. Her mother was trying to help her still, in whatever small way she could. Helaine pocketed the money, then followed Gabriel outside. She thought her mother might reappear and beg her to reconsider. But the street was silent behind them, except for the echoing of their footsteps.

When they reached the corner, Helaine looked back at the house. She saw her mother peeking through the curtains, her expression sad yet hopeful for Helaine. She raised her hand and blew a kiss before disappearing behind the curtains.

Gabriel turned to Helaine and took her hand. "Are you certain?" His eyes searched her face.

"Yes." Helaine worried that he was having second thoughts. "You?"

"Of course...it's just that you are giving up so much." He gestured toward the grand house behind her. "How can my world possibly be enough?"

It was not just enough. It was everything. Still, Helaine hesitated.

"I know I don't have much to give," Gabriel added.

"It isn't that," she replied quickly. Truly it wasn't. Gabriel's world of music and laughter felt so much richer than her staid home. Still, Helaine could not start a life with him with secrets between them. "There's one thing I have to tell you, though. The illness when I was young, it left me unable to have children. I wanted you to know, in case you were hoping for a family."

"That's it?" he asked. She nodded. "So you had a childhood illness." The way he described it made it sound like a minor event in her past, not something that had defined nearly two decades of her life. "I have a limp. I fell off my bicycle when I was nine and broke my leg," he said, offering the answer to a question she had been curious about but had not dared to ask. "It never healed properly. We are both imperfectly perfect for each other." Gabriel took both of Helaine's hands in his and smiled broadly. "Did you think I would love you less? Because that would never happen. My forever *is* forever."

"I'm sorry I didn't tell you sooner."

"I understand. Let's have no more secrets, though."

"I promise." Helaine threw herself into his arms.

When they broke apart, Helaine looked back, suddenly sad. The last thing she wanted in this world was to be estranged from her family, kicked out from the only home she had ever known.

No, that was the *second* to last thing she wanted. The last thing was to remain alone and a prisoner in her parents' house.

Helaine took one last look at the only home she had ever known and left.

5

Louise

London, 1953

I walk away from the jewelry shop, preparing to head back to Paddington for the journey home. Then as I near the Tube station, church bells in the distance chime eleven. I pause in front of a drugstore. I have been in the city for little more than an hour. It seems a waste to come to London for such a short time. If I cannot learn more about the necklace, at least I can enjoy a few hours out. Why not stay for tea and maybe go into a few of the shops? I can manage it and still have plenty of time to make it back to Henley before I need to pick the children up from school. The notion of taking a few hours for myself feels both alien and appealing. I start down the steps of the Tube station.

Twenty minutes later, I arrive at Oxford Circus, a wide, bustling thoroughfare of department stores and other shops. As I merge into the river of pedestrians who throng the pavement, I am overwhelmed. Having lived in bucolic Henley with Joe the past several years, I'd forgotten how big and chaotic the city is. The streets are choked with lorries and buses, and the sooty exhaust greets me like an old perfume. As I make my way down

Regent Street, my stride grows more confident with each step. Suddenly, I am *that* Louise, the wartime one who was independent with a life and purpose of her own, and it is as if none of the intervening years ever happened. Guilt nags at me. I love Joe and the children. How can it be so easy to forget?

Taken aback by the thought, I stop by a wall that is covered with old posters and placards, advertisements for cigarettes and sodas and West End shows. From amid all the paper, a familiar face looks out at me. I inhale sharply, feeling as if I am seeing a ghost. There, on a faded poster for a West End production of *Wild Rose* almost a decade old, is Franny. How is that possible? Half the city was reduced to rubble, yet her image is still here after all of these years. I stare at her beautiful face, violet eyes luminescent and pleading, even in the faded image. *Do something,* they seem to say. I am stunned. First finding the necklace, and now this. That I had stopped here and that the fragment of poster still exists seems a sign, like Franny reaching out from beyond the grave and imploring me not to give up.

I start walking, trying to get as far away from the poster as possible. But I cannot outrun my memories. I see in my mind's eye then the events before Franny died. I had glimpsed her from across a barren field, standing close to the fence of the POW camp, accepting something from a man, a musician with whom she'd performed in the camp, through the barbed wire. *Get away,* I wanted to shout. Taking something from a prisoner could mean her own arrest. I had not known at the time that something far more dangerous would befall her—and that not long after she would be dead.

Since finding the necklace, I have been thinking only about the piece of jewelry. Now my memory focuses in on Franny and the man with whom she was speaking. I realize in that moment that I am seeking answers not just about the necklace, but about what actually happened to Franny herself. Figuring out who the man was might be equally important in getting the answers I seek about Franny's death.

But how can I find out about things that happened a lifetime ago and a continent away? *Ian*, I think suddenly. My boss when I volunteered during the war pops into my head suddenly—along with that wobbly-at-the-knees feeling I used to get whenever I was around him. Ian was so much more than just my boss and heat rises within me as I think of him now.

I push those thoughts quickly away. I don't know why I hadn't thought of it sooner. Ian was there in Germany all of those years ago when everything happened with Franny and I had seen the necklace for the first time. He knows the history, knew Franny. And as part of the International Red Cross, he has connections and access to records, or at least he once had. If he could help me find out more about the man who had given the necklace to Franny, who he was and why he wanted her to take it, that might help explain what, if anything, it had to do with her death. Perhaps he might be able to help me now—if only I dare to ask.

The Red Cross is headquartered in Moorfield's, though, a few kilometers from where I am now. I don't have time to walk there, nor figure out the route by Tube. Instead, I go to the phone booth at the corner and connect to the operator. As I hold, I imagine the august Red Cross building with its marbled entranceway, a row of flags and engraved walls extolling the work of the agency, the virtues and sacrifices of its volunteers. My stomach tightens. I had been there only once in the course of my volunteer work, to complete required paperwork after I had returned from Europe and debrief what I had seen to a nondescript bureaucrat, who had pretended to listen and take notes. I had not worked there.

But Ian had—and perhaps he still did.

"International Red Cross, London offices," the receptionist chirps when the operator has connected me.

"Good day," I say. "I'm looking for a man who works there called Ian Shipley."

"We have no one here by that name," she replies in a clipped tone. My heart sinks. No, of course not. Eight years have passed since I last saw or spoke with Ian. My life has not stood still. Why would I expect that Ian's had? He might have left London or the country entirely. He might not even still be alive. This last awful thought catches me off guard. Ian had been just a few years older than me and healthy. There is no reason to think anything has happened to him. But the war had taken so many that the notion of premature death still comes quickly and by default, a conditioned response.

"He worked there at one time," I say, trying again. "Perhaps there is a forwarding address."

"I don't think so," the receptionist replies, making clear that she is not about to help. I start to hang up. "Wait a second while I ask someone." I bring the receiver back to my ear, not daring to hope. "There's a woman on the line asking for an Ian Shipley," I hear her say to someone nearby. Then she speaks into the receiver once more. "I've only been here a few weeks, but Betty in personnel has been here for ages. She knows everyone." I am surprised by her helpfulness, but doubtful she will learn anything useful. "Yes?" she says quickly, not to me. I hear a muffled voice behind her. "Mr. Shipley left the Red Cross some time ago and he is now employed by the Foreign Office," she says to me.

"Thank you." I hang up, then realize I should have asked her for Ian's number at the Foreign Office. Ian is no longer employed by the Red Cross. But the Foreign Office is just a short walk from where I now stand.

Impulsively, I start down Regent Street toward Westminster, grateful that the earlier drizzle has stopped instead of turning into a proper rain shower. As I walk, I cannot help but think of my mum. She still lives in South London in a tiny, sad flat she seldom leaves. We are not estranged exactly, just different and living separate lives. I have not seen her in nearly a year. I call her the last Sunday of every month, ringing the phone of her landlady downstairs, who rouses her to come talk to me so that I know she is alive. Most times in Henley, it is almost possible to forget that she is here. But now, it all comes back, the fact that she has no one, the ways in which we failed each other so many years ago. The way I am still failing her now. I should go see her while I am in the city, make sure she is all right. But there isn't time. I push the feelings down. I will call her when I get home, I promise myself, and set a time to come visit.

Twenty minutes later, I reach Whitehall. I stop, taking in the wide street lined with imposing government buildings, many with crumbling facades still bearing witness to the damage from the war. I turn right onto King Charles Street. The Foreign Office is located in a massive Victorian building occupying most of the block. Taking in its size and grandeur, I am daunted. What am I doing here? It is not just the audacity of walking into the headquarters of the nation's largest government agency unannounced and asking for someone I have not seen in nearly a decade. My time with the Red Cross during the war had not ended well and I felt cast out from service, betrayed. I still do. One of the plusses of leaving the city for Henley and my life with Joe was that I was able to put the past behind me. Now it rises up before me, larger than ever.

But this is the one place I might find more information and, given that Millie had not been able to help, is perhaps my very last chance. I steel myself and walk toward the entrance to the building. Then I stop, my doubts renewed. Now that I know it might actually be possible to see Ian, I am more hesitant than ever. Am I really going to see a man I haven't talked to in nearly a decade about a piece of cast-off jewelry? His life has surely moved on and he doesn't need to hear from someone from such a dark part of his past.

As I start to leave, I spy a group of men coming toward me on the pavement, all pinstripe suits and bowler hats and cigarettes. A familiar head looms above the rest. I see him then and the street around me seems to freeze, the needle on a phonograph screeching to a halt.

Ian. Recognizing the unmistakable cut of his jawline, I nearly gasp. Ours had not been just a working relationship—the connection between us had been powerful and real. The sight of him, mixed with all of the painful memories, is just too much. Suddenly, I don't want to see him at all. Overwhelmed, I turn to go. His eye catches mine, though, and an instant flash of recognition crosses his face. It is too late.

I stand frozen as he breaks away from the group of men and starts toward me. Then he stops a few feet away, staring as if seeing a ghost. "Louise?" The greeting comes out like a question, and I feel exposed, almost naked. He takes me in. Is he noticing the changes, the lines on my face that were not there nearly a decade earlier? Normally I am quite comfortable in myself, and I don't feel the need for a lot of makeup or fashion to impress others. But it has been eight years and I feel the passage of time, the sags and wrinkles, the lines. I hate that I care.

Ian has changed, too, although the gray at his temples only serves to make him more handsome. He wears a wool coat pulled up high at the collar and a dashing scarf tied smartly around it. His hair is now smoothed back with a pomade that gives off a faint mint scent. He is a more polished and sophisticated version of himself—and even sexier than I remember.

"Is it really you?" There is an odd twist to his voice and I know that this unexpected reunion brings up as many feelings for him as it does me. His gaze is deep, and our connection returns instantly.

"Do you have a few minutes?" I ask. He does not respond right away. We did not part on the best terms in Germany, I recall then. The events of the night Franny died and the few days that followed come roaring back at me like a freight train. Perhaps, despite the attraction that undeniably exists between us, he is still angry. I brace myself for the possibility that he might be too busy—or simply not want—to speak with me.

"Let me finish up with these chaps. I can manage a tea break in ten if you fancy a cuppa."

He returns to the group of men and they disappear inside the government building. I find a nearby bench and sit down, eyeing the dark gray clouds that have gathered low behind Parliament. I look up and down Whitehall, remembering London as it had been during the war, sandbags piled high at the corners, Londoners carrying small satchels of food and other essentials into the Tube stations and other air raid shelters, then returning to the street in the morning to see in the light of early day what of their lives was left standing. We were the lucky ones to have survived, but none of us would ever be the same.

I wait for what seems much longer than ten minutes and still Ian does not appear. I should just go, I think. It is getting late, and I have to be back to pick up the children after school. But just then, I see Ian coming down the street in my direction. This was a mistake, I realize the moment I see him. Along with the pain, I had buried memories of what had been between Ian and me, and I see it now, the attraction, as fresh and real as that last night we spent together.

"Sorry to keep you waiting. Some of the blokes from Whitehall never stop talking." He leads me to a tearoom down the street and orders tea for both of us, remembering that I take mine without milk or sugar. When the steaming cups are placed on saucers on the counter, he carries them to a table in the corner. "You look well," he says as we sit down. I reach for a cup and our fingers brush accidentally. I pull back, but my eyes are drawn to his fingers. They are long and thin, square-tipped at the end, just as I remember them. "What are you doing these days?"

"I live in Henley with my husband, Joe, and our two children," I reply, hating how boring that sounds. Who have I become? "And you?"

"I actually work for the Foreign Office now. I'm posted to the embassy in Paris presently. I'm just back here for a business trip and I'm headed back over this evening. You caught me by sheer luck." I'm surprised. Ian never really seemed to fit in when we went over to Europe with the Red Cross and it is hard to imagine him embracing a continental lifestyle. He's older now, though, more self-assured—and even more attractive than I remembered. "I switched from the Red Cross to the Foreign Office a few years back," he adds. I hope he might say something about his personal life. "But enough about me…how can I help?" he asks instead. He brushes at his forehead where the lock of hair used to fall, a reflex.

I decide to dispense with formalities and get right to the point. "I found a necklace. It looks exactly like the one…" I cannot finish the sentence. He looks at me with a puzzled expression, not understanding. Ian had never belittled me. He made me feel capable. Until the moment I needed him most and he hadn't supported me at all, which hurt more than almost anything, except losing Franny. Remembering now, I doubt I can trust him. "Never mind, coming here was a mistake." I stand abruptly, bumping the table and causing the teacups to rattle and hot liquid to spill over the edge.

He reaches up and catches my arm, urging me to sit back down. "Easy now, luv." There is a tone of familiarity, almost condescension, that makes me bristle. Once we had been, if not equals exactly, united in the same purposeful work. But the social contract was rewritten after the war: Ian had gone on to do bigger things while I was sent home. The inequity of our fates, laid bare now for the first time, is too egregious to ignore. "Why don't you slow down and explain this to me?" His expression is one of genuine warmth, eyes curious.

I sit once more, feeling the heat of his hand through the fabric of my blouse. Then I pull the necklace out of my bag. "I found this, the same half-heart charm I saw Franny with the night before she died."

Franny. It is the first time I have said or heard her name aloud in all of these years and the sound of it cuts through me like an electric current. Ian looks as if he has been slapped.

"The very same one?"

"I think so," I reply.

"Does it matter, really? A necklace?"

"You know it's about more than that. That night, I saw Franny take the necklace from a man at the POW camp, a musician who had performed with her. A day later she was dead." He listens intently, or seems to anyway. I tried to explain this years ago, but he had not heard me. It was the war and the rantings of a woman grieving her friend. We are older now and in a different place. Maybe now he will understand.

"It was surely just a coincidence." He still doesn't believe me. "The man gave Franny a necklace. He wanted her to deliver it to his wife in Paris as I remember. Franny was killed by a hit-and-run driver. The two are not related."

"I think they are. I think the necklace has something to do with what happened to her. And now that this necklace has turned up out of nowhere, I need to find out."

"Louise, no." His hazel eyes widen with concern. "You aren't going there again, are you? Why do that to yourself?"

Because I have never stopped doing that to myself, I think. "If we could find out where the necklace came from…"

"I don't understand. You've come to me to ask me to find out about a necklace? That's hardly my specialty."

"I didn't come to London to ask you. I actually brought it to a jewelry shop on Portobello Road. Millie, the proprietor, is the sister of my employer, Midge, and I thought she could help, but she wasn't able to tell me much. Anyway, I'm not asking you to help me find out about the necklace."

"Then what?"

I pause. "The musician." He looks at me blankly and I cannot tell if he truly does not remember or if he is being willfully ignorant. "The one I saw talking to Franny, who handed her the necklace the night before she died. Don't you remember?"

"Oh, yes. Sorry, it's been some years. Things fade."

Not for me, I think. "I need you to help me find out about him."

"Because...?"

"Because if we can figure out why he wanted her to take it so badly, we might be able to discover what happened."

"We know what happened," Ian says gently, leaning in close. "She was killed in a car accident. You can't possibly think there's more to it than that—or that the necklace and her death are somehow connected."

"I still think—" I pause for a breath "—that Franny's death was not an accident."

He holds up his hand. "That's a big leap. She was found struck by a car. You're now saying that someone hit her on purpose? That she was murdered?" I said it then, too, I think. If only he had listened. "Louise, sometimes, when something so out of our control happens, we want to create a story around it to help it make sense. But it was just an accident."

We have never agreed on what happened. I decide not to press the point now. "The man Franny was talking to, he was an accomplished cellist. Remember how beautifully he accompanied her? There can't have been that many. Also, he was in a camp for Allied prisoners. He may have had some connection to Britain. If I can figure out who he was and why he asked Franny to take the necklace, it might answer some of the questions I have about her death. You'll ask, won't you?"

He moves back almost imperceptibly. Now, as then, Ian has other considerations. He has a government position. He can hardly afford to get involved in some frivolous chase and risk his reputation.

He is going to say no.

"Why now?" he asks. "Why start asking questions about Franny now?"

Because the necklace turning up after so many years is like a sign, I want to say. *Like Franny calling to me from beyond the grave, reminding me of the promise I had left unfulfilled.* Of course, I cannot tell him that.

Ian continues, "We don't even know if the man who gave her the necklace made it out of the camps alive. Even if he did and you find him, he might not have the answers you are looking for."

"I know. But I have to try. You'll help me, won't you?" My voice is pleading.

Something inside him seems to break then. "All right, I'll try. Don't get your hopes up. Those records are almost a decade old. But I'll ask. I promise. And when we find nothing—because we are going to find nothing—you'll leave it alone, right?" I remain silent, unwilling to make a promise I know I cannot keep. "You should come over to Paris," he says suddenly.

"Paris?" I am caught off guard. "Why?"

"The musician, he was French, wasn't he? And he asked Franny to deliver the necklace to his wife in Paris. You could come over and we can look around and see if we can find out anything about the necklace." I'm puzzled by his sudden change of heart, his willingness to help now. Ian continues, "We could catch up on old times." There is a twist in his voice as he says this last part. I sense something more in his words and I try to ignore it. Ian feels the connection between us that lies beneath the surface still, even after all of these years. Our lingering attraction is undeniable, but I'm a married woman and I don't need complications, not now.

"What do you say?" he presses. "So are you in?"

His words are a refrain of our conversation years ago, the night I decided to volunteer to go to Europe with the Red Cross. Only, then I was young and brave. Now I am timid, shackled by my life and the wounds of the past.

"I'm married. I can't just leave."

"The old Louise would," he points out. Ian knew the brave, adventurous me, the one who would undertake an aid mission to wartime Europe on a few hours' notice. Not the one who has to rush home to make bangers and mash. Then he shrugs. "Suit yourself. I have to get back to my meetings. I'll let you know if I find anything."

"Thank you." I reach in my purse for a scrap of paper, then scribble down my contact information and pass it to him.

"And if you change your mind, you can find me here." He hands me his card. He kisses my cheek and a whiff of his familiar Dunhill cologne threatens to hurl me back through the years. He stands and buttons his coat, which, I notice then, he had never taken off at all. "Bloody good to see you, Lou."

And then he is gone.

⌘

Atlantic Ocean, 1944

The rain beat down heavy on the metal hull of the ship, tossing the hulking naval vessel about like a cork. I looked out across the darkened horizon and breathed shallowly, willing myself not to be sick.

Again. I had lost count of how many times I had leaned over the railing, retching into the swirling waters below. Thankfully, I had made it from the cabin where the other volunteers slept without disturbing anyone, and outside to the edge of the boat, and not incurred the wrath of the naval personnel of the SS *Embla*, who really didn't want us there anyway. I stayed on the deck almost all of the time, even now in the middle of the night, because I couldn't bear to be inside. I had stopped eating altogether.

Two days earlier, we had assembled in front of the volunteer center for our departure. There were a half-dozen girls including myself who boarded the bus for the port in Southampton, two of whom I recognized from my nightly volunteering. I carried with me a small bag of clothes and toiletries I'd cobbled together on short notice, not quite sure what I'd need for the trip about which I'd been told so little.

Looking up now, I saw a lone figure standing on the deck close to the bow. *Ian.* He was facing away from me, looking out toward the horizon, hand above his eyes. Ian did not seem to sleep, but paced the deck restlessly at night, as though solely responsible for our safe crossing. I longed to go to him and talk as we had in the volunteer center in London. But I didn't want him to see me sick.

As I tried to calm my stomach now, a burning stench mingled with the salt air. I turned and saw the tip of a cigarette glowing like an ember in the darkness about five meters away. I was surprised. Other than Ian from a distance and the petty officer on watch, I had not expected to see anyone else on deck at this hour.

Before I could consider further who the person might be, a wave of nausea overcame me and I lurched toward the side of the ship once more.

"You all right, hun?" an unfamiliar voice asked.

I wiped my mouth, then turned and looked up. Standing above me was a tall, willowy woman. Her luminous red hair was swept up in a knot, but pieces had escaped their moorings and whipped about wildly with the wind. I was certain that I had not seen her before on the ship. Yet she was oddly familiar. "I'm sorry," I managed, embarrassed to be sick.

"Try this." Still balancing the cigarette between her fingers, the woman pulled a small glass bottle from her purse. She opened the cap, then waved it under my nose. "Lavender oil. Inhaling it helps with the nausea." Closer, I could see that her eyes were an extraordinary shade of violet.

Smelling the herbal scent, my stomach calmed a bit. "Thank you." The ship lurched suddenly then, causing me to stumble and nearly fall.

The woman caught my arm to steady me, then led me to a crude wooden bench. After we sat down, she reached into her purse again, then pulled out a flask. "Now a bit of this." I hesitated. Liquor was the very last thing I needed right now. "It's ginger ale," she explained as she poured it into the cup. "Settles the stomach."

I took the cup gratefully. "I'm Franny," she said. "Franny Beck."

I recognized the name instantly. "The actress?" I blurted.

She dipped her chin in acknowledgment. "One and the same. Or at least before half of the West End theaters were damaged by bombs," Franny added wryly. That was why she looked familiar. Franny Beck was a famous actress, her image on placards and billboards for performances all over London. I had even seen her in a show once when I had scraped together some pennies for a standing-room-only ticket, and I had been mesmerized by her performance.

But what was she doing here? "I've been invited to perform for the officers," she explained, answering my unspoken question.

"For the Germans?" She nodded. I was appalled. How could she do such a thing? Was she a German sympathizer? Of course, I did not know her well enough to ask.

"I told them I would only do it if I got to perform for the POWs as well," she added. Her explanation did little to lessen my horror. In any event, I would not have guessed that meant someone of Franny Beck's stature would be down here among the volunteers.

"I'm Louise Emmons." I took a second sip, then handed back the cup.

"Better now?" she asked.

"A little," I replied sheepishly. Now that I knew who she was, I was even more embarrassed about being sick. "I just hadn't imagined." I gestured beyond the edge of the ship to the rough and dangerous waters.

Franny waved her hand dismissively. "You should have seen last time. Even the crew was ill."

"You've been before?" I could not imagine making the journey more than once.

"This is my third trip. Usually I travel with other performers, but some of them are too nervous to go anymore since the war had worsened." My stomach gave a little flip. If they were too afraid, how could it possibly be safe for us? "This is my first time traveling with volunteers like you. What made you decide to go?"

"I saw a sign at the center where I was helping with care packages and I wanted to do more. I was told they needed volunteers."

"Yes, there is a personnel shortage because several Red Cross workers were killed when their convoy was bombed."

I stared at Franny in disbelief. "But I thought when you are traveling with the Red Cross, there is protection."

"Not in this case. The Red Cross is considered neutral, but the Germans have given no assurance of safe passage, not to volunteers and certainly not to performers like me." She tried to joke, but her voice was grave. "And there's no protection if you are on the ground when an Allied bomb falls." I was suddenly terrified. I knew going into the war zone was dangerous, but I had not fully considered until now that, by signing on, I was risking my life.

"This is important work the Red Cross is doing," Franny added, seeming to read my thoughts. "There are thousands of prisoners needing help. We want to get to as many as we can." Though she was technically not a Red Cross volunteer, it was clear from Franny's words that she considered the mission her own. "But also, it is important to observe what is going on in-side the camps. The Germans need to know that we are watch-ing." I suspected then that I realized her work was about much more than bringing entertainment or even aid.

A sailor on deck patrol walked by us, his torch aimed low to the ground. "Good evening," Franny said, but he did not re-spond or acknowledge us. The naval personnel had made clear that our presence on the ship was a bother and that they did not think we belonged here.

"You would think the military would be more appreciative of what the Red Cross is doing for its POWs," I remarked.

"You would think," Franny repeated. "But they've decided we just get in the way of the fighting."

The ship lurched again, knocking me into Franny. I grabbed the bench to right myself. "Sorry."

"No worries." She reached into her pocket and I expected her to smoke again, but instead she pulled out a chocolate bar. She held it out to me.

"No, thank you." At the sight of it, my stomach roiled. "I've practically given up eating because I feel so sick."

"Well, that explains why I've never seen you in the mess." Franny took a bite of the chocolate bar and ate it with gusto. "So, what made you volunteer with the Red Cross?"

I tell her about the girl I saw sitting atop the rubble after one of the air raids. "I wanted to do my part," I explained. "Pack-ing boxes just didn't seem like enough. Before that, I was just working in one of the factories."

"You're so pretty you could be a stage performer yourself," Franny offered. I wondered if Franny was just being kind, but hearing the fullness of her voice, I could tell that her words were sincere. I flushed. I knew from a young age that I was attractive in a plain sort of way, with my wavy honey-colored hair and long lashes. But that was not at all the same as Franny's traffic-stopping starlet beauty, all violet eyes and red hair and dimples that flashed when she smiled.

"Have you been across to the Continent?" she asked. "Before the war, I mean." I was fascinated by the way she jumped topics in conversation, like a stone skipping across the surface of a lake.

I fought the urge to laugh. My childhood was not one of summer holidays to Europe, or anywhere at all, for that matter. "No. You?"

"Yes, I lived there for a bit as a child. My father was…" Our conversation was cut off by the ship's horn sounding long and low. Franny stood. "We should get some rest." She moved easily with the rolling ship. Then she held out her hand to help me up.

"I'm going to sit awhile longer."

She shrugged. "Suit yourself." She reached into her bag and pulled out a pack of Gauloises cigarettes. "Do you fancy a smoke?" I thought then of her wholesome image onstage. Now that I knew who she was, cigarettes seemed oddly out of place.

I shook my head. "No, thank you."

"Yeah, I gotta stop, too." She put the pack away and turned to go. "These things will kill you." Her last words faded along with her into the darkness.

6

Helaine

Paris, 1939

Helaine scraped at a speck of potato that was stuck to the bottom of the cracked, stained pot from the previous night's dinner. It refused to budge, so she dipped the pot once more in the sink of soapy water. The tiny kitchen, really just a corner of the single-room flat in Montmartre that she and Gabriel shared, was a far cry from the elegant one in her childhood home. She remembered, as if in a dream, the fine china and rows of copper pans suspended from the rack above the stove.

There were so many things about her childhood that Helaine had taken for granted; she knew that now. That someone would cook delicious food for her. That there would be food at all. She and Gabriel did not starve, but there always seemed to be just barely enough in the days leading up to when he was paid. More than once, Helaine had caught him dusting mold off a stale bread crust, or taking a smaller portion than he wanted so that she would have enough to eat. And it was not just groceries. Gabriel paid all of the bills late, cajoling the landlord and the shops to give them extra time and paying the most urgent only when there was no more grace to be had. Living without enough money was not something to which Helaine was accustomed and it often felt to her like sailing through the air without a net.

It had been more than a year since the night Helaine had left her parents' home with Gabriel. After she walked from their house, Helaine was flooded with remorse. What had she done? She had abandoned her family and home for a man she barely knew.

When they reached his flat, which was even tinier and grimmer than she recalled from her previous visit, her doubts redoubled. She had never been away from her parents' house. How would she manage with nothing? "I rushed you with all of this," Gabriel had said, noticing her unsure expression. "If it's too much, we can slow down and just be together."

"No," she replied. "I want to marry you." The hollowness she had felt at leaving him and thinking it was over made her realize how much she cared for him and wanted to share his life.

Gabriel laid a blanket on the floor in front of the window because he had no table. He produced a simple dinner of bread and cheese and a half bottle of chardonnay. They ate and then made love, and even though it was only the second time, it felt as natural and perfect as though they had been together in this way forever. After, as they lay entwined, Helaine experienced a contentment that she had never felt in her entire life. Her remaining doubts evaporated. She knew then that she was home.

They wed privately, a small ceremony at the town hall with just the clerk as witness. They did not have a honeymoon. Gabriel could not afford the cost, nor the time away from the orchestra during the concert season. "Someday soon," he said, "we will have a grand adventure on a ship to America." Helaine accepted the promise and tried not to think of the implausibility of his plan.

Their lives settled into an easy routine together after that. Helaine spent her days making the flat homier by searching the secondhand market for cheap items they needed, plus buying groceries and making their meals. There were many things she had to learn after coming to live with Gabriel, like how to budget to make the few francs they had stretch to the end of the week, how to get the best cut of meat and make sure the butcher didn't short them. Helaine often felt overwhelmed by her lack of practical experience in the world, having to figure out how to do everything for the first time like a child.

Helaine dried the pot now and set about preparing ingredients for their supper, a simple ratatouille made from the root vegetables she'd been able to buy at the market the previous day. Cooking, now that was the one thing she could do. Maman had taught her many recipes and techniques to keep her from getting bored, and Helaine could knead dough deftly and make a pastry thin enough that one could almost see through it. Each night, she made supper for Gabriel, who was so caught up in his music he might have forgotten to eat if she had not.

Of course, life with Gabriel was not all work. Every Friday evening, Helaine would go to the symphony and sit in the seat in the back that Gabriel reserved for her. She loved to listen to him play, hearing his cello alone amid the instruments. Over time, she had gained an even greater appreciation for his musical talent. Gabriel was not just a gifted cellist, though; he composed his own original pieces as well.

One night, Helaine entered the flat to hear Gabriel practicing a new piece of music. Unlike his usual confident playing, his bow strokes now were tentative. "I'm working on something. Do you like it?"

She nodded. "I truly do. It's a beautiful melody."

He smiled, his eyes crinkling, and she could see that her opinion meant a great deal to him. "Good, because it's called *For Helaine*."

"Oh, Gabriel!" She walked over and threw her arms around him. He was happy not just because she liked the piece, but because he had written it for her.

He returned her embrace. "The song, like our love, will last long after we are gone." It was, Helaine decided, the nicest thing anyone had done for her in her entire life.

On his nights off, they would take long walks down the sloped streets of Montmartre to the Canal Saint-Martin, getting to know one another in ways that there had not been time for before their impulsive marriage.

"When we first met, you told me that you liked to write," he remarked one night a few weeks earlier as they walked along the quay. "What did you write about?" he asked.

She smiled. "I wrote stories. Like I told you, my parents confined me to the house for most of my childhood."

"That must have been awful."

"It was and it wasn't. We had a wonderful home, but I sometimes felt like a prisoner. I know my parents did it out of concern."

"We sometimes hurt those we love most by trying to protect them," Gabriel agreed.

"When I was stuck at home, I created stories about a girl named Anna who traveled the world. I still do," she admitted, worried he would find that silly.

"You should write them again and publish them," he declared.

"But how do I know if they are any good?"

"I'm certain that they are." He put his arm around her shoulders.

"You haven't even read them. How can you be sure?"

"Because I know you." He stopped, drawing her into his embrace. "You must share your art with the world. Where does Anna travel?"

"Rome, Australia, New York. The places I've always wanted to go."

"Then we will go see those places so that you can write about them more vividly. Or at least, I hope we will when things are better."

"What do you mean?" Helaine asked. Gabriel had always spoken so brightly about their future. Why was he hesitating now?

"Darling, war is coming."

"I know." She had heard it on the radio and read the stories in *Le Figaro*. The Germans had amassed at the border. This was Gabriel's long-standing prediction and she had heard him repeat it a number of times since they had first met. Only now it seemed real and inevitable, a prophecy fulfilled.

"I sometimes wonder if we should leave Paris."

"Gabriel, no." Though Helaine yearned to travel, she could not imagine leaving for good. "Paris is our home. You have your work here." She expected him to argue further and was grateful when he did not. They had turned and started for home. Neither of them had spoken more about impending war since that night, but it hung over them like a storm cloud.

When the meal preparation was finished and the dishes clean, Helaine wiped her hands and took off her apron, smoothing the plain cotton skirt beneath. She'd had to find clothes after coming here, since she had left her parents' home with almost nothing. She had avoided the secondhand shops for this, instead finding fabric at a good price and making her own. The simple dresses were scratchier than the fine silks she'd grown accustomed to as a child, but also less constraining.

Helaine looked around the apartment, considering how to fill the time until Gabriel came home. Despite her happiness, she was often lonely. Left by herself in the apartment for long stretches while Gabriel taught and rehearsed and performed, Helaine yearned for her mother. Before this, Helaine had never been on her own or alone at all. Maman had always been close by, taking care of her and keeping her company. Helaine wondered how her mother filled her days now that she was gone, and whether she, too, was lonely. She had considered more than once writing to her mother but could not bear the thought that she might not reply.

Helaine went to the desk drawer to retrieve her journal and a pencil. She carried them to the cozy seat by the window and sat down. The one thing she regretted leaving behind in her parents' house was her journal. Gabriel had bought her a new one, a fine leather-bound book that cost more than he should have spent. But it was not the same. She had tried without success to re-create the story she had been working on before she left. Instead, she had begun sketching images of the Montmartre skyline, and of her grandmother's split locket, the one cherished thing she had brought with her from home.

Sometime later, Gabriel came in and she set down her notebook. Wordlessly, he swept her up in his arms, as though they had been apart for days and not hours. He was often like this after a long rehearsal, the music creating a kind of pent-up passion within him. But now his lovemaking seemed urgent, as though this time together might somehow be their last. He carried her to their bed, the intensity between them as strong as the first time they had been together.

After, Helaine stood and dressed and went to the kitchen area, pulling out two chipped porcelain bowls to serve the ratatouille she'd prepared earlier. As they were about to eat, a commotion came from the street below, a rumbling and then shouting voices. Gabriel stood. "Stay here. I will go see what is happening."

Helaine wanted to tell him not to go. If there was trouble, why run toward it? But Gabriel was already out the door, so she hurried to the window to see what was happening. People raced by; their faces were grim. Helaine wondered if there was a fire or other accident. Some carried bags as if setting out for holiday, but others looked as though they had been forced to depart without warning.

Gabriel returned a few minutes later, his expression somber. "France declared war on Germany in response to Germany's invading Poland. We are now at war."

A shock ran through Helaine. Although people had spoken of war, perhaps even expected it for months, the fact that it was now upon them felt surreal. Helaine and Gabriel stood silently for several minutes, as if unsure what to do. They ate by the window, watching the scene below play out like a movie. Helaine understood that if the French army did not prevail, the Germans might soon march into Paris. Still, she was puzzled by what all of the people were doing in the street. Where did they think they could go?

"Perhaps we should leave," Gabriel suggested as he had weeks earlier.

"But where would we go?" They did not have a great deal of money for traveling. "Surely many will be trying to do the same."

"The borders will be flooded," he agreed. "Getting visas to go anywhere will be impossible. We will stay put—at least for now."

The next morning, the streets were quiet, as though nothing had happened. Helaine dressed and prepared to go to the market. But as she reached for her coat, Gabriel came over and took her arm.

"You should stay inside." His eyes were dark with concern.

"But why? The Germans aren't in Paris." *At least not yet*, Helaine finished silently. Despite the patriotic talk everywhere in the months leading up to the war, there was also an unspoken understanding that the French military was no match for German might.

"I know, but I worry that those who dislike the Jews will be emboldened by the German declaration of war."

Helaine shook her head. Her freedom was recent and hard-fought. "I will not be kept prisoner again."

"Be careful, then," he said. Gabriel would worry about her because he loved her, but he would not try to keep her inside to protect her as her parents had done.

She started for the door and then turned back, a thought occurring to her. "Will you have to go and fight?" There had been talk of call-ups, all able-bodied men sent to the front.

"I already tried to enlist," he confessed.

Helaine was shocked. It was hard to imagine gentle Gabriel fighting in the army. And why didn't he tell her? Helaine considered that there might be other things about Gabriel that she did not know. "I had no idea."

"I'm sorry I didn't say anything. I didn't want to worry you. It doesn't matter anyway. They turned me down." He gestured toward his leg. Helaine scarcely noticed Gabriel's limp anymore. But to the military, it had been a detriment, excluding him from service. "I wanted to do my part," he said, his voice heavy with regret. Helaine realized he also had not said anything because he was ashamed at having been rejected from the military.

Helaine moved closer to him. "There will be other ways to serve as a civilian," she reassured. Inside, she was relieved. He would not be leaving her.

Helaine went to the market. She should hurry back, she knew, but instead she found herself lingering, savoring the sights and sounds in spite of any danger the looming war might bring. It was more than mere defiance. Gabriel's words had made her realize that her hard-fought freedom might not last forever. She wanted to enjoy it now, while she still could.

At first, nothing changed in Paris, and it seemed that the declaration of war might have been a bluff. "A phony war," some called it. Helaine held her breath all through that long winter, waiting to see what would happen, like some dreadful cliffhanger in a novel. Finally, in May of 1940, word came that Germany had invaded France. Still the fighting was by the border, hundreds of kilometers away. It often felt as if the war was not happening at all.

Throughout the early days of the war, Helaine thought often of her family. Helaine badly wanted to go check on them. That bridge was burned, though, her connection to her family irrevocably severed.

One rainy day as Helaine sat in the garret, trying to read and willing the hours of solitude to pass quickly, there came a commotion from the street outside. Alarm rose in her. She walked to the window and found people crowding the streets, seeming to run in all directions as they had the day France declared war on Germany. But Helaine could not make out what was going on. She put on her shoes and walked downstairs.

Outside, the sidewalk and pavement were packed with people, mostly women, since so many of the men had all gone off to fight. "What happened?" she asked to no one in particular.

"France has been defeated!" cried an elderly woman, tears filling the crevices of her wrinkled cheeks.

Helaine was stunned. She had known that the French army was no match for the Germans' tanks and steel, and that the Maginot Line, the fortification France had created after the Great War, would not hold them back. But it had been less than six weeks. She had not imagined it would be over so quickly.

"The Germans will be in Paris in days," the old woman added, her voice more fearful than sad now. "Those who can are leaving."

Leaving to go where? Helaine wondered. If the Germans had

defeated France, they would surely occupy the entire country. One could not simply go abroad. Helaine had so many questions, but the woman was already gone. Watching hordes of people flee the capital, Helaine questioned whether she and Gabriel should be among them.

In the days that followed, French soldiers, who had marched off so proudly less than two months earlier, straggled home, dazed and beaten. The city became engulfed in waves of people. First, those fleeing the fighting washed in from the north. But then the fear of the Germans coming sent people out of the city again in masses. L'Exode, they called it. People left in cars or bikes or on foot, carrying what they could on their backs or dragging belongings with them. One woman pushed a baby in a carriage, valise perched precariously atop it.

During her daily walks, Helaine watched the colors of the city change like leaves in autumn. The Germans arrived in Paris, tanks rolling down the Champs-Élysées. Within days, the street signs had changed to German and enormous red flags bearing black swastikas hung from every government building.

One night, Gabriel did not come home at his scheduled time and Helaine grew worried. Had something happened? Finally, close to midnight, he walked into the flat.

"You're late," she said, regretting the reproachful way it sounded. "Are you all right? I was afraid that something had happened."

"I'm so sorry to have worried you. I had an unexpected meeting and no way to send word," he explained.

"A meeting for the symphony?"

"Not exactly." He hesitated, then looked away.

"We said we would never keep secrets again," she pointed out.

He lowered his voice, as though there were others in the flat who might hear. "There are people organizing to defy the Germans, secretly of course. I want to be a part of that." He held out a leaflet that included a satirical cartoon of Hitler and a list of ways that ordinary people could help resist.

Helaine was worried. "Gabriel, that's dangerous."

"Even so, we must do something."

He was right, Helaine realized. They could not simply sit here and wait; they had to do something. "Then let me help, too."

"No, I won't put you at risk."

"So you can be brave, but not me?" He did not answer. Her frustration rose. "Why is it different?"

"Because," he said quietly. "You are a Jew." There it was, the truth, laid before them. No matter how much they loved one another, there were differences that made this so much worse for her. "And I am afraid for you."

"Do you regret this?" Helaine asked, gesturing between them. "I mean, being married to a Jew right now, it isn't easy."

"I'm not here for easy," he replied, and she remembered then all of the struggles they had faced to be here together. "I didn't take vows for easy. And I wouldn't trade this for anything. I only worry for your safety. With you," he added, "I regret nothing." He kissed her firmly on the lips, quelling her fears for the moment.

But even Gabriel's love could not keep the outside world at bay. The streets, which once felt like freedom, were now foreign and dangerous. The anti-Semitism that had bubbled beneath the surface in France for decades flourished in the light. *Death to Jews*, was crudely painted on a wall along Rue Berthe read. There were dreadful political cartoons in the newspapers portraying Jews as hook-nosed monsters, editorials calling for their expulsion from the country.

One Friday night, Gabriel and Helaine set out for the symphony. Helaine left Gabriel at the stage door and then started for the auditorium. Something was different, she noticed right away. There were two German officers in attendance, seated in some of the boxes with attractive young women as their guests. Uneasiness rose in her, but she swallowed it back and proceeded down the aisle. As Helaine neared her usual seat, she saw a woman two rows to the left pointing at her and whispering to one of the ushers. Helaine did not know them, but she recognized one of the women from the neighborhood where she had grown up.

The usher walked over to Helaine. "Excuse me, madam," he said. Helaine looked to make sure she had not taken the wrong seat. "Given the current political situation, I'm afraid that it is no longer appropriate for Jews to attend the symphony."

"Excuse me?" Helaine was stunned—and mortified. How had he known she was Jewish? The woman who had been pointing, Helaine realized. She must have recognized Helaine and remembered her religion. "I'm only here to listen to my husband play." Who was this man to cast her out? But everyone around her was staring, and arguing would only draw more attention.

Helaine walked out, cheeks flushed, feeling all eyes on her. Gabriel ran out into the street. "Darling, wait! I just heard. I had no idea. I'm so sorry." He took her arm. "Come, let's go home."

"But you have a show." He was ready to walk away from it all for her. "You can't just leave."

"If you cannot hear me, then I won't play," he declared defiantly.

"No, you must stay. I know that you are trying to defend me, but this is your career."

"How can I play for people who are rejecting us?" Gabriel, though not Jewish, was casting his lot with her and Helaine loved him even more for it. "I hate this."

"Me, too. But you must go back. I'll be fine." This last part was a lie. If she could not even go to see her own husband play, what else would she be forbidden from? What hope could there be for Helaine or their future together?

Gabriel kissed her and then reluctantly turned away and walked back into the concert hall. Watching him go, Helaine was filled with sadness. There was an undeniable gulf between them, people from worlds too different to bridge, no matter how much they loved one another. And with the troubles that were coming, that distance would surely only get worse. Helaine started for home, lonelier than she had ever been in her entire life.

7

Louise

Henley-on-Thames, 1953

My return train is delayed and it is almost half past seven when I arrive home. As I walk through the door, exhausted, the familiar space, usually so warm and welcoming, seems confining and close after the city. The children are already in bed, Joe reading in his chair.

Joe jumps up, and a bit of his scotch drips from his glass onto the end table. "Where were you?" he asks, his voice rising. I can see how worried he has been.

"I didn't mean to alarm you. I told you I was going to go into the city today." As is so often the case, he must have forgotten or not been listening in the first place. "I tried to ring you at work to leave word that my train was delayed. I called the school and asked Miss Eakley to mind them until you could get there." Miss Eakley, a teacher with no children of her own, did not mind babysitting after school for a quid or two.

"Still, I was worried. Plus, I still had to pick them up and fix supper." Joe makes the things I do every day sound Herculean.

"Ewen and Phed were asking for you and I didn't have anything to tell them. I put them to bed for you."

For you. As though they are my responsibility alone, and not ours shared together. As though he is doing me a favor just by helping out once or twice. I want to point all of this out, but I'm too tired for a row.

"What did you go to London for again?" Joe asks.

"Remember the necklace I showed you yesterday, the one from the thrift shop?" We had a whole conversation about it. How can he not remember? Not waiting for him to respond, I continue, "I wanted to know about its origin and Midge has a sister, Millie, who's a jeweler on Portobello Road..."

"London for an old necklace on a whim?" he repeats, sounding almost aghast. I hear in his voice how ridiculous it all must seem. "Lou, that isn't like you." No, of course not. Sensible Lou does what is needed. She would never go off on a lark to satisfy her own curiosity.

"The necklace, I thought I had seen it years ago during the war. I wanted to know if it was the same one."

"And?"

"And Millie said this type of necklace is English," I reply, a note of concession in my voice.

"Which means it likely isn't the one you saw in Germany during the war."

"Not necessarily."

"But if the necklace is English, what might it have been doing on the continent during the war?" His logic is undeniable.

He is asking for answers I don't have. My frustration grows. "A British soldier might have brought it with him."

"Lou, I think you're grasping at straws. Does this have to do with the friend you lost during the war?" His voice is gentler now. I am surprised. I have never told Joe the whole story about Franny and I had not realized he'd been paying attention to the part I had. "I know how hard it can be to remember the people we lost," he continues when I do not reply. "The chaps from my unit, I see them all the time in my dreams."

That isn't the same, I want to say. I know, though, that he is trying to relate, and I don't want to lose a moment of possible connection, which comes so seldom these days. "Anyway," I reply finally, "I'm home now."

"I'm sorry that this isn't enough for you," he says, gesturing to the house around us. His voice is sad, without a trace of reproach. How has he made the leap from the necklace to sensing the discontent with my life that I feel? But he is here every day, seeing more than I realize.

"It isn't that," I say, feeling equal parts guilty and frustrated. "I'm sorry, too," I say finally. "I didn't mean to worry you."

"It's all right," Joe replies, forgiving me instantly. I am reminded, not for the first time, of how kind and patient he is, and despite our disagreement, how much I love him.

The next morning when I reach the shop, Midge is already there, going over some paperwork. "How was London?" I tell her briefly about my visit with her sister and the fact that the necklace is English. "I'm sorry that Millie couldn't be more help," she says when I've finished.

"Not at all. Knowing it isn't what I thought is a kind of help, too." I gesture to the boxes stacked by the door. "Where shall I start?"

"There are more crates in the back of the shop to be sorted." I walk into the storeroom. It looks neater than when I was there two days earlier. Garbage day, I remember. I feel a tug of guilt that I was not there to help Midge put the boxes and crates out.

The crate. Suddenly, an image pops into my mind of the crate in which I'd found the necklace. It might contain clues about the necklace's origin. My eyes dart around the storeroom, but I do not see it. I race to the front of the shop. "Midge, the crate I was sorting the other day when I found the necklace, where is it?"

"It was empty and the bits that were left in it were rubbish," she says, "so I put it out."

My heart sinks. "It went with the garbage this morning?"

Midge shakes her head. "It was a solid crate and I thought someone might want it, so I put it out for the rag-and-bone man a little while ago." The rag-and-bone man collects things people don't want anymore to repurpose or sell. I run out the back door of the shop, hoping that he has not come yet. But the area by the back door is empty, the crate and other rubbish gone.

Midge comes to the door. "What on earth?" she asks as I begin to sprint down the road in the direction the rag-and-bone man would have gone.

I find him two streets over, collecting glass bottles from behind the grocery. "Excuse me." I stop, trying to catch my breath. "You picked up a crate at the secondhand shop."

"I pick up a lot of crates," he replies, a stub of hand-rolled cigarette hanging from the corner of his mouth. He bends down and lifts the long poles of the wagon he pulls himself without the aid of a horse. The rag-and-bone man is a toothless veteran in tattered clothes, a painful reminder of what Joe might have been without me. Why hadn't we done better as a country for all of those who served?

I gesture to the back of the wagon. "May I look?"

"Make it quick. I have a long route." I begin to rifle through the cart. So many crates and they all look alike. How can I tell which one the necklace came in?

Then I see the familiar broken slats of the crate I'd gone through two days earlier. I pull it out. "Two pence," the man says, and it seems preposterous to pay for garbage, much less the garbage Midge has just given him. But the man is only trying to earn a living and I am not about to quibble. I fish the coins from my pocket and hand them to him.

I carry the crate back toward the shop. It appears unremarkable and it seems in that moment that the whole chase and money spent might have been a waste. But as I near the shop, I turn the crate over and in the wood is etched a single word.

Lévitan.

I bring the crate inside and over to Midge, who stands behind the counter with her hands on her hips. "I just threw that out," she says, perplexed.

"I know." I hold up the crate to show her the bottom. "Any idea what this means?"

"Lévitan?" Midge repeats the word slowly. "I'm not certain, but it sounds familiar. Let me check something." She walks to the back of the shop. "Here it is," she calls a few minutes later. She returns holding a tattered magazine triumphantly. "I thought I'd read the word before." She gestures to an open page. Moving closer, I can see that the magazine is in French. She points to an advertisement for elegant women's hats. "Lévitan was a department store in Paris before the war." *Paris.* The word ricochets around in my mind. "It might not mean a thing," Midge cautions quickly, sensing my excitement. "People put things in random crates to donate all of the time."

I scarcely hear her words. The necklace, identical to the one I had seen during the war right down to the place where it was nicked, had arrived in a box from a Paris department store. This is no coincidence. The necklace came from France. "Still, it might mean something."

"It might," Midge repeats, but I can tell that she does not believe me.

Midge returns to her paperwork and I begin my sorting. As I work, I let the information sink in. I am more certain than ever that the necklace I now hold is the very same one that I saw in Europe during the war, the one the man had given to Franny right before she was killed. Finding its owner will surely provide answers about what had happened to Franny.

I think then of my conversation with Ian the previous day. *Come over to Paris,* he'd said. I pull Ian's card from my purse and turn it over in my hand, considering. At the time, the notion seemed ridiculous. But now, knowing that the necklace came from a Paris department store, and not from England, it doesn't seem so far-fetched. If I don't go, I've reached a dead end.

Ian appears in my mind. To be honest, he hasn't left my mind since I saw him the previous day. I picture him as he strode across Whitehall toward me, more handsome than ever. I still liked him—too much. And it was evident that he felt the same. Our connection, which had lain dormant beneath the surface for nearly a decade, reared up more powerfully than ever. The attraction feels like a breath of fresh air, welcome after the troubles Joe and I are having. I'm married and I love my husband; I have no intention of betraying him. At the same time, Ian has piqued my interest. Our time together years ago had ended so abruptly, and the last chapter of our story was never written. If going to Paris to look into the necklace provides a chance to understand what exists between Ian and me, then so be it.

I look around. How can I go? More to the point, how can I tell Joe that I am going? If it seemed foolish to him that I wanted to go to London, then a trip to Paris will seem preposterous.

That night, I wait until after dinner, then take a deep breath and jump right in. "Joe, remember that necklace I showed you?" He looks up from the newspaper. "Well, it turns out it came from a shop in Paris." Really I only know that it came in a box from the shop in Paris. But I am stretching, trying to bolster my reasons for wanting to go. "So I'd like to go to Paris for a few days to look into it." He is staring at me oddly.

"You want to go to Paris because of a necklace?" he asks with disbelief.

"Yes, this is important to me."

"First London, now Paris. Lou, how far is this thing going to go?"

"I need this, Joe." There is a note of pleading in my voice. I don't want to quarrel over this. "Plus, I could use a break."

"I know that the house and children can be a lot, but do you really have to go so far?"

"I know I'm asking a lot. But this is important to me, Joe."

"How long would you be gone?"

"Two nights," I say. "Three, tops." I'm guessing now. "Just long enough to visit the store and ask some questions." I leave out the part about Ian.

"I don't like it, Lou, you going so far alone. And we need you here. But if you insist, I won't try to stop you." His voice is reluctant.

"Thank you," I say, putting my arms around him.

"Do you want me to come with you?" he asks suddenly.

My heart breaks, because I want to say yes. A trip to Paris, anywhere really, might be just what we need. However, this is not that trip. "I love you for offering, but this is something I need to do for myself."

"Is it even safe?" Though I appreciate his concern, I am also annoyed. Once I went into occupied Germany to do important work for the war. Why am I seen as feeble or less than, now that I am married?

"I'll be fine. I'll ring your sister and ask her to watch the children while you are at work."

He hesitates and I worry that he will try to stop me. "Fine." I'm not certain if he is giving me the space I need or simply avoiding a confrontation. "Just be safe and please leave me all of your trip information. And hurry back," he adds. "I'll miss you."

"Me, too." I am touched and yet, at the same time, feel a twinge of guilt that I am leaving.

As I finish the dishes, I consider the notion of going to Paris. Even with Joe in agreement, it seems far-fetched, almost ridiculous. I am not one to leave. Despite my restlessness at the constraints of my current life, I love my husband and children, and I would not give them up for anything. And my memories of my time in Europe are not pleasant ones. In fact, the very last thing I want to do is leave my cozy world and open up the dark trappings of the past, to return and start tearing open the old wounds.

A plate slips from my hand and clatters to the ground, breaking into a thousand pieces. "Bugger!" I swear, unable to control my frustration. "Bloody hell!" I haven't cursed in years and the words leave an acrid burn in the back of my throat, like the cigarette habit I'd given up long ago.

The children stop playing and look up at me with wide eyes, unaccustomed to seeing me lose my temper. "I'm sorry," I say. They already have one parent who is neither fully present nor emotionally in control; they do not deserve a second. "Mummy's fine." As I clean up the mess, though, I know I am not fine. The past, which has returned suddenly and unbidden, has awakened a dark part of me I'd hoped was gone for good.

Later that night as I clean up the kitchen while Joe snores in his chair, the matter nags at me still. How can I possibly up and leave for Paris? I look around the house and think of Ewen and Phed, sleeping soundly above. I have a life and people who depend upon me. I cannot simply run off.

But I can't be any good for my family if I am not good myself. I have to sort out the past so I can put it behind me forever and move on. And there are some promises I had made, too deep and too long ago, to ever be broken.

The next morning I book the ferry to Paris.

❧

France, 1944

The aid convoy clacked northward with effort through the hills of occupied France, breaking the night silence. I rode in the front seat of a military truck, squeezed between the driver on my left and Franny on my right. Ian was in the truck in front of us and the other volunteers followed two vehicles behind. In the distance, I heard a rat-a-tat sound that I imagined was gun-fire. My heart beat faster with fear. I could not help but wish that Ian was here with us to reassure me or at least explain what was going on. We were passing through enemy territory now, under the auspices of German protection. But the guarantee of safety was an illusion, a promise that might be revoked at any time now. I shuddered, drawing my sweater closer around me.

The truck slowed as it passed through a village. Through the window of a house close to the road, I could see a mother and young child silhouetted against a backdrop of yellow light. Scenarios passed through my mind, creating a storyline for the scene. I imagined the child waking from a nightmare, the mother comforting him. What had they seen, bearing witness to war? The village receded in the background and the road grew long and deserted once more. "Almost there," the driver said. Franny shifted beside me restlessly and I could feel her wanting to get out and stretch her legs and smoke. She did not seem to do well in confined spaces.

The driver turned onto a side road and followed the other trucks stopping on the gravelly shoulder. "Halt!" a voice barked, the first German we had heard since coming here, speaking as harshly as though we were prisoners ourselves. I froze, the re-ality of our situation overwhelming me.

Franny, sensing my nervousness, slipped her hand in mine. "Come," she said gently, giving me a small smile. We stepped from the truck onto the side of the road. The caravan was in-spected thoroughly for weapons or other contraband. The Ger-mans, Ian had told me while we were in transit, were known to have impersonated the Red Cross to get information out of prisoners. It only stands to reason that they feared the Allies might use the aid mission to do the same.

The inspection was so extensive that I was afraid they might insist upon searching our persons next. But they waved us back into the trucks and we drove a few hundred meters farther until we reached the camp, a converted military barracks. The convoy stopped in front of a barbed wire fence. Through the faint predawn light, I could make out stone buildings, arranged in a U shape around an open courtyard.

The camp was an oflag, Ian had explained before we arrived, specifically designated for British officers captured as POWs and ostensibly better than the stalags where the enlisted men were kept. The Germans allowed the Red Cross in to inspect the prisoners' conditions and deliver limited aid here.

Ian got out of the vehicle ahead and came to the passenger-side door of ours and opened it. He held out a hand to assist Franny in stepping down and then reached out to me. "Here, allow me." His hand took mine and I felt a flash of electricity. I pushed down the reaction. I was here to volunteer for the Red Cross, not to get caught up in an affair with one of its workers. Yet when his hand lingered a moment too long after I had gotten down from the truck, I did not pull away.

At first, the camp on the far side of the fence appeared deserted. Then a shrill bell sounded. Men in gray prison uniforms, pale and skeletal and bald, stumbled from the buildings. They eyed us with interest, and I could tell by their confusion that we were the first aid convoy to reach this camp. They did not loiter or try to approach us, but went purposefully to other locations, breakfast or prison jobs, I imagined. I didn't know what I had expected coming over here to deliver food to POWs. But the sight of the emaciated men on the other side of the fence was almost too much to bear. I was suddenly angry. These were British citizens, men who had gone to fight for their country, just like Joe. And if things were this bad for the officers, I could only imagine what the conditions for the enlisted men must be like. Why wasn't our government doing more to get them out? There were reports, too, of camps a thousand times worse than this where the Germans imprisoned Jews. I was overwhelmed by the magnitude of the suffering. We could try to help from now until the end of time and it would never be enough.

Franny touched my arm. "We should unload the packages." She was right. Standing here and gawking was not going to help the men. The sooner we could get the aid packages into their hands, the better.

Franny began helping with the boxes. "Don't you have a show to get ready for?" I asked.

She shrugged. "It isn't for hours." She rolled up her sleeves and put her shiny curls up in a bun and worked alongside me, her hoop earrings jangling as we unloaded several dozen cardboard boxes containing basic supplies that would help the prisoners survive. We worked silently alongside one another. Despite the chill, I grew warm from the manual labor, moisture forming against my skin. Beside me, Franny glistened, her perfect makeup intact.

Ian supervised the volunteers, directing where the packages should be stocked, how wide and how high. I had wondered if his professor-like ways would make him ill at ease in the rough war zone. But with jacket off and sleeves rolled up, he seemed very much the commanding officer—and more attractive than ever.

Franny leaned close. "It's ironic, isn't it?" she whispered, gesturing subtly toward a German guard. "The men have guns, and we don't." It was always that way, I mused. The odds were always tipped in their favor. But the terrifying reality was that we were completely powerless here, at the mercy of the enemy.

"That's enough for now," Ian said when we had unloaded about two thirds of the pallets from the trucks.

"What now?" I asked. "Can we start giving out the packages?"

Ian shook his head. "They have to be processed by the Germans. They will be distributed tomorrow."

"Tomorrow?" It was only late afternoon. "But the men need this food now." I was eager not only to deliver the care packages so the men could receive the much-needed provisions, but also to do our job and leave.

"I know, but there's nothing to be done about it." He held out his arm to me. "Come, they're going to drive us to our rooms."

They set us up in temporary quarters down the road from the camp, an old, single-story hotel that had been requisitioned. "That's yours," Ian said, gesturing to one of the doors. I opened it and stepped inside. The room was cold and drafty with worn, spartan furniture. Ian lingered in the doorway a beat. "I'm just down the hall if you need anything."

I wouldn't have minded for him to stay a bit longer, but instead I said, "Thank you."

I was surprised to find Franny had the room adjacent to my own. I expected her, as a starlet, to have better accommodations, something more grand. But here, she was just one of us.

"Do you want to come in?" Franny asked from her own doorway.

"Don't you have to get ready?" Franny had told me earlier that her first performance for the men was that evening. "I thought you might want to rest before your show." I myself was exhausted from the long journey and the work unpacking boxes.

"I'm not at all tired. Plus, we should eat." She gestured toward the boxed meals that had been left for us outside our room doors.

"Sure," I said, picking up the meals and walking inside. Looking around the drab room, I wondered what Franny, with her glamorous London life, thought of it all.

But she sprawled on an old, worn chair as though it was the finest chaise at the Ritz. "This will do," she said with a smile as I handed her one of the meals. Inside, there were preheated noodles and small pie crusts filled with unidentifiable minced meat.

"I still don't understand how is it that you are allowed to perform for the prisoners," I remarked as we ate. Even though Franny had tried to explain it on the ship, it was a question that nagged at me still. "They barely have food, yet they are allowed music and entertainment?"

"Like I told you before, I was asked to come perform for the German officers. I insisted on performing for the prisoners, and I was surprised when the Germans agreed. I'm not the only one, though. Édith Piaf, the French singer, performed at a stalag near Berlin a few months ago."

"But how did you wind up with the Red Cross?"

"Once I agreed to go this time, my booking agent connected me with someone at the Red Cross. They figured a convoy that was coming across was the safest way to manage it so I was not traveling alone."

"I'm surprised the Germans would ask a British performer to come."

"I'm half French and I actually have a French passport, which makes it a little easier. And the Germans do it for the propaganda—so the Red Cross can go back and say, 'Look how well the prisoners are cared for. They even have entertainment.'" The very act of giving them a show is in itself theater.

Franny went to a round valise-style suitcase and opened it. Then she pulled out a black evening gown, long and jeweled, which seemed better suited to the finest nightclubs in London. I averted my eyes as she undressed without modesty in the middle of the room and shimmied into the closely fitted dress. "Zip me up?" she asked, turning away from me and lifting her hair to reveal a wide expanse of alabaster skin. After I had done so, she walked over to a cracked mirror, carrying a small leather case, and reapplied makeup and did her hair. Ten minutes later, she turned to me. "What do you think?"

"Beautiful," I answered honestly. Despite our long, weary trip, she had transformed into a glamorous starlet. I followed her outside, where a car waited to take her into the camp. She climbed into the back and gestured that I should join her. I hesitated. I would have to go inside tomorrow, of course, to deliver the aid packages. But I didn't know if I was ready. I didn't want to stay in the dreary hotel, though, or make her go alone, so I got into the car.

We drove slowly down the road, past where we had unloaded the packages, to a guard booth. A German soldier scrutinized us before opening the gate to let us inside the barbed wire fence. I did not see any prisoners as I had earlier, and it felt almost as though the camp was deserted.

The driver took us past the barracks to the back of the camp where a makeshift stage of wood planks had been erected in the courtyard between the stone buildings. I understood now why I had not seen anyone: the men were all here by the dozens, waiting for Franny. There were no seats, so the prisoners in front sat on the ground while others stood behind them.

Someone announced Franny and she came onto the stage. She stepped out and I gasped. I had seen her get ready, put on her gown and apply her makeup. Yet here onstage, she was larger than life, transformed. The men who had gathered lifted their eyes to take her in, faces rapt.

She began to sing an American song, "The Way You Look Tonight," and I was mesmerized. There was nothing overtly tawdry or sexual about it—she was wholesome, the girl next door. But she drew the men in and captivated them, their faces lit with awe and admiration.

Still, watching them, I was overcome by sadness. We could bring them a few moments of joy with Franny's entertainment and perhaps a care package. But the reality was that we would leave, and they would be forced to remain here as prisoners. We couldn't actually help them.

I spied Ian across the courtyard. I expected him to be watching the show, but his gaze was fixed on me. I looked away quickly. This was not the time or place. There was an undeniable attraction between us, though, that was impossible to hide.

Then just as quickly as it started, the show was over. It was not a full-blown concert, but rather a handful of songs before the whistle sounded for their curfew. After, the men surged forward to get an autograph or to be closer to Franny. I even saw one man pose with her while another prisoner snapped a photograph, and I could not help but wonder where they had gotten the camera. She was clearly embarrassed by all the fuss.

The whistle blew again, and the crowd dispersed. As the men walked away, their steps were lighter, spirits lifted. This had not been a thrown-together show on the edge of a prisoner camp. To them, she had been Ella Fitzgerald and Greta Garbo all rolled into one, the performance of a lifetime.

After most of the men had returned to their barracks, one man lingered by Franny's side, as if he had not heard the bell or was not worried about getting in trouble for failing to heed it. He was talking to Franny with great intensity and I knew there was something more to it than mere admiration. I tried to catch her eye to see if she needed me to rescue her. But Franny was engrossed in whatever the man was telling her and did not see me.

"What did that man want?" I asked her when she finished and walked over to me.

"Just a fan," she said vaguely, and I suspected she was lying.

I noticed for the first time that she was holding a camera, the same one I had seen the prisoners using to take photos. "That's yours?" She nodded. "It's rather macabre, don't you think, taking pictures in a place like this?" There was a new sharpness to my voice. "I mean, these men are suffering and here we are acting like tourists."

"The photos aren't for me."

"Then who? You can't possibly get them to the men."

"You're so naive," she said, putting her arm around me like a big sister. She lowered her voice. "The photos can be used to make new documents for the men to help them escape."

"Escape?" My mind whirled. Franny was secretly helping POWs. If she was caught, she would be arrested and possibly killed. We all might be. I was seized with fear for her—and myself.

She nodded. "We take the photos and crop each for an identification card. Then someone else will smuggle the card back in to the prisoner along with a compass and map to help them try to escape." I remembered then how she stood slightly apart in the pictures. I had thought she didn't want the men getting too close, but looking back now, I could see that she was trying to get a photo that could be cropped to show the man alone so that it would work on an identification card. Franny continued, "Last time we performed in a camp we were able to smuggle out a few prisoners by pretending they were part of the musical ensemble. Unfortunately, we don't have a big enough ensemble to manage that this time."

I tried to comprehend what she was telling me. Franny had not come just to perform; getting inside the camps was a way to help the prisoners. There was so much more to her than I had ever guessed. "How on earth did you ever come up with this?"

"I didn't, really. It was a personal assistant of mine back in London, a Jewish refugee. Her brother was involved with the resistance work, and when they heard I was coming over, they asked me to get involved."

She explains this as though it was the most natural thing in the world. I can imagine it, Franny being asked to help, and saying yes without giving it a second thought. "But Ian said if we angered the Germans…" I began.

"Ian's an ox. He has no idea what I am doing. The Germans are killing people by the thousands. Do you think it matters if we anger them or not? For goodness' sake…" She stopped midsentence and turned abruptly. "Smile," she whispered to me under her breath. My gaze followed hers to where a German guard stood watching us, looking suspicious. "Dodgy, are we?" she whispered through gritted teeth. I froze. But Franny jutted out a hip in an exaggerated pose and blew him a kiss. The officer turned away, crimson appearing around his collar.

"We should go," Franny said. As we were driven from the camp, I felt a sense of relief.

"Good night," I said reluctantly when the car dropped us in front of the hotel. I didn't want to be alone and wished that Franny and I shared a room.

"Do you want to come stay?" she asked, gesturing toward her door. I realized then that she did not want to be alone either.

I collected my things from the room I'd been assigned, then went to join her. We lay down, pressed close in the narrow bed. I thought of the camp and the prisoners we had seen. "It's so awful here," I remarked.

"It's an abomination," Franny agreed glumly.

"I thought there were rules of war to ensure prisoners are treated humanely."

"In theory. In reality, the prisoners, even the officers, are subjected to brutal conditions. Unheated barracks, little food or medical care. Hard labor."

"The British government, why isn't it doing more?"

"There's a prisoners' department in the War Office in London. But it's poorly staffed and organized with no funding. The government is focused on fighting battles and winning the war. Trying to repatriate soldiers and giving the Germans their own in return goes against that. You know, the British dislike the Red Cross," she added, lowering her voice even though we were the only two people in the room. "They regard them as interlopers, meddlers who hinder the war effort and whose efforts cannot be trusted." I was surprised. I had imagined the Red Cross volunteers as heroes, angels of mercy bringing aid. I had not realized they would be subject to criticism or disdain.

Overhead, there came the rumbling noise of an airplane, followed by the whinnying sound of a bomb dropping. Moments later, I heard it explode in the distance. The ground shook. I bolted upright in bed, terrified. But Franny remained non-plussed. "It's just the Allies."

"But if they bomb the camps, we'll be hit."

She shrugged. "Maybe, but I don't think so." I realize once more that by coming to help, we might be killed, not just by the Germans, but inadvertently by our own side, because of our proximity to the enemy.

Franny drifted off to sleep, breathing heavily. A moment later, she began to snore. Hearing it the first time, I had to laugh. The glamorous starlet snored like a pissed sailor—a secret that only I knew.

The next morning, we awoke early and dressed in preparation for delivering the packages. "Be nice or I'll tell them you snore," I teased as we walked from the room.

"Oh, Louise!" She laughed, but then her face grew serious. "You see, that's the problem with getting close to someone— you let them expose all of your flaws."

"I was just joking," I said quickly. "I would never tell any of your secrets."

"I know," she replied darkly, and I could not help but wonder what other secrets she might be keeping.

After being driven from the hotel to the camp, we walked to the place near the gate where the trucks stood and continued unloading the packages. They were handed to German guards for distribution, and I regretted that we did not get to give them out ourselves in order to make sure they found their way to the hands of the prisoners.

I reached for another pallet of boxes, these unlabeled, but Ian put his hand on my arm, halting me. "That's all we are permitted to give out."

"But why are we stopping? There are more packages in the trucks and more people who need them."

"The Germans only permit us to deliver packages addressed to specific prisoners. We only have so many names of prisoners, given to us by the War Office. We are only allowed to deliver one package to each of the named men."

"And the rest?" I asked, placing my hands on my hips.

"The rest we send back."

"That's senseless!"

"I don't make the rules," Ian replied, "but I am obliged to follow them. You must understand, the Red Cross has to be sensitive to state interests while firmly pushing ahead its mission." It was in itself a kind of diplomacy—perhaps the hardest kind. "Do you understand how precarious this is? The Red Cross is not allowed access to POWs in Asia or even on the Eastern Front. The belligerent nations, they get to tell us yes or no as to whether we can come across their borders and they can tell us to leave."

"But you saw those men." I moved closer, looking deep into his eyes, imploring him to do more. "The conditions they're being kept in are inhumane. If someone doesn't help them soon, many will die. We must do something."

"We are doing something with these care packages, getting them to as many as we are able. The practical, that's what concerns us. Food, water, clothes if we are able. Little things that give people a chance to survive until this awfulness is over."

But what about those who had no chance at all? "Doing something for some," I countered. I liked Ian and I did not want to quarrel with him. But this was too important to let go. "What about the others?"

"They get nothing, I'm afraid. We are helping as many as we can. I'm trying to get more names. I've lodged a formal protest."

"That will do a lot, I'm certain." My voice was riddled with sarcasm.

"I'm sorry, but we have to play by their rules or be denied access entirely."

I stormed away, frustrated, tears stinging my eyes. Franny appeared then and followed me. "What is it?"

I explained to her what Ian had said. "These packages will go to waste because we don't have the names."

She cracked her gum. "So get more names."

"How?"

"Talk to the men and ask them what they're called."

As if it were that simple. "Ian said that's against the rules. If we break them, our access will be cut off and we will not be able to help anyone. There's no way to do more."

"There's always a way," Franny said curtly. Then she walked away without speaking further.

8

Helaine

Paris, 1941

Helaine stepped from the apartment building onto the pavement. It was a warm June day and the linden trees that lined the sidewalk were flush with green and the birds that flitted among them chirped defiantly. Much had changed in the city since the Germans had come the previous year, with Nazi flags billowing from the Hôtel de Ville and German military vehicles at every corner. But here in Montmartre, the sloped, winding streets were still pleasant in spring and it was possible to forget for a few minutes that anything had happened at all.

Helaine set out for the local boulangerie, hoping to find a few rolls reduced to half price because it was later in the day. But when she reached the shop, it was already closed. There were fewer baked goods to sell now that butter was nonexistent and there was only coarse chestnut flour, not wheat. Helaine berated herself for not having gone earlier. She started home.

Across the street from the boulangerie, Helaine noticed a group of people in the park. At first, she thought they might be parents with children, playing. But closer, she could see that they were all grown women. Many were kneeling on the ground. Curious, Helaine moved closer. The women were digging at the earth.

One of the women noticed Helaine and stood. "Do you want to join us?" she asked. She looked to be about Helaine's age or a year or two younger, with dark braids crisscrossed around the back of her head to form a kind of bun.

"What are you doing?" Helaine asked.

"Gardening."

"I can see that. But why in the park?"

The woman nodded. "We've been given permission by the city to use the park for gardening space. We are going to grow vegetables so that our families have enough to eat. The shortages are only going to get worse." Helaine understood. She had seen firsthand the lack of produce in the stores and had heard stories of entire herds of cattle making their way across the border into Germany, crops requisitioned to feed Axis soldiers at the front. "We are going to divide up the harvest among everyone who works. We could use another pair of hands."

"I would like to help." The extra food would come in handy for feeding herself and Gabriel. She was bored, too, of trying to fill her days while Gabriel rehearsed and played and taught. "I'm Helaine."

"Isa." She handed Helaine a pair of gardening gloves and gestured to a patch of dirt. "You can start by weeding there."

Helaine knelt uncertainly on the hard earth. Another woman working beside Helaine eyed her with disinterest. Helaine faltered. She had helped Maman pot houseplants but had never worked in a garden. She tried to pull up a weed, but it snapped in two. The woman beside Helaine looked at her disdainfully now. Isa bent down beside her to help. "You have to pull from the root, so the whole thing comes up," she explained.

"Have you lived in Montmartre long?" Helaine asked Isa as they worked side by side.

"My whole life. My parents are artists and they raised me and my four younger brothers here. The littlest two are still in school. I hoped to be a painter myself. Of course, being an artist does not bring in much of a pension, so it falls to me to find work and pay the bills." Isa spoke matter-of-factly, no hint of sadness or resentment in her voice. "And you?"

"I moved to Montmartre when I married my husband, Gabriel, a few years ago."

"Gabriel Lemarque, the cellist?" Helaine nodded. "I know Gabriel! We've been neighbors for years. I live on your street. How is it that we have not met?"

"I don't know," Helaine replied. "But I'm glad that we have now."

Helaine worked alongside Isa for about two hours. "I should go," she said finally when the sun began to drop behind the row of houses to the west. "But I'll come again tomorrow if that's all right."

"You are always welcome," Isa said warmly.

Helaine rushed back to the flat, filthy from gardening, but exhilarated from the sense of purpose and having met Isa. When Gabriel returned, Helaine told him about Isa. "She's a good person," he remarked. "And I'm glad you found a friend. You shouldn't be alone so much, especially if anything were to happen to me." There was an ominous note to his voice and Helaine grew worried. What did Gabriel expect to happen to him?

Helaine went to work in the park every day that the weather permitted to till the soil and plant seeds in long, even rows. She and Isa became fast friends. When it was too rainy to garden, Isa came around to the flat for tea. She also showed Helaine the hidden shops in back alleys that had the goods that were growing harder to find, like sugar and coffee, and the makeshift stands where scarce items could be purchased on the black market for a price.

At first, Helaine approached Isa's friendship uncertainly. After a childhood alone, friendship was like a foreign language and Helaine was not sure why anyone would want to spend time with her. But she came to welcome their long conversations that skipped topics easily.

"Are you Jewish?" Isa asked as they worked in the garden together on a cloudy June morning. Helaine nodded. Though it was not something she tried to hide, they had never discussed it before. How could Isa tell? "Are you worried?"

"About the Germans?" Helaine considered the question. "Yes, of course."

"There was a roundup of many men last month."

Helaine nodded gravely. "I understand the arrests were of Jewish immigrants, non-French citizens." More than a third of the Jews in Paris were foreigners, having fled persecution from other countries. Not that those poor souls being taken was any better, but thinking the arrests were limited to non-native French people gave Helaine a kind of comfort. Surely it could not happen to her. "Terrible, of course. But I should be safe."

"I don't know. Still, you must be careful, Helaine."

The next day, Helaine could not work in the park because it was raining and Isa was staying away because of a cold. The door to the flat opened just after lunch and Gabriel stormed in. Helaine looked up from her journal, startled. She had not expected him for hours. "Was your rehearsal canceled?" she asked as he entered, carrying his cello. His expression was grim. "Darling, what is it?" Helaine asked. "What's the matter?"

"I was fired!" he burst out unceremoniously.

"That isn't possible." Gabriel was one of the symphony's most gifted musicians, a rising star.

"We were to play a smaller engagement at the Salle Pleyel." Helaine recognized the name of the once-prestigious theater, now frequented almost entirely by German officers. "At the instruction of the Propaganda Stauffel, they added Bruckner to the program. A shameless attempt to appease the Germans. I refused to play it, so they fired me." This was not the first time Helaine had heard Gabriel talk about the politics of music. He and some of the other instrumentalists did not want to play the German pieces, which seemed to appear on the programs with more frequency now.

"But, Gabriel, this is your career—and your livelihood." Gabriel's salary from the symphony was their primary source of income and Helaine could not imagine how they would live without it. And she was not worried just about the money. Though Helaine did not want to say it aloud and appear cowardly, she worried that there might be repercussions for his refusal to play certain music.

Gabriel would not be swayed. "It will give me more time to work on my own music." Composing his own pieces was truly Gabriel's heart. It did not, however, pay the bills.

Helaine was torn. She was proud that Gabriel stood by his anti-German principles so steadfastly. On the other hand, the Bruckner concerto was a piece of classical music that had been around for years. What would be the harm in going along and playing it? Helaine was not one to rock the boat. "Perhaps if you apologize..." Helaine began.

"Apologize?" Gabriel exploded, and it was the first time Helaine had ever seen him angry with her. There suddenly seemed a side to him that she did not know at all. "They should apologize to me. I won't do it!"

"You must. What choice do you have? If you refuse, what will become of us?"

"I can't. They are using our music as instruments of propaganda and I won't be party to that. I'd sooner stop playing altogether than help them." He carried his cello purposefully to the window and opened it, and Helaine realized with alarm that he meant to throw the cello out and smash it on the street below.

"Gabriel, no!" Helaine rushed to him and took the cello from his hands. She set it in the corner, then wrapped her arms around him and led him to the small sofa she had found at a secondhand shop just weeks earlier. "This isn't the way."

"How, then?" Gabriel looked into Helaine's eyes, searching for answers she didn't have. Helaine didn't speak but held him silently. Her mind turned with worry. She understood his principles. But his music was their only source of income. If he didn't play with the symphony, she was unsure how they would live. Their only item of value was Gabriel's beloved cello, and she couldn't ask him to sell that. Even if she did, she did not know how much it would fetch. If she had to, she would bring herself to ask her parents for money.

After Gabriel was dismissed from the symphony, Helaine thought he would be around the flat more often. At first, he went out to give lessons and play in small groups. But his private teaching and concerts also soon dried up. It was as if others, learning that he had been blacklisted, were afraid to have anything to do with him.

Helaine continued with her own daily routine, mornings gardening with Isa and the other women, and walks through the city as the weather permitted. One day, when the autumn air was particularly pleasant, Helaine strolled farther than usual and found herself crossing the Pont Neuf into the Latin Quarter. The Left Bank was not a neighborhood that was as familiar to her, but she enjoyed the energetic vibe of the university students who gathered defiantly in the cafés.

In an alleyway between two buildings, Helaine spotted a stall with some chocolate croissants in the front case, the kind she had not been able to find for Gabriel in months. They were being sold on the black market, undoubtedly; such things were no longer found in established shops. As she fished a few coins from her purse to buy two, she heard a commotion from across the street. Looking up, Helaine saw a police officer detaining a man. She wondered if he was a pickpocket or some sort of thief; petty crime was not uncommon on the streets. But the man was well-dressed and did not seem likely to cause trouble. What had he done?

"Jewish," she heard a young woman behind her in line whisper to her friend, and Helaine wondered how she knew.

The man fumbled for his papers and handed them to the officer. "I'm a French citizen," he offered. But that did not seem to satisfy the policeman. Helaine could not hear the exchange, but the officer's voice was angry, the man's pleading. A few minutes later, he was escorted roughly into the police car, all pretense of civility gone.

As the police car sped away, Helaine fought the urge to cry out. How were such things happening here on the streets of modern Paris? Before now, she had kept her head in the sand. She had wanted to believe the lie that it only happened to others and not to people like her. But the truth was before her now, impossible to ignore. No one was safe, not Helaine herself, nor her family.

She was suddenly seized with the urge to go see her parents. To check on them, warn them and make sure they were all right. Even as she thought this, she worried that they might not want to see her. Surely they would put the past aside after everything that was happening now. And even if they did not and still refused to speak with her, she had to see them and know that they were safe.

That night as they lay in bed together Helaine broached the subject with Gabriel. "I saw a terrible arrest today."

His face grew somber. "Things are getting so much worse for the Jews." Once he would have told her that things would not come to their part of the city, that she was safe. Now he did not bother to mince words. "Perhaps we should consider leaving France." He raised the topic with more urgency this time. "I can seek an invitation to play in England and we can just go and not return."

"Gabriel, no! This is our home." Helaine had spent her entire life in Paris. For all of the awful changes, she could not bear the thought of leaving. "Your whole career is here. How would you live?"

He shrugged. "We would find a way. Your safety matters most."

Not her safety alone, Helaine thought. "No," she said softly. "I don't want to leave. But I do want to go see my parents. I need to make sure they are all right."

"Darling, no. It's too dangerous to go across the city anymore. Surely you understand that after what you saw today. Promise me you won't go," he said. She did not answer and neither of them spoke for several seconds. Then he drew her close, as though the matter had been resolved. Soon he was fast asleep. But Helaine lay awake, thinking.

The next morning, Helaine slipped from bed. Gabriel snored lightly beside her. "I didn't promise," she whispered before leaving the flat.

The autumn air was crisp as she made her way from Montmartre toward her parents' neighborhood. The walk was a reminder of that first day she had set out from her childhood home. Only, now the lively cafés were somber, and the shop windows that once had been filled with bright and colorful goods were sparse and drab. How had life changed so much since then?

The streets grew busier as she neared her parents' neighborhood, the familiar patchwork of stores still bustling with people going about the business of feeding their families and otherwise trying to survive. But the once-convivial atmosphere was tense and businesslike; everyone was trying to do what they needed to quickly and get home. As she neared the corner of Rue de Navarin, Helaine saw why: there was a checkpoint, a police car blocking the street and two officers checking papers of the passersby.

Panicked, Louise started to turn around. Though her papers were in order, she was terrified of being confronted by the police, especially after she had seen the Jewish man arrested on the Left Bank. Behind her, a police car had parked at the corner. She was trapped. One of the policeman at the blockade, noticing her abrupt action, started toward her. "Papers," he demanded.

Helaine fumbled in her bag and handed the officer her identification card. He scanned it. "You don't live in this neighborhood. What are you doing here?"

"My parents…" she began nervously.

"Laina!" a voice boomed. Helaine froze, terrified of having attention called to her when she could afford it least. But it was Gabriel, his face red from running. He must have awoken and realized she had gone to see her parents, then come after her to try to stop her. He stood panting, assessing the situation. The policeman was between Gabriel and Helaine. Gabriel could do nothing to help her.

In spite of this, he raced toward her. "Laina, the doctor called. Your test results are in and you must come at once." He had risked everything to save her.

The policeman stepped backward. "Doctor?" he asked with a worried expression.

Gabriel nodded gravely. "Quite serious. We don't know if it's contagious." He took Helaine's arm and started to lead her away.

The policeman moved even farther away, giving them a wide berth. "Do not leave the house again until you are well," he ordered.

"Laina, what were you thinking?" Gabriel said when they were away from the checkpoint. "When I woke up and found you gone, I was so worried."

"I wanted to go check on my parents."

"I know, but it's too dangerous. Surely you see that now." Helaine nodded. She did, but she was more worried than ever about her parents.

After that, she shortened her daily walks, not venturing farther than the market or the gardening plot at the park. But things seemed to change overnight, the city becoming less hers. The streets that had once seemed a wonderland to her now felt dark and menacing. It was as if unseen dangers lurked at every turn.

One afternoon, Helaine returned from her walk to see Gabriel sitting on the windowsill, staring out over the rooftops. She expected Gabriel to be playing his cello. Despite war or politics, his love of the instrument would not change. But his cello still lay in its case, untouched. There was a folded piece of paper next to him. Helaine's heart seized. She had heard of deportations to forced labor camps in the east. "What is that?"

"I went to try to make amends with the symphony. You were right, we cannot survive without my income." Gabriel was willing to swallow his pride in order to provide for them. "A small group of the musicians are going to tour Germany. A show of so-called goodwill from the Vichy regime." Helaine nodded. The French government was little more than a puppet of the German occupiers. "They've invited me to come with them."

"Invited?" An invisible hand seemed to close around Helaine's throat.

"More like ordered. I have to go."

"No!" Her eyes burned and the tears spilled forth, splashing hot against her cheeks. "You can't leave me." Helaine felt ashamed of her cowardly reaction. There were so many bigger things to think about than her own happiness now. But it seemed so unfair. She had finally found Gabriel and this life, and it was being snatched out from beneath them by the war. "You can't go to Germany, not now. It's too dangerous."

"What choice do I have? We must stay in the good graces of the Vichy regime." Still, Helaine was surprised. Gabriel had always been so staunchly anti-fascist; it was hard to imagine him going along with this. "I could be sent to compulsory service in Germany anyway," he added. Helaine nodded, recognizing the truth. Men were being ordered to Germany for forced labor as part of the Service du Travail Obligatoire, and those who refused were arrested.

Gabriel continued, "You told me to play along. We can't have it both ways." Surely there was a way to do just enough without becoming complicit. Going to Germany felt like a step too far. But Gabriel was right, cooperation was a slippery slope, and once he started, he was in too deep to stop.

"Don't you see?" he pressed. "If I go and do this for them, we will have special status and be protected."

"No one is safe anymore," Helaine countered. "They have taken artists and intellectuals. You won't be any different."

"I've received assurances that you will be left alone while I am on tour." As ever, he was not thinking of himself, but of her.

"Reassurances?" What good were they? The Germans had broken every promise they had made. That they would not invade France. That French Jewish citizens would be safe. But Gabriel could do nothing but agree and hope for the best that this time it would be different. "And what then?" Helaine asked, seeking answers he did not have. Surely he could not stay on tour until the war was over. "Let me come with you." Even going to Germany, she thought, would be better than staying here alone once more.

Gabriel took her hands. "Darling, that is impossible. And even if I could bring you, Germany would be more dangerous for you as a Jew, not less. It will be a few weeks, a month at most. And it isn't combat. It's music." How could he not see that even music had become an act of war?

"You know, you don't have to report. You could go abroad on tour to the States or Britain," Helaine suggested. Her heart broke at the notion of him going even farther away, but at least then he would be safe.

"And leave you behind in France? Never." Helaine wanted to tell him that by going off to play for the Germans, he would be abandoning her just the same. But she understood what he meant. "I will go play on the tour and get back to you as quickly as I can."

Helaine knew he would not be dissuaded. "When do you leave?"

"Tomorrow, first thing."

Helaine started to protest further. She could not bear for him to go, especially so soon. She sank to the windowsill beside him.

"Perhaps you should go back to your parents," he said.

"No!" Helaine was aghast. How could she possibly return to her parents' house? She had broken so severely with them. That would mean negating all that she and Gabriel had built, admitting that she had been wrong, when that was the furthest thing from the truth. "I will stay here." Even as she spoke, Helaine saw what lay before her: endless days of waiting and nights alone. She dreaded it. But what other choice did she have?

"After I'm gone, it might not be safe for you here," he fretted.

"This is our home," she insisted. "I can't leave it."

"I won't insist upon it." Helaine was grateful that Gabriel, as ever, would let her decide for herself. But it did not quell her unease about his leaving or about their future. "But you must be careful," he added.

"I shall. You should rest now."

"I know, but I hate to waste a minute of the time we have left."

"Me, too."

Gabriel drew her to him and closed his eyes. Soon he slept, but Helaine lay awake. She propped herself up on her elbows and looked out the window at the city below, knowing that it would somehow look different when he was gone.

Then Helaine got up and began to prepare a satchel of things he might need for him to take with him. She added a change of clothes, some canned beans. She wished that she might have prepared some meals for him to take. But she hadn't known.

When the skyline above Notre-Dame began to pinken, Helaine reluctantly nudged Gabriel awake. He reached for her. But his movements were rushed now, as though his mind was already set on the journey before him.

He sat up and reached under the mattress and pulled out a small wad of cash. "Where did you get that?" she asked as he handed it to her.

"I took my money out of the bank. I wish I had more to give you, but that's all I have and you must make it last." Helaine nodded solemnly. Though it would have been a paltry sum during her childhood, it was more money than she had seen since coming here. She could manage if she was careful and budgeted.

"Why did you withdraw it?"

"In case the banks become unreliable. Because they might not give you the money as a Jew. Or if something should happen to me and they impound my account." So many ifs.

"I should go."

"No, wait." Helaine had known that this moment was coming, had dreaded it. Now that it was here, she was desperate to stop time and hold on to Gabriel for a little longer.

He put his arms around her. "Darling, I know. It is unbearable. But we must be strong. We have no other choice." She did not answer but lingered in his arms, trying to memorize the feel of his arms around her and the scent of his skin.

Finally, he broke away from her and reluctantly stood. A few minutes later, he walked to the door of the flat, dressed and packed, but not wanting to leave.

Helaine remembered then her grandmother's necklace. She had taken it with her the night she left home. She reached into the cupboard where she had stored it after she first arrived and pulled it out. She didn't want to part with it—at least not all of it. But she needed to give him something before they said farewell. She separated the two halves, then gave him one.

"You keep one and I keep the other until we are back together," she said, trying to convey that it was not just a necklace, but a promise they were making to one another.

He took the necklace and placed it solemnly in his breast pocket, then put his hand over his heart. "I shall keep it right here until we are together again."

Tears sprang to Helaine's eyes. "I can't do this without you." She had vowed to herself not to cry and make this harder on him than it already was. She was ashamed of herself for being so weak. It was so selfish to think of her own needs now. But she had given up her whole world for Gabriel and now he was leaving.

He placed his hands on both sides of her cheeks. "You are stronger than you know." It was the first time anyone had ever called her strong, the very opposite of what she had been raised to believe. All of the things she had been told her whole life before him about her weaknesses welled up inside her and threatened to spill forth.

Before she could speak, Gabriel kissed her firmly once. And then he was gone.

9

Louise

England, 1953

I slow the car, a Ford Anglia with a dented bonnet that Joe had purchased on installment, as we near the Herefordshire farm where Joe's older sister, Beatrice, lives with her children.

Earlier that morning, I'd hastily packed the children up for three days' time (I couldn't fathom being gone longer than that) and piled them into the car with their small overnight bags. "You're going to spend the weekend with Auntie Bea and your cousins. Won't that be fun?" Phed, a creature of habit, seemed perturbed by missing school, but Ewen was excited.

Joe had lingered awhile longer than usual before work that morning to see us off. "I can take the children to Bea's for you, if you'd like," he'd offered, surprising me.

"I appreciate that," I said, giving him a quick kiss. "But I want to make sure they are settled." As excited as I was for my trip, it was going to be hard to leave them, even for a few days.

As I'd driven through the countryside, the once-lush Chiltern Hills withered in late autumn, my doubts had grown. Was

I really going to leave for France, just like that? What were the chances I'd find out anything at all about the necklace? But if I didn't go, a voice in my head reminded me, the chances of learning anything were exactly zero.

I pull up in front of Bea's farmhouse now and her two yellow Labrador retrievers come toward the car, barking but friendly. The sprawling, dilapidated farmhouse, with its sloped, peeling roof, stands in sharp contrast to our own modern, trim cottage. Her house is larger but in need of so much work and with fewer of the modern conveniences. Bea is in the front yard, wrangling laundry over a large tub with tongs. She has Joe's auburn hair; only, hers is long and pulled back in a knot at the nape of her neck. I study my sister-in-law curiously. Bea did important things during the war, too, manning an antiaircraft gun on the rooftops of London. But she lost her husband, Fergus, to fighting in Ardennes and is raising their three children alone. She seems to unquestioningly accept her life, consisting only of childcare and all the menial work that comes with that. More than once, I have considered whether she minds her situation, if she wants more like I do. But even after all of these years, I don't know her well enough to ask.

I open the door and the children bound from the car, Phed starting toward the house to find her older cousins and Ewen making a beeline for the pen of goats. Bea sets down the tongs and walks over. "Good to see you, Louise."

"You, too. Thank you for taking the children on such short notice."

"Of course. But you didn't say much about why." It had seemed too much to explain over the phone, so I had only mentioned that I needed to go out of town for a few days. "Is it your mum?" I shake my head. "Joe, is he all right?"

"He's fine," I reply, not at all sure if that is really true. "I need to go out of town for a quick errand, and Joe, well...he has to work." Bea nods with understanding at the real reason I need her help. Having the children on his own would be overwhelming for him.

"Where are you going?" Bea asks.

I hesitate. "Paris." I didn't want to tell her, but I couldn't lie, not when she is watching my children.

"Paris, really?" I can hear my own doubts echoed in her own voice. Paris is so far away and the last-minute trip sounds random, even ridiculous. "By yourself?"

"Yes."

"Joe doesn't mind?"

"Joe doesn't notice," I say, a queer twist to my voice.

Bea pauses for a beat. "You can't outrun your problems," she says evenly.

I look at her, considering how much she knows, or has guessed. My sister-in-law is a good person, but we aren't close and I haven't told her much about my past. "I know," I say finally.

"Joe's a good man," she adds. Bea is Joe's older sister and I can hear the protectiveness in her voice. Joe and Bea are close in a way that, as an only child, I sometimes envy. Even with their parents gone, they still have each other as family, something that I do not. "Fergus and I had troubles. It wasn't perfect. But you work it out." She isn't prying. Rather, she is implicitly asking me not to give up on her brother despite his struggles.

I want to tell her that I would never leave Joe, but the words stick in my throat. "It's only a quick trip," I say instead. "Three days, no more, I promise." Even as I say this, I know that it is unrealistic. It will take me a full day to get to Paris and another to return; what can I possibly hope to accomplish in such a short time in between?

She dips her chin slightly in acknowledgment. "You know,

it's funny, I worried about Joe so much when he was away, just like Fergus. And now..."

"You worry about him in a different way," I finish for her. We stand silently for a moment, united in our concern for her brother and my husband.

"Anyway, it's fine of course to leave the children." Adding my two to her large brood will be nothing. Still, I feel a twinge of guilt at saddling her with the extra burden.

"Thank you. I need to go if I'm to make my train." I start for the car.

As if on cue, Ewen breaks from the goats and comes running to me. "Mummy, don't go!"

My guilt swells. I kneel and kiss him on the head. "It will only be a few days, I promise. Be good for Auntie Bea," I say, "and I will bring you something special."

Bea walks over and holds her hand out to him. "Come, I've got some treats you can give the goats—and maybe a biscuit or two for you as well." He takes her hand and follows without looking back.

I turn and get in the car before I can stop myself. My eyes sting. I feel so selfish, like I am abandoning my family. But I need to do this for myself so I can come back and be good and whole for them.

As I drive away, my guilt and sadness are replaced by excitement, not just to be solving the mystery, but to be on my own again and free. The thought is a dangerous one, though, and I know that I mustn't let it grow too large.

I return the car home. Not stopping to go inside, I take my small bag, which I brought with me earlier, and head for the rail station, making it just in time to book the ten-o'clock train to London. It is less crowded with commuters than it had been on my previous trip and I have the cabin nearly to myself.

In London, I travel by Tube from Paddington to St. Pancras,

intending to board another train, this time heading south for Dover.

Inside the station at St. Pancras, I stop. I should let Midge know that I will not be coming to work. I ring the thrift shop and Midge answers.

"It's Louise," I say. "I won't be in for a few days."

"Everything all right?" Her voice sounds concerned. Other than when I went to London, I am not one to call out.

"Yes, fine. Only, I'm going to the department store in Paris to find out more about the necklace." There is a silent pause and I wait for her to chide me as the others had.

"Be safe," she says instead. "There's a small hotel in the 2nd arrondissement Millie stayed at once. Le Petite Meridien, I think it's called."

"Thank you. I will try to book there." I hang up and hurry to my train.

As the train leaves the city and chugs southeast through Kent toward the coast, I catch a glimpse of myself in the window. I'd done my hair and makeup more carefully than usual, sprayed a spritz of L'Air du Temps on my neck and wrists. I told myself I was primping to look well-heeled as I travel. Not because I was going to see Ian.

Ian. I wanted to ring the previous night to tell him I was coming, but it had been too late. I hope that he will make good on his promise to help me—and that going to see him, with so many feelings still there between us, is not a mistake.

The ferry is large and well-appointed with a café for lunch. The seas are calm, nothing like the wartime voyage on a naval ship I had made almost a decade earlier. We can cross the Channel directly, unimpeded by war or blockade.

Still, as I look out across the Channel, I cannot help but see Franny and ghosts of the trip we had once made. Ahead, the European continent looms like a reckoning. I had not wanted to come back here. I had avoided it for years, always demurring when anyone suggested a holiday, saying I preferred somewhere closer to home. Joe hadn't protested; Europe bore its own painful memories for him that he was happy to avoid. But now, here I am, chasing the same past I had tried so hard to outrun.

It is midafternoon when the coast of Calais becomes visible through the mist. We disembark and clear customs, and I join the others on a bus that will take us south to Paris. But as we bump along the road, still marked by craters in the earth and snapped trees where the fighting had been, my mind reels back to the war, and the long nights crossing the countryside to reach the next camp. With Franny.

We reach Paris in the late afternoon. I convert some of my money to francs at the kiosk beneath a Dior ad in the bus station and then go to the taxi stand outside. "Hotel Le Petite Meridien," I request, hoping the driver will know the address and that the hotel is not altogether far from the department store I need to visit the following morning. The department store. I still cannot imagine what it has to do with the necklace and Franny's death.

The taxi whizzes through the streets of Paris, weaving between the old green prewar buses. It is the first time I have been here, and despite my uneasiness, I am still taken by the beauty of the famous city, which I have until now known only in books.

The driver lets me out in front of the hotel. It is midway down a quiet street lined with narrow buildings, boutiques and other small storefronts at the ground level, well-kept apartments on the floors above. As I start for the hotel, I notice a phone booth on the corner. Instinctively, I walk toward it and ring Joe's office. The secretary says he is gone for the day, so I leave the name of the hotel where I plan on staying and ask her to give it to him.

Then I dial again and tell the operator the number Ian had given me. The phone rings several times and I realize that the office has already closed. But then a receptionist answers. "Ian Shipley?" I ask.

"I'm afraid he's gone for the day."

I consider hanging up. "This is Louise Burns, I mean Emmons," I say, correcting myself. Ian would know me by my maiden name. "Would you please tell him I'm in Paris and staying at Le Petite Meridien?"

"I'll make sure he gets the message."

"Thank you." I hang up, then start down the street.

I go to the hotel desk to check in and ask for a room. "Madam, will your husband be joining you?"

"No, I'll be staying alone." He raises an eyebrow. I hand the man some francs as a deposit for the room. Joe's income takes care of our needs at home. But I have a modest amount of savings of my own from when I worked in London before we were married. I've always kept it for a rainy day and today seems as rainy as it gets.

❧

France, 1944

The night after we arrived at the POW camp, I watched from a corner behind the makeshift stage as Franny performed a second show. She began to croon "I'll Be Seeing You" in a sweet-but-sultry, wistful tone. As she sang, her eyes traveled over the crowd, as if searching for someone. In the back, I saw Ian. But he was not looking in Franny's direction. His gaze was once again fixed on me. Our eyes met and held. I looked away, heart pounding.

The first song ended, and Franny segued seamlessly into a second one, a happier, big band tune from the States. I looked at the prisoners watching her, and as we were swept away by Franny's voice, I felt the divide between us widen to a chasm. I was free. These men were not, and they might never be again. Some of them might surely die here.

After the show, Franny lingered again among the audience to sign autographs. She took more photographs with the prisoners, too, one man holding the camera while she posed with another. Now that she had confided in me, I understood that there was so much more going on with her beneath the surface. She was trying to help these men, right under the Germans' noses. What if she got caught? I was terrified for her.

Yet at the same time, her bravery made me determined to help, too. I stepped forward and took the camera from one of the men. "Here, let me help." With me holding the camera instead of passing it around, we could get more photographs taken before the guards shooed the prisoners back to their barracks.

Franny mouthed a silent "thank you" in my direction, then took a picture with another man, careful to stand a few inches apart so it could be cropped later.

When there were no more photos to take, I returned to the hotel to pack while Franny lingered for a few last autographs. We had delivered the bundles we could, and the caravan would be moving out at first light. As I remembered the refusal to let us deliver the remaining packages, my anger continued to burn. The prisoners were rail thin and there were many more whom we might have helped with food. Instead, they stood hungry because we did not dare cross the arbitrary rules of the enemy we were fighting. I cursed my own cowardice and that of an organization that could not keep its promise.

A short while later, Franny appeared in the doorway. Her skin glistened from washing, but traces of her stage makeup still lingered around her eyes. We got ready for bed and lay beside one another in the darkness. Franny tossed and turned, seemingly too restless to sleep. Thinking back to our conversation the previous night about the camera and how she was taking photos to secretly help the prisoners, I realized how little I knew about her. "Your family," I said, "what were they like?"

"My mother was a stage performer." Franny paused hesitantly. "But not the reputable kind, if you know what I mean." I nodded, recalling the street in Croydon, not far from our flat, with the posters of scantily clad women in the windows. Franny continued, "After my father died, she brought us back to England and we lived in a really dodgy part of South London. She brought men to our flat from the club where she worked—men who were sometimes more interested in my little sister, Bette, and me."

"Oh…" I am horrified by her revelation and how much Franny and her sister helplessly suffered. "It must have been awful to be trapped in such a childhood."

"It was. I was able to fend them off, and usually I could protect Bette as well, but once when I was not at home, one of the men raped her. She got pregnant and Mum sent her away. My mother told people that Bette died, to avoid the truth and embarrassment of what had happened."

"Franny, that's awful. Where did she go?"

"I don't know, and I'm still trying to find her."

"I'm so sorry."

"Since then, I've always hated to be by myself. My mother used to go out at night and leave us by ourselves. I was terrified that one of the men would come back, but my little sister was so brave. Then suddenly I didn't have her anymore and I really was alone."

I squeezed her hand. "You aren't alone now."

"I have an older brother, too," she added. "But he left when my sister and I were younger. So he wasn't there to protect us. Bette and I were on our own." It wasn't a sibling's job to protect you, though. I thought with anger of the mums like Franny's and mine. Why hadn't they done more?

I started to ask what had become of her brother, but before I could get the words out, she turned away, signaling that she didn't want to discuss her family or her past any further.

"I understand what it is like, having a difficult childhood," I said. "My mum was a drunk—is a drunk," I corrected. "I always had to be the grown-up and figure out a way for us to eat and pay the rent."

"What about your father?"

"I never knew him. Not even who he was. I'm not sure my mum knew either."

"So neither of us spent Sundays sailing paper boats in the park with a doting parent, then," she observed, a note of irony in her voice.

"I suppose not." Mums were supposed to protect their children. Yet both of ours had failed. "So what do you think of Ian?" I offered. The transition was an awkward one, but I needed to change the subject and lighten the conversation.

"I don't." She shrugged dismissively. "You like him, don't you?"

"Is it that obvious?" I was embarrassed, but I sensed that I could trust Franny. "It's silly, really, to think about such things when we are over here doing vital work, but I think that I do."

"It's human," she replied. "And I'm quite certain he likes you as well."

"No, he couldn't possibly," I protested. I had noticed Ian looking at me, felt that the connection might be more than one-sided. But I had convinced myself that I imagined it, or that he was just lonely in the field. Nothing could, or should, come of it.

"I'm sure of it," Franny insisted. "But what do I know? Men are not my cup of tea, if you know what I mean. I'm gay."

"Oh." I considered the gravity of her confession. The world was not accepting of such things and it was brave of her to be open about it. Surely she trusted me to reveal something so personal about herself.

"It's pretty common in the theater community. But I have to keep it under wraps because of my stage persona." I understood what she meant. Franny's image was that of feminine beauty, desired by millions of men on stage and film. To learn that she liked women instead would have been career ending. The irony was that Franny, adored by thousands of men, didn't like men at all.

"I've never talked about it much," Franny confessed. "My mother certainly would not have understood. I don't really want to be with anyone, if you know what I mean." I nodded. After everything she had told me about her painful childhood, it made sense.

"Were you ever in love?" I asked.

"There was someone once, an older woman who worked backstage at the Theatre Royal. But she broke my heart, and I haven't let myself get hurt again since." I could not imagine anyone not wanting Franny. "It's just as well," Franny added grimly. "I learned a long time ago that the only one sticking around is me. How about you?" she asked, turning the tables. "Have you ever been in love?"

I considered the question. "I don't know," I said honestly. Joe's face popped into my mind. "I was dating someone before the war and I was rather fond of him. But that's all done now. He binned me."

"I'm sure it wasn't like that," Franny protested.

I shrugged. "It doesn't matter. It's over now." I paused. "I'd like to fall in love someday for sure." I wanted a home and husband, a family, everything that had been missing from my own life growing up with a single, alcoholic mum.

"It's getting late," Franny remarked. "We should probably get some sleep."

I nodded in agreement, though in truth I had always been something of a night owl. "It's so hard to sleep here," I said. "It's such a strange place, and so far from home."

"I've been on the road so much touring, I can sleep pretty much anywhere. Anyway, you should try. We head out tomorrow." I wanted to ask her more about the route from here, the way home. But she rolled away to face the wall. "Good night."

Moments later, I heard Franny snoring. I watched her sleep. How was it possible that this woman, beautiful and gifted and charming, concealed so much pain? I supposed we all carry the secrets of the past, buried.

The next morning, I awakened to find Franny gone, the space beside me empty and cold. I got out of the bed, but before I could leave the room, the door opened and she strode in. "Here," she said, thrusting a scrap of paper in my direction.

"What is it?" I took the paper and scanned it. It was some sort of list.

"We can only deliver packages to people whose names we have, right?" She continued before I could answer, "You need names. Here are names."

I looked in disbelief at the roughly two dozen names she had amassed, people we would now be able to help. There were enough here to distribute most of the remaining packages before we left. "But how?"

"Does it matter? Give those to Ian," she added.

I walked to Ian's room and knocked. "Coming," he said. His voice was sleepy and I wondered if I had woken him. But when he opened the door, he was freshly washed and dressed, his collar a bit damp. A whiff of his aftershave tickled my nose. "Lou…" he said, sounding surprised but not unhappy to see me.

"Here." I handed him the paper.

"She shouldn't have done this," he said with a frown, seeming to know without my saying that it had been Franny.

"We have names. We can deliver the rest of the packages." I started for the trucks, more than a little satisfied that we could play by the Germans' rules and still win. The aid packages we brought would not actually save anyone. No one box could contain enough food to sustain a person in these conditions for any length of time. But they contained a kind of hope that might give a prisoner the strength to go on for one more day.

An hour later, packages had been distributed to all the remaining prisoners. "That's it," Ian said.

I pointed to the truck behind ours, which contained more packages. "What will be done with those?" I asked. I wished that we might leave the extras for the prisoners to have when the ones we had given them ran out.

"Those are for the next camp," Ian explained.

"Next camp? But I thought we were going home."

"You and the other volunteers are. But I'm continuing on with one of the trucks to a camp in Germany."

I felt an unexpected pang at leaving him. "Into Germany. That's so much more dangerous."

"It's the work," he said, his voice unwavering. "It has to be done." I admired his bravery.

"Do you want me to come with you?" I asked without thinking. If there was more work to be done, then I should help, too.

"I could never ask that of you." His voice was torn.

"I don't mind." I was committed to the work and to making even more of a difference to ease the suffering so many faced. But the undeniable truth was that I did not want to leave Ian either.

He shook his head. "You should go back to London. But when I return..."

"Louise!" Before Ian could finish, Franny bounded over and threw her arms around me. "I wanted to say goodbye."

"You're going to Germany as well?"

"Yes, I'm going to give performances at a couple of camps in Germany."

"Why didn't you tell me?" They were going deeper into Germany, and they were sending me back without them. I felt abandoned and betrayed.

"It was all arranged last-minute. I wasn't even certain I could get authorization until Ian confirmed it this morning."

"Let me come with you," I implored, not fully understanding what I'd be getting myself into.

"You would want to?" Franny asked. "I mean, we are going into Germany. Everything will be so much more dangerous."

I hesitated. I was only supposed to be gone for a short time. *A week at most*, Ian had promised. But there was nothing waiting for me back in London, no one who would be worried if I took longer. "Yes," I said, seeing the hopeful faces of the poor men we'd helped here. I wanted to do more. And if Ian and Franny could be brave enough to press on into Germany, so could I.

"So you'll come with us?" Franny asked, confirming.

I nodded. "If I'm allowed." I turned to Ian. "I'd like to come with you to Germany and help."

"If you're certain," he said, "I'll make the arrangements to have you added to the schedule."

"I am."

I turned to Franny. "It's all settled. I'm coming along."

"Hooray!" Franny hugged me again, this time with a whoop. "I'm so glad." Her great weakness, I had come to learn in the short time that we had known one another, was that she couldn't stand to be alone. I had grown up largely by myself; I was trained for it, immune to loneliness. But to Franny, it was simply unbearable.

"What about your family?" she asked. "Do you need to let your mother know you are staying longer?"

"No," I replied candidly, and a look of understanding passed between us.

The truck idled, waiting to take me home. I considered going one more time, back to my life in London, boring and safe. But then I saw Ian and Franny, and I knew that my place was here. I waved off the truck, then turned away and started back toward my friends and the work that awaited us.

10

Helaine

Paris, 1942

Gabriel was gone. Helaine's heart screamed.

Alone, Helaine's days became long and empty. The space they had shared and filled with laughter and love felt small and drab without him, a shell of what it had once been. Helaine had not minded being alone in their apartment during the days when she knew Gabriel would come home to her. But now the emptiness was interminable. The world they had created together was gone, as though it had never existed at all. Sometimes Helaine feared she had imagined it.

Being in the apartment was unbearable, so Helaine started walking through the neighborhood once more. She strolled aimlessly for hours. But she was mindful of German soldiers and military vehicles that lined the streets, and stayed on high alert, careful to avoid checkpoints or other places where she might face scrutiny. As the occupation dragged on, there were new orders barring Jews from the cafés and markets and the Metro. They had to affix crude yellow stars to their clothing.

Because Helaine was a Jew, she was unable to visit the stores and markets she once had. But it did not matter. There was no need to go to the market because there was no one to cook for. And what was the point in shopping for inexpensive treasures across the city if she could not show them to Gabriel when she brought them home?

Nights were the worst. Helaine lay awake hour after hour, staring restlessly out of the window at the city with its now blacked-out skyline, thinking about Gabriel, missing his touch. Looking up at the stars above their tiny apartment in Montmartre, she could feel his presence. But where was he? She worried about whether he was safe, when he would come home. *If* he would come home. Though he had not gone off to fight, he was touring through war-torn Germany, subject to all of the same dangers as the ordinary people there. She could not bear the thought that something might happen to him. When Helaine did sleep, she heard Gabriel's music in her dreams.

In her loneliness, she thought not only about Gabriel, but also her family. Would they all have cast one another aside so heedlessly if they had known what was to come? They should be together in trying times like this. Maman, or possibly both of her parents if Papa was not abroad, was here in the city, just a few kilometers away. Helaine considered reaching out, extending an olive branch. After all, it was her father, not her mother, who had rejected her marriage to Gabriel so wholeheartedly. But Maman had chosen to remain by his side, rather than stand up for Helaine. And reaching out to her mother would mean repudiating Gabriel and all they shared because, even now, her parents would never accept him. Helaine could not do that. Maman might have found and checked on her as well, given everything that had happened in the city, to see if she was all right. She had not. No, even now in war, they were unable to put their personal differences aside. Helaine could not return home. This was the life she had chosen.

Months after Gabriel had gone on tour, Helaine set out for the market one morning with her ration coupons to try to buy some flour, if there was any to be had. Though she took no joy in cooking for herself, she still had to eat. Shortages were everywhere and she did not have the money to buy things on the black market. She was not permitted at the local bakery she loved but had to go to one of the distant markets in Le Marais that allowed Jews.

She returned to find a letter from him waiting in the entrance-way to their building. She tore it open, drinking in Gabriel's familiar script. But inside, there were just a few lines.

Performing close to the front, but doing well. I miss you. Be safe, my love. G.

The censors, she decided, were the reason he had not written more. However, she could already sense the distance beginning to pull them apart. Helaine touched the paper, feeling for him. She wanted to write back, but there was no return address. She searched the envelope in vain for some indication of its origin, something about the stamp or the way it had been canceled that might give a clue from where it came. Gabriel was simply beyond reach.

And then there was nothing.

After that first letter, Helaine did not hear from Gabriel again. Months passed. She was confused by the lack of communication. He would not have forgotten her, Helaine told herself. Something must have happened to him. Pushing the very worst thoughts from her mind, Helaine prayed for his safety and that he would return to her soon. But with every day, her apprehension for his well-being grew.

Not that things in Paris were so much safer. German soldiers were everywhere on the streets, patrolling and watching. During her walks, Helaine saw terrible things, innocent civilians harassed, people arrested. She froze every time a siren wailed. Helaine learned of the first raid of a Jewish neighborhood in Le Marais and another in the Jewish section of the 11th arrondissement, people arrested in their homes in the middle of the night with only the clothes on their back and imprisoned God-knows-where. Hearing the news of Jews being arrested, Helaine considered leaving the city. But where would she go? Gabriel would not be able to find her if she fled.

Helaine thought of her parents even more, worried if they were all right. They were scions of Paris society, Helaine tried to reassure herself. Surely no one could hurt them. One night, she dreamed that she had started toward her parents' house. She reached the end of the block where she had grown up. She could see her mother in the window. But as she started toward home, a black car pulled up at the curb and her father started to get out. Fearful of seeing him again, Helaine ran in the other direction. She awoke from the dream, smelling her mother's cherry vanilla scent, as if she had actually been there. Helaine rolled over in the empty bed, feeling more alone than ever. Helaine's heart ached.

After Gabriel left, the garden became a lifeline. She went to work with Isa and the others every day, eager to fill her time while he was gone. However, one morning, there was a new placard on the gate. *Jews forbidden.*

Helaine stood motionless, stunned. She knew the restrictions against Jews were growing by the day. She was already banned from the stores where she once shopped, from the orchestra where her own husband had played. But now she was being excluded quite literally from the outdoors, from fresh air and nature. How much more could they take from her?

Helaine started away. "The only place for Jews is in the earth," she heard one of the women remark. The words were a punch to her stomach. Helaine knew anti-Jewish sentiment had existed in Paris, even before the occupation. But to see it unmasked now from the very people she'd worked alongside was sickening.

Isa rushed up to the low fence surrounding the park. "Helaine," she said. "I'm so sorry." A tear rolled down her cheek. Helaine waited for Isa to tell her that it did not matter, that they would ignore the German decree so that she could keep working in the garden. "You must understand, I need this garden to feed my family. And if I defy orders and get arrested, they would have no one. Here is your share." She handed Helaine a small satchel of turnips. It was a fraction of what she should have gotten for her labor if the harvest had been divided equally as was promised. But she was in no position to argue.

Isa was turning her back on Helaine as surely as her family had. Helaine started to race off. "Wait!" Isa called after her, but it was too late. Helaine was already running down the street. She walked blindly, turning this way and that, not realizing quite where she was headed until she arrived at the park in the city center. It, too, had a sign barring Jews. Suddenly, it seemed to Helaine that the Germans were erasing her life, one memory at a time.

That night, there was a knock at the door to the apartment. "Helaine, it's me, Isa. Can we talk?" Isa could not have her in the garden but was able to come visit her—at least for now. But Helaine was too conflicted and hurt to see her. She remained silent and did not answer her friend. Finally, she heard Isa's footsteps retreating down the stairs, growing fainter, followed by the click of the front door.

After being banned from the garden, Helaine was lonelier than ever. A few days later, desperate to fill her time, Helaine set out for the distant market where Jews were still permitted to shop.

After walking for more than half an hour, Helaine reached the Marché des Enfants Rouges. The once-grand covered market was now a sorry affair, half of the stalls closed and the rest with little on their wooden carts and tables. There was no flour to be had, so Helaine purchased the last remaining stale baguette. She turned to go.

As she neared the exit to the market, Helaine spied a familiar figure at the corner. *Maman.*

Helaine froze. Her first reaction was relief: Maman had not been arrested but was safe and well. She was surprised, too; she had not expected to see her mother. She looked out of place in her fine clothes in the middle of the dismal market. But her parents' house was not far from Le Marais, and it made sense that Maman, a Jew, also had to shop here.

Seeing her mother after so long, Helaine's heart pounded. Helaine started toward her. She wanted to hug her mother, throw her arms around her. *Come home*, Helaine imagined her saying. She would accept Helaine and her new life, see that it had not been bad or wrong after all. And for a split second, Helaine thought that she might go home, just for a time until Gabriel returned. She would go on her own terms, though, no longer the overprotected prisoner she had once been.

"Maman," Helaine breathed. Her mother stood before her like a ghost, and for a moment, she was terrified. She wanted to run away. But Maman saw her.

"Laina." Helaine's own conflicting emotions, apprehension, joy, uncertainty, were mirrored on her mother's face. Maman stepped forward, arms half-raised, as though she wanted to embrace Helaine. Helaine stepped back instinctively, then immediately regretted it. She yearned to hug her mother as well.

"Thank God you are well," her mother said. "I was so worried."

Not worried enough to come find me, Helaine thought.

"And Papa?"

"He was overseas on one of his trips when the war started. His firm has been expropriated." It made sense. Jews were no longer allowed to own businesses, even powerful ones like Helaine's father's. But now her father was out of the country, unable to get back into France.

"Gabriel, he is well?" Maman was trying to be polite, but she said Gabriel's name with effort.

"Gabriel is touring abroad."

"So you are all alone?"

"Yes." Helaine yearned to reach out and embrace her mother. Once, they had been so close, and Helaine wished that it could be so now. But too much had happened between them.

"You know, you can always come stay with me again." Helaine wanted to say yes.

Helaine might have returned to her parents' house and they could have been together as they once had been. That was not Helaine's world anymore, though. The apartment she and Gabriel shared was her home now. She couldn't abandon that and give away the life she'd fought for. Helaine was filled with distrust. Her mother had turned on her once. Helaine would always be afraid that she would do it again.

"How could you go?" her mother asked suddenly. "How could you leave us like that so easily?"

"It wasn't easy. It still isn't."

"It was not easy for me either," her mother bristled. "You put me in an impossible position and you forced me to choose between you and your father."

"But I'm your child," Helaine said. "You should have chosen me."

They stood silently, separated by their respective positions. "I should go," her mother said finally.

"Wait." Helaine threw her arms around her mother. Maman

stiffened with surprise. Then she embraced Helaine as well, and it was as if all of the acrimony evaporated and they were as close as they had once been. Despite their differences, they still loved each other. They clung together, silently understanding that it could be the very last time they saw one another. Helaine leaned her head and nestled in against the warmth of her mother's neck like a child, inhaling her familiar scent to capture and keep it forever.

Maman pulled back slightly and studied Helaine's face for several seconds, as though wanting to etch the image deep into her mind. She reached up and stroked Helaine's cheek lovingly. "Goodbye, Laina." Then she broke away and started walking. It was as if she could not bear to watch Helaine leave again.

Helaine turned and ran from the market, her eyes burning. A while later, she stopped, trying to get her bearings and decide what to do next. She could not in that moment bear to go back to their Montmartre apartment and deal with all that she had learned alone. Helaine wished Gabriel was there to help her make sense of it all. If only she knew how to reach him.

The Conservatoire de Paris, she remembered then. The music school, which was housed in a corner building on the Avenue Jean Jaurès in the 19th arrondissement, was where Gabriel had practiced and taught. Perhaps they might have information regarding his exact whereabouts on tour. She started in that direction.

Forty-five minutes later, Helaine neared the conservatory. At the sight of the building, memories overwhelmed her. She walked closer, as if being near the building might bring her nearer to Gabriel himself.

Closer to the conservatory, she could hear the sound of string instruments playing. They still made music here, but it was not Gabriel's.

A man walked out of the conservatory, and Helaine recognized him as Monsieur Bolois, the director of the symphony. She doubted that he would remember her, but perhaps he had news of where the performers were touring currently, or even about Gabriel.

"Hello…" she started. Monsieur Bolois turned in her direction. "I'm Helaine Lemarque," she said, using her husband's surname, though she had not taken it formally.

"Oh, yes, Gabriel's wife. How is he?"

Helaine was puzzled. "What do you mean? I haven't seen him in months. He's on tour."

He looked at her quizzically. "Tour?"

"He was sent to Germany to play with the symphony," Helaine insisted. "In fact, I was coming to inquire about the symphony's exact whereabouts so I can reach him."

"I have no idea what you are talking about. The symphony is not touring. It has been disbanded due to the war."

"But…" Helaine was stunned. How had she not known? "Are you certain?"

"Quite. I'm the only one still here to take care of the building and forward the mail. Most of the musicians have gone south to Rennes to wait out the war. Alas, Gabriel was not among them."

Gabriel was not touring as he had told her. Had he been tricked into going to Germany under false pretenses? Or had he lied to her? Helaine realized then how much she had taken at face value. She had no idea whom Gabriel was touring with or where he was going. He had, quite literally, disappeared. And he had left her alone in Paris to fend for herself, despite the fact that she was vulnerable as a Jew. A sense of betrayal rose in her. "Thank you," she said, retreating.

"You might try the police station," Monsieur Bolois offered, his voice softer now. "He might be playing with a smaller group of musicians. If Gabriel went abroad, he would have had to file for permission to travel."

Helaine hesitated. Going to the police station was no small task now, not as a Jew. But she had to find out where Gabriel had gone. She started in the direction of the police headquarters.

The Préfecture de Police was located on the Île de la Cité in the shadow of Notre-Dame Cathedral, several kilometers and almost an hour walk from the Conservatoire. Jews were banned from the buses, so she had no choice but to walk. As she made her way toward the Seine, she thought of all she had learned about Gabriel. He was not touring in Germany, at least not officially with the orchestra. Where was he and what was he doing?

At last, she reached the river and crossed the Pont Notre-Dame. The police station was an imposing arched building, built nearly a century earlier as barracks for the Garde Républicaine. She took a deep breath and walked inside.

"I'm trying to find some information on my husband's whereabouts," she said to the policeman behind the desk. "He's gone abroad and I'm told he may have filed travel papers."

The police officer looked down at the yellow star affixed to her coat. "I'm sorry, madam, but police records are confidential," he said dismissively, then started to turn away.

"I'd like to speak to Chief Gateau," she said, using her most authoritative voice. Henri Gateau had been one of her father's closest friends and she hoped the connection might be of use now. She had worried that the police chief might have been replaced, as so many French officials had in the Vichy administration. But his photo still hung above the reception desk, which meant that he was still here—and likely sympathetic to the Germans.

The police officer turned back toward her and looked at her strangely. "You are asking for Chief Gateau?"

Helaine saw how ridiculous she must have sounded. But she did not waver. "Yes. Please tell him that Helaine Weil is here," she said, using her family name. "He knows me." Though Helaine might have been too proud to return to her parents' house, she was not above using them to help find her husband.

"Very well." The police officer stood and walked into a back room. A moment later, he returned, so quickly that Helaine doubted he had checked at all. "I'm sorry, but Chief Gateau is presently unavailable."

Helaine folded her arms. "I'll wait."

"He is not available," he repeated firmly, making clear that the chief's unavailability wasn't a temporary situation. Did it have something to do with the fact that her family was Jewish? There was no one who would help her now.

As she turned to go, she glimpsed a familiar figure through the window of the office behind the reception desk. "Pardon," she called, waving her hand. She pushed past the policeman at the desk and knocked loudly on the window to get the chief's attention. "Chief Gateau, I'm Helaine Weil, Otto's daughter," she said, loudly so that he could hear her through the glass.

Recognition, then displeasure, crossed his face. He walked out of the office toward her. "Helaine," he said with familiarity, but the warmth that had once been in his voice was missing. Though she had not seen Chief Gateau during the years of her confinement, she had known him her whole life. He had sent her holiday and birthday presents as a child. Now he was cold and businesslike, a longtime family friend turned stranger. "What brings you here?"

"My husband, the cellist Gabriel Lemarque, went on tour to Germany. But the orchestra had no record of the tour or his whereabouts. I was hoping you could check for travel papers."

Chief Gateau hesitated. "That would take time and I'm terribly busy."

"Perhaps your secretary could check," Helaine pressed. "I'm sure it would only take a few minutes."

Chief Gateau paused, as if searching for another reason not to help. "Fine," he said. "I'll take a quick look." He walked into the back office.

A few minutes later, he returned. "I'm sorry, but there is no record of your husband applying to go abroad."

Gabriel had simply disappeared. It was as if he had fallen into the abyss.

"Your parents, they are well?" Chief Gateau asked, his tone more prying than concerned. He had not heard about her estrangement from them. "They are still in their house?"

"Yes, of course." Uneasiness rose in Helaine. By making inquiries about Gabriel, she might actually be drawing attention to her family and placing them in greater danger. Quickly, she thanked Chief Gateau for his help and hurried from the office.

As Helaine neared the door to the police station, she heard someone call her name. She stopped, thinking it had all been a mistake and that Chief Gateau had found Gabriel's travel papers after all. But when she turned, a man in a German uniform she had not seen before was walking toward her.

"You are the wife of Gabriel Lemarque?" he asked sternly.

"Y-yes," Helaine replied, suddenly flustered. "Do you know where he is?"

"That is what we need you to tell us."

"But I don't know where he is. I came here to inquire."

"So your husband is missing?" The officer's voice was hostile now. "A fugitive from the Reich?"

Helaine was stunned. "That's ridiculous. He is a cellist with the Orchestre National." *Was*, she silently corrected herself. Suddenly, it seemed that while Helaine wasn't looking, the whole world had changed.

Helaine was seized with the urge to flee the police station. She was a Jew and now the wife of a wanted man—a target twice over. "I'm sorry, I really need to get home." She gestured to her bag from the market. "My groceries…" She turned to leave.

But the German caught her arm and held on firmly. "Madam, come with me. You are under arrest for conspiring with an enemy of the Reich."

11

Louise

Paris, 1953

Late morning the day after I arrive, I step out of the hotel and onto the brisk autumn street. I had planned to get an early start but, exhausted from the journey, had slept much later than I intended. Dark clouds hang to the west, threatening a storm. Up close, Paris looks different than I imagined it. The once-elegant buildings are worn and pockmarked, the shop windows still half-empty from shortages. Other than a lone Citroën idling at the corner, the street is devoid of cars, owing to the lingering gas shortages. The women who pass by are well-coiffed, their hair and makeup done impeccably, but they are rail thin from the years of having to survive on rations. Even the tiny dog who passes by on the end of a tattered leash looks tired and skinny.

I walk to the phone booth on the corner and ring Ian's office once more. The same receptionist answers as the previous evening. "Ian Shipley, please."

"I'm sorry, he's not in."

"Do you have any idea when he will be?"

"I'm afraid not. He didn't come in today."

I leave my name and hotel information once again, then hang up, annoyed. Ian is not there. To be fair, I did not tell him I was coming in advance. But I hope he has not gone out of town and my whole trip is for nothing.

I do not have much time in Paris and I cannot afford to wait for Ian to turn up. I walk back to the hotel. "I'm trying to get to a department store called Lévitan," I say to the clerk.

He shakes his head. "That store is not in business anymore."

My heart sinks. "Can you at least tell me how to get to where it used to be?" He gives me walking directions too quickly for me to follow in French and I do my best to keep up.

I start down the street in the direction he indicated, turning right at the corner, then left, hoping I am going the correct way. As I walk, I pass scaffolding at every turn. Despite its tattered appearance, Paris is a city under construction, with those who can afford to rebuild attempting to erase the weariness of the war and begin anew. The streets are strangely quiet, save for a few pedestrians and an elderly woman who pedals by on a dilapidated bike.

Soon I reach Rue Faubourg du Saint-Martin, the wide boulevard where the department store is located. The word *Lévitan* is still engraved in the granite above the doorway. But it is no longer a department store, I note with a mix of surprise and disappointment. Instead, it is an office building of some sort, converted and modern, not at all the same kind of business it had been during the war. I question, not for the first time, whether my coming here for answers will be in vain.

I walk inside the building, where a young woman with a sleek bob sits behind a reception desk, clacking on a Rooy typewriter. "Can I help you?" she asks, still typing. I admire her easy, confident way. Women still have jobs here. Not everyone had let that be taken away.

"I've come to ask about the department store that was once here, called Lévitan."

"I'm afraid it went out of business years ago." That was not unusual. So many livelihoods were disrupted by the war and many never returned. "Or at least that's what my mother told me," the receptionist adds. "I was too young to remember much before the war."

Of course, there is a whole generation that has largely been raised since then. "I've got a necklace from the jewelry department. I was hoping to learn about its origin. Are there any records?"

"Not that I know of," she says. I hope that she might offer to check, but she does not.

"Is there someone else who might know?"

"Maybe the managing director, but he isn't in yet."

Deflated, I start to go. Outside, I look across the street at a pharmacy with a clouded glass window. *Pharmacie Dupree, Established 1912*, the sign reads. The pharmacy had been here during the war. Perhaps someone there knows something more about Lévitan. I try not to get my hopes up. Just because the pharmacy was here doesn't mean the people who work here now are the same ones who had been here then.

I cross the street and go into the pharmacy. The man behind the counter, who wears a short white coat and looks to be in his twenties, eyes me warily. "Can I help you?" the pharmacist asks. He is young, too, and I begin to lose hope that anyone here will know about things from the wartime.

I look at the medicines, pretending to be interested in buying something. "Some aspirin tablets, for headaches," I request. He ducks under the counter and pulls out a bottle, counts some pills into it. "I understand the pharmacy has been here since before the war," I remark after he hands me the package and I pay. "That's quite a history."

"Before the First World War," he corrects with a note of pride in his voice. "Not me personally, of course, but my father and my grandfather before him."

"How remarkable," I say. He nods. "The building across the street," I continue, trying to sound nonchalant, "do you know what it was before the firm took it over?"

"A department store. But I'm sorry to say that during the war, the Germans imprisoned Jews there," he adds.

I struggle to contain my surprise. "Really?"

"Yes, it's dreadful, I know. They actually used it as a kind of concentration camp." My heartbeat quickens. I had come here to find out about the necklace, whether it might have been purchased at Lévitan. I had not imagined that the store had such a direct and immediate connection to the war.

The pharmacist continues, "My father owned the pharmacy then. I was just a teenager. But I remember he and my mother speaking of people kept in the department store when they thought I wasn't listening. My father prepared medicine for them more than once." His eyes narrow a bit. "Why are you asking?"

"I'm studying architecture," I lie. "And I'm interested in the history of the building."

"My mother might know more. Maman?" he calls into the back of the shop. There is a silent pause and then a protracted rustling as a stooped, older woman appears, walking with the aid of a cane. "This is..." He hesitates. "You didn't mention your name."

"I'm called Louise Burns," I say. "I'm from England."

"I'm Paul Dupree and this is my mother, Celeste. Maman, Madame Burns is asking about the Lévitan building."

Madame Dupree eyes me skeptically. "You aren't interested in the architecture." She must have been listening from the back room, her hearing sharp despite her age.

"No," I confess, then pull out the necklace. "I'm sorry for not being more forthright. I found this necklace in a crate marked Lévitan and it looks like one I saw during the war. I'm trying to find out more about it, including where it came from and to whom it might have belonged. But I wasn't able to learn anything when I stopped in there just now. Do you know about the history of the building? Your son said that it was used as a prison during the war." Even as I say the words aloud, they sound impossible to believe.

"Yes, the building has a very shameful history, I'm afraid. The Nazis used Lévitan as a kind of camp. They kept Jews in the department store during the war as prisoners, and if you can believe such a thing, they had them sell items plundered from Jewish homes to the Germans." Though the woman seems lucid, the explanation is so strange, I wonder if she is confused with age. It doesn't make sense. How could a department store serve as a prison? What on earth did they sell? But her son nods gravely beside her, confirming her account.

And something about what the woman said resonates: the night before Franny died, she had been talking to the cellist, who was a French prisoner of war. Might he have some connection to the camp that had been here in the department store?

"The receptionist in the former Lévitan building did not seem to know anything about it," I say.

"Of course not." Madame Dupree waves her cane dismissively. "Come with me." Without waiting, she hobbles out of the pharmacy and across the street into Lévitan.

Seeing us enter, the receptionist stops typing this time. Remembering what Madame Dupree and her son told me, I'm incredulous that the receptionist did not know about the building's history. Was she lying or really that young and naive? "I'm here to see Georges," Madame Dupree informs her. Without waiting for a response, she starts past the front desk and into what had once been the center of the store. Beyond the reception desk, the store opens into a massive indoor courtyard. It is four stories high and ringed with balconies, their rails and balustrades white marble. The store could have just as easily been a museum and I can only imagine how grand it was in its heyday. "Georges!" she bellows. I expect the receptionist to protest or try to stop her, but she sits helplessly, as if she has seen this all before and can do nothing. "Georges!" The old woman's voice ricochets through the cavernous hall.

A spectacled man in a pinstripe suit appears on the stairwell. "Bonjour, Madame Dupree," he says with feigned patience. "What can I do for you?"

"For me, nothing," she replies tersely. "But for this woman, you can answer some questions about the history of Lévitan. Your infant receptionist was, of course, useless." The receptionist seems to sink lower in her chair, as if trying to disappear entirely.

The man turns to me. "I'm Georges Larent, managing director of Chateau Design. How can I help?" His voice is calm, but beneath the surface I can sense tension. I realize then that just asking questions is not enough. No one is going to give me the answers I seek. I need to see the history for myself.

I lift my chin to meet his eyes. "If you please, I would like to see the department store."

"Madam, you are in it."

"The whole store, I mean, including the upper floors." I am curious now, not just about the necklace, but the people who were kept in the store, how and where they lived.

"I'm not certain that I can do that during working hours," he begins, and I am sure that he will say no. But Madame Dupree is still standing there, arms folded, and I know he will not refuse her. "Very well, but we must be swift. I have a meeting in thirty minutes."

"I will take twenty and not a second more," I promise.

"Come with me." Monsieur Larent turns and walks deeper into the store.

I follow, as does Madame Dupree. "I have helped his family with medicines late in the night more than once," she explains to me in a low voice. "He owes me."

The managing director stops in the middle of the store and turns to us. "As you may know, this building housed a department store called Lévitan before the war," he says, sounding like a tour guide. "You can see how our architect preserved the original stalls in which goods were displayed."

"I was told that people were imprisoned here during the war, that it was a kind of labor camp."

Monsieur Larent shifts uneasily. "I think labor camp might be overstating it. The Germans forced Jews to sort and sell goods in Lévitan."

"Goods that had been taken from Jewish homes," I interject. I marvel that he can be so dismissive about the building's horrific past.

"I'm afraid so. When we first renovated the building, we did find some bed frames here, so it is possible that people had stayed here for a time to sort goods. But I would hardly call it a camp."

"It was a camp," Madame Dupree says firmly. "My husband and I saw the faces behind the windows, the Jewish prisoners who were held here for months, if not years. Can you imagine it, people living here, sorting Jewish belongings for sale?" Her eyes cloud. "And it was not just the Germans who did it," Madame Dupree adds. "There were plenty of French who helped, like the police and the moving companies. It was the shame of our nation. My own husband was arrested for trying to smuggle medicine to the people inside the store. Later, when he was freed, he told me about the poor souls he had seen close-up at the store. They were rail thin and pale from lack of sunshine. After that, the police were watching me constantly, and it was impossible to help." She is trying to explain to me, I realize, why she had been close enough to see everything, yet powerless to do more.

"It must have been a very difficult position," I say. I want her to know that I understand, even though absolution is not mine to give. "You mentioned something about the moving companies... What did they have to do with all of this?"

"The French moving companies were complicit. The big

ones, and the same ones that you see moving furniture today. They carried the goods from the Jewish homes to Lévitan. One could say, what choice did they have? Someone had to transport. But they did the work and they were paid handsomely for it."

"May I ask why you wanted to see the store?" Monsieur Larent interjects.

"I found a necklace and I am trying to learn more about it." I pull it from my purse and hold it up. "It was in a crate marked with the name Lévitan, so I thought perhaps it came from the store."

Monsieur Larent shakes his head. "Lévitan didn't sell jewelry before the war. It was primarily a home goods shop."

"What about during the war?" Madame Dupree asks. "Could the necklace have come here then?"

"Not then either," he replies. "They sorted housewares and furniture here. Valuable jewelry would have been confiscated by the ministry and other pieces melted for their metal. Jewelry was not sold in Lévitan."

That stops me in my tracks. The necklace was not sold at the store. What other reason could it have possibly come from there or been in the crate? Of course, I knew it was possible that the crate had just been used as a container without any connection to the store whatsoever, but I didn't want to believe it. Now it suddenly seems I have reached a dead end. I am no closer to finding out about the origin of the necklace than I was in London. I turn around, dejected. I should just go home.

"I'm sorry not to be of more help," Monsieur Larent says, trying to steer us toward the front entrance.

But Madame Dupree then asks, "What about the dormitory?" Monsieur Larent looks at her blankly. "On the fourth floor where the prisoners slept."

"Yes, of course," he answers, too quickly. "That's a storeroom now."

"You'll show it to us." Her words are not a request.

"As I mentioned, I have a meeting."

"You have a meeting in ten minutes," she replies. "We will only need seven."

Defeated, Monsieur Larent leads us to a lift at the back of the store. We step inside and he closes the wire gate behind us. The lift is deep, and I imagine the large pieces of furniture that might have been moved in it during the war. None of us speak as the lift groans and creaks its way to the top.

When the doors open, we step out into a long room filled with storage boxes. "You see," Monsieur Larent says. "Not much interesting history here."

I take in the room with the sloped ceiling, imagining dozens of people forced to sleep here in the drafty, bare space. "Look at this," Madame Dupree says, pointing to the wall where there is what looks like graffiti. Closer I can see that they are hash marks, I assume, made by a prisoner, marking off their days.

I turn to Monsieur Larent. "And you still do not call this a camp?" I demand. He does not answer. "Are there any documents? Records of who stayed here?"

"I'm afraid not. Lévitan was one of three satellites of the larger camp Drancy, which was just outside Paris, so they were all listed there." Listening to him provide this information so readily, I grow angry. He must know so much more than he is pretending to. He continues, "Who was detailed to this specific shop and when, I'm afraid, remains a mystery."

"It's ironic," Madame Dupree remarks, "that the Germans cataloged all of the people's belongings so very immaculately, but not the people themselves."

"So there was a register for goods, but not people?" I ask.

She nods gravely. "They recorded those which had value to them."

"Even if there had been records, the Germans destroyed just about everything before fleeing at the end of the war," Monsieur Larent adds. "The records would've been burned."

I can see that I will get no further with the managing director, that I have learned all that there is to learn here. I take a long
last look around for clues, and finding nothing, I turn to leave.

Madame Dupree and I walk from the store. "I'm sorry not
to be of more help," she says. "We had almost no contact with
the people in Lévitan and even less so after my husband was arrested. But we could see them. They occasionally came near the
windows, and I glimpsed them on the roof sometimes. I wish
I knew more. There was another half to that necklace, yes?" I
nod. "What do you think became of it?"

"I don't know. I assume it was lost to the war—along with
whoever possessed it."

"Not necessarily. This half survived the war. Why not the
other? Of course, finding it would be a needle in a haystack. So
many unanswered questions and the truth will never be brought
into the light."

"Not at all. You've been extremely helpful." I am still trying to sort through it all, but there doesn't seem to be anything
more to say. I take out a scrap of paper and write down my name
and hotel information, as well as my address at home. "I'll be in
Paris for another day or so and then I'm headed back to England.
Please contact me if you think of anything else."

Discouraged, I start away. "There is one more thing," Madame Dupree says. I turn back. "I just thought of it. After the
war, Henri Brandon, a man who had been prisoner in the store,
came here to the pharmacy as a customer."

"Did he live nearby?"

"I suppose so, yes. I would have wanted to get as far away from
such an awful part of my life as possible, but it was almost like
he couldn't leave. He eventually moved out of the city, though.
Wait here." She goes into the pharmacy, and through the glass
window, I can see her rifling through a cabinet in the rear of
the store. She pulls out a sheet of paper, then copies something
from it onto a small pad before ripping off the top sheet. She

walks from the shop and hands the paper to me. "Here." The address is in Belleville. "That's located in the 20th arrondissement, but a bit farther out."

"Do you have a phone number?"

"I don't. I'm sorry. I'd be surprised if he has a phone."

It is just as well. It would be easier to ask for help in person—and harder to tell me no than it would be by phone. "You've been so helpful and I'm forever grateful."

Madame Dupree squeezes my hand. "There was so much I couldn't do during the war. Helping you now won't change that, but maybe it will be a little easier to bear. Good luck." She turns and goes back into the shop. I marvel at her candor. If more people were like Madame Dupree and took responsibility for what they had failed to do during the war, the world might be a very different place.

I study the address Madame Dupree has given me, considering. Though I would like to go right now, I have to think about how I will get there. Perhaps the front desk at the Meridien can give me directions or even help me arrange a car. I start back toward the hotel.

When I reach the lobby, I go to the front desk. "I need to arrange a car to Belleville," I say, showing the receptionist the address.

"The soonest I can do this is tomorrow."

"But..." It is early afternoon and I hate the idea of waiting and wasting time. I need to see if this man has the answers I seek so that I can get home to Joe and the children.

The receptionist shrugs. "There are few cars now and a petrol shortage. If you would like to go by Metro, you would have to transfer."

Listening, I am overwhelmed. My head swims. "The car tomorrow morning sounds fine." I will take a night to myself in the hotel, I decide. The idea is suddenly appealing. It is not just that I am exhausted from travel. I am also eager for the room that is all mine for the evening, without anyone asking me to help them, or to do or get something for them. I worry fleetingly about the children, whether they miss me and if they have what they need. I push the thought away. This is the first time I've had real time to myself in nearly a decade and it is like getting to know someone I've never met. I'm going to make the most of every minute of solitude this trip affords.

I decide to go for a walk, perhaps find something to eat. I step outside the hotel onto the pavement once more. "Which way is the city center?" I ask the doorman.

He points. "Go left at the corner and keep walking down the boulevard until you reach the Seine."

"Thank you." I start in the direction he had pointed. As I make my way down the unfamiliar streets, I find that I enjoy the anonymity of a city where I know almost no one, and am largely unknown. In the distance, the Notre-Dame beckons. I walk faster, as if doing so will allow me to outrun the ghosts of the past and the uneasy questions about my own life now.

I travel much farther than I planned, strolling the quay along the river and even crossing the bridge into the Latin Quarter. Only when the sun begins to sink low behind the Eiffel Tower do I make my way back in the direction of the hotel.

At last I reach the street where the Meridien is located.

"Louise!" a familiar voice calls as I near the hotel door. Hearing my name, I stop short and turn.

Coming toward me with rapid strides is Ian.

❧

Germany, 1944

We neared the second camp after nightfall, having crossed into Germany in the darkness. We were a smaller group now, just Franny, Ian and myself, plus the driver. The other volunteers had started for home, as I would have if I had not chosen to come with Ian and Franny. We rode now in a lone truck, Franny stretched out on the small second-row bench, snoring. Ian sat next to me, too close, our legs pressed warm against one another. His head was tilted back and I thought he might be sleeping. But when I looked over, his eyes were open, alert. His fingers brushed against mine and I expected him to pull back. He did not. Instead, he put his hand atop mine and held it gently.

Though we had been in occupied territory for days, there had been an ominous feeling as we entered Germany. This was truly in the belly of the beast now, behind enemy lines and far from where anyone could help us. I was suddenly paralyzed with fear. We were in Nazi Germany, under the control of the enemy. Despite the assurances that the Red Cross was neutral, we might be detained at any second.

The new camp was a stalag, designated for enlisted men and not officers. It was in the forest, away from prying eyes of civilians, and any pretense of decency was gone. The buildings were ramshackle wooden huts with broken windows and gaping roofs, scarcely providing any shelter at all. Barbed wire fencing ringed the camp and bright searchlights scanned the ground. In the distance, a guard dog barked menacingly.

Our quarters here were converted railcars, leaky and windowless, parked on an abandoned stretch of track just outside the camp fence. The message the Germans sent by housing us in such a place was clear: we were inferior and unwelcome. I watched Franny, wondering how she would react to the grim accommodations. "Want to share?" she simply asked. I nodded, and we carried our bags inside one of the railcars, which sat low to the ground, wheels removed. The interior was bare except for two metal cots and a basin for washing. There were no showers and the toilet was an outhouse behind the train. We put our things away and prepared to go to sleep on the hard cots inside without speaking.

I turned to Franny. "How is it that they let you perform for these men?" I asked. "The POW officers in the last camp are one thing. But the men in this dreadful place seem beyond hope."

"I insisted," she said. "If I was coming for one prisoner, I was coming for all of them. I wanted to see it all, to bear witness and help where I can. Not just what the Germans wanted me to see. After all, who needs our help more than those who have no hope?"

Still, taking in the new camp through the barbed wire, I was seized with the urge to leave. *Go now,* a voice seemed to say. I had promised Franny I would stay, though, and I would not abandon her, nor the work that might mean the difference between life and death for some of these men. I lay awake feeling very much a prisoner myself.

The next day, I awoke to a steady rain beating against the railcar. Franny was not in her bed. She was up already, standing in the doorway of the railcar and peering outside. She seemed to be searching across the barbed wire, as though looking for something or someone.

Outside, the heavy downpour had turned the dirt to a thick mud. I lay in the uncomfortable bed, not wanting to face the grimness ahead. But Franny gamely pulled on high black Wellingtons and a bright red poncho. "Come," she said brightly. "There is work to be done." We spent the morning sorting and delivering packages to guards who took them from us at the gate without speaking. The rain slowed to a mist. I watched Franny work in her red poncho, which made her stand out like a beacon amid all of the drab gray and brown.

Around midday, we stopped and returned to the railcar for lunch that Ian had left us, thin cheese sandwiches on stale bread and a cold, watery stew. "I have to go," Franny said when she'd finished eating. "There's a rehearsal."

"A rehearsal?" I was surprised. At the previous camp, Franny had simply gone onstage.

"Yes, I'm playing with an orchestra here. Well, not an orchestra exactly, but a few chamber musicians, a violinist, a flute player and a cellist, who are prisoners themselves. Want to come watch?"

"Sure." In truth, I did not want to go inside the camp. But I also did not want to be left behind in the railcar, alone. I followed her down the muddy road, which ran parallel to the barbed wire fencing of the camp. The prisoners I glimpsed through the fence were bald and emaciated beneath their khaki uniforms, bespeaking months of starvation. We walked to the gated entrance of the camp, where Franny showed her identification card and we were let inside. Prisoners, who seemed to be lining up for work details, eyed us strangely, whispering.

A guard escorted us past rows of ramshackle wood huts to an old barracks that served as the practice hall. There, three men waited. I took a chair in the corner as they began to practice without introduction. I marveled at their instruments. Though they were worn and likely not the ones the musicians had played before coming here, they still looked like treasures, fragments of light in this dank and hopeless world.

The musicians came from different places and had not played together before their imprisonment. Their skill levels were different, too, the most gifted being the cellist. Though I was not trained in music, I could see that he led the others, and seemed to follow Franny's singing and cues effortlessly. It was the difference between simple playing and art.

The rehearsal ended and I waited, thinking Franny and I might walk back together. But she waved me off. "You go on. I need to go over some notes." She walked to the cellist and conferred with him, heads leaned close, voices low. There was a familiarity between them, as if they had met before. Dismissed, I walked to the door of the practice hall where the guard who had brought us in waited. He escorted me from the camp and I went back to the railcar where Franny and I slept.

When a half hour passed and Franny did not return, I set out to find Ian in his railcar. There was work to be done distributing Red Cross care packages and I wanted to be useful. I neared Ian's railcar and stopped. Franny was there, I noted with surprise. She must have gone straight from her rehearsal. Through the doorway, I saw Franny and Ian talking. No, not talking. Arguing. Franny pleading with him, close to tears.

Still, I moved closer, curious to know what they were talking about. "What do you mean, you can't help?" I heard her ask him, her voice equal parts demanding and beseeching. Help with what? I wondered.

Soon after, she broke away from Ian and started toward me. "Are you all right?" I asked. She did not answer but stormed past me into our railcar. I followed her inside. "Franny, what's going on?" I demanded.

Franny pulled me to the corner of the room. "There's a prisoner who has asked me to deliver something to his wife in Paris."

"Franny, that's so dangerous." It was one thing to take photographs for making illegal identification cards. But secretly carrying something for a prisoner seemed even more risky, a step too far.

"I know, but he begged me and what other choice do I have? I'm not headed back to Britain straightaway because I have performances scheduled on the French Riviera. So I'm trying to see if Ian will arrange to have it delivered for me. Of course, he doesn't want to."

I could see her frustration with Ian. He was balancing the competing demands and where he could do the most good. "Do you want me to talk to him?"

"Do you think it would help?" Even as she asked this, we both knew that it would not. Ian might be fond of me, but no amount of attraction would deter him from the mission or doing what was best for it.

"Never mind," she said. "I'll think of something else."

Neither of us spoke for several seconds. "Sure, you invite me here," I said. "But what about the French Riviera?"

She laughed at my feeble attempt to joke. "You could come if you wanted." She was not entirely kidding. For a moment, I could almost see it, going along with Franny for her performances, the two of us having adventures. But I could not follow her forever. I needed to go back to London and figure out what my own life would look like after the war.

As evening fell, we returned to the camp. The audience began to gather for Franny's show, I hid in the wings of the makeshift stage, peering out. The POWs stood subdued around the back, the seats reserved for the German guards. Despite the prisoners' downtrodden state, there was a buzz of excitement about them, as though they could not believe this very special thing was for them, a bright spot.

The musicians she had practiced with sat in a semicircle behind Franny. It was the first time I'd heard her playing with accompaniment and the music was even richer, the chords from the instruments lifting her voice.

A commotion in the audience tore me from the music. A man in the audience was having a coughing fit and a guard was trying to remove him so that he did not interrupt the show. "I want to stay," the man wheezed. Franny and the musicians stopped mid-song. The guard yanked him roughly from the crowd and smashed a club down on his head.

"No!" I cried, horrified by the brutality. I expected the others to protest, but they kept their eyes low, fearful that they would be next. The guards beat the man mercilessly. Sickened, I wanted to look away. But I could not. This was not the fair treatment that was required by the rules of war. Here, the pretense of civility was gone. And if they were willing to treat an enemy combatant like that, what might they be doing to the Jewish prisoners?

When the man had been dragged away and the show resumed,

I marched from backstage, searching for Ian. Not seeing him, I left the camp and went to find him at his railcar. I knocked but did not wait before walking through the open door. Ian looked up from where he was seated on the edge of his cot, sorting papers. "Did you see what just happened to that man?" I asked. He nodded slightly. He must have left just after the incident as I had. "We have to do something."

He looked up, brushed his hair from his eyes. "We will issue a letter of protest," he said evenly. Despite my anger, I could not help but feel drawn to him in the intimate, too-close space.

I pushed my feelings of attraction aside. "A letter? That won't do anything." Once, Ian had seemed so very committed to helping. Why wouldn't he do more?

"It will send a statement."

"A statement?" I repeated, my voice rising with disbelief.

"Well, what do you expect?" he exploded, standing up. "Shall we call the police? We aren't in Britain anymore, Louise! We are behind enemy lines and we are powerless." I saw his frustration. He shared all of my same anger and pain at the situation in the POW camps, but at the same time he had the extra responsibility of seeing that the mission was fulfilled and we all made it home safely.

I remembered then Franny's argument with Ian. "Franny said you wouldn't help her deliver something for one of the prisoners."

"Franny doesn't know when to stop," he said darkly. "It's complicated, Louise. We must all be careful. Things are very bad elsewhere. The POW camps are the best of it. There are camps filled with people, Jews mostly, and you can't even imagine the atrocity of what's happening there."

"Why doesn't the Red Cross do something? The Red Cross is a humanitarian operation—how can it bear witness to barbarism so contrary to its mission and do nothing?"

"It's complicated. We're doing all we can. *I'm* doing all I can."

A wave of empathy came over me then. Ian had so much responsibility put upon him, for delivering the packages and helping people, and for trying to keep us all safe.

"I'm sorry," I offered, putting my hand on his arm. "This can't be easy."

He dipped his chin in acknowledgment. "It isn't easy—for any of us."

Ian and I stood in silence, staring out across the field. Our shoulders pressed against one another. "What do you miss most?" he asked suddenly. "From before the war, I mean."

I considered the question. "I miss oranges," I replied finally.

He looked puzzled for a moment. Then he smiled. "Oranges." Citrus had always been scarce. But now with rationing and shortages, they were nonexistent.

"I miss the quiet," he said. "Long walks in the countryside with nothing but the sound of the larks, you know? When I was a child in Wales, you could walk for a day and not see or speak to anyone." I see him then, not as the head of our mission, but as a boy, not so very much older than myself. He was, like the rest of us, just trying to find peace and go home.

"Ian…" I found myself moving toward him. I looked up into his eyes and the connection between us was undeniable. Our faces were just inches apart and I wondered if he might try to kiss me.

"This can't happen," he said abruptly, straightening. "I've seen it a half-dozen times, men and women spending too much time together in the field. I like you, Lou. But I have to focus on the work at hand. I've got an operation to run and people to care for, and you…you get in the way and you cloud my judgment." His words stung.

"I won't bother you again." I hurried away, feeling foolish.

When I returned to our railcar, Franny was already there. I waited for her to share a story as she always did, witty or sad. But tonight she was silent. Outside I heard a guard walking by.

Footsteps paused by the window and I held my breath. We were in enemy territory and might be apprehended at any moment. The danger seemed more acute now that I knew about Franny trying to help one of the prisoners. I fully understood in that moment that we might never make it home.

"Fancy a smoke?" she asked, holding out the pack. I took one and accepted the light she offered. I smoked now, too, a way to manage all the danger and stress.

I thought that Franny would get ready for bed. But after she took off her makeup, she reached for her coat. It was a subtle gray and, unlike the bright poncho she had worn earlier, designed to make her blend in with the drab surroundings.

"Where are you going?" I asked. We were not allowed inside the camp and there was nothing else around for miles.

"Just walking," she said. I wondered if she was lying and had planned to meet the man who had asked for her help.

"You shouldn't walk alone at night," I said.

She tossed her head and laughed. "I'm not afraid of the dark."

"But it's dangerous."

"Bloody hell, it's all dangerous!" Now Franny was angry. "You can't just keep your head in the sand. We give out packages and we sing and none of it matters at all."

Franny stormed away, her hair fanning behind her like a kite tail. I started to follow her, but I knew when she was in a state, it would do no good. I would wait until she came back, I decided, and try to talk to her again.

I drifted off but slept fitfully. I dreamed that we were on the boat once more. I lost Franny to the dark, stormy sea. I awoke in a sweat, calling her name. She had not come back yet.

Restless, I walked outside. I spotted a figure in the distance. Franny, I realized with relief. Only the picture was all wrong; Franny was where she should not have been, pressed up close to the fence, talking to a man. I recognized the man as the cellist who had accompanied her performance. He was handing her an object. He must be the one who had asked her to carry something to his wife.

I started toward her, wanting to warn her, to call her back. We were not permitted to interact with the prisoners, other than during the shows, and being that close to the fence was dangerous.

Then I stopped. Something told me that it was not my place, Franny would not want me there. But I was curious, worried even. Franny was always pushing things and it was only a matter of time before she went too far.

Reluctantly, I returned to the railcar and forced my eyes shut. Eventually, I fell asleep.

At some point during the night, I was awakened by a rustling as Franny settled in beside me. "What were you doing?"

"So many questions," Franny said, trying to sound light and chiding.

But I was unwilling to let it go, would not let her dodge the question. "I saw you talking to one of the musicians and he handed you something. What was it?"

"It's none of your affair." Franny's tone was cold and I was taken aback. "I need to get some sleep before tomorrow's show." She was shutting me out, keeping me at a distance, and the rejection stung.

"I'm sorry," Franny said later. "I didn't mean to snap. This is just all so difficult and stressful. The truth is, I'm glad you're here. I've never had many female friends. After my sister left, I was alone. And then in the theater, there are not so many genuine people. It's hard to know who to trust, you know?"

"I do." Having a difficult childhood like Franny, I had never developed many friendships. It was as if I had formed a protective outer shell that kept anyone from getting close. Only Franny and I had gotten close, and it was both wonderful and scary. "But I'm glad you're here and that we met."

"Me, too. Letting someone in, though, it's bloody terrifying." We both laughed softly.

Later, when she was snoring soundly, I crept to the far side of her bed. I hesitated. Franny and I had just talked about trust and I felt guilty snooping. But I had to know what she was doing. I peeked into her bag. There, wrapped in cloth, was a necklace charm, a half heart with the words *watch* and *me* inscribed upon it, and it had a nick in the top arch of the heart, as if it had been somehow chipped. It did not look particularly valuable, yet at the same time I could tell that it was precious, unique. I fingered it, curious. Why did the man want Franny to take it to his wife?

The next morning when I awoke, the events of the previous evening came rushing back. I rolled over, half-afraid that Franny would be gone again as she had the previous evening. But she was sleeping soundly beside me, as if none of it had ever happened at all.

12

Helaine

Paris, 1943

Lévitan.

After the lights went on, Helaine stood bewildered with the other women who had been brought from the police station in the middle of what had been one of the grandest department stores in Paris. She looked around the cavernous, arched hall in disbelief. She was familiar with the shop, where her family had once purchased the finest goods. But why had they been brought here?

Of course, Helaine had never really shopped at Lévitan. When she lived at home, she was not permitted to go out to the stores. And later after marrying Gabriel, she frequented the secondhand markets. But Helaine had passed Lévitan's broad windows before, seeing her own reflection among the furniture and other goods displayed. And she had seen the name on shopping bags and labels. The department store had gone out of business at the start of the war. But to Helaine's surprise, it was not empty.

The shelves were stacked neatly with apparel and home goods, as though still open for business.

"What are we doing here?" Helaine whispered to the woman beside her. She received no answer. Their group was larger now than it had been at the police station, and Helaine guessed that they had been joined by prisoners from a second truck.

"Welcome," the guard who had herded them inside said mockingly, "to Camp Lévitan."

He led the women across the store, past the elevators to a narrow stairwell in the rear. They followed upward single file, their collective breath growing heavier as they reached a landing. Through a doorway, Helaine glimpsed large piles of blankets and clothing. They began to climb the stairs again, bumping against the narrow walls and one another as they went. At the top, the man opened a door and let Helaine and the other women into a long room. Inside, there were two rows of narrow cots, per-haps forty in all. A curtain ran down the middle, as if to separate the room for privacy. Some of the beds were already occupied and the people in them stirred, awakened by the new arrivals. A washbasin stood at the far end. "The toilet is one floor down," the guard informed them.

"We are to sleep in the store?" Helaine asked.

"Yes," the guard snarled. "If this is not grand enough for your tastes, you can always go to Drancy."

Helaine bristled with fear. She had heard about Drancy, the transit camp the Germans had erected at the old military bar-racks outside the city, the crowding and starvation and hard labor Jews endured there. Even from this cursory glance, she could tell how much better life would be here.

"You will report downstairs for work at dawn," the guard said, closing the door behind him and disappearing. There did not seem to be anything to do but choose an unoccupied bed and sleep in it.

The women who had just arrived looked from the bare, stained mattresses to one another. "Is this where we are to sleep?" Helaine could not help but be horrified.

"Of course," an older woman snapped. "You were expecting maybe a canopy bed?" She sat up. "At Drancy, we slept on wood pallets, on straw. Have you no idea what we have endured, how much better this is?" The other women looked at Helaine with a mix of pity and disdain.

Helaine opened the door and walked down the stairs to the floor below where a large pile of sheets lay in a heap and a few of the others followed her. "What about these?"

"Taking from the deliveries is forbidden," the older woman said, following her.

"They will never notice if we just take a few," Helaine pressed. She fingered a fine silk sheet, reminiscent of the ones she had in her childhood room.

"We are not going to risk getting in trouble just because you think you are too good to sleep like the rest of us." Helaine understood then that there was a collective responsibility—all might be punished for the infraction of one. She set the sheet down reluctantly.

Back upstairs, each of the women who had just arrived claimed a bed on the right side of the curtain. Helaine was horrified at sharing a room with a bunch of strangers, and even more appalled that some of them were male. She selected a bed at the very end of the row, close to the far wall.

"Here," a voice said behind Helaine. She turned to see the older woman from earlier holding out a large, rough piece of fabric. "The linens you wanted to take have been cataloged and the guards will know if any go missing. Use this instead." It was an old drapery, Helaine realized, not a blanket. But it would do the job.

"Thank you."

The older woman sat down on the bed beside Helaine, which Helaine realized already happened to be hers. "Miriam," she said by way of introduction. Her skin was papery, her complexion ashen.

"I'm Helaine. Where did you come here from?"

"Our house was on Rue Charlot." Helaine recognized the address from the Jewish Quarter in Le Marais. "But I was arrested two months ago. Then we were sent to Drancy." Helaine could not fathom what Miriam must have experienced at Drancy; she could see the haunted look in the woman's eyes. "I was brought here a few weeks ago. Thank God they opened the department store. It's for those with some sort of privileged status whom they don't dare to deport east. My husband was a decorated officer in the Great War." A note of pride crept into her voice. "So I've been given special designation as a veteran's wife, even though he died years ago." She blinked back tears, the memory clearly still painful. Then she cleared her throat. "And you? How have you come to find yourself here?"

"I honestly don't know," Helaine replied. "I'm not even certain why I was arrested." As she was taken from the police station, she had tried to argue: she had only come to inquire about her husband; she had done nothing wrong. But her pleas had been ignored.

"You're a Jew and that's enough reason to be arrested these days." Helaine had heard rumors that Jews were being taken from Paris in greater numbers, but she had assumed it was limited to the immigrant community. She had not realized that it extended to Jews who were French citizens. It seemed that Isa's prediction that they would eventually come for all of the Jews was now coming true. Helaine could not help but worry for her parents.

"My husband is a cellist, and my father owned a substantial

business, so perhaps it has something to do with one of them," Helaine offered.

"Don't question it further," Miriam advised. "Do the work and don't complain, because being here is as good as it is going to get." Miriam coughed and her face turned grayer.

"You sound sick." The deprivation and hardship had most certainly taken a toll on Miriam at her age. "If we tell the guards, surely you can go see a doctor."

"No," Miriam snapped angrily. Helaine was taken aback by her response. "Those who are seriously ill are sent to Drancy and deported. Leaving would be a death sentence. I'm never going back there again. I'm not sick."

"I was sick as a child," Helaine confided. "I nearly died."

"My son was sick as a child." She paused and her eyes grew hollow. "He did die." Miriam's voice cracked at the end. "He was my only child." A tear rolled down her cheek. Helaine reached instinctively for her handkerchief. Then, realizing that she did not have one, she used the corner of her sleeve to gently dry Miriam's face.

"I'm so sorry for your loss." Helaine reached out and took Miriam's hand. Helaine felt so much sadness at being separated from Gabriel and her mother. But Miriam had lost everyone she loved forever.

"It was during the flu epidemic of 1919. We couldn't get medicine. But enough about that," she said, swiping at the corner of her eye to prevent more tears from falling. Helaine saw that she had buried her sadness down deep beneath a crusty exterior to survive. "Anyway, if I wanted to see a doctor," Miriam added, "I could get a pass."

"You mean people leave here for appointments?" Helaine was incredulous.

"Yes, for doctor's appointments and such. People are allowed visitors once a week as well."

"But why?"

Miriam shrugged. "Perhaps because everyone here has some sort of privileged status. Also, Lévitan is in the middle of Paris. They don't want the locals to know what's really happening here, so they give the illusion of treating us better. There is not even that much security, just a single guard at the door."

"Then why don't more people try to escape?"

"Believe me, I have thought of it. But really, where would we go?"

Hours later, after they had gone to bed, as Helaine lay awake on the bare mattress, her mind raced, trying to understand all that had happened. She had been arrested and imprisoned. She remembered the abject fear of being taken against her will, not knowing where she was going. She could not leave. As a child, she had considered herself a prisoner. But now she saw that staying in the comforts of her parents' house, surrounded by love, was not at all the same as the horror of being detained in these dreadful conditions. Gabriel was missing, doing who knows what and where. She had been separated from everyone she loved and everything she knew.

Run, a voice inside her seemed to say. Helaine considered the option, replaying in her mind her earlier conversation with Miriam about the relative lack of security. She could check if the exit to the dormitory was unlocked and sneak downstairs, or perhaps climb out the fire escape. What would stop her from simply leaving? She could return to her and Gabriel's apartment or even run to her parents' house. But at the same time as she thought it, Helaine knew she did not dare. The streets were heavily patrolled, and even if she could get out of the store, the chance of her making it across the city without being recaptured was slim.

Helaine rolled over onto something hard. The necklace. After she had been arrested, she remembered in the police car that she was still wearing it and quickly hid it in her pocket. Thankfully, she was not searched and was able to conceal it in the lining of her dress, so she had it with her still. But she needed to find a better place to stow it. She looked under the bed. However, the space was too open and exposed. Then she turned toward the wall beside her. There was a piece of cracked drywall low beside the cot and Helaine pulled at it, revealing a narrow space where it had separated from the bricks. She wedged the necklace in there and then replaced the drywall as well as she could.

Helaine turned over on the hard cot. She heard a rustling and knew instinctively that there were mice in the walls. She rolled toward the wall and scratched a line in the plaster to signal her first night there. Each day she would keep count until she was free again. She closed her eyes, trying to black out the sound and pretend she was home.

It seemed to Helaine that she could never sleep under such dire conditions. But at some point, she must have drifted off, because the next thing she knew, they were being awakened by bright lights.

"Up quickly," a voice barked, and the women obeyed. They did not have fresh clothes to change into, and so the prisoners rose from their beds and stumbled down the stairs. As they passed the third floor, Helaine slipped from the group to use the toilet hurriedly. There was no shower or bath and she worried how they would ever get clean.

When Helaine rejoined the group, they were headed out the rear of the shop onto a shipping dock. A large truck had just pulled in beneath the arches of the Passage du Desir. It was marked with the insignia from *Le Castagne*, one of the largest moving companies in the city. The back of the truck opened, and workers began to pull out various household items from the truck, chairs and dressers and smaller items like lamps and bedding. Helaine was confused. The store had been closed for some time, so what were these items and why were they here?

"It's called Operation Furniture," Miriam whispered as they were directed into a line. "The goods will be passed down and you sort them."

"So, we are workers in the department store now?"

"Workers?" she spat. "Workers get paid a wage. We are slave laborers, nothing more. There are two other satellite camps for sorting the belongings as well," she added, "one at Austerlitz in a warehouse behind the train station and one in an elegant town home in Bassano in the 16th arrondissement. All are considered sub-camps of Drancy."

It was not until the first item, a silver candelabra, reached Helaine's hands that she understood what they were doing. She ran her hands over the engraved Hebrew lettering, recognizing it from her family's own Shabbat candlesticks. A mix of horror and sadness washed over her. The "goods" were the contents of Jewish homes that had been emptied by the Germans because their owners had been sent to the camps. Helaine had known that Jews were being taken, glimpsed it with her own eyes. But some part of her had believed that this would all end at some point and people would be going home. Here, right before her, was evidence that they would not. Jewish homes were being robbed of their belongings with the absolute certainty that the owners would never return again.

Helaine stood frozen, trying to absorb this information. "Keep going, keep going," Miriam urged in a whisper beside her. Helaine's hesitation was causing a bottleneck in the line and the guard at the end had noticed and was looking at her. "If we don't work well, we will be sent back to Drancy, and no one stays there long." Helaine could hear the fear in Miriam's voice. Helaine placed the candlesticks in a bin. For each type of household item, there were three piles: items that were broken and would be discarded, those that needed repair and finally those that were in good enough condition to be used.

"And the goods, what happens to them from here?" Helaine asked in a whisper.

"Most of the quality items are sent to Germany by train. The furniture is sent east, the office pieces to offices of the Reich, and the beds and such to new estates given to high-ranking SS by Hitler as a reward for loyalty. But the very best items will be displayed downstairs for the German officers to purchase," Miriam added. So that explained why the shelves of the defunct department store were filled with goods. The Germans were using the store to sell the belongings that they had taken from the Jews.

Miriam turned back to her work and did not speak further. The sorting continued endlessly, box after box. They did not take breaks. Helaine hoped they might stop for lunch, but at midday, pieces of stale bread were passed down the line and the workers ate quickly at their stations. Just when it seemed they had sorted the entire contents of the moving truck, another pulled into the loading dock and the process began all over again. Helaine thought about the moving companies: Did they know what kind of work they were really doing and simply not care?

As she worked, Helaine marveled at the goods that she sorted, an endless stream of fine silver and china and linen. No doubt these were expensive and valuable objects; many of them had probably been cherished by their owners. There were practical items, too, pots and small appliances, can openers and clothes irons. The things that people had once needed in their daily lives, until their daily lives were gone.

A lump formed in Helaine's throat as she thought of her mother. Surely she would not be able to remain in her home for much longer—if she had not been taken already. Maman might have been arrested and Helaine would never know. Helaine wished that she could reach out and warn her. But even if that was possible, where would she go?

At the end of the day, a bell sounded. Helaine's bones ached from the hours of kneeling and bending over boxes. She followed the other workers back to the fourth-floor dormitory, where they were given watery bowls of soup.

"Where do they make the food?" Helaine asked.

"The department store has no kitchen, so the UGIF sends food over from their central kitchen on Rue Guy Patin." Helaine nodded. The Union Générale des Israélites de France (UGIF) was the organization overseeing the Jews in Paris under the auspices of the Vichy government.

There was nowhere to eat, so they pulled back the dividing curtain and sat on the floor in between the two rows of cots.

Later, Helaine lay awake, unable to sleep. It was only her second night in the department store, and it already felt like an eternity. She thought of the people she loved: Her mother—did she wonder what had become of Helaine? Her father was likely somewhere abroad, powerless to help. Mostly Helaine thought of Gabriel, worrying about where he was and whether he would come for her or work to secure her release. He could not possibly know she had been arrested. Surely if he did, he would do something to try to help. She retrieved the locket from its hiding place in the wall and wrapped her hand around it, praying that he could feel her as well.

On the other side of the curtain, a man snored. The department store was stifling hot, especially the fourth floor, which heated up all day and only cooled a few degrees at night. Helaine stood and walked from the dormitory, then climbed the stairs toward the roof. The German guards thankfully kept to the perimeter of the store. They did not often come inside and never up to the dormitory, so the prisoners moved with relative ease. There was an overseer, Maxim, who was half-Russian.

Himself a Jew, he had been put in a position of authority over the Jewish prisoners and everyone despised him for it. He was lecherous, Miriam had warned, saying that more than once she had seen his hands on the other women in places that they did not belong.

Helaine had been told that prisoners would be given the chance to go upstairs for fresh air once a week, though that had not in fact happened yet since her arrival. Sometimes the prisoners sneaked up there to smoke. But surely coming up here at night was not permitted.

Helaine stepped out onto the roof terrace and then stopped, surprised by the panoramic view of the city, as grand as any she had ever seen. The department store was in the center of Paris, right across from the mairie, or town hall, for the 10th arrondissement. The Eiffel Tower was so close it seemed to loom over her. Its lights did not twinkle as they once had, but had been blacked out, another casualty of the war.

Helaine looked out forlornly across the rooftops at the Paris skyline. The view made it almost possible to forget she was in a labor camp. It reminded Helaine of the first night Gabriel had taken her to his apartment above the city. Her eyes filled with tears of longing. She knew that she had it so much better than those in the other camps and that she had no business complaining. But she yearned to be free again and to walk the streets that had been hers ever so very briefly.

A whiff of smoke from below tickled Helaine's nose, causing her to sneeze. She looked around anxiously, hoping that the guard below had not heard. Every night there was a bonfire in the alley behind the store where they burned the goods that were not fit to keep. Across the street, she glimpsed a woman in an apartment. Their eyes met. Helaine wondered how much the woman knew about who she was and what she and the others were doing here. The woman saw them. Yet she said nothing.

Did nothing. Helaine took a last look at the Paris skyline, then returned to the dormitory below.

Life in the department store fell into a pattern after that. The prisoners were expected to be at their workstations at seven in the morning and worked without a lunch break until seven in the evening. Other times, though, their regular schedule was disrupted by the arrival of the delivery trucks. As soon as a truck came in, it had to be unloaded. More than once, the prisoners were awakened in the middle of the night and ordered to assemble a sorting team. When the trucks came faster, they worked longer days, fourteen and even sixteen hours without rest.

But the nights were their own. After their meager dinner, one of the women would use coffee they had bribed one of the movers for to make weak coffee on the lone electric burner by the washbasins. Every evening, they huddled around a contraband radio that one of the prisoners had pilfered from the sorted goods, listening for bits of news from London. Occasionally, someone would sing a childhood song, or one of the tunes that was popular before the war, taking them back to happier times. The prisoners would talk long into the night in hushed voices. No one spoke aloud in the daylight of the things that had happened to them, as if their communal suffering would have been too much to bear. But sometimes they whispered from cot to cot in the darkness, sharing their horrific stories of families torn apart, lives shattered without warning.

Lévitan, Helaine came to learn, was a study in contradictions. They were in the middle of the once-elegant department store, but their living conditions were spartan. In addition to not having a kitchen, the department store also had no bath or shower. Once a week, the prisoners were permitted to visit a vacant apartment in the adjacent building and given five minutes to bathe. They did not have to wear uniforms, but were allowed to remain in their street clothes.

One night a few weeks after she came to Lévitan, Helaine lay awake thinking as she so often did about Gabriel. She felt so alone without him. She pulled out the locket and ran her fingers over the letters, feeling part of the inscription: *The Lord watch over thee and me.* Of course, her locket contained only half of the quote; the other half was engraved on the locket Gabriel carried. Helaine felt stronger and more connected to Gabriel when she held it.

From the bed beside Helaine, Miriam eyed her necklace. "Where did you get that?" she whispered.

"It was my grandmother's." She showed it to Miriam. "It is actually one of two parts. My husband has the other half."

"Just don't let them catch you with it." Helaine knew the necklace could be taken from her at any second. "What happened to your husband?" Miriam asked.

"I'm not certain," Helaine admitted. She hesitated, not wanting to mention that Gabriel had claimed to be abroad playing for the Germans. It sounded somehow wrong, and she didn't know if it was even still true.

"There are visits allowed on Sundays, if he is able."

"I know." The previous Sunday, Helaine had peered enviously over the rail at prisoners waiting for family members to appear. Watching the other families reunite, Helaine could not help but long for her own. Helaine shook her head sadly. "He's much farther away." She hoped that Miriam would not ask her where. "I would like to get a letter out, though."

Miriam nodded. "We are permitted to send one letter per week and to receive mail when it arrives. Just remember anything you say may be read and censored."

But Helaine didn't know where Gabriel was or have an address to send the letter. She decided to send it to the Conservatoire in case they learned of his whereabouts. That night, Helaine wrote a letter on a piece of paper that Miriam provided.

Dearest Gabriel,

I'm writing with the news that I have been arrested and taken to the department store Lévitan as a worker. I am well. Please write back and let me know that you are safe. I pray that we will be together soon.

With all my love,

Helaine

Helaine gave the letter to Maxim. "I'd like to send this," she requested, trying to ignore his leering expression. She felt as if she was sending a message in a bottle that might never reach Gabriel, or anyone at all. Helaine thought about sending a letter to her mother as well but did not want to risk her safety by bringing attention to her.

The next morning, she awoke and dressed. On the loading dock, Helaine was put to work sorting glassware and packing it in wood crates filled with straw. "Do it this way," a young red-haired woman called Ruthie instructed beside her. She put the glasses in at an angle so that they leaned against one another.

"But I am doing it the way I was told," Helaine protested.

"Exactly." Ruthie lowered her voice. "Don't. Look, if you place the straw just so, the goods will break in transit."

"Oh…" Helaine understood then. *Sabotage.* "We have to put our prisoner numbers on the outside of the crates," she said, gesturing to the small tag that had been affixed to her dress since shortly after her arrival: *L186.* She was no longer a name, but a number. "They will know it was me."

Ruthie shrugged. "Very hard to blame someone for a little straw shifting in transit."

Helaine did as Ruthie told her, angling the glassware. Ruthie nodded with approval.

After that, Helaine noticed a dozen other acts of sabotage. One worker had a tiny hammer and she would hit the furniture when no one was looking. People removed screws so items would fall apart, removed knobs on drawers. Others shredded and cut holes in garments. Each was a small symbol of defiance, a stand for their side against their jailers. It was a marvel that any goods made it to Germany at all.

The next night, Miriam nudged Helaine from sleep. "Here, we need you to take this pile of silver goods and leave it near the loading dock out back." She held out a small silver tray with some cutlery upon it.

Helaine rubbed her eyes. "Me? Why?"

"Because you are relatively new and no one suspects you. One of the movers who is secretly helping us will take it and get it to the partisans—for a cut, of course." Miriam paused, eyeing her warily. "We can trust you, can't we?"

"Of course."

"I said as much. And Ruthie vouched for you because you put the glasses in so they would break like she told you. So you'll do it?"

Helaine hesitated. She wanted to keep her head low in the camp and wait until she could be free and find Gabriel. But she could not refuse. "Yes."

"Good. Take it down to the loading dock. And don't get caught."

Helaine stood and eyed the silver. She could not just carry it openly, she decided. She tucked the smaller pieces into her clothes, then put the tray behind her back. She walked to the door of the dormitory and peered out to make sure neither Maxim nor the guard were nearby.

Helaine crept down the stairs. Her footsteps seemed to echo too loudly through the empty store. Her heart pounded and she was certain that she would be apprehended at any moment. When she reached the ground floor, she hurried to the rear of the store and opened the door slowly, so that it would not creak. She set down the tray and pulled out the pieces of silver she had hidden.

After depositing the silver, Helaine raced inside and started back upstairs. Then she stopped again. She had not seen much of the store since coming and she was curious to have a peek now. The first floor of the department store and its window displays had been left largely unchanged, and to a passerby who happened inside, it might look as though they were still in business or temporarily closed. The center of the grand hall was filled with counters displaying smaller goods, scarves, gloves and the like. Around the perimeter, there were stalls, each the size of a small room, displaying furniture like the set of a play. Helaine was struck with a sudden sense of nostalgia and longing.

As Helaine crept through the makeshift living rooms, she could almost hear the voices of those who had sat in these chairs and cherished these objects, crying out in protest. Some of the prisoners avoided the main floor of the store as much as possible. Too many ghosts, she'd heard Miriam say once. But Helaine did not mind. Walking among their belongings, she almost felt as though she came to know them.

Walking farther, Helaine discovered a small alcove toward the back of the store. She stopped and gasped when she saw it: a toy shop, with beautiful objects, dolls and trains and balls and wooden soldiers. She remembered it now, having come to the toy room as a child and leaving with a doll. But hers had been new, the dress crisp and unstained. The toys here now were all gently worn and loved, bearing witness to the children who were no longer here to hold them. Unable to stand the sight, Helaine turned and ran back up to the dormitory.

On her way back upstairs, Maxim appeared suddenly. "What are you doing?" His large frame filled the doorway and he stood over her too closely.

"I was just going to the bathroom." For an awful moment,

Helaine thought he had seen her with the silver. But he let her go without saying anything further.

Helaine hurried back to the dormitory. "Did everything go all right?" Miriam asked.

"Yes. Except for seeing Maxim. He didn't suspect anything, but he makes my skin crawl."

"Maxim is a lech," Miriam said darkly. "And there are plenty of prisoners who give him what he wants in exchange for favors. He would rather have someone young and pretty like you, though. You must be careful to never be alone with him."

A few days later when Helaine reached the line, the spot beside her was empty and Ruthie was nowhere to be found. *Gone*, Miriam mouthed when Helaine asked. Helaine wondered whether Ruthie had escaped. But seeing Miriam's grim expression, Helaine knew that she had not. Rather, she had been taken to Drancy for certain deportation. She might have been caught packing the glassware wrong or smuggling the silver for the resistance, or sent for some other perceived infraction. There was a rumor that she and several others had been taken in reprisal for another prisoner trying to escape.

There was a quiet vulnerability among the prisoners after that. Before, Helaine had felt a false sense of security, when the truth was that they could be snatched away at any moment. Their safety here was promised by no one and their sanctuary might be taken for no reason, just as suddenly and arbitrarily as they had been stolen from their lives and brought here in the first place.

Helaine realized then how very fragile her existence was and she could not afford to take risks. Instead, she would do what she must in order to remain here, alive, until she and Gabriel could be together once more.

13

Louise

Paris, 1953

"You're here," Ian says, his voice a mix of surprise and happiness.

"Yes." I shift awkwardly. "You invited me."

"I did. I just never thought…" His voice trails off, but his eyes do not leave mine.

"That I would dare to come?" I finish for him.

"Yes," he admits.

"I'm here to find out more about the cellist," I say, making sure there is no confusion about why I am here.

"I'm so glad you did." His voice is warm, and a sea of emotion rises in me. Being here with him feels strange, like characters in the wrong story. "I was going to reach out to you. I did some checking and I found out some information about the cellist in the POW camp," he says.

"Really? And?"

He shakes his head. "Not here." I'm frustrated, eager to know what he has learned. But Ian will not tell me until he is ready. "Shall we have dinner and talk?" he proposes. He gestures toward the hotel. "I've heard the restaurant is quite good."

I hesitate. I had come to Paris to find answers and I need Ian's help. But the prospect of sitting across from him, looking into his eyes, is almost too much. "Certainly," I manage finally. "Let me freshen up first." I walk into the bathroom just off the lobby.

After I use the toilet and wash my hands, I peer into the mirror, wishing I was not so worn from the trip. My face is pale and dark circles ring my eyes. I reach into my purse for my powder and lipstick. As I do, the necklace falls out and clatters to the ground. I pick it up and turn it over in my hand, discovering for the first time a faint crack along the edge of the charm. My curiosity rises. It is a locket. How had I not noticed before? The opening is so fine that even Millie had not spotted it. I try to pry it open, but it is stuck with age.

I reach into my purse for a thin metal nail file. I wedge the file into the crack and the locket opens with a pop. The necklace is actually a locket with a tiny place for storing things inside.

Something tiny falls out and flutters to the ground. I pick it up and examine it, trying to figure out what it is. It is smaller than my thumbnail and translucent. It appears to be a piece of film, so I hold it up to the light, trying to see what tiny image it holds. It is impossible.

Another woman walks into the bathroom. I scramble to put the locket and film back in my purse. Then I walk out into the lobby. Ian is waiting for me by the hotel bistro.

We find our way to a small table in the corner. A tiny candle flickers in the center of the table, its shadows dancing on the pressed white tablecloth. "You haven't given up on chasing this thing," Ian observes wryly once we've sat down.

"No," I admit. "At first, when I learned that the necklace was English, I thought that maybe you were right and there was nothing more to it. But then when Midge told me that Lévitan, the name on the box, was a Paris department store, I suspected there might be a connection. So I came." I hear how far-fetched my own explanation sounds.

"You went to the department store already?"

I nod. "It's a design firm now, but you can still see the original architecture of the shop. I didn't learn much at first. It turns out that the store didn't even sell jewelry, and I thought I'd hit a dead end."

"So you see, there really is nothing to all of this. I hope this wasn't a waste of a trip for you."

"It wasn't. You see, as I was about to give up, I met a woman whose family owns a pharmacy across the street. She has lived there since before the war." I put my hand to my temple, overwhelmed and exhausted by what I had learned and the whole day. Ian is watching me intently as I speak. "So, what did you find out about the cellist?"

Before he can reply, a waiter comes around and Ian orders for us in flawless French, chardonnay for me and a scotch neat for him, plus a tray of meats and cheeses. I consider asking for tea instead. But after everything that has happened today, I could do with something stiffer. "You remember what I drink," I say, a touch flattered.

"Some things don't change," he says evenly, giving me a long look.

"But some do. When did you learn to speak French so well?" His French had been terrible when we were in Europe during the war.

"I've needed it for my job. I've had a few assignments abroad." I realize how little I know about him or what he has done in the years since the war. Neither of us speak. It seems so odd to be seated here with him. Ours had not been the world of bars and cafés. Rather, our backdrop was the war, rolling boats and jostling trucks. After all of the feelings we had between us and the terrible circumstances under which we parted, the ordinary does not feel right.

"The man, I found out who he was," Ian says when the waiter has set down our drinks and left again. "He was a well-known cellist, Gabriel Lemarque. He was half-English." Which might explain the Mizpah, I think. Or perhaps why it had wound up back in England. "And as I said, it turns out he lived in Paris. He was an up-and-coming star of the French classical musical scene before the war." I try to figure out how this information might connect to Franny and the necklace. Ian continues, "But, Lou, there's more. It turns out that he was a collaborator."

"No..."

"The records are clear. He was performing for the Germans and their propaganda effort."

A terrible thought comes into my head: If Franny was helping him, was she also a traitor? The war had been filled with stories of double agents, people betraying their countries on both sides. Still, it was hard to imagine Franny, who had been so fiercely intent on helping the prisoners, collaborating with the other side. "How is it possible that Gabriel was working for the Germans?" I press. "At some point, he was arrested and put in the POW camp, which is where Franny met him. He wouldn't have been there if he was working for the Germans."

"I suppose not." Ian pauses a beat, thinking, brushes at his forehead.

"Franny said that he asked her to get the necklace to his wife in Paris," I say. "I wonder, why did he want her to do that?"

He shrugs. "Maybe to tell her that he was alive or to make sure she was all right."

Or maybe, I think, *to develop a piece of microfilm*. I am more curious than ever to know what is on it. Yet I still do not mention it to Ian.

Ian continues, "Franny never said why. I'm not sure she knew herself."

"Any idea what became of the cellist?"

"I'm afraid there's no record of him after the camps. He very well might have died during the war." Consigned like so many, I thought, to an unmarked grave. "I checked the postwar emigration records, even looked through the phone directory for Paris on the off chance that he survived and stayed here. But there was nothing."

The waiter returns with a tray of cured meats and cheeses. "Please," Ian says, gesturing to the food. I take a piece of baguette, my mouth watering. I, too, am famished. Other than a crepe I'd hastily grabbed when first arriving in Paris, I haven't eaten. But it is more than that: my head is light from the wine, and I need something in my near-empty stomach to balance it out or it's going to go to my head—which is the last thing I need when I'm here alone with Ian after all of these years.

As we eat, my thoughts turn back to Franny and the cellist. "Franny asked you to carry the necklace for the cellist. But you refused. Why?"

"It was more complicated than that, Lou." His voice is plaintive, asking me now, as he did then, to understand the difficult position he was in. "You have to remember that the Red Cross was in those camps by the grace of the German government."

"You mean the Nazis."

"I do. And if we made waves, they would no longer allow us to deliver the aid packages. You understand, don't you?"

I pause for a second, considering. "Yes." How could I judge Ian for not helping Franny deliver the necklace when I had refused to do so as well?

There does not seem to be more to say, so he pays the check and we start from the bistro.

"So what now?" he asks. I start to reply that tomorrow we will go see the man Madame Dupree told me about. But I realize he is not asking about our plans tomorrow. Rather, he wants to know about the two of us, right now.

"I suppose you'll want to turn in," he adds. "You must be knackered from the trip across. Unless you fancy a cup of tea..." he suggests.

"You could come up to my room and we could talk awhile

longer." I know that it is the wrong answer the moment I speak. I am playing with fire. "Just for a bit," I add, as if this will make it somehow better. "A quick cup of tea and then you need to go."

"I'd love that." He smiles, and I regret extending the invitation even more. I want to change my mind. But it is too late. He has started across the lobby to the lift. And when the door opens, he holds it for me and then follows me in.

The lift begins to rise. Then it stops suddenly, jostling us awkwardly together. "Darn lifts." He lingers a second before pulling away. "Nothing from before the war works as it should." At his closeness, my breath catches. In addition to trying to find out about the necklace, I'd come here to put whatever was between us to rest. Instead, our connection looms larger than ever.

When we reach the door to my room, Ian follows me inside. My dress from the previous day lies across the back of a chair and my toiletries are at the sink. Intimate things, reminding me that he does not belong here. I should ask him to go, but I do not.

I scan the room. "No kettle, I'm afraid."

Ian walks to the small liquor cabinet in the corner of the room. "No wine either." He pours two drinks, then crosses the room and hands one to me. "To the old days," he proposes. I raise my glass in acknowledgment but do not repeat the toast. I take a sip of the brandy, wincing as it burns my throat sharply. He reaches into his pocket, and I expect him to pull out a cigarette. "I quit," he says, reading my mind, but he twirls his fingers as though he wishes one was there, the old vices gone but not forgotten.

"Can I see the necklace?" he asks. I take it out and hand it to him. He holds it in his palm, turning it over, considering. "Why do you think Franny was so determined to help the man deliver the necklace?" He drops into one of the chairs and sets the necklace down carefully on the table beside him.

"Because she was Franny." She always cared so much about the conditions the prisoners were forced to live in. About all of it.

"So, you never did tell me what you learned at the department store," Ian says.

"At first, nothing. The current occupants of the building were not eager to talk. But there was a pharmacy across the street from the store, and I met a pharmacist whose parents were there during the war. The pharmacist's mother made the managing director of the firm take me around and show me everything. It's unbelievable, really. Jewish people were forced to live above the store and sort through the plunder of their own people and sell it. And then the pharmacist's mother gave me the name of one of the Jews who was imprisoned there. I had hoped to visit, but he lives outside Paris, and I didn't think I could get there in time today."

"We'll go first thing tomorrow, then." *We.* I'm not sure if I am ready to be a "we" with Ian, even just for this project. But I'm grateful for his help.

"There's a car coming for me at nine, if you'd like to join me," I relent.

"I will." He pauses. "I almost forgot," he says. He reaches into his pocket and pulls something out. He tosses it at me and I scamper to catch it. "At your pleasure, Lou."

"An orange!" I exclaim.

"Yes, I saw a woman selling oranges on the street, so I brought you one. I remembered that you missed those most."

"Almost the most," I reply, a catch in my voice. I can't believe he remembered. I peel back the skin of the orange and bite into it. The taste is youth and freedom, something just for me that I am not obliged to share or give to anyone else.

The juice trickles down my chin. Ian pulls out his kerchief and steps forward to blot it. The gesture feels somehow too intimate and I step back awkwardly.

"You never really said when we met in London what you've been doing since the war," I say, changing the subject.

Ian shifts, uncomfortable as ever talking about himself. "I

stayed at the Red Cross for a while and then moved over to government. I had to do something to keep busy. Never married, no kids," he adds, though I have not asked. Ian never seemed to be the marrying type, too much of a lone wolf, and independent. "It's just not the same, though. During the war, there was so much purpose, a clear sense of wrong and right. It's all muddled now with the Cold War and the Soviets. And it's hard to fit back in to everyday life."

I nod. This is exactly how I have felt in the years since the war. "And you?" he asks.

"I'm married with two children in Henley. An exciting life, I know." My voice contains a note of bitterness. I love my husband and the twins. And I feel disloyal and spoiled complaining when others have so much less. Marriage and children had once been my dream, the very thing I wanted. "They're lovely. My husband, Joe, is a veteran, and my children are five. Really, I wouldn't trade it for anything. It's just…"

"Different, I know."

"Yes." I am grateful to be here in this space where time stands still and someone else understands the way war changed us and the ache that never eased.

There is a radio in the corner of the room and Ian turns it on. An old, familiar tune, "The Way You Look Tonight," begins to play. The same song Franny sang in one of her shows. Tears fill my eyes. Ian holds out his arms, and I hesitate. I shouldn't want to dance with him, but I do. Eager to escape my painful memories, I step closer, and he puts his arms around me. Suddenly, I am a young woman again, a time when I was sure I knew what I was doing, and that it was all going to work out. How had I been so wrong?

As the music plays, my troubles seem to melt away with the years. Being here with Ian is a welcome respite from the problems that linger at home. Time seems to melt away and it is just the two of us once more. It is almost possible to forget everything—including the fact that I am married.

We shouldn't be here, I realize suddenly. "I'm too warm," I say, stepping away.

"Me, too. But it's a beautiful night. Shall we walk?" he asks, misinterpreting my words as an invitation to do something else. "Come on, then." Before I can protest, he leads me from the room and downstairs.

We step out onto the pavement and start down the boulevard. Paris at night is a glittering jewel once more, the wartime blackout cast off. Gargoyles from the corners of buildings look down like sentinels, casting long shadows. We walk in the direction of the Champs-Élysées, neither of us quite knowing where we are going, both feeling our way. A while later, we reach the banks of the Seine and step out onto the Pont Neuf. The Eiffel Tower stands in the distance, unreachable.

I look from the beautiful skyline to the man beside me, who isn't my husband. This is not why I have come to Paris, not really.

I force myself to focus on Franny and the necklace. "We never did find out what happened to her," I say, a note of recrimination in my voice. "You said there would be an autopsy. But it never happened, at least not as far as I know. They took her body and she just disappeared."

"You have to understand, it was the war. The military investigative unit had jurisdiction, and once they removed her body, it was out of my hands."

"I told you something more happened to her. You didn't believe me, Ian. You didn't believe *in* me."

"I was scared," he confesses. "Scared of losing the whole operation and of something happening to you."

"And then afterward, you just forgot about it and moved on."

"Not at all. I wanted to reach out after it had happened, to apologize and explain. But I couldn't. Too much time had passed." As angry as I was for what had happened, I understand what he means. It was all different once we came back, like a dream too odd to articulate into words.

"I made mistakes," he admits. "I was twenty-four years old, for Christ's sake. And I was leading an operation in wartime Europe. I was in over my head."

"Which mistakes?" I need more than an apology from Ian. I need him to acknowledge what happened—and to tell me everything.

"That's the thing, Louise. The Red Cross knew and they did nothing. Not just about the POWs, but about the Jews." He is talking about the larger failure of the Red Cross to report the Nazis' atrocities it witnessed. It had all come to light after the war, the terrible truth about the camps where millions of Jewish people were imprisoned and killed. "They made a few inquiries, issued some protests. But when the Germans said no, they accepted it. And we were no better. We saw what was happening in the POW camps. We did nothing, said nothing. I did nothing. You tried to warn me when that man was beaten, and I refused to listen. And I justified that to myself because we were helping others. But the guilt has eaten me alive. They could have done more. *I* could have done more." His expression is heavy with remorse and I can see how torn up he is inside. The Red Cross mission had been everything to Ian and its failure was his greatest regret.

"You can't change the past, but you can help me now. Help me, Ian." My last words come out a plea.

"Louise, this business with Franny, you should leave this alone. There's no point to it."

"That's rubbish. How can you say that? Why did you invite me to Paris if you were only going to talk me out of it?" I am suddenly angry. He claimed to have information and instead he is trying to stop me. Again.

"Why can't you let this go?"

"Because I failed her, too!" I burst out. "Franny had asked for my help, and when I said no, she was forced to do it alone. And she died because of it. I turned away from my friend at the moment she needed me most. Something happened. There's a connection between what she was trying to do and how she died. Of that I am certain." The weight of guilt atop my grief nearly buckles me. "If I had helped Franny, she would still be here."

"No, Lou, don't say that. We still don't know her death had anything to do with that man. And even if it did, helping her wouldn't have changed anything."

I am suddenly overwhelmed by all that has happened. I lean into his chest then, letting all of my grief and guilt pour forth. He puts his arms around me and I look up awkwardly, then take a step back. "I'm sorry," I apologize. But when I look at his face, he is staring at me intensely.

"I sometimes thought," he begins, his voice tentative and pained, "that the two of us, under other circumstances..." The meaning beneath his words is undeniable and I wonder what might have been if the war had not come between us.

"Me, too," I admit. "But you told me you couldn't get involved."

"I couldn't afford to get distracted from the mission. That didn't mean I didn't want to. And then the night after Franny died..."

"It was just a night." I try to sound dismissive. But we both know it was more than that. "Two grief-stricken people finding comfort."

"Not for me."

"We were in the field, and we were lonely."

He shakes his head. "It would have been the same anywhere and you know it. My feelings for you were real. They still are." Ian leans in to kiss me and I freeze, too stunned to move.

His lips are on mine. It's wrong, I know that instantly. At the same time, a long-forgotten passion wells up within me, threatening to sweep me off my feet. I am kissing him back, unable to stop.

Then my senses return to me and I push him away. "Ian, no."

"I loved you, Lou. I think I still do. I didn't realize it until I saw you again in London. But it's all still there. And I think you feel it as well."

I am stunned. Of course, there is a tiny part of me that is flattered, and an even tinier part that wishes I was a carefree young woman, able to entertain such notions. But I am not. I love Joe.

I should tell Ian that I am a married woman, say something to mute the intensity of our words. He moves closer. Together now, I know that it was not just loneliness or isolation that had drawn us together. The attraction between us is real—and would have been anywhere.

"I have to go," I say, backing away. It is not just Ian. A part of me wants this, too—which is why I absolutely cannot be here.

"Lou, wait…" Ian says.

But it is too late. I am already turning and running away, the clacking of my heels against the glistening pavement echoing through the Paris night.

Germany, 1944

The next evening before the start of the show, a worried ripple spread backstage: Franny, the star of the show, was missing.

"Find her," someone hissed. The men had assembled, and their impatience grew as they waited for Franny to take the stage. I ran back to our railcar, half-afraid that she wouldn't be there. There had been something bothering her since we had gotten to the second camp, a growing darkness. I had tried to ask her about it more than once. At first, she brushed it off lightly, told me I was being silly. But as I pressed, she became annoyed, then angry.

I found her behind the railcar, staring off into the distance. "Franny, what's the matter?"

"Help me," she said, her voice imploring.

"Are you ill? What do you need?" I would help her, of course, but first I needed to know how.

She opened her mouth, as if to explain. Then she blinked and the cloudiness in her eyes cleared. "Nothing. Forget it. Is it showtime already? I must have lost track of the hour." She tried to appear composed, but her eyes were glazed and a faint coat of sweat covered her skin, smearing her makeup.

"Franny, we can postpone or cancel if you are unwell. You don't have to do this."

"Of course I do," she replied, managing a smile. "After all, the show must go on." There was a trace of irony in her voice. Without speaking further, she turned and started for the stage as though nothing had been wrong and we were all so silly for worrying about her.

She was a professional, and so she shook off whatever was bothering her and began to perform. I watched her from the wings. But her haunted look when it had been just the two of us seared deep into my mind. Even before her current melancholy, there were little things about Franny that signaled her anxiety. The way that she tugged at her hair or would repeat a certain note over and over again obsessively, certain that it was not right. To the public, she was light and beauty, perfection. But in private, the demons that held her were too great to outrun. That was why she kept people at a distance, so they could not see the cracks beneath. I had gotten close enough to know the truth, though.

At the end of the show, Franny raised her hand in a kind of wave. And then she stepped back and disappeared into the darkness.

Later that night, she did not come to the railcar and I went looking for her once more. I felt a tug of uneasiness. I was afraid of being out at night, of getting caught where I was not supposed to be. But I was deeply concerned about Franny.

I found her standing by the field again, looking out, as if searching for something or someone. "Come to bed. You must be exhausted." Franny did not answer me but remained motionless, as if she had not heard. I prayed that she might snap out of it as she had before she went on to perform. But she stood rooted this time, too firmly caught in the grasp of whatever darkness or worry held her mind. I started to give up and walk away.

"Wait," she called. I turned back, hoping she would explain everything.

"What is it?" I asked, growing frustrated. Franny had everything, or so it seemed. I could not imagine what she might need from me. "I can't help if you don't talk to me."

"I need you to take this." Franny's voice was pinched and pleading. I saw then that she held in her hand the necklace the man had given her. "Take it with you and deliver it."

"What about you?" I asked instead. "Can't you just take it yourself?"

"It will be too late. Anyway, I'm not going home." There was an unmistakable note of darkness in her voice.

A chill went down my spine. "Whatever do you mean?"

"Just that my tour has been extended, like I told you." She cocked her head and looked me in the eyes. "What did you think I meant?"

"Nothing," I said, but I could not shake the uneasiness.

"After my tour, it will be too late. You must take it to Paris."

"Paris? But I'm not going there," I replied, feeling confused.

"You'll be leaving through France. You'll find a way." It was one thing for her to ask me to deliver the necklace on her behalf, but this was something more. She wanted me to risk everything.

"Franny, why all of this fuss for a necklace?" A strange look crossed her face. I wanted to plead with her to tell me more, but I knew that she would not.

"So you'll help?"

"Franny, smuggling contraband is against the law. I could be arrested." What she was asking was more than I could manage. It was too much. A braver soul would have done it. But I was not a rule-breaker. I wanted to do my job and get out alive.

"I got the names for you. I helped you when you needed it." Her voice deepened with anger. "I always thought you would do the same for me."

I wanted to argue that this was different, more dangerous. But Franny did not see it that way. To her, a favor was a favor, to be owed and paid.

"But why this person? You can't save everyone. You can't even save him. Sending the message won't free him."

Franny stood, her lips pressed tightly together, refusing to say more. That Franny, intensely independent Franny, was asking me for help should have told me something. I should have sensed the depths of her desperation, her need. But in that moment, scared and isolated behind enemy lines, I was too afraid. This was so much riskier. If caught, we could be arrested or worse, and no one, not Ian nor the British government, would be able to help us.

"Why should I do it?" I pressed.

"Because I'm asking you. You have to trust me."

But I could not. "I'm sorry," I said, suddenly terrified. I walked swiftly back to the railcar, leaving Franny standing alone.

As soon as I walked away, I was racked with guilt. I had been wrong to doubt her, I realized as I got ready for bed. I would apologize when she returned. I lay down to wait.

Except she didn't come. The hours passed and the bed beside mine lay empty. I wondered where she had gone. Was she staying out because of our earlier quarrel? No good would come of my playing mother hen and trying to bring her back, and it might only anger her more. I went to bed, sleeping restlessly. I dreamed that I had gone after her. Only instead of being spring, it was a blizzard, and when I started after her, she disappeared into the storm.

I woke sometime later and listened for her in the darkness. Perhaps she had come in. But the railcar was still, and when I reached over, the bedsheets were smooth and untouched. My heart sank. She had never come back. Something was wrong. I rose and dressed hurriedly.

I raced from the railcar. "Franny..." I called quietly. My toe caught on a rock and I stumbled, falling and banging my shin. Heedless of the pain, I stood and continued forward in the darkness. "Franny!" I cried, louder now, not caring who I disturbed.

About fifty meters from the railcar, a few people had gathered by the roadside, too many of them to be awake at such an hour. A man whom I recognized our driver waved me over. "Louise, come quickly!" Nearing them, the pit in my stomach grew.

Lying there on the ground was Franny's lifeless body.

14

Helaine

Paris, 1943

It was an unusually difficult day at the store. The elevator was broken and so the workers had to carry the pieces up from the loading dock, the women using cumbersome baskets that caused them to scrape their knees, the men wobbling precariously under pieces of furniture. Maxim seemed to watch more closely than usual, shouting angrily when people worked slowly. Helaine kept her eyes low and struggled to keep up.

Helaine had been assigned to a group of women sorting cookware that had recently arrived. She lifted a pot and felt the inside. It was still sticky from a recent meal. She imagined the person, a mother making porridge for her children's breakfast. A day like any other, until the knock had come that was to change everything.

Beside Helaine, Miriam was sorting cutlery and silverware. The women had grown close in the time since Helaine came to the store. Miriam had taken Helaine under her wing, treating her as she would a daughter. And though Miriam was nothing like Maman, Helaine looked to her as a mother figure and was glad to have her there. Miriam had been a scion of the Jewish community in Le Marais before the war. She knew everyone. Though it had not stopped the Germans from arresting her, it gave her an elevated status among the prisoners of Lévitan. And because she accepted Helaine, the other prisoners did as well.

Helaine watched Miriam slip a silver ladle from one of the boxes into the waistband of her skirt. Helaine was surprised. She had not seen anyone steal from the line since Ruthie had been transferred.

But Miriam's eyes met Helaine's, unrepentant and unafraid. *For the resistance*, she mouthed. Then she coughed, face reddening. Miriam's cough had grown ominously worse over time in a way that suggested more than flu or some other passing illness. Yet she still refused to seek medical help.

"But if you are caught," Helaine said, "they will send you back."

Back. That was the word that haunted the prisoners' days. Though the prisoners enjoyed the relative liberty of the department store, they might be hauled away to Drancy without notice, either to fill a convoy or as punishment for some minor transgression. Each prisoner worked zealously to avoid that fate. There were a series of unwritten rules: Keep your head low. Do nothing to draw attention. And whatever you do, do not get sick. Anyone who was ill for more than three days was immediately sent to the larger camp. It was a one-way trip. Once someone went to Drancy, they never returned to the department store but were slated for deportation to the camps in the east.

As Helaine worked, her thoughts turned to Gabriel. She wondered, as she so often did, where he was and whether he had any idea what had become of her. Sometimes it felt like they had been apart longer than they had been together. Helaine loved Gabriel more strongly than ever, but sometimes in her darkest moments, she worried that they might never be reunited.

The previous night, as she lay awake on her hard cot, she

heard the furtive steps of a man sneaking to the women's side of the dormitory, followed by the rhythmic sound of sex. Love flourished even here—or at least the need for warmth and companionship. Seeing the couplings that formed so casually among already-married prisoners, Helaine worried about Gabriel. Who was he with, and might he seek warmth on those long, lonely nights? Thinking of her father's infidelities, Helaine could not help but be afraid that Gabriel would be unfaithful to her as well. Gabriel had loved her in a wholly devoted way, or at least he had, before he'd gone away. She could only hope the bond they had shared and the life they had built would be strong enough to sustain them through the war.

Helaine tried to concentrate on the pile of cookware before her. But out of the corner of her eye, a flash of silver caught her attention. She turned to see Miriam lifting a silver tea set, tray and pot. It was grander than any of the other pieces they'd unloaded, and despite the rough transport getting here, it still shone. Helaine froze. She was struck not only by the elegance of the set. She recognized it as her own family's tea set, the one that had sat in the china cabinet.

"Can I see that?" she asked. Miriam passed it to her, and Helaine took it. The set was too ornate to be mistaken. The embossed leaves on the handle had been custom-made for her grandmother's wedding. It was so valuable that Helaine didn't even know how it had made it to sorting without some German picking it off.

Helaine's heart leaped into her throat. "This belonged to my parents." She reached over into the box Miriam had been sorting, curious what else from their home might be found. She could not keep any of it, of course, but she wanted to touch it, as if finding a piece of the past would bring her family closer to her.

She found nothing else. Their tea set was here, though, and that could mean only one thing. "My mother must have been taken."

"Perhaps it is a mistake," Miriam said, trying to offer Helaine comfort. But there was no conviction in her voice. "This could be a similar tea set." Helaine shook her head. The engraved initials on the bottom of the tray left no doubt. Her mind raced as she searched for another explanation. She hoped in vain that only their belongings and not her mother herself had been taken.

Helaine stood and walked from the sorting floor to the administrative office for the department store. Here, the overseer kept the *Wohnungsbefund,* the book listing all of the homes that had been emptied and their contents. She had to get in there and check if her parents' home was listed. But doing so could cost Helaine her life.

The office was empty, so she crept in and opened the ledger, which sat on the desk. She was amazed by the pages and pages of neatly written rows detailing the theft of various objects. Perfect evidence if someday after the war the Germans were to stand trial for this. Helaine scarcely dared to dream of such things.

"What are you doing?" A harsh voice startled Helaine. It was Maxim, the overseer. Except for the night she'd secretly carried the silver to the loading dock, Helaine had managed to avoid him since coming to Lévitan. But now she was alone with him in the small office. He stood between her and the door, blocking her escape.

She froze. "Nothing."

He came closer, looming above her. "Don't lie. Why were you snooping around my office?" She could smell his breath, a foul mixture of cigarettes and rotting teeth.

Helaine swallowed. "I found my family's tea set among the boxes. I wanted to see if their house was listed as having been liquidated. If my mother has been taken."

Helaine braced herself for Maxim to deliver his sentence for her actions. "Did you find them?" he asked, sounding more curious now than angry.

"I didn't have the chance to look before you came in," Helaine confessed. "Can you check for me?" Helaine hated having to ask Maxim for anything at all, but she had no choice. "Please."

Maxim did not answer right away but leered at Helaine, clearly enjoying his power over her. He walked closer and leaned in so his face was just inches from hers. Helaine willed herself not to move, terrified of what he might do next. He stared at her for what felt like forever, seeming to breathe her in. Then he took the register, opening it slowly. "Her name?"

"Annette Weil."

He scanned the register. "I don't see her listed."

Helaine dared to hope. "Perhaps just the tea set was taken." Helaine heard how implausible the words sounded as she spoke them. Still, she desperately wanted to believe her mother might remain free.

Maxim shook his head. "If a person's belongings are here, then they've been arrested and their home liquidated." He spoke bluntly, not mincing words. "The records probably have not been updated yet."

The pit in Helaine's stomach grew. Her father might have been away on business, but Maman would certainly have been home when the Germans came. Helaine had to get to her mother. "Taken where?" she asked, dreading the answer she knew would come even as she asked.

"Drancy."

Helaine's heart screamed. The notion of her mother withstanding the horrors of the camp was unbearable. "Tell me how I can get to see my mother. Please."

Maxim set down the ledger, laughed harshly at Helaine's plea. "You can't. It's impossible."

But Helaine would not be dissuaded. "I know people leave here on passes sometimes for the doctor and such."

"Yes, but this is different. To go to Drancy would mean death for you. You would not come back."

"My mother can't possibly stay in Drancy. She won't last. Can she be brought here as a worker?" Helaine's voice trailed off at the end. Without special skills or connections, there was no way to make that happen.

Maxim shook his head. "That's ridiculous. Only those with the official designation are eligible." Sadness engulfed Helaine. She could not save her mother.

He took a step closer to her. "But I could help you check on her, send word." He reached out and brushed a lock of hair from her forehead with his filthy finger. It took everything Helaine had not to slap him. He was asking her to do the unthinkable simply to send word to Maman. But it was the only hope she had, a lifeline, and for a moment, Helaine considered it.

Miriam appeared then in the doorway to the office. "Helaine!" she said with mock harshness. "Where did you go? You are needed on the sorting line." She stepped into the office and reached around Maxim. Then she grabbed Helaine's arm and pulled her away out of ear shot. "What on earth were you doing in Maxim's office? I told you never to go in there. If I hadn't come just then…"

"I know. But I needed to find out more about what happened to my mother." Tears filled her eyes. "Maxim said she's likely been sent to Drancy. I have to go to her."

"You can't possibly," Miriam chided.

"But I cannot just leave her."

"If you go to see her, you will not be allowed to leave. You must understand, Drancy is a transit camp. Thousands of Jews pass through there, but no one stays long. There's a very good chance to think she has already been sent east, or will be soon."

Helaine's mind reeled back to the day she had seen her mother at the market. Maman was gone now, likely forever. She thought of the moment they embraced, tried to conjure the smell of her. It was almost as if they had known then it was the last time that they would be together.

"But my mother, she's not strong enough to endure the

camps." Maman was a grand lady who had always been sheltered and surrounded by comfort. She was simply unprepared for such a life.

Miriam put her arm around Helaine and stroked her back lovingly. "This war has forced all of us to face circumstances we did not expect and find strength we did not know we had."

"I have to do something. Maxim said I could send a letter."

Miriam shook her head. "Maxim is a liar. You must never trust or rely on him. The prisoners at Drancy cannot receive regular mail like we do here." She paused, thinking. "Still, you could try to reach her. Sometimes the truck drivers can be bribed to deliver packages or messages for a price." Miriam looked back into the office to make sure Maxim was gone, then walked in and snatched a piece of paper and a stub of pencil. "Write your mother a letter and I will do my best to get it delivered."

That night after the others had gone to sleep, Helaine carried the paper and pencil over to the windowsill. Her heart broke as she imagined her mother in a place a thousand times worse than this. What could she say to give her hope?

Dearest Maman,
I know you have been taken. I'm in the department store Lévitan and things are not so bad here. Be strong and I will come for you if I can. I am sorry for everything.
Love,
Your Laina

Helaine finished writing, then set down the pencil sadly. Her mother had loved her more unconditionally than anyone, except perhaps Gabriel, ever had. Why had they wasted so much foolish time on anger? They never should have stayed apart when they could have been together.

Helaine fell into a deep depression after that. She had no family left except for Gabriel and she had to find him.

One day, as she passed by the hall during Sunday visiting, Helaine spied a familiar face at the counter, checking in. "Isa?" she said with disbelief. Despite the fact that they had not parted well, Helaine was overjoyed to see her friend.

"You're here!" Isa threw her arms around Helaine, then pulled back to look at her. "Are you all right?"

Helaine considered the question. Nothing about Lévitan was all right, not the heavy labor nor the limited food. She knew she looked far worse than when Isa had last seen her. But she could not complain aloud. "I'm fine. What are you doing here?"

"I had not seen you in the neighborhood and I became worried. I had no idea you were arrested." No, of course not, Helaine thought. Because she had been taken from the police station and not her home, no one would have seen. It was as if she had simply disappeared. "But it took me a bit to realize you were gone, and even longer to figure out where."

"So how did you find me?"

"I went to the police station and asked. They told me nothing, of course. But a contact of my father's who formerly served as arts' minister in the prewar government made inquiries." Helaine was touched that her friend had gone to such lengths to find her.

"Here, I brought you this." Isa pulled out a small cloth bag, then looked around surreptitiously.

"It's all right. We are allowed to receive parcels." Helaine had seen other prisoners receive small packages of food and toiletries from visitors. The guards and Maxim were willing to look the other way as long as they were given a share of anything useful.

Helaine took the bag and opened it. Inside was some food, bread and cheese. "I gathered what I could," Isa explained. "And I brought you something else." She reached into her purse and pulled out a small, familiar leather book.

"My journal!"

"Yes, when I went to your apartment looking for you, the door was unlocked." Helaine did not know if she had forgotten

to lock the door accidentally or whether the Germans or someone else had been inside since it was vacant. "I hope you don't
mind. I saw your journal and I remembered how you loved to
write in it. I thought you might be glad to have it."

"I am." Helaine held the journal in both hands and pressed
it against her chest, savoring the connection to her past and the
outside world.

"How can I help?" Isa asked.

"You want to help now?" Despite Helaine's happiness at seeing Isa and her gratitude for Isa's offer, she could not forget that
her friend had turned her back on her, and the painful memories sprang up now. "You kicked me out of the garden, went
along with their rules."

"I know. I didn't help you before and I'm sorry. I was afraid.
Only, I see now that no one is safe. But I'm here now and I will
do whatever I can. Tell me what you need."

Helaine thought of all the assistance she needed. Isa could not
get her out. She could not help Helaine find or free her mother.
But perhaps she might be able to get word to Gabriel. "I need
to find Gabriel."

"Yes, of course. But how?"

"Gabriel is supposed to be on tour. Only I found out he isn't
touring with the symphony, so I don't know with whom or
where he has gone. Please use your father's connections to find
him and tell him where I am."

"I will try," Isa promised. Then she paused and her forehead
crinkled with consternation. "But there's one thing. There are
rumors about Gabriel."

"Rumors?" Helaine stiffened, fearing Isa would say she had
heard Gabriel had been with another woman.

"Yes, that he is working with the Germans."

"That's ridiculous," Helaine scoffed. She recalled how Gabriel
had run off to his secret resistance meetings, refused to play the

works of German composers, even if it meant not playing at all. There was no way Gabriel was a collaborator.

"Helaine, he went to Germany to play music for them."

"I know, and I know how that must look. He was forced to go. He had no choice." Gabriel would never in a million years conspire with the Germans; of that Helaine was certain. But the questions, not just about where he was but what he was doing, bubbled up. Helaine needed to find him. She needed to know that he was safe and she needed answers. "Please, you must try to reach him for me."

"I will do my best. I have to go now. Stay safe and I will be in touch soon."

Helaine felt an immediate pang of regret at parting from her friend, the only person she still had contact with beyond the walls of the department store. "Thank you."

Isa squeezed Helaine's hand and then she was gone.

Helaine returned to the dormitory, which was empty at midday. She paged through the journal, rereading. Each entry was not just a story. They read now like a precious chronicle of all that she had lost. A tear fell from her eye, dropping to the page and staining it. She closed the journal, overwhelmed with sadness.

Then she opened the front cover once more and added Gabriel's surname after her own. *Helaine Weil Lemarque.* It made her somehow feel more connected to him, more whole. But she couldn't leave the journal out, in case someone found or confiscated it. She pried back the piece of drywall where she had hidden the necklace, digging at it to widen the space enough for the journal, and tucked it away, out of sight.

15

Louise

Paris, 1953

I awaken early the next morning. As I look around the hotel room, I recall all that had happened the previous night: Our conversation and quarrel. Ian's confession that he once had feelings for me—and I for him. Our kiss. I push that last part aside; it has no bearing on why I have come to Paris or finding out about the necklace or the truth about Franny's death.

Franny. Her death, and my grief about it, arises in me anew, stirred up by all that I have learned in Paris. I had not known Franny long before she died. We had formed an instant connection, though. That—and the sudden way she had been taken—made my grief outsized beyond our brief friendship. How could someone as young and vibrant as Franny be snuffed out like a candle? Struck by a car, that had always been the official answer. But her death, right after I saw Franny take the necklace from the man, had shortly made me suspect there was something more.

As I dress, my thoughts shift to what Ian had told me about the Red Cross the previous night: they had seen what was happening in the camps. After the war, governments had claimed not to know what was happening to the Jews of Europe as a justification for failing to help. The Red Cross had been inside the camps, though, not just the POW camps like the ones we had visited, but some of the camps where the Germans imprisoned and killed the Jews. Its representatives had witnessed the atrocities firsthand. And still they did nothing.

But that has nothing to do with Franny's death, and I need to focus on that. Franny had been angry with Ian because he would not help deliver the necklace for the cellist. She had been angry with me for the same reason, I think, my guilt redoubling. She was determined to deliver it herself. If someone wanted to stop her... I pause, then dismiss the far-fetched idea.

The necklace, I am still certain, is the key to finding out what had happened to Franny, more so than any conspiracy theories about the Red Cross. It had disappeared—seemingly forever—the night Franny died. Or at least it had until it appeared in the charity shop where I work, out of the blue, like a hand reaching down from the heavens and tapping me. I have to find out where it came from.

In the distance, cathedral bells toll nine. I start down to the lobby. In the lift, I consider what I will say about the previous night. Part of me wants to tell Ian that we need to put all of this silliness between us aside and figure out the secret behind the necklace. Perhaps he will not bring it up and we can forget all about it.

The lobby is bustling with businessmen and other visitors starting their day. But Ian is not there. He is probably sitting in the hotel bistro eating a big breakfast, I decide, when we really need to get to the business at hand.

I walk to the bistro and scan the patrons seated at tables. Ian is not among them.

I go to the hotel front desk and give my name. "Are there any messages for me?" The clerk shakes his head.

Perplexed now, I start from the hotel. I walk to the phone booth at the corner and ring Ian's office.

"This is Louise Burns, I mean Emmons," I say when the receptionist answers. "Is Ian Shipley there?"

"He isn't in," the receptionist replies. My heartbeat quickens. Ian was supposed to help me today. Perhaps he had taken the day off. But then why isn't he here?

Now I am annoyed. Ian has not even given me the consideration to leave word that he wouldn't be here as promised. He knew we were going to see the man who had been imprisoned at Lévitan first thing. I consider waiting a bit longer to see if he returns, then decide against it. I don't need Ian for this. This is still my mission and I am happy to manage it alone. The man might be less likely to talk if I bring a second person anyhow.

I return upstairs to my room to retrieve the necklace before heading out. I check the nightstand, but the necklace isn't there. Panic rises in me. Had I lost it? I remember then how I had given it to Ian the previous night. He had set it down on the nightstand and I had forgotten to put it back in my purse. It should still be there, but I do not see it.

Stay calm, I think. Ian must have put it somewhere for safekeeping. I walk to the nightstand and open the drawer. Except for a copy of the Bible, it is empty. I check the floor around the nightstand in case it has fallen to the ground. Nothing. Ian likely took it with him. But why? And where is he? I look at the clock on the wall. It is after nine o'clock and the car I arranged will be outside now. I cannot wait any longer. I will have to go without him.

I set out, and as I cross the street toward the hired car waiting for me, I berate myself for being so careless. I never should have left the necklace behind. Now I have to go see the man who was imprisoned in the department store without the very thing I am going to ask him about.

Twenty minutes later, I step out of the car onto Rue Sainte-

Marthe. Far from the polished city center, Belleville is a working-class neighborhood. The houses are more dilapidated and narrower, seeming to lean on each other. Laundry hangs from the wrought iron fire escapes above and the smell of something garlicky cooking wafts from a half-open window.

I walk to the address Madame Dupree gave me, then hesitate. I feel bad calling unannounced, but I didn't have a phone number. Even if I did, the man might have been less likely to speak with me if I rang.

I scan the column of door buzzers, then push the bottom one, which has the name *Brandon, H.* listed beside it. There is no answer. Perhaps the address Madame Dupree gave me is outdated and the man no longer lives here. When I push it again and there is no response, I open the door to the apartment building. The lobby is dusty and the wallpaper peeling. I ascend the stairs, my footsteps echoing too loudly through the open space. I expect someone to emerge from one of the apartments, ask what I am doing there and tell me to leave. No one does.

I reach the top landing, my breathing slightly heavy from the climb. There is a lone door and I knock softly, wondering if there will be no answer once again. "Monsieur Brandon?"

"Oui. Who is it?" a raspy voice calls. I hear in it an apprehension, left from the wartime days when an unexpected knock often meant trouble.

"I'm Louise Burns and I've come from England. I was given your name by a woman at the pharmacy on Rue Faubourg du Saint-Martin."

There is a pause. "Come in," the voice says at last. Inside, a man is seated in a chair in semidarkness. I cannot tell how old he is for the war had aged so many before their time, but his hands and face are flecked with brown age spots.

"Monsieur Brandon?" He nods in acknowledgment. "I'm sorry to disturb you. Madame Dupree sent me."

He smiles. "She's a good woman." He gestures to a chair close to his. "Please, sit down." Then his expression turns puzzled. "Why have you come?"

I lower myself into the chair before replying. "I wanted to ask about Lévitan."

There is no response for several seconds and I worry that he will refuse to speak with me.

"The camp?" Monsieur Brandon seems to shudder. "No one has talked about that in years. I'd rather forget it, personally." His voice wobbles and his eyes dart away. "It was hell."

"I'm so sorry." I regret having to bring up memories so painful to him.

"They put us there because of our so-called 'privileged status' or special skills, and we did have it better than those in the camps in the east. But it was horrendous. Many suffered and died. And afterward, it was as if we had no right to talk about what happened to us among those who had been through worse."

I should just go, I think remorsefully. In trying to put my own questions about the past to rest, I have stirred up painful memories for others. But I have come too far to give up without trying now. I need to ask my questions and then leave this man in peace. "Monsieur, I'm terribly sorry to come here and bring up such painful memories. But I was hoping that you could help me. You see, I found a necklace in a box that was marked Lévitan and I came to Paris to learn more about it. In my search, I met Madame Dupree and discovered what went on at Lévitan during the war. I'm trying to see if there is any connection between the necklace and the store."

"Can I see the necklace?"

"I'm afraid I don't have it with me," I say, feeling foolish. "A colleague of mine has it and he's...not here. It is gold and shaped like a half heart."

"I see." The man scratches his chin, as if thinking. "I don't think the necklace would have come from Lévitan. The department store was used to sell Jewish goods. But it was mostly housewares, china, that sort of thing. There wasn't a jewelry counter, though, so the necklace wouldn't have been sold in the store." His words are a refrain of the managing director's the previous day, confirming the lack of a connection.

"Perhaps it belonged to one of the Jews imprisoned there," I suggest.

"That would have been impossible," he replies. "Most of the Jews were thoroughly searched upon arrest, and their valuables were confiscated. And even if someone was able to smuggle something past the guards, they would have kept it hidden. In any event, I'm certain that I never saw a necklace like the one you describe during my time at Lévitan."

My shoulders slump with disappointment. "Thank you anyway." I stand to go.

"Wait a moment," Monsieur Brandon says. He gestures for me to sit once more. "Why is finding out about the necklace so important to you? If you tell me more, then perhaps I can be of some help."

His wide brown eyes peer out at me from behind his spectacles, demanding an explanation as the price for my coming here and interrupting his solitude. "Because I think the necklace is the same one I saw a man give my friend in one of the camps just before she died. And I'm hoping that finding out its origin will give me some of the answers I seek about her death." I brace myself for the skeptical expression that always comes when I tell someone this, followed by condescending or dismissive words.

But his face remains somber and attentive. "Tell me about your friend."

"Her name was Franny Beck and she was a great stage actress. She was singing for the prisoners in the camp. A musician, a cellist who was accompanying her, had given her the necklace."

"Wait a moment. Did you say cellist?"

"Yes, why?"

"Mon Dieu!" he exclaims. He pauses, rubbing his chin in

thought. "There was a woman in Lévitan who was married to a cellist. I remember because there was an article in the news-paper, which one of the prisoners had, that said the cellist was playing in Germany. There was some allegation that he was a collaborator." Ian had said as much, I recall, my excitement ris-ing. We were talking about the same man. "There was a rumor that he might have even come to see her once at the store."

"Was his name Gabriel Lemarque?"

His eyes brighten with recognition. "Yes, that sounds right. I'm afraid I don't remember his wife's name, though. It was something like Helen or Elaine. I'm sorry not to have more information, but memories escape me." He rubs at his temple. "I've blocked so much out from those years." I understand; like Joe, forgetting is a form of self-preservation. "I wish I could be of more help."

"That's all right. You *have* helped, a great deal, and I appre-ciate it. But if you think of anything else, please send word." I scribble down my contact information on a scrap of paper and hand it to him. "This is my address back in England. I'm staying at the Meridien hotel, but for how much longer, I do not know."

"Good luck. Whatever answers you are looking for, I hope that you find them."

"Thank you."

I hurry from the apartment building and into the car that is waiting for me at the curb. As the driver pulls into traffic, I gaze out the window as the Paris streets roll by, considering all I have learned. The connection is now clearer: the cellist had tried to get Franny to take the necklace to his wife imprisoned at Lévitan, though I do not know why. Maybe he was sending a message to let her know he was alive. But Franny had died almost immediately after, yet the necklace had somehow made it to Lévitan. How had the cellist managed to get it to his wife after Franny died? And why was it so important to him that she receive it?

The film, I remember. Perhaps Gabriel was not only trying to deliver the necklace, but what was inside. I had taken it out of the necklace and put it in my purse. So even though Ian has the necklace, I still have the film. I lean forward to the driver. "Pardon, but do you suppose you could take me to a camera shop or somewhere else that can develop film?"

"Oui, madam." If he is surprised by the unusual request, he gives no indication. "I know of one not far from your hotel."

Ten minutes later, he pulls up alongside the curb in front of a shop with *La Photographie* etched in the glass window. "Shall I wait for you?" he asks.

Recognizing the street we are on, I know that my hotel is just around the corner. "I'll walk back, but thank you." I go into the store and a bell tinkles overhead, announcing my arrival. It is small and cluttered, with different cameras and other film apparatuses placed precariously on the crowded shelves.

I walk to the counter in the back of the store, where a man with a trim goatee looks at me, not speaking.

"Bonjour," I say, then hold out the film. "Can you develop this for me?"

He takes the film from me and holds it up to the light, studying it. "It's somewhat old and I will need special equipment to manage it. Two days."

My heart sinks. I do not have two days. I need to get home to Joe and the children. And while I can take the film back to England with me and have it developed there, something tells me that any answers it contains will be most helpful right here in Paris. "Is there any way you can do it faster? Please. I can pay extra." I reach into my bag and pull out a few of my precious remaining francs, then pass them to him.

The man sniffs and takes the francs. "Come today after four."

I leave the store and set out down the street, eager to find Ian and share all I have learned. But where is he? I pull his business card from my purse and turn it over. On the back, Ian had scrawled his home address: *29 Rue de la Hutchette #2*. Wishing I had not sent the hired car away, I walk to the taxi stand at the corner, get into the first waiting cab and give the driver Ian's address. "Is it far?"

"Across the river in the Latin Quarter," the driver says. The cab pulls away from the curb and accelerates through the street.

As we start to cross the Pont Neuf and the Seine, I take in Notre-Dame, bathed in sunlight. Paris, more so than ever, seems a city of buried secrets. I know now that the cellist was trying to get the necklace to his wife in Lévitan. But I am no closer to learning what that has to do with Franny's death.

After the bridge, the cab drives into the tangle of streets that make up the Left Bank. I am surprised that Ian lives here and not in a more posh neighborhood close to the embassy.

We pull up on a side street lined with row houses. I pay the driver and get out and then walk up to the door of the address Ian gave me. Inside on the second floor, I find the apartment marked #2 and knock. There is no answer.

Across the hallway, a door flies open and a woman in a house-coat appears. "What are you doing here?" she asks rudely.

"I'm looking for Monsieur Shipley. Have you seen him?"

"Non." She shakes her head. "I'm the owner of the house and I rented the room to him, but I have not seen him this morning."

"My name is Louise Burns. I'm a friend from England. I've knocked and he isn't answering and I'm concerned. Can you let me in so I can check on him?"

She eyes me warily and then returns into her apartment and gets a set of keys. She unlocks the door to Ian's apartment. "Hello?" she calls inside. There is silence. She turns to me. "As you can see, he isn't here."

"Yes, but…" I stall, searching for some pretext to get inside the apartment and look for the necklace, or at least a clue as to where he has gone. "I left my scarf last night. If I can just see if it's here."

She eyes me warily, then takes a step back to let me pass. "Two minutes. I shouldn't be letting you in."

Inside, the apartment is bare.

"It looks like he left," the landlady remarks. "He better still pay me for the last month's rent."

For a moment, I wonder if I have made a mistake. I double-check the address on the card. It is correct. But the place where Ian claims to live looks as if no one has ever lived there at all. I am confused, about so many things. But I know one thing for sure.

Ian is gone, and so is the necklace.

CD

Germany, 1944

"No!" I cried. "Franny!" She lay lifeless on the side of the road, close to the draining ditch. Her limbs were splayed elegantly, a show woman even in death. A few of the guards from the camp stood nearby, staring but keeping their distance.

I looked away from her, unable to bear the sight. My mind raced, searching for answers. She might be unconscious, I thought desperately. Perhaps she had fallen and hit her head. "Call the medics!" I cried, but the guards did not move.

"She was struck by a car," a voice I didn't recognize said behind me. But it didn't make sense. Franny always walked after dark. She knew not to walk in the road so as not to risk getting hit. The car engine would have been loud in the night silence. She would have moved out of the way if it got too close. And most importantly, if she had been hit by a car, there would have been bruises and broken bones. Instead, Franny's beautiful appearance was perfectly intact.

I forced myself to look at Franny once more, searching for answers. She was lying in the same peaceful position I had seen her in so many nights as she slept. Her arms were splayed above her head in a kind of surrender. I watched her chest, willing it to rise and fall with breath. Though I knew she could not be asleep, I prayed that she somehow was.

"No!" I cried again, dropping to the ground beside her. I wanted to rewind the scene and go back to the moment when I had left her alone in the field, refusing to help. If I had said yes, she might have come to bed, instead of going out walking. Could I have stopped this from happening?

My cries had drawn others and someone behind me pulled me away. A siren wailed in the distance, growing louder as an ambulance neared. Of course, it was too late. The medics came, but they didn't rush. Their movements were slow and methodical, and they lowered a stretcher beside her. Why weren't they doing more? They should be working to resuscitate her. Instead, they lifted her onto the stretcher and covered her with a blanket.

"Lou…" Ian rushed up behind me. Though I didn't take my eyes from Franny, I could feel the same emotions cascade over him as they had me: shock, then horror and devastation. He wrapped his arms around me and turned me toward him. I buried my face in his coat, not watching as the military police carried Franny away on the stretcher.

Someone led me away from Ian and into one of the buildings, wrapped a blanket around me and brought me tea. Outside I could see Ian directing people, taking charge, his eyes dark knots and his face creased with pain.

I sat numbly, unsure how much time had passed. Finally, Ian came into the room, and I ran to him and threw myself into his arms, not caring who noticed. "What happened?"

"A car hit her while she was walking." I noticed that his eyes were red as though he had been crying. "The road was dark, and the driver must not have seen her."

"Do they have him?" Why, I wondered, did I presume it was a man? "The person who hit her, I mean."

"No. I'm afraid he drove off before anyone arrived."

"Did anyone see the car?"

"No one."

"Then how do we know it was an accident?"

Ian looked genuinely puzzled. "What else could it have been?"

"I don't know." The notion that someone could have hit Franny on purpose sounded too preposterous to voice aloud. But nothing about this situation made any sense.

"Come, we have work to do. Another pallet of packages arrived and they need to be distributed before it rains." I stared at him in disbelief. Did he really expect us to press on with operations just hours after Franny had died? But he was right: the work was the work and it had to be done. Lives depended on getting the rations contained in the care packages.

I tried to carry on as best I could that day delivering the rest of the care packages. Franny would have wanted it that way. But her absence was a gaping hole in our world. Tears streamed down my face and my limbs were leaden. I thought ahead to the evening when Franny normally would have been getting ready to perform and the stage that would remain forever dark.

When we neared the end of the workday, Ian came to me. "Where will you stay tonight?" he asked.

"What do you mean?"

He gestured toward the railcar. "After everything that has happened, I didn't think you would want to be in there alone." I had not thought of it before, but I could see his point. The railcar had been Franny's and mine. How could I be there without her?

I followed him wordlessly to his railcar, a duplicate of our own, except for his belongings. I considered the impropriety of us staying in the same space. But after what had happened to Franny, right and wrong didn't matter anymore, not here.

I sat down on the bed and he looked at me uncertainly. "It's all right," I said, indicating the space beside me.

"Are you certain? I don't mind sleeping on the floor."

"It's fine." I knew it was not proper. But nothing was as it should be anymore. And why had I come here, if not to be close to him?

We lay side by side, not touching.

As I lay awake beside Ian, little snippets of the past few days began to appear in my mind: Franny talking to the man by the fence, the necklace she had asked me to carry. I gathered the scraps together like a bird building a nest, trying to make sense of it all. Franny would have been performing now. I saw her face, illuminated on the stage, and heard her voice, soaring across the sorrowful camp and bringing joy. Then the image flickered and was gone.

My grief rose up like a wave. I moved closer to Ian for comfort. Mistaking this for something else, he reached for me then. His lips were on mine, body pressed close. I wanted to tell him that we should not do this. It was the wrong thing and the wrong time, for all of the wrong reasons. I was not entirely naive about men. I had dated Joe. We'd had some stolen moments, kissing in the darkness of the park, in the movie theater. I'd even been back to his dormitory once or twice. But I'd always stopped short. I'd seen what wrong decisions had done to my mum. I didn't want to wind up alone with a baby and no way to support myself.

But passion exploded inside me then, eclipsing logic, and I kissed Ian back with equal intensity. I needed to feel alive. This was not just about our shared grief. The attraction between us was undeniable and real. We tore off each other's clothes and I let myself be carried from this terrible place to somewhere that pain and suffering no longer existed.

Afterward, I was filled with remorse. What had I done? My friend was gone not a day and I was engaging in some silly affair with my boss in a place that could not be more inappropriate.

I gathered my clothes and slipped from his railcar. I returned to the space I had shared with Franny just a day earlier, feeling sadder and more alone than ever.

Then I put my face in my pillow and sobbed.

16

Helaine

Paris, 1944

Helaine looked out of the window now, across the gray slate rooftops of Paris. It was March and the days were getting longer, she noticed. "Spring is coming," Miriam remarked, coming up behind her and seeming to read her mind. Helaine's favorite season had always been spring, especially after marrying Gabriel and enjoying their evening walks as the weather began to warm and the willow trees along the Seine grew buds. But the prospect of pleasant weather beyond the walls of their prison seemed a taunt now, and the memories of walks she could no longer have brought more pain than joy.

"I've been tasked with cleanup," Miriam said, coughing. "Help me?" Cleanup was the job of going through the store in the evening and straightening all of the displays. It was not the most onerous job, but Helaine hated that elderly, sick women like Miriam had to work at all.

They walked down to the main floor of the shop and began to refold a pile of silk scarves that had been carelessly scattered by a German visitor. Behind a counter on the floor, there was a lone silk glove, white and unstained. Helaine picked it up. It was too pristine to have come from among the plunder. She guessed that it was left behind by the days of the store's grandeur, a relic from times gone by.

Helaine looked up at the vaulted ceiling of the shop. "I remember coming here as a child and it felt like the grandest place in the world." She gestured widely. "Now look at it."

"Ah, yes, Lévitan in its heyday." Miriam smiled at the memory.

When they finished straightening up, they returned to the dormitory, where the others had gathered to eat. Helaine noticed a woman whose name she could not remember at the far end of the room pointing at her and whispering. "What is it?" Helaine asked the woman loudly, suddenly nervous.

"How is it that you are here?" the woman asked. She stood and walked toward Helaine, arms crossed. She was called Chava, Helaine recalled then, though they had seldom spoken. "What status has kept you from Drancy?"

It dawned on Helaine then what she was asking. All of the other prisoners had been assigned to Lévitan due to a special status, wife of a foreigner or military officer, etc. Something that made them worthy of better treatment, even protection. Chava was demanding to know what Helaine had done to deserve that. "My husband is a musician," Helaine offered, realizing even as she said it that the explanation was not enough. Being married to a cellist did not accord her a status that was worthy of the department store. "My father is a prominent businessman. Perhaps it is because of that." But if that were the case, Helaine reflected, her mother would have been able to come to the store as well.

"Or perhaps," Chava said, "it is because your husband is a collaborator." She nearly spat the last word. A collective gasp went up among the others in the room. Indignation rose in Helaine. How dare she? Collaborating with the Germans was the most serious of offenses among prisoners. It also was not an accusation one dared to make lightly, though, and Helaine knew immediately that she must have a basis for the claim. Isa had suggested it as well.

Helaine opened her mouth to protest, but before she could respond, Chava held up a newspaper, several weeks old and undoubtedly left behind by a guard or Sunday visitor. "This." She pointed to an article announcing that a group of French musicians were playing in Germany. Gabriel's name was listed among them. "Your husband, he isn't missing. He's playing for the Germans. He must be sympathetic to them, or perhaps even helping their cause."

"You believe that rag?" Miriam scoffed. *Paris-Soir* was a collaborationist newspaper, little more than a puppet of the Germans. But it was one of their only forms of access to information about the outside world and many at Lévitan read it.

Helaine shifted uncomfortably. "That's a lie." But she scanned the news story; the truth in front of her was impossible to ignore. "He is performing for the POWs in the camps. He was forced to go. He was not given a choice." Her words were a refrain of the explanation she had given Isa when she visited.

"Your husband," Chava repeated, "is a traitor."

"No!" Helaine cried. "He only does as he is ordered." Helaine heard the hollowness of her own words. "Following orders" was the excuse of the French police and others who did the Germans' bidding. She hated that it was the only alibi she had for Gabriel now. Helaine remembered Gabriel's melancholy at the start of the war, the way he had almost smashed his cello rather than use it in service of the Germans. He could not be helping them. But there it was, a photo of him at a concert in Germany, looking well and smiling. Although she was relieved that Gabriel was alive and safe, her anger rose. Gabriel was performing willingly and he looked glad to be doing so. How could he be happy and free while she was in here?

"How do you think your husband avoided the same fate as the other artists?" Chava sneered. "He is a collaborator!"

Shaken, Helaine stormed from the dormitory. Miriam followed her. "Pay Chava no attention. She's terrible." Miriam paused. "Your husband, how long were you married?"

"A few years," Helaine replied. Inwardly, her doubts grew. They had married so quickly, though. She really had not known Gabriel at all. And there was no one from his past life, no parents or siblings. What secrets might he have kept from her?

Helaine tried to push away her doubts. She loved Gabriel, knew him. But still her questions persisted. What was he doing and why? She needed to see him and learn the truth.

A few days later, as they were preparing to begin the day's work, Helaine saw Miriam toying with something over by her cot. Helaine approached and Miriam tried to hide the object, but it was too late. She had seen it was a metal file. "What are you doing?" Helaine demanded in a low voice.

"Leaving. I'm going to get out of here," Miriam replied. Her voice was steely with determination. "I'm going to climb down the fire escape and ride one of the trucks out of here, then jump."

"And the file?"

"In case the door is locked and I need to open it."

Helaine's eyes widened. Escape was one of the things she dreamed about most often, second only to reuniting with Gabriel. But contemplating it was one thing; actually planning to attempt it quite another. Though Miriam had talked about it on several occasions, Helaine had not thought she was serious. "They will kill you if you are caught. And if the Germans discover you missing, the rest of us will pay. Don't you remember what happened with Ava?"

Helaine's mind reeled back to weeks earlier, when she had seen another woman about the same age as herself prying open one of the windows. "Ava, don't!" If she wasn't caught, she might fall to her death from the high ledge outside.

"I'm sorry," the girl said as she hoisted herself over the window ledge. And then she was gone.

The next day, Ava's bed was stripped bare. "Caught and deported," Miriam said. How far had she gotten before she was captured? In reprisal for Ava's escape attempt, the other prisoners had their rations halved and their work doubled for one week. Helaine shuddered now at the memory of hunger on those terrible days.

But Miriam would not be dissuaded now. "I will make it," she said resolutely. She did not see the limitations of her age, nor the obstacles in her path to freedom. The possibility of escape was the fuel that sustained her and the hope that kept her going. "I don't know how much time I have left." Though they had not discussed it openly, Miriam's cough had worsened over the time they had been imprisoned in Lévitan, signaling a more dire illness. "I'm not going to spend it in here. I'm going to get out somehow."

"Miriam, no!" Miriam had to be close to seventy. How could she possibly manage it? The department store, however terrible, was surely better than where she would find herself if she was caught.

"You think they are going to keep us here forever?" Miriam asked. "Wherever they send us, it will be worse. We have to leave now before it is too late. You should come with me. You know the only way you are going to find out what is really going on with your husband is to get out of Lévitan and find him."

Helaine shook her head. She wasn't brave enough to try to escape. She could not.

Later that afternoon as Helaine worked, she was summoned from the sorting line. She leaped up, praying that she was not in trouble or worse. "You are needed on the second floor," the guard said tersely. Helaine froze with fear. She had never been pulled from the line before. What could this possibly be about? The second and third floors were a storage space between the main floor of the department store, where goods were displayed, and the dormitory above. When she ascended the stairs, another guard pointed Helaine toward the back of the floor. Helaine's heart pounded as she walked with dread through rows of plunder too large or broken to be displayed, mattresses and mismatched armories. Farther back, there were grand pianos and other musical instruments. Despite her worry at being summoned here, Helaine could not help but marvel at the work the Germans had put into stripping Jews of such unwieldy items. What could they possibly hope to do with all of this?

Suddenly, Helaine heard a commotion from the back of the storeroom. She jumped, fearing some sort of attack. She expected to see Maxim lunge out at her, her worst nightmare finally coming true. Before she could turn and flee, a familiar voice called out her name. "Laina!"

She spun in the direction from which it had come. As if in a dream, her husband appeared before her eyes.

"Gabriel!" Helaine cried. She ran to him, touching him to make sure he was not a figment of her imagination. Without a word, Gabriel drew Helaine into his embrace. His lips met hers. His beard was matted and his scent was pungent from not washing. But it did not matter. Everything she had been longing for all of this time had suddenly and unexpectedly come true.

He kissed her passionately. "Thank God I found you."

"But how?"

"Isa managed to get word to me. I had no idea you had been arrested."

"I tried to send a letter."

"Did you? I never received it. But when I learned of your arrest from Isa, I knew that I had to come and make sure you were all right. I left straightaway. I made my way to Paris on foot."

"But how did you get in here?" Sunday visitors were permitted, but to sneak in unannounced was another thing entirely.

"I bribed one of the movers who had a key and was able to

go up the stairs. That and a bottle of schnapps for the guard did the trick." He smiled. "And here I am."

Here he was. The reunion that Helaine had dreamed of for so many months had now come true.

"Gabriel..." Helaine hesitated. The last thing she wanted to do now was quarrel with him. But she had to know the truth. "When I went to the Conservatoire, they said that you were not touring with the symphony, that they were no longer playing due to the war. How can that be?"

"It is true that the symphony disbanded. But I was invited to Germany to play with a smaller group of musicians and I felt that I couldn't refuse. I'm sorry if I didn't make that clearer before I left." His explanation was so simple that Helaine fleetingly doubted whether she should believe it. But it was Gabriel, *her* Gabriel, telling her this and looking deeply into her eyes, so how could it possibly be untrue? "What matters now is that we have found one another. Are you all right?"

"I'm fine," Helaine said, pushing aside the months of work and deprivation. Complaining about Lévitan was not how she wanted to spend their precious time together. "But my mother is in Drancy." Helaine's eyes teared as she thought about the terrible conditions she'd heard of at the camp.

"I'm so sorry. I wish that there was something we could do to help her. But I thank God that you are all right."

"I am now that you are here," she said, pressing herself close to him.

Neither of them spoke for several seconds. "The necklace, do you still have it?" she asked.

"I do." He reached into the collar of his shirt and pulled out the chain. "I wear it always close to my heart."

In that moment, she knew that she could trust her husband. He was a good man, and he loved her deeply. He gestured toward the necklace. "I'm never without it," he said.

"I have my half hidden in the dormitory where we sleep," she explained. "I don't wear it when I am working because I don't want the Germans to see it. I would be devastated if they confiscated it from me. And I don't keep it on me in case we are inspected and searched. I must be careful."

"When we reunite after the war, they will be together," Gabriel said.

"When will that be? And where?"

"I don't know," he replied honestly. "But they say things are going very badly for the Germans, so hopefully it will be soon."

It *needed* to be soon, Helaine thought. She pictured her mother in the camp, thought about her own precarious situation. None of them could hang on for much longer.

"But I might not see you again until the end of the war," Helaine lamented. *Or ever*, she finished silently.

"You must have faith." Helaine had never considered Gabriel a religious man. He was talking about something larger now, though, a belief that they were meant to be together when all of this was over.

"But where will we go after?" Helaine fretted. She saw the garret in Montmartre like a long-forgotten dream. Surely it had been taken or destroyed by now. Even if they made it through and found one another, their home was gone.

"*Laina*, we will have each other. Nothing else matters. Let's not worry about it now."

Still, Helaine's doubts remained. "How will we find each other?"

"Whatever happens, stay here and I will come for you," he pledged.

"But how?" Helaine asked with a note of desperation in her voice. "And from where?" He did not answer. How could he possibly know? "I'm glad you still have the necklace," Helaine confessed. "I sometimes worry, with so much time apart, that you might not want to be married anymore."

Gabriel looked at her with disbelief. "You think I might want to be with someone else?" he asked. He shook his head. "I can't even conceive of it. I only wish that you and I could be together now," he said bluntly.

It was their only moment together; who knew where and when they might be together again? But it was impossible here. The guard might come by on patrol at any time. She'd heard of a place in a back storeroom where couples sometimes went to be intimate. "Come with me," she whispered, taking his hand. Helaine led him to a spot in the very back corner of the storeroom, where no one could see. Nearby there was a pile of dusty blankets. She arranged them beneath one of the pianos so that they could lie down. Then she pulled him to her, not caring that it was the middle of the day or that they might get caught. They were alone together for the first time in more than a year, and she could feel his longing, as strong and deep as her own. Their clothes seemed to fall off of their own accord and their bodies met in a fiery crescendo unlike anything Helaine had ever experienced. Though she had longed for Gabriel in his absence, she had not realized how much she had missed and needed his touch. Here, in his arms, all of the suffering and hardship seemed to fade away, and she felt loved and beautiful again.

Afterward, they huddled beneath the piano. Gabriel drew one of the blankets around them, wrapping them in a cocoon. Helaine leaned her head against Gabriel's chest. Helaine could not help but lament how they had gotten here, making love on the dirty floor of a dusty, desolate storeroom. It seemed like just yesterday when they lay together in their Montmartre apartment, the city splayed below them and a canopy of stars above.

They lay in each other's arms until Helaine realized that Gabriel had dozed off, as if the effort of getting to her had taken all of his energy. Helaine might have slept, too; the long hours working in the store and restless nights in the dormitory left her constantly exhausted. But she did not want to waste a single moment of their precious time together. Instead, Helaine studied him, imagining his days and the things he had seen in the time they were apart. Gabriel looked like the same man she had married, but something had changed. He seemed older, eyes sunken, skin worn. She could only imagine how different she appeared to him than when they had last been together.

"Gabriel…" At last, Helaine roused him. She could not stay here too long without someone noticing that she was gone. He opened his eyes, and his face registered surprise, as though he was not certain where he was or why they were together again. Then, seeming to remember, he smiled broadly and drew her into his embrace once more.

Helaine did not know if they had much time left, and she did not want to ruin it. But she thought back to his earlier explanation of what he had been doing in Germany. It felt vague and somehow did not make sense. "Where have you been and what have you been doing this whole time?" Part of her was not sure she wanted to know the answers.

"Touring and playing in Germany. Mostly for senior officers at gatherings and parties. There are not so many larger concerts now that the halls have been bombed." Helaine had heard that the Allies had stepped up the air raids over Germany and was glad to know it was working. But Gabriel sounded almost remorseful. "When I rejoin the orchestra, we will be headed further into Germany to perform at a Wehrmacht base near Köln."

"How can you keep playing for them?" Helaine asked. The last thing she wanted was to fight with Gabriel during their precious time together. But Helaine had to know.

"What choice do I have? You've heard about Drancy. The camps in Germany are even worse. If I refuse, I will be imprisoned—and you could be deported to the east." He paused.

"Laina, there's more to it than that." He lowered his voice. "The truth is that we are not just playing. There is more to it than it seems. You must trust me."

"Tell me," Helaine demanded.

"I can't. For your own safety and for the safety of others." Gabriel spoke in a hushed tone, his voice urgent. "You must understand, this is complicated. There are things that I cannot discuss."

"What?" Helaine demanded, desperate to understand the truth. "I am your wife. You can tell me!" she pleaded.

"I'm sorry, I can't, not even with you. If you think me a traitor because I can't tell you, then so be it. The lives of too many depend on it. And it is best for your own safety that you do not know." Helaine folded her arms stubbornly. Gabriel was treating her like a child, being overprotective just as surely as her parents had. He continued, "I am the same man you fell in love with. We are the same. You must believe me."

"Then don't go back. Stay with me." Seeing him and having him leave again almost hurt worse than not seeing him at all.

"People vouched for me. They would pay with their lives if I did not return. Darling, come and let's enjoy our last few minutes together. Please," he said, taking her face in his hands. "I hate that you are here and we cannot be together. But you must hang on for a little longer and then I can come for you."

Helaine felt a pang of remorse. How could she possibly fight with him when they might never see one another again? She moved closer, pushing her questions away, and let Gabriel envelop her once more. He was here, but in just moments, he would be gone again. Her tears fell then, and she sobbed for all that they had lost and might never have again.

"No matter what happens, I will come for you. I love you." He lifted her chin, then wiped the tears from her cheeks. He pulled away reluctantly, then stood and started to get dressed.

When he finished, he knelt to kiss her once more. "Goodbye, Helaine." He straightened and turned to leave. His footsteps grew fainter as he walked away. Helaine wanted to run after him and wrap herself in his arms one more time, tell him that she loved him, too.

Of course, that was impossible. Gabriel was once again gone.

17

Louise

Paris, 1953

Later that afternoon, I find myself in yet another place I never thought I would go: the police prefect.

Earlier, after looking for Ian at his apartment, I'd stepped out onto the street, uncertain where to turn next. Ian was not at work, and his apartment looked as though no one had been there at all. I was out of leads. Annoyance rose, mixing with my concern. What if something had happened to him? He could have had some kind of accident, or worse. It seemed more likely that, after we had parted badly the previous evening, he might have decided not to help me at all. I had come here to find out about the necklace, if there was a connection to Franny's death. I would have to proceed on my own.

So I made my way to the local police prefect, situated in a small building on Rue Chauchat. It looks like any police station in Britain (or at least what I imagine—I've never actually been to one). There are metal desks and file cabinets, and cigarette smoke hangs in a halo below the ceiling. "I'd like to report a missing person," I tell the very young officer behind the front desk. "He's called Ian Shipley."

"How long has he been missing?" The policeman takes out a notebook and pencil.

"About twelve hours, I think."

I expect him to start writing down the information, but he does not. "That isn't missing. That's going out for a walk." He seems pleased with his own joke.

"This is serious. My friend disappeared rather quickly and I'm concerned for his safety."

He looks at me like I am a silly woman. "Maybe he simply left." He has seen this before, a woman abandoned by a man, wanting to make it into something more.

"There's something else," I press. "My necklace is missing, too."

"Did Monsieur Shipley give it to you? If so, perhaps he simply took it back."

"No, I brought it with me from England to France. And now it's gone."

"Are you saying that Monsieur Shipley stole it?" The policeman is looking at me evenly now. He reaches for his pencil. "For that, we can file a report."

"So for people, you have to wait longer than twelve hours, but for objects, you can search right away?" I ask. It is a refrain of my conversation with Madame Dupree the previous day, recalling how the Germans logged the belongings that came through Lévitan more precisely than the people to whom they belonged. The policeman does not reply. "Then, yes, I would like to file a report." I'm not certain that Ian took the necklace intentionally, but if saying so will get the police to help find him, I'll do it.

The policeman holds out a pack of Gauloises to me, and when I shake my head, he lights one for himself.

"Description?"

"He's about six feet tall with brown hair."

"No, I meant the necklace."

"Oh." I'd nearly forgotten for a second that the necklace is what the police are searching for, not Ian. "It's gold and shaped like half a heart. It has the words *watch* and *me* engraved on it."

"And the man you think took it?"

"His name is Ian Shipley," I say again.

"He's English as well?"

"Yes. I knew him from London. He works here in Paris now for the Foreign Office at the British Embassy. He worked for the Red Cross during the war."

"What kind of work does he do?"

"I'm not certain." I had not thought to ask. I realize then how very little I know about Ian and what he has been up to in the years since we had seen one another. How very little I really know about him at all.

"Did you come over to see him?"

"In a sense." I consider explaining the locket and Franny to the policeman, then decide against it. It occurs to me then that telling the police about the locket and my errand here may not be the best idea. I am loath to trust anyone right now, and bringing up Franny's death seems likely to only complicate matters when I need to be done here as soon as possible. If the people closest to me in the world do not understand the connection I see between the two, there is no point trying to explain it to a stranger.

"When did you see him last?" the policeman asks.

"Last night, we were at Le Petite Meridien. That's the hotel where I am staying."

"He was in your room?" The question seems too prying, irrelevant to the investigation.

"Yes." The policeman raises an eyebrow. "And in the lobby and we took a walk," I add hurriedly. "Why does that matter?"

"I'm only trying to understand your relationship so we can

figure out where he might have taken the necklace. Was it in your room?"

"No. That is, yes." I take a breath, trying to figure out the best way to explain it all. "I was carrying the necklace and I showed it to him. I thought he set it on the nightstand. Only, when I looked for it this morning, it was gone." *And so was Ian*, I think.

"So you gave it to him?"

"No, I *showed* it to him." My frustration rises. I am getting nowhere here. I pull out the business card Ian gave me and pass it to the police officer. "This is his home address." He copies down the information.

"We will look into it. You are staying at the Meridien?"

"Yes." I stand to leave.

"There's one other thing, madam," the officer says. "You ought to check if he has an address in London, if you have not already. Most often in times like this, missing people have simply gone home."

"Thank you." I take back the card and leave the police station quickly, eager to be out in the fresh air once more.

In the distance, cathedral bells toll six. The film, I remember suddenly. The man at the camera shop said to pick it up after four. Surely the shop is closed now.

I start back in the direction of the hotel, feeling my way through the unfamiliar streets. My mind races. Ian has disappeared without a trace—and he has taken the necklace with him. Why had Ian come to Paris in the first place? Maybe his motives were altogether different than I realized.

Ian is gone, I think as I reach the hotel. And so is the necklace. I will never really know the truth about what happened to Franny. I should pack up now and go back to England, resume my life. Upstairs in my room, I sink onto the bed. "I never should have come," I say aloud. What was I thinking coming here? I am a mum who should be with my family. Not in another country, trying to solve the mystery of someone's death. It is time, I decide, to go home.

I go back downstairs to the front desk of the hotel. "I need help booking passage to London," I say to the clerk.

"Let me check with our travel bureau." He goes to the office behind the desk and picks up a phone, and I can see him talking in a low voice, but I cannot make out what he is saying. A few minutes later, he returns to me. "The next ferry is tomorrow at three from Calais. I can book you on a train at ten in the morning from Gare du Nord."

"That will be fine, thank you." I hate the idea of spending another night away from Joe and the kids, but there is no other choice. At least this will give me time to try to pick up the developed image from the film I left at the camera shop.

I hand him the money to pay for my trip and then walk to the bistro and order a sandwich for takeaway. When my food is ready, I take it back to the room and lock the door. I eat, then pack the few things I had brought. I imagine the children, waking up to another morning without Mummy. With any luck, I can be there tomorrow for bedtime.

I do not change into my nightclothes but sit atop the still-made bed, fully dressed with the lights on, too nervous to sleep. To pass the time, I think of my family. I brace myself to go home and make things right with Joe, planning how I will apologize for leaving and explain everything that happened. I pray that he will forgive me, that it isn't too late. I am prepared to put the past behind me and live my life. I only hope it will still be there waiting for me now that I am ready to take it.

Despite my nervousness, my eyes grow heavy, and I doze off as the hour grows late. Sometime later, I awake with a start. I do not know how much time has passed. The lights are still on in the room. But through a crack in the window curtains, I can see the faintest pink, the gray sky lightening above the rooftops. It is morning, or almost. Time to go home.

As I stand, I hear footsteps in the hallway, drawing nearer. I imagine that it is Ian and his disappearance was a terrible dream. I expect to see him holding the necklace and talking about our next steps in finding its owner. I start for the door, then stop myself again, calming my expectations. More likely it is another guest, walking to their room. Or housekeeping, though it seems too early for that.

The footsteps stop outside my door. But the person on the other side does not knock. Instead, they turn the knob. Whoever is trying to get in has a key. I search frantically for a weapon but find nothing except a parasol. Desperately, I pick it up and raise it above my head, prepared to strike whoever stands on the other side of the door. It won't be enough to do any real harm, but maybe it will stun the intruder for a few seconds so that I can flee. This is no longer just about the locket and the fate of the person who had owned it. There is a larger truth from the past that it held and someone who will stop at nothing to keep me from finding it.

I stand motionless, on edge, and prepared to strike.

ॐ

Germany, 1944

I barely slept that first full night after Franny died. When dawn finally came, I awoke and dressed. Outside, the accident scene had been cleared. It was as if it had never happened.

Except that it *had* happened. Franny was dead. One minute, Franny had been vivacious and alive on the stage and the next minute gone. To have someone as young and beautiful as Franny, who had always seemed so invincible and larger than life, snatched in an instant felt stunning and wrong.

I went to see Ian in his railcar once more. In the doorway, I stopped. Images of the previous night flashed before my eyes and I was suddenly too warm. I pushed the thoughts away.

"Where is she?" My question sounded as though Franny might be alive and walking around the camp somewhere. I could not bear to think of her lying cold and alone in a hospital or morgue.

"She's been transported home." I was stunned. The war had made everything so much slower and I had not imagined it would be possible to send Franny's body home overnight. A new wave of grief washed over me. Although I had known she was gone the moment I saw her lying on the ground, the fact that she was no longer physically here made the loss all the more real.

"Will we be having a memorial service?"

"I don't think so. This is a German POW camp, Lou."

"So it's as if she was never here at all."

"This is complicated. You know that." I saw then that Ian's eyes were red-rimmed, his face haggard with grief.

"But we are going to find out what happened to her, aren't we?" I pressed.

"She was hit by a car."

"That doesn't seem very likely, does it? I mean, the area is practically deserted and there are so few vehicles out here at all, especially at night. Plus, what was she even doing out at that hour?"

"There's a rumor she was meeting a man." I thought maybe he meant the prisoner she had been talking to earlier through the barbed wire. "Like an affair," he added.

"No," I said, thinking of that night when Franny had confessed to me that she was a homosexual.

"Why not?" Ian pressed. "Can you really say you knew her all that well?"

"I can." In truth, Franny and I had only been friends for a short while. I did not know much about her background, other than what she had shared. But I knew this much to be true: Franny had not gone out to meet a man. "That doesn't make sense. You see, Franny didn't like men."

I could see him processing the idea, trying to understand. He cleared his throat. "Anyway, she was walking and was hit by a car. End of story."

It could be, I reasoned. It was dark and the roads were terrible. I had warned her as much myself. Even as I thought this, I knew it wasn't true. Something else had happened. It was not the end of the story for me.

"Hardly. There were no bruises or broken bones," I persisted. "How do you account for that?"

"I don't know!" he burst out, exasperated. "Can you please stop?" He reached out to touch my arm, but I stepped back, any warmth that I'd felt between us the previous night gone in the harsh light of day. His expression hardened. "Louise, we're in an odd position here. Best if we ask these questions when we are all back home. There will be an investigation and an autopsy, I'm sure."

I knew then that it would never happen. "We need to know now, while we were still here on the ground," I insist. Here, the evidence was fresh and any possible witnesses within reach.

"We're in Germany, enemy territory, for Christ's sake! We can't afford missteps. You need to leave this alone. I understand that you are sad, and I am, too, but there are much larger stakes at play here." Before I could ask what those were, he walked off.

I walked aimlessly for much of the day. I could not bear to stay in the quarters that Franny and I had shared. But I also did not want to go inside the camp. As my grief set into place and my initial panic subsided, the questions and the pieces that did not make sense loomed larger than ever. I thought back to the days right before she had died, the sense of purpose. I had to find out why.

Ian was not going to help me, though. I started out to find the prisoner I'd seen her speaking with the night before she died, the cellist who had given her the necklace. But to go see him, I would have to go into the camp. My stomach churned. Entering the camp, even just for Franny's concert, had been terrifying. To return there alone now, without a legitimate reason, was unthinkable. It was my only hope, though, if I wanted to find out more about what happened to Franny.

I went to the truck parked just outside the camp fence where the remaining packages were stored and took two. Then I walked to the gate of the camp. The guard, holding the leash of a fierce-looking Alsatian, eyed me warily.

"I'm with the Red Cross delegation and I've brought a package from Ian Shipley for one of the musicians, a cellist," I said. I prayed he would not ask me the name of the cellist or notice that I carried two packages. The Alsatian growled.

"The musicians rehearse in barracks nine," he said, stepping back to let me pass.

"I know where that is," I said, hoping he would not insist on escorting me. He pointed in the direction of the practice hall, where I had previously accompanied Franny.

I kept my head low as I walked down the main road of the camp, partly to avoid drawing attention and also not wanting to see the horrific conditions around me. Then I remembered what Franny had said about bearing witness, and I forced myself to look up. The camp was almost deserted, the prisoners already at their daily jobs. Inside one of the barracks, I could see a man lying on the bottom pallet of a hard wooden bunk bed, too sick or weak to go to his job. Impulsively, I walked to the doorway of the barracks. "Here," I said, handing him a care package. "It isn't much and I'm sorry it is not more. But I hope it helps a bit." Though he did not speak, his eyes widened with surprise and he gave a small nod of gratitude.

I continued on to the barracks where Franny had practiced with the musicians. Inside stood a man I recognized as one of the other musicians. "Pardon me..."

"Yes?" He looked apprehensive, but then he seemed to recognize me. "I'm sorry about your friend," he offered.

"Thank you," I said. I couldn't believe how quickly the news about Franny had spread throughout the camp. "I'm hoping you might be able to help me. There was a cellist who played with Franny. I'd like to speak with him." I noticed a cello leaning against the wall in the far corner.

"I'm afraid that's impossible. He's gone," the man said, all but confirming my fear. "He was transferred out of here yesterday morning before dawn."

Just hours after Franny's death, I thought, a chill running through me. "Transferred?"

"Deported, really." I questioned if his involvement with Franny had resulted in being sent east as a punishment. "To another camp, closer to the French border."

"But why?"

"With our star performer gone, they claimed there was no need for a cellist. At least that's what they said."

"Were others transferred as well?"

The man shook his head. "Just him. And it was quick. Usually, you know a few days in advance. But he said nothing about it last night and today he was gone."

He was transferred so suddenly, I felt certain it had to do with Franny's death.

Just then I saw a guard eyeing me suspiciously through the window. "I should go," I said. I did not want to cause trouble for this man. I handed him the care package I carried.

"Thank you." He took the package from me and I started to go. "Wait, there is one other thing." I turned back. "Did he give your friend a necklace?"

"Yes," I said, surprised that he knew. "To deliver to his wife in Paris. Why?"

He ignored my question. "Do you know what became of it?"

"I can check among her belongings," I replied, "but she may have been carrying it when she died."

An urgent expression crossed the man's face. "Please check

and let me know. If it isn't there, I can bribe one of the guards to check her personal effects."

I started to ask him why the necklace mattered, why he would go to such trouble for a sentimental piece. But before I could speak, I noticed a guard striding purposefully toward the barracks, as though realizing I did not belong there. "I have to go."

"That way," the man said, pointing toward a door at the back of the barracks. I raced out. As I reached the front gate to the camp, I realized that I still did not know the cellist's name. I had not asked and his friend had not offered it—perhaps a reflex of a prisoner to protect another. I wanted to go back and ask, but it was too late.

Once out of the camp, I rushed to the railcar where Franny and I had stayed. I wondered if they had taken her things. But all of her belongings were there just as she had left them, from the open makeup to a dress strewn across her bed. As if she might walk in at any second. Choking back a sob, I went to her bag and opened it. Once, it had felt like a violation of her privacy, but not anymore. I looked inside.

The necklace was gone.

18

Helaine

Paris, 1944

Inspection.

The word reverberated through the dormitory, loud enough to wake Helaine from sleep before roll call. "Inspection" meant that one or more high-ranking officials would be visiting Lévitan, led by Oberführer von Behr, who was in charge of the department store. They came ostensibly to view operations, but the real purpose was to sift through the plunder and take the best of what was there.

Despite the alarmed state of those around her, Helaine roused slowly. Her days had settled into a gray haze since the day Gabriel had come and gone again. She felt his absence more acutely than ever. Without him, there seemed no future, no hope.

"Inspection," Miriam hissed, her voice a mix of anticipation and terror. "Get up! And look sharp, if you hope to still be here by day's end." In theory, the inspections were supposed to be unannounced, but von Behr always sent a warning so that the workers could have things in order and put the very best appearance on the shop for whoever accompanied him.

Helaine joined the other workers as they dressed quickly and silently in the semidarkness. They hurried from the dormitory, but instead of going to the warehouse to sort with the men, the women walked down another flight of stairs to prepare the main floor of the department store for visitors.

"You help with the china," Miriam instructed. Helaine obeyed and joined a woman she did not recognize to polish and carefully arrange the dishes. They worked quickly, but precisely. Everything had to be perfect.

When the shop was in order, most of the women started toward the loading dock to begin their normal sorting duties. But when Helaine went to join them, Maxim grabbed her arm.

"You!" he yelled. A knot of dread formed in her stomach. Had she done something wrong in the preparation of the shop? "One of the shopgirls is out sick. A replacement is needed. You are to go get ready."

"Shopgirls" were the ones who had to work on the department store floor when the Germans came. Until now, Helaine had always managed to remain in the warehouse, out of sight. She had not planned to be seen on inspection day.

"Come, we must get you dressed," Miriam whispered, leading Helaine to a room adjacent to the dormitory where clothing hung from a rack. She gave Helaine a proper dress, folded but still smelling of its previous owner, as well as powder for her nose. Helaine went to the sink to wash and fix her hair carefully in the cracked mirror above it. She paused, studying her reflection. To the outside observer, she looked like a normal sales clerk, a little thin perhaps. They couldn't know that she lived and worked under harsh conditions and had almost no food. No, they would not see the differences. But Helaine herself was acutely aware of her gray skin color and sunken eyes and the way her cheekbones protruded too sharply. The woman in the mirror was someone she did not recognize anymore.

Helaine hurried downstairs. "Go to porcelain," the shop overseer, an older woman named Deidre, instructed. Each woman had a station, and she was responsible for cleaning and polishing the goods until they looked like new and displaying them artfully, showing them if a visitor asked. Helaine stood behind the display, repeating the instructions she'd heard several times in her head: *Smile, but do not make eye contact. Your chin should be at a proper height, deferential but not subservient. Become part of the scenery, yet draw no attention.*

Helaine had barely gotten settled at her station when the front door to the department store opened and von Behr strode in, flanked by three other men in uniform she did not recognize. The men walked through the shop, talking as they studied the goods. They carried with them the cold, sooty smell of the outdoors, the smell of war but also of the freedom beyond Lévitan. They ran their hands crudely over delicate dishes and other goods. But they did not see the history of the belongings, any more than they saw the women selling them.

"Face them at all times," Miriam whispered, "even if you have to turn around." Helaine recalled hearing once that von Behr did not like when prisoners had their backs to him. She hurriedly tried to comply. As she did, she noticed that one of the porcelain vases was very close to the edge of the counter, about to fall over. She lunged for it, and as she did, the display rattled, sending two other vases crashing to the floor. Both shattered into a million bits.

The store grew silent. All heads swiveled in Helaine's direction, and she willed the earth to open up and swallow her whole. She could feel the stunned horror of the other women, waiting to see what would happen next. She knelt hurriedly to pick up the pieces with her bare hands, heedless of the way the porcelain shards cut into her skin.

"Halt!" von Behr shouted. Helaine looked up to see him looming over her, his face twisted with anger. It was the first time he had ever spoken to her. Helaine braced herself. Surely, she would be beaten or worse.

But then, seeming to remember the other officers and the need to give the best impression of Lévitan, von Behr knelt and offered her a hand to get up. "Accidents happen," he said. Helaine could see him seething beneath, faking civility for the sake of the visitors. She knew that there would be hell to pay later, out of sight.

One of the other Germans stepped forward. He looked older than von Behr and more senior in rank, with graying temples beneath his hat and an array of medals and ribbons affixed to his uniform. "You look familiar. What is your name?"

"Helaine Weil." Helaine gave her maiden name, the one she had been imprisoned under.

"Weil," he repeated, seeming to recognize her surname. "Any relation to Otto?"

Helaine dipped her chin in acknowledgment. "He is my father."

"I knew him before the war, did business with him." The officer's tone was amiable, as though they were speaking to one another on the street. "I saw a photo of you in his office once." Helaine had not known that her father displayed a photo of her. She wondered what had become of it, of Papa's office. Of everything. "He is well?" the German asked.

The question was so ridiculous that Helaine nearly laughed aloud. "He was abroad when the war started." *But for the grace of God*, she wanted to say, *or he would be in Drancy with my mother.*

"Please give him my regards if you speak with him. Oberführer Frantz."

"I shall." Did the man not realize that Helaine was a prisoner here, who had little communication with the outside world, much less her father, who was abroad? Still, Helaine's hopes rose. This man knew her father. Perhaps he could be an ally. Helaine imagined that he would help her, and maybe even help her mother. Helaine considered throwing herself at his feet for mercy, asking for aid for her mother and herself. But she did not dare. If she was wrong, it would spell the end for their whole family.

"You see," von Behr interjected, turning to the other officer. "We have the finest of Jewish aristocracy working here." There was a note of mocking in his voice. But when he turned back to Helaine, his expression was serious.

"I haven't seen you before," he said accusingly.

Helaine fought the urge to correct him. He had seen her a dozen times when he passed through the store. Only this was the first time he had *noticed* her. "I'm normally in the warehouse."

"Someone as beautiful as you should not be in the warehouse," von Behr said. Helaine recoiled. She had heard stories of Germans using their power to coerce young women into affairs. She would sooner die than betray Gabriel with this Nazi scum. But she didn't want to make things worse for the other prisoners, so she stood motionless, lips pressed in a fake smile. "You will work on the showroom floor from now on instead," von Behr announced.

Helaine waited until the Germans had finished shopping and had left the store before running over to Miriam. "The shop floor?" she said with disbelief. "I can't possibly."

Miriam shrugged. "It's not so bad. The work is not as difficult, and there is sometimes a bit of extra food to be had. Anyway, it isn't as if you have a choice."

The next day, Helaine rose as usual. However, instead of going to the loading dock to sort with the others, she put on the borrowed dress and combed her hair, then made her way down to the shop floor. Deidre told her to go work in cutlery. As Helaine straightened up the counter, she realized that she should not mind so much. Despite the aching in her feet from the too-tight dress shoes she'd been given, standing behind a counter for hours each day was better than the backbreaking work of lifting and sorting the boxes.

Among the cutlery, Helaine spied a tiny spoon, designed for a baby. She imagined the child and the mother so carefully feeding them. She could not help but wonder what had become of the child, whether they were still with their mother, or somewhere alone—or worse.

Once Helaine had her counter ready, there was nothing to do but wait. It was hardly a normal department store with the usual flow of customers. An officer browsing, a courier with a special order for someone's wife or girlfriend. Other than that, there was too much time to stand around and worry and think. The hours stretched long.

After that, Helaine found herself on the shop floor every day, part of a small group of women who manned the stalls even when there were no customers. Though the work was less taxing on her body than the warehouse, she longed for the camaraderie and conversation of the sorting line. Occasionally, Helaine would talk to one of the other shopgirls quietly across the distant counters. But they were too spread out for real conversation. Helaine missed sorting the newly arrived items, when she could still see the scratches and imagine who might have owned the objects. Though the work had been unfathomably sad, it had provided a kind of connection to other Jews. By the time the items reached the displays here, buffed and polished, they were indistinguishable, all signs of the past gone. They might have belonged to anyone—or no one at all.

A few weeks after Helaine began working on the shop floor, the bell over the front door tinkled unexpectedly one morning. Helaine lifted her head from the scarves she had been arranging, startled, as two Germans walked in. Helaine could tell from the insignia on their uniforms and the medals on their chests, as well as the overconfident way they carried themselves, that they were high-ranking Wehrmacht.

Helaine looked around for von Behr, or another German, to come and greet them, but there was no one. "May I help you?" Deidre asked from her place at the porcelain counter.

The officers ignored her question. One walked to Helaine's counter and picked up a scarf with rough hands. He pushed it in Helaine's direction. "Wrap it and send it here," he ordered rudely, scribbling an address in Germany. The name he scrawled was a woman's and the surname different than the one on his uniform. Helaine suspected that he was sending it not to his wife, but to his mistress.

As she wrapped the package, the officer turned his back to her, addressing the other man. "Did you hear about the melee at the base near Köln?" Helaine's ears pricked up. Gabriel had mentioned a Wehrmacht base near Köln during his visit to see her. Surely they were referring to the same one. "There were several spies arrested for treason during a supposed performance. One was even a musician. Who would have thought?"

She cleared her throat, unsure if she dared to ask. "Excuse me, sir. But I was wondering, what kind of musician?"

He turned to glower at her. "A cellist. Not that it is any of your concern."

Her heart pounded. A cellist playing at the base near Köln had been arrested for treason. They could only be talking about Gabriel. The news hit her like a rock. She was filled with terror for Gabriel and the fate that would surely befall him. Reprisals against those who were found to defy the Germans were swift and severe. And the Germans shot traitors without exception. His arrest was nothing short of a death sentence. Was he even still alive?

Helaine recalled how Gabriel would not tell her what he was doing in Germany, how he had steadfastly refused in order to protect her. Now she understood, at least in part, his mysterious behavior and why he could not explain it to her. He was playing for the Reich, but he really must have been helping the POWs or the Allies in some way. Helaine filled with pride. Gabriel had been fighting for the right side all along, using his position to work against the Germans.

And in the midst of all of that, he had still found time to come see her, to check on her and reassure her that he was all right and had not forgotten her. Her response had been to accuse him of collaborating. Helaine's guilt rose. How could she have doubted him?

Helaine finished wrapping the package and showed it to the German for inspection. He nodded, satisfied. "The men who were arrested," she managed, "do you know what happened to them?" She prayed he would not be angered by her question— or want to know why she was asking.

"The article says they were taken to a POW camp called Wann."

She hoped the men would not shop further. When they left the store, she sank into a chair, overcome by all that she had learned. Gabriel was not a traitor.

Miriam, who was passing through the shop with an armful of cookware, saw Helaine sitting and came over. "What is it? What's wrong?"

Quickly, Helaine relayed the new information about Gabriel. "I don't know whether he is all right," she finished, her voice frantic. *Or even if he is alive*, she finished silently, unable to share the thought aloud. Gabriel was hers and true, but at the same time she recognized the awful reality that she might not see him again. She looked up at Miriam. "Isn't there anything you can do?"

"I will make inquiries, of course." Miriam's husband had been highly placed in the French army before his death and Miriam still had a network of contacts who could sometimes be helpful in procuring needed items and information.

"Can you do that?"

"Yes. Because Lévitan is not a typical camp, but here in the middle of the city, we have many more connections with the outside world. As I've mentioned before, some of the men from the moving companies can be bribed. But if he was deep inside Germany when he was arrested, the chances I can learn anything are slim. I would not get your hopes up," Miriam added.

Hope. The word seemed ironic, the furthest thing from what Helaine was feeling. Her thoughts turned to Gabriel's visit and his promise that he would return for her. All of this time, Helaine had assumed that to be true and that the safest thing was to wait in the store until Gabriel came for her. Now, in addition to her sheer worry for him, another realization crashed down upon her: his arrest meant that no one was coming to rescue her. If she were to survive, it would be up to Helaine to save herself.

19

Louise

Paris, 1953

The door opens a crack and I lunge forward. Then, inches from raining down a blow on the intruder, I stop. "Lou?" a familiar voice calls.

There, standing before me, is Joe.

"Joe…" He does not speak but stands looking uncomfortable and out of place, in the doorway of a Paris hotel room, holding a small overnight bag. "What are you doing here?" My surprise is instantly replaced with happiness. Joe is my husband and, despite everything we have been through, the love of my life. Especially now, after everything that has happened, I am happy to see him.

"I was worried," he says finally.

"I told you where I was going."

"I rang the hotel, and when I couldn't reach you, I grew worried. I regretted not coming with you. And I know it sounds silly, but some part of me was afraid you had gone for good."

"It wasn't like that," I reply. "I would never leave you, or the children." But I see now how it must have looked. To me, it had been just an errand. But to Joe, still carrying the pain and scars of the war, it had felt like abandonment and total loss all over again. "Joe, I'm terribly sorry. And I'm so glad you're here."

He stiffens and pulls away a bit. "Are you certain about that?" He hesitates. "When I called the hotel and asked for you, they said you were with your husband. Who was that, Lou?"

I realize that he is speaking of Ian and I'm amazed that the hotel front desk had so readily disclosed my personal affairs. "It's not what you think," I say, understanding how it must seem to Joe, that I was with another man at this hotel. "I ran into an old supervisor from the Red Cross," I add.

A flash of recognition crosses his face. "Ian?" he asks.

"Yes." I had mentioned Ian once or twice when I talked about my work during the war. I had not realized that Joe was listening— or would remember.

"I had asked Ian for help finding out about the necklace and its possible connection to Franny's death. I thought because of his government work, he might have the connections to find out more about the person who owned the necklace. Only, Ian went missing and the necklace is gone, too… Please, you must trust me." I press into him and his familiar scent envelops me. There has been so much distance between us. But now that he is here, there is no one else I would rather be with.

Joe pulls back. "When you needed help, you asked him and not me."

"Oh, Joe, never! I was in London to see Millie about the necklace and I ran into…" I stop, unwilling to lie again. "That is, I remembered the Red Cross and I thought Ian could help, so I went and asked him. It was never about choosing him over you."

"Where is Ian now?"

"I don't know. He's disappeared and I think he has the necklace with him. I went to the police, but I'm not certain that they will help. I was just packing up to come home this morning.

I seem to have hit a dead end here in Paris. But I still need to find out what happened to Franny."

"I don't like this," Joe says, his brow furrowing with concern. "If Ian left and took the necklace, there's probably a reason. It could be dangerous, Lou. Why can't you just let it go?"

I consider the question. I have spent my life laboring under the delusion that being safe might save me. All of my life, I have played by the rules, and it has gotten me nowhere. Not this time. "If there's something that Ian was trying to keep from me about the necklace and Franny's death, then that's all the more reason I have to find out. I'm sorry, but I can't."

"In that case, let me help."

I am surprised. "Really?"

"If that's what you need to put all of this behind you, then yes."

I expected Joe to insist we go home, but instead I see a glimpse of the old Joe, the man I fell in love with. "I won't let you do this alone," he adds.

I start to tell him no. This was my friend who had died and my mission, and I need to finish it myself.

"I know you can do it on your own," Joe says, seeming to read my thoughts. "But you shouldn't have to. It might seem like I'm not paying attention," he adds. "But I understand what it took to come back from all you did during the war and care for our family, to carry the weight when I can't. Now it's my turn to be strong. I'll help you. We're a team, Lou."

I realize then that not letting Joe in was what had nearly destroyed our marriage in the first place. I cannot afford to do that again. "I would like that very much." I throw my arms around him. "Thank you."

I take his hand. "I'm so glad you came. I thought after everything that happened, you might be too mad."

"What did the war teach us if not about second chances?" he asks. "Believe me, the last thing I wanted to do was come to Paris." I realize then how hard it must be for him to return to Europe and all of his painful memories as well. "But I know how important this is to you. You've always needed to know what happened to Franny. It's partly self-interest, too. How can we move forward with our lives until you've made your peace with the past?"

"Then let's figure this out so we can go home," I reply.

He takes my arm protectively. "So what now?"

"I don't know," I admit. "The necklace I found is gone. Ian had it and he must have taken it with him. It seemed like a dead end anyway."

"But what about the other necklace?"

"The necklace with the other half of the heart?" Millie had mentioned the other half when I visited her jewelry shop in Portobello Road; so had Madame Dupree. I have been so focused on the one I had seen years ago, though, I have not stopped to think about where the other half might be—or the fact that it might have the answers I am looking for. "I have no idea. But even if I did, I'm not sure it would help. This is the half I saw during the war, I'm certain of it. It has the same half of the inscription and everything."

"I understand. But if the man had one half, then surely his wife had the other." The logic is as simple as it is brilliant. What if the one bearing the truth is still out there? "And perhaps the other half might contain the answers you are looking for," Joe offers.

"Yes, but where in the world would that be? The cellist had the half I found. The other half was with his wife…" I remember then what Monsieur Brandon told me about the woman he knew at Lévitan—the one who was married to the cellist. My mind goes to the dormitory in the attic of the department store. "I have to go back to the store where she was kept prisoner during the war. If that's the last place she lived, then perhaps there is some clue there about the necklace that I might have missed. I wasn't thinking at all about it when I was there."

"I'll come with you," Joe volunteers.

"No, you can't," I snap. He looks hurt and I realize it sounds as though I am rejecting him all over again. "That is, I need you to do something else." I explain about the film and give him the address of the shop that is developing it. "It should be ready by now."

"I will get the photograph while you go to the store." It feels good to be working together, a true partnership.

I start for the door and then turn back. "Are the children still at Bea's?" Their faces appear in my mind. I want to be home and holding them.

"They are now. But after you left, I brought them home from Bea's and took care of them myself." He smiles. "I was actually kind of good at it." There is a note of pride in his voice. He can help, I see now, if only I make room to let him. "It's been good for us in a way," he adds. "We missed you, but it's good for me to spend time with them and have them see that I can take care of them. That I'm capable. And for me to see it, too."

"I know what you mean."

Then he smiles. "Who am I kidding? The house is in shambles and we are desperate for you to be home."

We take the lift down to the lobby. I look at Joe out of the corner of my eye. His gaze is fixed ahead with a kind of determination, his fingers are laced firmly with mine. He is here, and present now, in a way that he has not been since the war. In that moment, I know we are going to make it.

"Go get the film," I say as we step outside. "I will check the store and I will meet you back here straightaway."

"Promise?" I can sense his apprehension, and I kiss him squarely on the lips.

"Promise," I respond. Then I set out.

⁊

Germany, 1944

My breath caught. The fact that the necklace was missing did not mean that someone had taken it. Franny could have had it with her when she was killed.

I set out to tell Ian all that I had learned. Surely now he would believe me. He would have to see that something was not right. But as I walked into his railcar, his face was a thundercloud. "I'm glad you're here. Sit down." He gestured to the lone chair across from his cot. I was surprised. I had come here to see Ian on my own, but he was acting as though he had summoned me.

He looked away and I wondered if he felt as awkward as I did about what had happened. "I know what you are going to say. I agree. It can't happen again. It never should have happened in the first place."

"I agree." Though I had said as much, his acknowledgment still stung. I brushed it away. "But that's not what this is about."

"Then what?"

"I need to talk to you," I began, but he raised his hand.

"No, me first. I don't need to tell you how disruptive this situation with Franny has been." My anger flared. It was not a disruption. She had been killed and he was boiling it down to some kind of inconvenience. "But we really can't let this situation interfere with our mission. It's become too much, you see, and it has to go away."

I realized then that the mess he was talking about was not Franny's murder. The mess he was talking about was me.

"You went and tried to talk to one of the prisoners."

My confusion turned to alarm. How did he know about that? Then I remembered the guard who had been watching me. He must have told Ian. "I did. I was trying to find out the truth about what happened to Franny, which is more than I can say for you!"

"Louise, how could you?" he exploded. "I explained to you the constraints under which we operate here. You've gone too far and it's out of my hands now. I can't protect you." *Protect me from what?* I wondered. Ian continued, "You must understand, I'm thinking of the lives of thousands of people. People who we will not be able to help if we are found meddling and sent home. It's not that I'm not sad about Franny. I cared about her just as much as you. But I have to think of the greater good."

He turned to some paperwork on his desk. "You'll want to go home now, I expect. After everything that happened with Franny, the last thing you would want is to stay here."

I looked at him in surprise. "No." I was grieving for my friend. But I was more committed than ever to the work—and to finding the man with the necklace. "Ian, did Franny have anything on her when she died?"

He shook his head. "Not that I know of. Just her Red Cross identification card. Why?"

"The cellist gave Franny a necklace to deliver to his wife. She asked you to make sure it got delivered, didn't she?" He did not say anything, but I already knew the answer. "I looked in Franny's belongings, but the necklace is gone. Don't you think that is strange? Or that maybe it has something to do with Franny's death?"

I saw from his weary expression that he did not, and that he also didn't believe me. "I think Franny got hit by a car because she liked to walk at night and it was a darkened country road," he said, repeating the theory I would never believe. "And I think that I've got a dead actress." I cringed at the coldness of his words. "And I've got prisoners who need our aid packages if they are to survive and a worker in the war zone who won't follow instructions." He would not sacrifice his work to help me. His principles and commitment, the very things that drew me to him, were the things that would in the end tear us apart.

He was looking squarely at me, an accusation. "I told you to leave this alone. And you didn't. You should go home, Lou."

"I'm not leaving until I find out what happened to Franny."

"No," he replied quietly. "You're leaving now." His expression hardened then. "Louise, you don't understand, you're being sent home." He had been trying to give me the option. But now the truth was laid bare. I was being forced to leave. They weren't giving me the choice.

In truth, we would have all been going home soon anyway. Still, it was upsetting to be told that I was no longer needed or wanted, that the trouble I was causing was greater than any help I could possibly offer.

"But why? I don't understand."

"When you asked about Franny, I told you to leave it alone. But you didn't, did you? You kept asking questions when I asked you to stop, going places where you weren't supposed to. The guards saw you talking to a prisoner in the barracks. You've been ordered to leave the country immediately."

He slid a paper across the cot. Government orders, sending me home. And they had been signed by Ian himself.

20

Helaine

Paris, 1944

One morning as Helaine was preparing her counter in the department store, she heard a commotion coming from outside the shop. She and Miriam exchanged puzzled glances. What was happening? Miriam moved cautiously toward the front door. "Don't!" Helaine whispered. The windows were blackened, but prisoners were still not permitted to go near the glass and she didn't want her friend to risk getting in trouble. But Miriam waved her off, curious, and pressed her ear to the window. A moment later, she returned. "People are saying that the Allies have landed at Normandy," she said quietly. Her eyes were damp.

Helaine moved toward the front of the store now, too excited to remain cautious and heed the rules about staying away from the windows. Through a space in the window where the black paint had worn away, she saw a new wave of Parisians fleeing with their belongings. This time, it was likely the collaborators running, the ones who had reason to be afraid when the Allies came because of what they had done during the war.

News that the Allies had crossed the Channel filled Helaine with hope. "The landing," Helaine whispered, squeezing Miriam's hand. "It's happened. It won't be long now." Surely the Allies would soon reach Paris and free them. If only she and the others in Lévitan could hold on. She prayed that Gabriel, if he was still alive, could survive until liberation as well.

But Miriam's expression changed slowly, the lines around her mouth deepening. "We will have to leave sooner than I thought."

Miriam was still talking about trying to escape, Helaine realized. Didn't she understand that help was on the way and they would soon be free? "Miriam, we don't need to escape now. The Allies will liberate us."

"Hah!" Miriam waved her hand dismissively. "You think the Germans are going to just leave us here for the Allies to find? No," she said, answering her own question without waiting for Helaine. "They are going to try to erase all evidence of what they did here before the Allies arrive." Helaine's blood chilled. "We are only useful as long as the store goes on. And maybe not even then. Things are going to get much worse before they get better."

"What are you going to do?" Helaine asked, already knowing the answer. Her eyes traveled through the window beyond the edge of the rooftop to the horizon.

"I don't know. I'm still thinking of the best way to go."

That night, the news on the contraband radio, hidden in the dormitory, spoke of the Allied forces landing at Normandy. And yet, the next morning, the prisoners were sent to work as if it were any other day. They continued working in the store as spring turned to summer and the days grew longer and the nights in the stuffy attic grew hotter. Helaine could tell that Miriam was still determined to escape. She saw the older woman studying the doors and windows, calculating the best way to go. Weeks passed. The Allied advance across Europe was far from steady. The battle lines moved slowly and there was word of setbacks. It seemed as though they would never reach Paris, or if they did, it would be too late.

But there were little signs that the Germans were weakening and the Allied offensive was taking its toll. The Allies had bombed the rail lines, and with the tracks destroyed, the Nazis could not ship plunder to Germany as efficiently as they wanted. There were fewer trucks bringing household goods to the store, too, though Helaine was unsure whether this was due to the war or the simple fact that there were almost no Jewish homes left to loot. The war had to be nearing its end. The remaining Nazi customers were rushed and looking only to buy goods they could carry with them. But with the shelves of the shop growing barer by the day, the undeniable reality, whispered among the prisoners, was that the department store would not remain open much longer.

What then? Helaine considered one night as she lay awake, unable to sleep in the stuffy dormitory. If the Germans closed the store before the Allies reached them, the possibilities were too awful to contemplate. No one went home; Helaine knew that now. All paths led east to places a million times worse than here. There were rumors of camps in Poland where the smokestacks were the only way out.

Escape. Helaine was overwhelmed at the notion. But the end of the war was coming, and so, too, was the end of the department store. Gabriel was not coming to save her. Helaine had always believed that if she waited, he would come for her. He had sworn it. With Gabriel arrested, though, his promise to come for her was simply one he could not keep. If she were to live, she was going to have to save herself. There was no hope left here.

All of the old doubts, her mother's words, which Helaine had not thought about since leaving home, reverberated now in Helaine's head. She was weak from her childhood illness. Not strong enough to survive. Except she had survived, Helaine reminded herself. She had survived these many months in the camp. She could do it; she had to, because there was simply nobody else anymore. She was not the same person she had been when Gabriel left.

The next morning as they prepared for work, Helaine approached Miriam. "Take me with you," Helaine whispered.

Miriam looked at her with surprise. "You always refused before."

Helaine dipped her chin in acknowledgment. "I know. I'm ready now." She felt the words as she spoke them.

"So what changed?" Miriam asked.

"Because now," she said slowly, only fully realizing the words as she spoke them, "there is no other choice." She straightened, filled with newfound resolve. "Tell me," Helaine said to Miriam. "When do we go?"

"We have to plan it," Miriam said grimly. "I would have used the window to climb out onto the ledge and down. But I'm not strong enough now." Miriam gestured toward her own emaciated body. It was not just the meager rations that had caused her weight loss. Miriam's cough had worsened to near incessant and she wheezed all night trying to breathe. They both knew she had cancer or something equally dire. Yet she was still determined to try to escape, rather than living her remaining time in captivity. "We need a different way," she added.

Helaine looked at the shop with a new eye, calculating the best route out. "What if we wait until the guard is asleep?" she asked, referring to the one gendarme who was supposed to stand watch downstairs at night. In reality, he always found a comfortable chair in the furniture department to rest in, his snores reverberating through the high ceiling of the store.

Miriam nodded in agreement. "We can sneak down the back stairwell and out." There was a second set of stairs that led to the side alley. The prisoners seldom used them except when accessing the adjacent apartment building for their weekly showers.

"But where will we go?" Leaving the department store itself

was not hard; that was the ironic part. It was surviving after escape that would be the most challenging. Paris remained a city under siege, there was hardly a single Jew left nor a friendly house where they might find shelter. Once they went, they had to leave Paris for good.

"I don't know," Miriam replied honestly. "But if we wait until we have all the answers, we will never get out of here and then it will be too late. We will go tomorrow after bedtime," she added decisively.

"Miriam," Helaine said, one more question occurring to her. "You've been talking about escaping for so long. Why now?"

She smiled. "Because I was waiting for you."

The next night, Helaine lay awake. She looked around the department store and listened to the familiar chorus of people breathing in sleep. She would not miss Lévitan, to be sure. But it had protected them from so much worse. If she lived to tell about it, Helaine vowed, she would never forget this strange place.

An hour after the dormitory was settled and still, Miriam nudged her. It was time. Helaine slipped from bed and started for the door. She looked across the room and hesitated, then raced back to the hole in the wall near her bed. The necklace. She had nearly forgotten it. She fastened the locket around her neck, then pulled out her journal. She could not bear to leave it.

Miriam looked down at the journal and Helaine worried that she would object to her bringing it. Carrying objects would only slow them down. "I feel bad about the other prisoners," Miriam said to Helaine instead. Surely there would be repercussions when it was discovered that they were gone. But there was no other choice—they could not take everyone and they could not stay here. And if they warned the others, they might try to stop them or perhaps even tell the guards.

They walked to the back stairwell door as planned. It was open every night, leading to both the lower floors and the roof. Prisoners accessed it frequently when they went up to the roof to smoke or breathe the fresh air. But when Helaine tried it now, it was locked. Was it just bad luck that the door was locked tonight, or had someone overheard their plans and told the Germans? Helaine's eyes met Miriam's in panic. They were trapped.

Suddenly, there were footsteps on the main stairs below. There was no other way down and the door in front of them was locked. Any minute the guard would be here and see that they were trying to escape.

From the landing below, someone shined a torch upward in their direction. "Who's there?" It was not the guard, but Maxim.

"Just me, you fool." Only Miriam would dare talk to the overseer that way. "Helaine is with me as well."

Maxim shined the flashlight at Helaine, illuminating her body and leering. Normally, this would have bothered her. But she was too scared about being caught to notice or care.

"What are you doing up and about?" Maxim asked.

"She felt ill," Miriam lied smoothly. "We were going to get some fresh air."

"You can't. Doors are locked from now on, von Behr's orders. Air raids make it too dangerous." Helaine did not know if that was a lie. Why should the German care if the prisoners lived or died? There was hardly any merchandise to sort anymore. Most likely, he did not want anything to happen to the Jews under his watch because it would be a stain on his military record, injurious to his future career aspirations. "Use the toilet if you need to be sick," he added. "And don't make a mess." He turned and walked back down the stairs.

After he left, they stood silently as Helaine tried to calm her racing heart.

"That was close," Miriam whispered. "Maxim is terrified of prisoners escaping on his watch and what would happen to him if they did. He is going to be watching us like a hawk. I'm afraid there is nothing more to be done."

"Is there another way?" Helaine whispered. She had already begun to taste freedom, and it felt like they were so close.

Miriam shook her head. "Anything else is too risky. The elevators are noisy and the front stairs visible. And I can't manage the window ledge." Helaine thought she could make it from the window ledge, but she would never abandon her friend.

Their escape plan foiled, they returned silent and defeated to their beds in the dormitory. They would be forced to remain at the department store, at least for now. Reluctantly, Helaine returned her journal and the locket to their hiding place and added a hash mark to her count of days upon the wall.

21

Louise

Paris, 1953

When I reach the department store, it is still early and I worry
that they might still be closed. But I try the door and am relieved to find that it opens. I race inside and past the receptionist.
"Pardon?" she calls, but I keep going, hoping she will not stop
me. I sprint up the back stairwell without waiting to find out.
I open the door to the dormitory and dash to the spot where
we had stood on my previous visit. I scan the room, looking
for clues. Nothing. Everything that had been in here during
the war is gone.

My eyes lower to the hash marks we had seen last time where
a prisoner seemed to have been marking the days. I scan the wall
around the markings, noting how the plaster is cracked with
age. My eyes are tracing the cracks when I notice a place on the
wall where the paint is darker than the rest and a bit uneven. I
run my hand along the wall, then tap on it. There is a spot that
sounds different. Hollow.

I start digging at it, plaster caking under my fingernails and
cutting the skin. The managing director is in the doorway now,

starting toward me. "Madam, you must stop! You are destroying our property and I will be forced to call the police."

Ignoring him, I tear at the wall. A moment later, it gives way, revealing a hole. I reach in through the dust and pull out a small journal. I open the cover.

There is a name inside: *Helaine Weil Lemarque.*

Gabriel's wife.

My breath catches. Hurriedly, I reach into the hole once more, stretching farther, feeling for the locket. My hand closes around emptiness. There is nothing else.

I sink back, disappointed. The other half of the necklace is surely gone, and so, too, is anything I might have learned from it.

The managing director looks over my shoulder, more curious than angry now. "What is that? If it is some sort of artifact from the war, it must be turned over to the government. There is a law."

Not responding, I open the journal and begin to page through it. There are stories, fiction by the looks of it, about a girl named Anna, and a few sketches, the words of a person trying to express themselves to survive their days in captivity. I don't have time to read it all. I start to close the journal. Then on the inside cover, I see a sketch.

It is of a necklace with a half-heart shape.

There is no doubt that the owner of the notebook and the locket are one and the same. I still do not have the necklace. But it is a connection. It is something.

I study the name once more. *Helaine Weil Lemarque.* Our mystery woman has at last been identified.

But can she be found?

I race downstairs and start from the store. The managing director calls after me, insisting that I leave the journal. I keep going, half-afraid that he will follow me. He does not.

I step outside. I have the name of the cellist's wife, but she could be anywhere, or even no longer alive. For a fleeting second, I think of Ian and his connections. If he were still here, he might help me track her down. But I have to do this myself now. No, not completely myself. Joe is here. I decide to ring the hotel and see if he has returned yet. Perhaps we can figure out how to find Helaine together. I start for a telephone booth at the corner.

I dial the hotel and the front desk clerk answers. "This is Louise Burns. I'm staying at the hotel and I left a short while ago with my husband, Joe. I'm wondering if he has returned."

"I have not seen him, madam, but I've just come on shift. I can check your room."

"Please do." There is a pause. I wait impatiently, my fingers ruffling a thick phone book on the shelf below the telephone.

A moment later, the clerk returns on the line. "I tried the room, but no one answered."

"Thank you." Joe is not back yet. I pause, considering what to do next. I know now who the cellist's wife was. Is. Hopefully she survived the war and is alive somewhere. My mind races as I consider where she could be. People left in droves after the war. She might be anywhere. But people also went home. Most often went home, the policeman had said about Ian. And Helaine's last known whereabouts were the department store.

What if she stayed right here in Paris?

I look down at the phone book. I try not to get my hopes up as I open it and thumb hurriedly through the pages. She might not have survived the department store. And even if she did, there was no reason to assume that she remained so close to her painful past.

Unable to stay calm, I continue paging through the phone book. I look first under Lemarque, checking both *H* for Helaine and *G* for Gabriel, just in case. Then I go to the *W* listings. There is nothing for *Weil, H.* My heart sinks. No, of course not, even now women are not considered important enough to be listed separately. But there is a *G*: Is it possible that Helaine is listed under her husband's first initial, but her own surname? It seems unlikely, but it is my only hope, and the only clue I have. I scribble down the address, then step from the phone booth.

On the pavement, I pause, trying to decide what to do next. I want to go right to the address to see if Helaine is actually there. But I promised Joe I would meet him straightaway, and if he comes back and does not see me, he might worry.

I hurry back to the hotel, but Joe has not returned. Perhaps the film is taking longer than expected to develop. I scrawl him a note.

Found address for Gabriel's wife at 8 Rue Petrelle. Going there. Meet me and let's finish this so we can go home. Xo Lou

I fold the note and then set out once more.

22

Helaine

Paris, 1944

The dormitory lights went on brightly. "Raus!"

Out. For a moment, Helaine hoped that the day for which they had waited so long had finally arrived and that they were being liberated. But the men waking them wore German uniforms.

"They're closing the shop," Miriam whispered. "Taking everyone." Their worst nightmare had come true. They had tried to escape. But they had failed. Now their chance to leave had evaporated. It was too late.

Helaine jumped up, and as she did, something fell to the ground. Her necklace. She remembered looking at it the previous night, thinking of Gabriel. She must have fallen asleep holding it. She picked it up and hurriedly shoved it in her pocket.

As the prisoners were herded toward the door, Helaine turned back and looked once more at the attic where they had been imprisoned for so many months. They had known deprivation, pain and hunger. Yet it had been their shelter from greater unknown horrors beyond the walls of the department store. Helaine would not miss the department store, but she was terrified of what worse horrors might lie ahead.

"My journal!" Helaine realized aloud. She looked back across the room to its hiding place in the wall, desperate to get it.

But there was no time. "Come," Miriam whispered, tugging at Helaine's arm as the rest of the group started to leave. Helaine was forced to leave the journal behind.

They were hustled downstairs and onto two small buses, packed tightly to fit them all. "Where are we going?" someone asked aloud. There was no response.

The buses rolled silently through the nighttime Paris streets. It was a warm summer evening, and through the poorly blacked-out bus window, Helaine could make out a canopy of stars above the Seine. Would she ever be free to view the stars again? Miriam sat beside her, hands clutched tightly in her lap. Helaine had never seen Miriam look scared before, but she could see the fear in her eyes, her face pale and drawn. Helaine put her arm around her friend.

In the distance, Helaine heard what sounded like machine gunfire, sharp and rattling. It was followed by a louder boom. The prisoners from the department store were being evacuated just steps ahead of liberation. The Germans did not want to leave anyone behind. As Miriam had said months earlier, they wanted to ensure that there were no witnesses to what they had done.

She and the other prisoners could not allow themselves to be taken from Paris, Helaine realized then. Escape was impossible, but at the same time, it was their only hope for survival.

Helaine looked around the bus desperately, trying to figure out what to do. She had no idea where they were being taken or how much time they had before they got there. But if they reached their destination, they would certainly never return. The bus slowed in traffic, the road ahead clogged with people trying to flee by car and on foot. This was their chance. Once the bus really started moving again, they might not stop. The bus they were riding on was once a regular passenger bus. The bell cord, which one would pull to signal their stop, was intact.

Helaine nudged Miriam and their eyes met. Helaine tried to signal to her friend what she intended to do. Miriam's eyes widened with recognition. Did she dare try to pull the cord and see if it still worked? Surely it would do no good. But Miriam, seeming to recognize the futility of their situation and the lack of other options, acknowledged Helaine with a slight nod.

Taking a deep breath, Helaine reached out and tugged the cord. The bell rang, cutting through the bus and startling the other prisoners. There was a moment's hesitation and then the driver screeched to a halt. People froze uncertainly, so used to staying in place until told to do otherwise. "Go!" Helaine cried urgently. They were farther from the front than she had realized and there were too many other prisoners blocking the way. They could not get past unless the others got off the bus first. Then someone close to the front pushed the door open and they surged forward, a pressure valve released.

As Helaine neared the door to the bus, someone grabbed her arm. It was a guard, trying to stop them from escaping. Even now, when the Germans were about to lose everything, his concern was making sure no Jew went free. Desperately, Helaine brought up her knee, striking the guard in the groin. He reared back, howling. But he did not let go of Helaine.

Miriam lunged forward and gave the man a mighty shove, and Helaine was able to break free. Helaine fell backward into the street, hit the ground. She leaped to her feet and ran several meters from the bus. Then she turned back, looking for Miriam. Her friend was trapped. The guard had caught several prisoners and secured them inside the bus once more. Helaine started back toward the bus, trying to signal to her friend. Their eyes met. Miriam had not abandoned her the night they tried to flee the shop—how could Helaine leave her now?

Miriam shook her head, waving Helaine away. "Go!" Miriam

screamed imploringly. How could Helaine abandon her now, when Miriam had risked so much for her. There was nothing she could do, though, and if she tried, Helaine would surely be rearrested. The whole escape attempt would have been for nothing. No, she owed it to Gabriel, to her mother, to Miriam herself to keep going and do everything she could to survive. She looked back once more gratefully at her friend. She turned and ran into the night.

Six days.

That was how long Helaine hid on the streets of Paris, crouching in deserted alleyways and sleeping in garbage dumpsters and eating the scraps she found in them, as the last bits of the war played out around her. She did not dare go to her childhood home or the apartment she had shared with Gabriel, and she didn't know if it was possible to leave the city. So she stayed out of sight while the gunfire rattled and the Germans fled, until at last the streets were silent.

Only when she heard the cheers did Helaine unfold herself stiffly from her hiding place and walk into the light. The tanks that lined the Champs-Élysées were American now, festooned with red, white and blue flags and flowers, and surrounded by Parisians who wanted to see, touch and kiss their liberators.

Weak with hunger and from hiding, Helaine found a man with a red cross on his armband and asked for help. He directed Helaine to a makeshift facility in a school gymnasium where those who needed it were being given food, shelter and medicine. A short while later, the Joint Distribution Committee offered Helaine space in a displaced persons camp in Hénonville, northwest of the city. She did not have to go, the woman representing the organization said. She was free now and going was an offer of aid, a choice. But it was recommended until everyone could be checked for disease and fed.

Helaine didn't want to accept. "Camp" was the very thing she had dreaded and avoided while at the department store. Technically they were French citizens, not displaced from their own country. But in Paris, she had nothing, no family or home. There was no one to send for her from abroad, other than her father, who likely did not know that she was even alive. The liberators tried to give people some dignity in choosing their own path, but in the end there really was nowhere else to go, no choice to make at all.

The displaced persons camp offered shelter and good food. But it was not a permanent home. It was a respite while Helaine figured out where she might go next. Already others were emigrating to America and other countries, leaving the past behind. Helaine questioned if she could, or should, do the same.

The first thing Helaine did when she reached the displaced persons camp was to go to the special office set up for survivors trying to find their loved ones. It was her only hope of finding Gabriel and her mother. She waited in a queue of camp residents making inquiries. Behind her in line was a woman a few years older than herself. Her face was drawn, her eyes sunken. She looked grief-stricken.

"Did you lose someone?" she asked the woman. The question was a foolish one, Helaine realized as she asked it; everyone had lost someone.

"I was separated from my twins when we were arrested in Lyon." The woman's voice, barely a whisper, was numb with disbelief. She seemed to relive the horror of the memory as she spoke. "I was freed from an internment camp in the north of France. When the camp was liberated, they tried to put me in a DP camp there, but I insisted on leaving and coming here because this is the closest camp to where they were taken from me." Her eyes were near frantic.

"How old are your twins?"

"Four." The woman's face crumpled with pain. "My babies are four. They were two when they were taken from me."

"No…" Helaine was struck. She could not imagine the horror of having been separated from one's children—nor how children so young might have survived without their mother. "I'm so sorry," Helaine said helplessly. There were no words she could offer that would adequately reflect the woman's suffering. "You should go in front of me," she said, stepping aside.

"Thank you. I'm called Dania," the woman managed feebly, as though ordinary conversation was an effort.

"Helaine." The line moved forward. Helaine held her breath while Dania asked about her children at the desk.

The woman behind the desk shook her head. "I'm sorry, but we have no lists of children here. They were all sent east."

A small cry escaped Dania's lips and she swayed backward. Helaine leaped to support her so she did not fall.

"I'm trying to find news of my husband, Gabriel Lemarque," Helaine said, still holding on to Dania.

"Was he a prisoner at Drancy or one of the other camps?" the woman asked.

"Neither. He was in a POW camp."

"We don't have access to those kinds of records here, but if you give me his name, I will make inquiries for you."

Helaine scribbled down Gabriel's name and date of birth, as well as the camp he had mentioned the day he visited her in the department store. "I do have another missing person," Helaine said. "Annette Weil." Her mother's name sounded almost foreign. "She was imprisoned at Drancy." The woman paged through the records. Her eyes scanned lists and lists of people. At first, Helaine hoped that her mother's name might be on the list. But then she realized those were the names of those who had died. Helaine held her breath, praying that her mother would not be among them. The woman stopped reading and her expression grew somber. Wordlessly, she pushed the paper across the desk, allowing Helaine to see the news herself.

"No…" Maman was gone. Helaine's eyes filled with tears, blurring her vision as she stared at the page with disbelief. Some of the names had a cause of death beside them. But typed beside Maman was simply the word *Undetermined*. Dania put an arm around Helaine and the two women supported one another in their pain as they walked away.

Miriam was gone, too, Helaine later learned from another resident in the displaced persons camp. The prisoners who had not escaped the bus had been shot immediately in reprisal for the escape attempt. Helaine bowed her head and gave silent thanks to her friend. Without her help and sacrifice, she would not still be alive.

But there was no information whatsoever about Gabriel. There was no record of him, because he had not been imprisoned as a Jew at one of the concentration camps. The lack of news or any way to learn more was excruciating. It was as if he had simply fallen off the face of the earth. It seemed to Helaine that she might spend the rest of her life not knowing what had become of him.

Dania came to her after breakfast one morning, her expression grave. "What is it?" Dania had spoken little since learning the likely fate of her twins.

Dania carried a newspaper and showed her an article about a fire at Wann, the POW camp where Gabriel had been imprisoned, caused by an Allied bomb that hit the barracks. All of the remaining prisoners there were gone. "I'm so sorry. But I thought you would want to know."

"No…" Helaine buried her head in her hands. Even after hearing of his arrest and leaving the department store, she had held out so much hope that he would live, and they would find one another again and reconcile. Now that dream was gone like everything else. This last piece of news, on top of everything else, was almost too much to bear.

For days, Helaine scarcely got out of bed. Dania and a few others, understanding her need to mourn, brought her food.

People left the camp daily, those who had someone to claim them in America or elsewhere. The number of camp inhabitants dwindled. But Helaine remained. She had nowhere to go. Helaine knew that she had to decide her next step, not just wait for a sign. She put her name on the lists to emigrate to the United States and Canada, but without papers or relatives to claim her, it was impossible. There were courses in the DP camp, designed to help prepare the people for the next chapter of their lives. Helaine decided to learn to type and take dictation, practical skills that she never would have learned in her previous life but that might come in handy now.

A few weeks after she began the course, as she left the makeshift classroom where she learned to type one afternoon, Helaine spied a small pile of writing tablets. "May I have one of those?" she asked the instructor, who nodded. Helaine took the notebook back to her room and began to write. The stories about Anna that she had written before the war came back to her anew. She reconstructed them, wishing she had the journal she left behind in the department store. There were new stories, too, and she began to see that the things she had once only dreamed about doing through her fiction, travels and adventures, might be possible once the war was over. Only without Gabriel, starting over seemed pointless.

The next morning, Helaine was scanning the board where people posted messages looking for loved ones. There was a postcard from her father searching for her mother, though not for her. Helaine felt the pain of rejection all over again. She should contact him and let him know that she was alive. But she was too afraid. What if he didn't want her? He might still be angry about her marriage to Gabriel. Helaine's father had rejected her once; she could not bear it again. Whatever future she made, she would start over on her own.

She took the postcard and shoved it in her bag.

As the days passed, Helaine found that she was beginning to feel unlike herself. She was exhausted, even more so than usual. She could not eat. Though she welcomed the wholesome Red Cross meals after so much hunger, the sight of food turned her stomach. Helaine assumed it was an aftereffect of the starvation she'd endured. But other former prisoners ate ravenously, whereas Helaine could not hold down so much as a morsel. Something was wrong. Helaine panicked. She could barely summon the strength to go on as it was.

"You should go to the infirmary," Dania suggested. Dania had stayed after learning the news about her children. She was trying to gather the strength and money to travel east and start her search for her children anew. Helaine started to protest. When they were at Lévitan, serious illness was a death sentence and telling those in charge would result in being sent to Drancy and deportation east. "It's safe to get help now," Dania added, reading her thoughts.

Helaine allowed Dania to take her to the infirmary, a small but clean building. In the crowded waiting room, she feared she might become sick with something even worse than what she had.

Finally, she was escorted in to see a doctor, a young Dutch man with tortoiseshell glasses and a serious but friendly expression. He examined her and drew blood. "When was your last period?" he asked.

Helaine blushed at the question. "I can't remember. Few of the women still menstruated because of starvation."

"I think you are just fine and that your condition will improve in a few months." He smiled.

"I don't understand."

"You aren't sick. You're pregnant."

Helaine was stunned. "That isn't possible."

"Not just possible, but true. You didn't notice?" He pointed to her stomach. Helaine had thought it was distended. However, it was, in fact, a baby.

Still, Helaine could not believe it. "But I'm not able to have children. I had a serious illness as a child and a high fever. The doctor said..." Helaine began, then stopped. The doctor had not told Helaine she was infertile. Her mother had. Was it a lie? Had her mother been trying to keep her from wanting—or attempting to have—more than she could handle? Even if that were true, Helaine understood that her mother had been trying to protect her, and despite all of her anger, Helaine could not help but love her still.

The time to stop talking about what she could not do had ended, Helaine realized. It was time to start focusing on what she could.

A child of her own. A new beginning. Helaine was filled with joy and yet sadness. Gabriel would never know his child.

Faced with the news of her pregnancy, Helaine's mission to find a new place to live took on increased urgency. She did not want her child to be born in the displaced persons camp, but a real home. She decided to pen a letter to her father after all. Family, no matter how estranged, was a precious and scarce commodity now that so many had been lost. She hated asking for his help, but she had no choice.

Papa,
I am sure by now you have heard the news of Maman. I am in the displaced persons camp and I would be very grateful if you would send for me so that I can leave.
Your daughter, Helaine

She paused after writing the note, added the return address for the camp. She considered making mention of her pregnancy. The prospect of a grandchild might soften her father's heart. But knowing that it was Gabriel's might make him even more remote.

Helaine was pulled from her thoughts by music being played nearby. The arts flourished in the camp and there were concerts and plays, musicians returning to their passion and finding new life in it. Helaine never went to them because they reminded her too much of Gabriel. Now she heard the unmistakable strains of a cello and a wave of sadness washed over Helaine as she thought of Gabriel and the music he would never play for her again.

Something about the music became familiar, the notes of an original piece she had heard only once. It could not be. Surely there were dozens of musicians in the camps. Gabriel was gone. But only one knew the melody he had crafted just for her long ago. Only one could play *For Helaine*.

Helaine walked toward the building, scarcely daring to hope. Through the door, she could only see his fingers, but even then she knew.

She was home.

23

Louise

Paris, 1953

I reach the address I'd found in the phone book, a row home in the 9th arrondissement with bright chrysanthemums in the front window boxes. Outside the door, I stop, suddenly nervous. This is my last chance at finding out the connection between the necklace and Franny's death. What if the answers are worse than I thought? Or worse yet, what if there are no answers at all?

There is only one way to find out. I ring the bell. My heartbeat quickens.

I hear footsteps growing louder. The door opens slowly, and a slight woman appears. She looks to be about my age, though her face has deeper lines, and her hair bears a streak of premature gray. This surprises me; I always imagined the cellist and his wife to be much older. But their history during the war happened at the same time as my own.

"Yes?" she says, eyeing me suspiciously. She looks puzzled and even a little alarmed. I am not surprised, considering the trauma she has lived through. Of course she would be fearful of a stranger at her door.

"Are you Helaine Weil?"

She stares at me nervously. "I am. Who are you?"

"I'm Louise Burns. I'm hoping you can help me…" I hesitate, trying to think of the best way to describe my quest. "I am looking for information…about a necklace shaped like a heart. It was broken into two halves." I wish that I had the necklace to show her now, but the half I had is long gone. I pull out the journal and turn to the image of the necklace sketched inside the cover. "Do you recognize this?"

"My notebook!" Her eyes widen. She is taken more by the journal it is sketched in than the image itself. "I lost that during the war. How do you have it?"

I try to think of where to begin the story that I have told so many times in the past few days. But now that I am actually here with the person who lived the story, my words stick.

Helaine seems to sense my unease. "Would you like to come in?" she asks, stepping aside. She ushers me into a small sitting room. The narrow house is modest but homey, with simple furniture. She gestures to a rose-colored sofa with fabric worn slightly where it is pulled tight along the edges. "Now, why don't you tell me everything? How did you find my notebook? And why are you asking about the necklace?"

I take a deep breath. "I was a Red Cross volunteer during the war, and I traveled from England to the continent to deliver packages to prisoners of war in the German camps. One day in a camp in Germany, I saw a man give a necklace to my friend with a locket shaped like half a heart and ask her to deliver it to his wife. That necklace recently turned up in a box in England."

"What an unusual coincidence," Helaine remarks. "That must have been quite a surprise."

"It was," I admit. "I've been trying to find the owner of the necklace to learn more about it. Is that you?"

"Yes, my husband, Gabriel, was trying to get a message to me to let me know that he had been arrested, by sending a necklace to me at the department store in Paris where I was imprisoned. We each wore a half-heart locket on a chain." She reaches into the neckline of her blouse and pulls out a chain bearing the other half of the locket.

I stifle a gasp. "You still have yours."

"Yes, I was able to hide it with me when I was imprisoned and take it with me in the end. By sending me his half, Gabriel was trying to tell me that something terrible had happened to him and that he might not be able to return."

Before I can ask her anything further, the doorbell rings. "Another visitor?" Helaine remarks, surprised. "This is more company than we've had in years."

Through the lace curtains that hang from the front window, I can see Joe on the doorstep, waiting uncertainly. He must have returned to the hotel shortly after I left and received my message. "It's my husband. I asked him to meet me here," I explain apologetically. "I hope you don't mind." She does not seem angry, but a little taken aback by this sudden and unexpected invasion of strangers.

I open the door, and Joe and I smile at one another. I am glad to see him, grateful that he is here. Joe walks over to where Helaine has risen from the sofa. "Ma'am, I'm Joe Burns, Louise's husband. It's a pleasure to meet you." I can see her relax slightly. Joe has a wholesome, trustworthy manner that puts people immediately at ease.

"You were telling me about the necklace during the war," I prompt gently when we are seated. "How Gabriel used it to send you a message."

"During the war, Gabriel and I were separated. I was imprisoned in a former department store in Paris called Lévitan and he was sent to Germany to play his cello. We had no way to reach one another or know where the other one had gone. He was able to visit me one time during the war and he swore he would come for me in the end. But shortly after, he was arrested.

Gabriel was desperate to get word to me. He wanted to send me the other half of the split locket we shared and tried to get someone to deliver it to me. Only, the necklace never arrived."

"But if the locket never reached you, how do you know all of this?" Joe asks.

Helaine does not answer him directly but looks over her shoulder. "Darling," she calls. A man with a trim gray beard and moustache steps into the room and moves to her side protectively. "This is Gabriel." I look at him in surprise. The very man I had seen speaking with Franny at the camp fence all those years ago stands before me now, slightly older, but unmistakably the same. I had assumed all along that he had died during the war, but he is here in front of us, alive and real. His expression is guarded.

Then Helaine rises and introduces us and explains why we had come, and Gabriel relaxes. "A pleasure to meet you." I can tell from the way they stand close and look deeply at one another that they are very much in love.

"How long have you been together?" Joe asks.

"Gabriel and I were married a few years before the war," Helaine replies.

"You never took his name?" I ask.

"Not legally. At first, I just never got around to it. And well afterward, I wanted to keep something to remember my family by. Something for myself." She pats his hand lovingly and Gabriel smiles. She turns to Joe and me. "In fact, Gabriel changed his last name to Weil."

"I wanted to honor my wife's family, which had been destroyed during the war," Gabriel adds. That explains why I could not find him in the phone book under Lemarque, I think.

Helaine continues, "So as I was telling you, after Gabriel went off to play his music, I was imprisoned in the Lévitan department store."

"I was able to visit Helaine once in the department store,"

Gabriel adds, picking up for her. "But after I left Lévitan and returned to Germany, I was arrested and put in a POW camp. You see, we musicians were not just playing for the Germans. We were using our position and our ability to get inside the camps to gather information for the resistance. But while I was gone seeing Helaine, someone betrayed us. I was immediately arrested upon my return. I wanted to send word to Laina to let her know what had happened, why I might not be able to come for her in the end like I had promised. She needed to know so that she would save herself. I sent the locket."

"But it never arrived," I say slowly. I realize that for all of the time we have been talking, I have not yet explained the reason.

Gabriel's eyes grow troubled, as if reliving the memory. "I had no way to tell Laina where I had gone, why I wasn't able to return for her as I promised. But that wasn't all. After I was arrested, I learned about a traitor who was getting inside the camps and disclosing information from the Allies. I needed to relay that message as well. I knew, though, that Helaine, no matter how strong and capable, was a prisoner as well. She wouldn't be able to get that information into the right hands. So my mission was twofold—deliver the necklace to Helaine and make certain that what was inside it got to the right hands in the French or British government."

"The information inside," I say, "was it on a piece of film?"

Gabriel's eyes widen. "Yes. You have it?"

"We had it developed," Joe offers. He pulls an envelope from his jacket and passes it to me. I take out the photograph and study the image, trying to make sense of it. It is Gabriel, standing by the camp fence. Some other prisoners and a few German officers mill around in the background.

But there seems nothing else noteworthy in the photo. "I don't understand." I assumed that the photograph was what Gabriel had needed Franny to deliver. But why was it so important? There seems nothing remarkable about it.

"Look," Gabriel says, leaning over my shoulder. He points to men in the background of the photo, a German military officer and a civilian. The civilian is handing an envelope to the officer. "Do you recognize this man?"

I look more closely at the image and gasp. "Ian."

"He was using the cover of the Red Cross to provide classified documents to the Germans," Gabriel confirms. "And also to feed false information from the Germans back to the Brits."

My mind whirls. "I had no idea," I say. Ian was at the volunteer center when I met him. He led the mission to deliver the care packages. To me, Ian *was* the Red Cross. Anything else is unthinkable.

I listen to what Gabriel is saying, stunned. Franny had only told me about delivering the necklace—not about the information it carried.

Gabriel continues, "When my sister came to perform and I saw her secretly helping so many, I saw my chance to send the locket to Helaine and deliver the information."

"Excuse me?" I interject. My heart skips a beat. "Did you just say that the person who took the necklace was your sister?"

"Yes, I'm sorry, I thought you knew. She is called Franny." I recall Franny talking about a brother. But I had no idea that she had found him or that he was in the camp we visited. "We were very close as children, despite the age difference. We also have a younger sister, Bette. Our home life was not ideal, but I did the best I could to take care of both of them. Really, Franny and I took care of each other. We both loved the arts, me the cello and her the stage. But then I went abroad, and we lost touch. Time and life got in the way. Apparently when she was touring, though, she caught wind of a cellist in one of the camps and she found her way to me."

The answer appears before me then. That was why she had seemed so purposeful and desperate when we reached the second camp—and why she was willing to risk everything to help him. Franny had found her brother, but in the end, she had been powerless to save him, or herself.

"When she found me, I had already been arrested for helping the resistance. Franny wanted to try to get me out. But it was impossible, and I didn't want her to risk herself. Instead, I asked her to get the necklace to Helaine and to deliver the information about the traitor. Our resistance network had crumbled at that point. Asking Franny to carry the message was my only choice."

"Only, the necklace never arrived," Helaine interjects.

"And I never heard from my sister again." Gabriel's eyes darken.

Because Franny died, I think. Gabriel does not know about his sister. I take a deep breath. "I'm so sorry to tell you this, but Franny died."

"No!" Gabriel cries, and his wife moves closer to comfort him. "When?"

"Shortly after you saw her in the camp and gave her the necklace. They said she was hit by a car outside the gate." I pause. I do not want to cause Gabriel more pain. I need to tell him the truth, though, if I am to get answers. "But I never believed that was what really happened. That's why I came here," I explain. "I always thought that the necklace had something to do with Franny's death. And when it turned up again in the box, I knew I had to finally find out the truth." The pieces of the puzzle come together in my mind as I speak. "She must have been killed to stop the information in the necklace from coming to light."

Tears form in Gabriel's eyes now as he thinks about the loss of his younger sister. "I never meant to put her in harm's way." He shares my guilt in Franny's death, I realize as he leans his head sadly against his wife's. "I was transferred out of the camp so quickly that I never knew she died. When I learned that she did not deliver the necklace, I feared that something had happened to her. Still, I never imagined this. All she knew was that there was important information to be delivered. I told her to relay the message with the film that the man seen with the German officer was a traitor. I didn't tell her the specifics about the traitor's identity because I thought it would be safer that way."

"So she inadvertently took the information to Ian for help delivering it, not knowing it was he himself who would be implicated by the information getting out," Joe adds. "And he killed her to protect himself."

"Or had someone do it for him." I still cannot believe it. Ian thought that getting rid of Franny would keep his secret safe. "Only, then I started asking questions and he sent me home. Why didn't he have me killed?"

"Maybe two deaths would raise too much suspicion," Helaine suggests.

Or perhaps he could not bear to kill me because of his feelings, I think. I want to believe that despite everything else that was a lie, Ian's feelings for me were real. "After I went back to England, Ian's secret lay buried. He almost got away with it—until I found the necklace. When I came and asked questions, he must have started getting nervous." I pause, putting the pieces together before speaking. "He invited me to Paris in order to control the situation and feed me information so I would think the necklace had no connection." The answers come to me as I speak. "He didn't count on me meeting the pharmacist and his mother, or the survivor from Lévitan who could link the necklace to Gabriel and the store."

"There's one thing I don't understand," Helaine says. "Franny was not able to carry the message. So how was it delivered such that it turned up in Lévitan?"

"The other musician," I remember. "After Franny died, I went looking for you, Gabriel, to find out more about the necklace you had given her. Another musician told me that you had been transferred. He asked me what had become of the necklace and seemed very intent on finding it."

"Marcel," Gabriel says, smiling at the memory. "He was a gifted violinist and also very committed to the resistance. And he had connections in the camp. He must have been able to find the necklace among Franny's personal effects and send it on to Helaine."

"But before the necklace could reach me, Lévitan was liquidated, and we were all taken from the camp. We never knew what became of the other half of the locket, until today."

"It must have arrived at the department store after you left," I say. Somehow it had wound up in the crate that made its way to the secondhand shop, swept up like so much of the past, like rubbish, its secrets buried forever.

"Now you have the photo," Joe says. "You can share it and bring the truth to light."

"Would anyone believe it?" Helaine asks. "Do they even care anymore?"

"Ian is a traitor and a war criminal who still has access to the highest levels of British intelligence," Joe replies. "I assure you that the government will care very much."

"Except that he's gone," I lament. "He could be anywhere by now. And he's got the other half of the necklace. I'm sorry I lost it."

"It's all right," Helaine replies. "I've learned not to hold on to things. What's important is the truth, and thanks to you, that's been revealed."

I notice then pictures of a girl on the mantelpiece. "You have a daughter?"

"Yes." She beams with pride. "I found out I was pregnant shortly after Paris was liberated. I was told I couldn't have children, so we were surprised and overjoyed."

"How did you find one another again after the war?" Joe asks.

"After Gabriel visited me at the department store, I learned that he had been arrested. Later, after I had left the store, I read about a fire at the POW camp at Wann where I'd been told

Gabriel was taken." Helaine's face clouds at the memory. "I assumed Gabriel had been killed."

"In fact, I was transferred out of Wann before that," Gabriel adds. "In the end, being transferred saved my life. I was sent to a POW camp in the north of France. When the camp was liberated, I made my way to Paris to find Laina. But by then, the department store had been liquidated and I was told that all of its former occupants had been sent east to the death camps.

"I wanted to go find her, but the war was still being fought in Germany and Poland," he continues. "Our apartment in Paris was gone and I had nothing, so I went to a displaced persons camp to stay and try to figure out what to do next. I played the cello as a way to bring comfort to the other camp residents. Each day, I played the piece I had written for Helaine as a way to feel close to her." He smiles at his wife. "And then one day when I was playing it, she appeared, as if in a dream."

Gabriel puts his arm around her, and they look so in love that I can almost see them as they had been when they were young, back when it all began. "It hasn't been perfect," Helaine admits. "Even after all we went through, we were just two people trying to build a life together with all of our flaws and differences."

"But because of the struggle, we also knew what was really important," Gabriel chimes in, squeezing her hand. The connection when they look at one another is powerful. "We're very lucky." *Lucky.* The word reverberates in my head. If people like Helaine and Gabriel, who have been through so much, can say that, then surely Joe and I can remember what's important. I move closer to him.

Helaine's face grows somber. "But even though I survived and went on to have a wonderful life, I never quite moved on." I understand. There are still things that stop me in my tracks, hurl me back. The sound of a police siren, crowds gathering. They make me want to run and hide in a basement. None of us are whole.

"So how do you do it? Not just make it through each day, but really live?"

Helaine smiles. "I remember all that I still have. What happened to you during the war?" Helaine asks, and I realize it is the first time anyone has posed that question to me. Until now, no one has recognized the battle I fought or the scars I bear from that time.

"After Franny was killed, I tried to find out what happened to her. But the Red Cross didn't want me asking questions, and when I refused to stop, I was sent home and forced out of the organization altogether."

I stop talking, but the scene continues to play out in my mind. I was given thirty minutes to pack my belongings. A military escort waited outside my railcar the entire time, though I could not imagine what they thought I might do or take. I gathered my few things. I wanted to take Franny's, too, but I didn't dare. Instead, I looked over once more sadly at the space we had shared, wishing so many things. *I'm sorry*, I mouthed silently. Sorry that she was gone and that I had not been brave enough to help her. Things might have turned out so much differently. Then, with no other choice, I left.

I was escorted over the border to Switzerland and then put on an airplane home, my first and only flight. I should have been relieved. I had wanted to go home. But by choice, when the job was finished. Not like this.

I was required to go to the War Office for debriefing. Red Cross neutrality or no, I was a private citizen now and they wanted to know what I had seen in Germany, any intelligence that might have been of use. I complied; even after all that happened, I wanted to do my part if I thought it would help. But I did not mention the necklace or the cellist, because what good would that have done anybody? I was let go without pay or commendation, and they gave me a strict warning not to talk about what I had seen and done.

And so I hadn't. *Until now.* Now I see that it is okay to tell my story and that my suffering is as real as anyone else's.

"I had no idea you were forced to leave," Joe says, putting his hand on mine. "That must have been terrible."

"I know. I should have told you sooner." I regret keeping so much from Joe and realize it was driving a wedge between us. Sharing our pasts, our suffering and our truths, is the only way that we can grow together.

"Thank you for bringing me this," Helaine says, holding up the journal. "I always wondered what had become of it. I even considered going back to the store to look for it, but I assumed it had been taken or destroyed, and the notion of going back there was just too painful. I'm so glad to have it again."

"You're a gifted writer," I say.

"Thank you." She smiles. "Just the musings of a young girl. Stories mostly."

"Perhaps," I reply. "But you have so much more to say. You should write about your life and your loved ones and whether they survived and found one another again. People's stories matter, and how they end, matters."

She touches the necklace. "I swore I would never forget, that I would tell the stories of my family and friends—and what I lived through in Lévitan."

"Why don't more people know about that?"

"A prison in a department store? Who would believe it? Lévitan and the two satellite camps housed a few hundred Jews for a little over a year. We were, at most, a footnote in the history of the war. At first, I felt guilty talking about it when others had suffered so much worse. And later, well, France wanted to claim credit for liberation, not remind people that French policemen had loaded Jewish children onto trucks and then shopped among their plunder."

"It's important," I insist. "You should write about it."

"I did want to be a writer when I was young," Helaine admits.

"You should," her husband says. "You are terrific at it."

"I only write children's stories," she says with a note of self-deprecation.

"Write those," Gabriel urges. "Or write your own story. Write what is in your heart."

"Why not?" I urge. "Think of everything you've seen."

"Maybe." She tries to sound offhand, but I can tell she is seriously considering it. A tiny spark of possibility.

I turn to Gabriel. "Did you ever find your youngest sister or learn what became of her?"

Gabriel shakes his head remorsefully. "Bette. I tried to look for her but had no luck. But maybe I can try again. Perhaps you could help me."

"Me?" I repeat, confused.

"You did such a good job solving the mystery of the necklace and finding us. Why not take on another case?"

I start to tell him that I am a housewife, not a detective. But I realize then that I am more than just a housewife. I made a real difference during the war, and I could have done even more if I hadn't been silenced and sent away.

"There's an idea, Lou," Joe chimes in. "You could help people not just find items but one another, or at least learn the truth about what had become of their loved ones during the war."

Of course, Bette is not just anyone. She is Franny's sister. Perhaps by finding her and reuniting her with her brother, I think, I can help Franny after all.

"I believe," Helaine says, "that you have your first case. Perhaps you could help me find my father, too. We lost touch during the war. I sent him a postcard from the displaced persons camp, but never heard back."

"I'll think about it," I promise. "And I'll be in touch." Even as I say this, I know that I will help.

Joe and I say goodbye to Helaine and Gabriel and step outside.

"Ready?" Joe asks.

I nod. I'm ready not just to go home, but to do things better. I think suddenly of my mum, alone in her London flat. "I should have done more for my mum," I lament.

"But she's still alive," Joe points out. "And you still have time to make things right. How many people would give anything to be able to say that? Say, here's an idea: Why don't you bring her out to the country to stay?" I start to protest. I cannot imagine my mum living with us. Surely she would refuse to leave the city, and our relationship might be too far gone. An image pops into my mind then of my mum once doing a jigsaw puzzle with me. She had loved it. Perhaps she might share that with her grandchildren. Getting to know Ewen and Phed might be just the change she needs to fix things. And it would be a help that might let me pursue the career I want. All I can do is try.

Joe turns to me. "Thank you," he says lovingly.

"For what?"

"For letting me in. For letting me help. I was so unhappy when you left for Paris. And I hated coming over. But I'm glad that I did. It has helped me, in a way, to start to heal as well."

"I'm glad. But it isn't enough." I pause. I need to set things right now if we are to start again—even if the words are hard to say. "Joe, I know how much you still hurt from the war. I hear your cries at night and I see your nightmares."

"I'm fine," he insists stubbornly. He is always too proud to admit weakness.

"You aren't."

He pauses for a beat. "Never mind that now," he says brusquely. "We can talk about everything when we get home."

"We don't talk!" I burst out, and Joe looks surprised. He has never seen this side of me before. "That's the thing about it, we never talk about what happened during the war."

"We're here together and we've put all of this business with the necklace behind us. Why waste more time talking about the past?" he asks, a flicker of apprehension in his eyes. Even now, it is hard for him to open up old wounds and talk about the past.

"Because it's part of us, part of our story of who we are and how we got here. Not talking about it doesn't make it go away. It just pulls us further apart. You need to get help, real help, so you can be a proper husband and father. And for your own good. Because that's the thing, we can't fix us until you fix you. So, what do you say?"

"All right, I'll try. I'll try for you and our family." Joe, I see then, is doing the best he can. And with that understanding, the anger I have been holding on to begins to subside. Things aren't fixed, but somehow the promise that he will try is enough for now.

"I'll be here with you every step of the way." I lace my fingers with his and the distance between us begins to close. We are not the same as we once were, but I have renewed hope for us.

"Are you ready to go home?" Joe asks.

"Yes." I realize now that the truth does not lie in some mystery or far-off quest in another country. The answer has been right here in front of me all along. *That is something*, I can hear Franny's voice say. *That is enough*. It will have to be.

"Let's go," Joe says. "I know two little people who will be most eager to see you."

"Wait," I say. The children are well cared for and they can wait a little longer. "First let's take some time here in Paris for us."

Joe holds out his arm and I take it. We set out, together.

Epilogue

Louise

England, 1953

The kettle whistles and I put water into two chipped teacups, one for me and one for Midge, and carry hers to the front of the shop where she is sorting. Then I return to the back office and sit down at the desk I'm using for my new venture. I feed a piece of crisp stationery into the typewriter. *Louise Burns, Private Investigator,* the heading reads. I've got half an hour until I have to leave to pick up the children from school and I want to finish the letter I've started to Gabriel, updating him on what I've learned so far about his youngest sister, Bette, during the war. I plan to write to Helaine separately, seeking details about her father so I can try to help her find him.

It has been nearly a month since I returned from Paris. I decided in earnest to help people find loved ones and other truths they are seeking. It has been slow going, just one case of a woman wanting to know what happened to her fiancé, who was missing in action during the war and never returned. I've made records inquiries and I will go to Europe if it turns up anything promising for her. I suspect I will never have another case as meaningful to me as discovering the connection between the locket and Franny's death. But there is something fulfilling in helping people put together the pieces of their lives.

A bell tinkles in the front of the thrift store and I assume it is a customer. But a moment later, Joe appears in the doorway of the office. I stand. "What is it? Is everything all right?" He should be at work and I'm concerned.

"Perfectly fine." He crosses the office and kisses me quickly on the lips. Things have been so much better since we returned from Paris. He is seeing a doctor to help him deal with the trauma of the war. It isn't perfect or easy. Sometimes, examining the past will stir things up and he will cry for no reason or wake up yelling. Occasionally, we have an honest-to-goodness row about something silly. But I understand better now what he is dealing with and we are closer for it.

"It's just that I have some information. The policeman from Paris called to tell us that Ian has been arrested. They caught him trying to flee to South America. He's being extradited and sent back to Britain. And he will stand trial for his crimes—for the war crimes and for murdering Franny."

When I think of Ian and his betrayal, a torrent of emotions comes washing back over me. How had I been so wrong about him? I had liked him, admired him. In the end, I had not known him at all. I wonder if his feelings for me had been a ruse. But when I see him in my mind's eye, I know that they had not.

"So, it's over?"

"It's over." I exhale with relief.

Except that it will never really be over. "If he stands trial, that means I will have to testify, won't I?" And face him in court, I think, and relive it all again. I'm petrified of seeing him again, this time across a courtroom, of speaking the truth as he watches.

Joe pauses. "Probably. You don't have to do it, of course. No one will force you."

"But if I don't testify, Ian could be exonerated."

"They have very little evidence without you," he concedes. "Just the photo. They will need you to put together all of the pieces of what Ian was doing in the camps, how he responded when Franny died."

I square my shoulders. "I can do it."

"And I'll be there with you every step of the way," Joe promises. "Anyhow, it's over. We're safe." I fold myself into his arms, wanting to believe we are safe, but not sure I can ever feel that way again. We stand in a close embrace, letting the weight of the past and all that has happened wash over us and fade away. "There is one other thing," Joe adds. "When Ian was arrested, they found the other half of the necklace among his possessions. They asked for our address so they can return it to you."

"Tell them not to."

Joe looks surprised. "You don't want it back?"

"It was never mine in the first place." I take a piece of paper and write down Helaine and Gabriel's address in Paris. "Can you have them send it here instead?"

"Yes, of course. Anything for you. You must be so relieved to put this all behind you."

"I am. It's time to move on."

Joe looks around the shop. "Are you almost done here?" he asks.

"I am." I clear my teacup. The letter to Gabriel can wait until Monday. "I want to stop on the way home and get some of that bread my mum likes."

I had reached out to my mum, but she had not wanted to come live with us. Her life in London, while dreadful to me, is her life and she does not want to leave it. But she has stopped drinking and comes to see the children often on weekends now. Joe and I plan to let her mind them overnight next summer when we take a night at the seashore just for us. "I'll buy you your very own candy floss," he promised teasingly when proposing the plan.

"What about you?" I ask. "It's not even three. Do you have to go back to work?" Joe never misses time at the office—or at least the old Joe hadn't.

He shakes his head, then holds up a package wrapped in brown store paper. "I've taken the rest of the day off. I bought a new kite and I thought that Ewen and Phed might like to go to the park and try it out. You could join us, too, if you would like."

"I would love that." I take his hand and together we leave the shop behind us and start the journey home into the light.

★ ★ ★ ★ ★

Author's Note

If you've heard me speak about my previous books, you may know that when I am looking for a book idea, I'm looking for what I call the Gasp. If I find a piece of history that is so untold that it makes me gasp after more than a quarter century of working with the Second World War, then I'm hopeful I'm onto something about which readers will feel the same way.

In the case of *Last Twilight in Paris*, the Gasp was learning about a former furniture store in Paris called Lévitan, where Jews were imprisoned and forced to sort, display and "sell" objects plundered from Jewish homes to German officers. I was curious about this piece of history and wanted to construct a story around a fictitious occupant of Lévitan. And so Helaine was born.

In addition to telling the story from the point of view of Helaine living through the horror of the Holocaust in real time, I also wanted to construct a more "modern" narrative (in this case set in 1953) that connected another woman who had lived through the war from a different perspective to Helaine. And so we meet Louise, who is not Jewish and was not a victim of the Holocaust, but who lived through her own difficult wartime experience, both as a Red Cross volunteer and through the tragic and mysterious death of her best friend, Franny. Bringing in Louise allowed me to explore the complex role of the Red Cross in Europe during the war. I was also inspired to include Franny, a theater actress who traveled to occupied Europe, ostensibly to perform for German officers and Allied POWs, but in fact to help with important war efforts, by the real-life story of Édith Piaf, who was rumored to have done the same.

But how to connect the two stories? I wanted Louise to find an object that dates back to the war. I have always been fascinated by Mizpah charms, hearts that break into two so that lovers or other beloveds can each wear a half when they are separated. The necklace provided a link between Louise in the 1950s and Helaine's wartime story.

As ever, the balance between history and fiction is a delicate one. I always say that I am, first and foremost, a novelist, and that my work is inspired by, rather than based on, actual events. Thus, while attempting to remain true to the integrity of history, I have taken certain liberties for the sake of the story. I have characterized prewar Lévitan as a department store, when in fact it was a furniture store. I have focused on a small group of people who were imprisoned in the store, but it is important to note that close to eight hundred prisoners were kept in Lévitan for varying amounts of time while it was operated by the Germans. I have made the first camp Louise visits in occupied France an "oflag" (officers' camp) when it really would in that region have been a "frontstalag" (temporary camp close to the front lines) and I have fictionalized the locations of both camps and military bases. I've also taken liberties with some of the details of the Red Cross relief efforts and with the timing of the displaced persons camp after the liberation of Paris.

To learn more about the real-life history that inspired *Last Twilight in Paris*, I recommend *Witnessing the Robbing of the Jews: A Photographic Album, Paris, 1940–1944* by Sarah Gensburger and *Nazi Labour Camps in Paris: Austerlitz, Lévitan, Bassano, July 1943–August 1944* by Jean-Marc Dreyfus and Sarah Gensburger.

Acknowledgments

There are so many people without whom this book would not have been possible. I'm forever blessed by my agent, Susan Ginsburg; her assistant, Catherine Bradshaw; and everyone at Writers House. I'm so grateful to my dream editor, Erika Imranyi, and her entire team, including Emer Flounders, Rachel Haller, Lindsey Reeder, Randy Chan, Craig Swinwood, Loriana Sacilotto, Margaret Marbury, Amy Jones, Kathleen Oudit, Nicole Luongo, Justine Sha, Brianna Wodobek, the Sales team and everyone at Park Row Books, Harlequin and HarperCollins. I'm grateful to historical fiction fact-checker Jennifer Young, copy editors Nancy Fischer and Bonnie Lo, and proofreader Kristen Salciccia. Enormous thanks to my book counselor, Andrea Peskind Katz, as well as to Cara Black for reading for my accuracy on Paris. As ever, the mistakes are all mine.

The book community continues to grow and amaze me in its energy and generosity. I want to offer thanks to the (too many to name) booksellers, librarians, bloggers, influencers, podcasters, reviewers, fellow authors and readers who make this life possible.

I've long said that launching a book takes not a village but an army. I'm so thankful for my mom, Marsha, who helps us eight days a week, my brother, Jay, and my in-laws, Ann and Wayne. Love and gratitude to my friends Stephanie, Joanne, Mindy and Brya, who keep me sane while I am endlessly driving, as well as to my camping crew, the Kathleens, Lili, Kristin, Dava and Shira. Thanks also to my coworkers at Rutgers and my supportive communities in the public schools and libraries, the Jewish Community Center, BBYO and doggy day care (no, seriously!).

Finally, my very deepest love and appreciation is reserved for my husband, Phillip, and my three not-so-little muses, without whom this journey would not be possible—or worthwhile.